The Wizard's
Butler

ISBN-13: 978-1-940575-18-6

Second Printing: April, 2021

For more information or to leave a comment about this book,
please visit us on the web at:
www.solarclipper.com

For Christopher Weibe.
He had this crazy idea when I needed something crazy.

Thanks, Chris.

The Golden Age of the Solar Clipper

Quarter Share
Half Share
Full Share
Double Share
Captains Share
Owners Share

In Ashes Born
To Fire Called
By Darkness Forged

Milk Run
Suicide Run
Home Run

South Coast
Cape Grace
Finwell Bay

Tanyth Fairport Adventures

Ravenwood
Zypherias Call
The Hermit Of Lammas Wood

The Wizard's
Butler

NATHAN LOWELL

Durandus

CHAPTER 1

Roger Mulligan stopped in front of the house and stared up at its gabled windows. The wrought-iron gate and fence suited the place but looked completely at odds with the trust-fund-baby gentrification on a street paved with silver spoons. He checked the address on his phone against the number on the house—4185. They matched, and his GPS agreed, so he pushed through the gate, mildly amused that it didn't squeak like the lid of some mummy's coffin.

A fragrant herb grew between the stones of the paved walk, the scent wafting around him as he walked. The grounds seemed well kept, lawn manicured. Looking up at the house, he didn't see so much as a loose shingle or flake of paint on the ornate, if somewhat monochrome gray, façade. The place gave off an old-money vibe. Very old. He reached for the doorbell and pushed it. Nothing happened. He looked again and realized his mistake. He pulled it. When he let go, he heard a faint tinkling—like an old-time shopkeeper's bell—from inside. He revised his estimate of the house's age upward by a couple of decades.

Tapping heels approached the door a moment before it swung inward on silent hinges. The woman behind the door knew how to dress to impress. She posed, knee bent, head tilted at just the correct angle to be coy without being a come-on. The four-inch red stiletto heels spoiled the effect, but Roger didn't mind. "Yes?" she said, stretching the word out so he wasn't sure if it was a question or an answer.

"Hi. I'm Roger Mulligan?"

"You don't sound sure of that," she said, stepping back and ushering him into a two-story foyer. "Come in, Mr. Mulligan. You're in the right place."

He took in the wainscoted walls, old paintings in heavy frames, and a crystal chandelier hanging a dozen feet over what had to be honest-to-God wood parquet flooring, gleaming with fresh wax. "Thank you, ma'am."

She swung the door closed behind him with a solid thump and held out her hand. "Naomi Patching. We spoke on the phone."

For a moment he wasn't sure if he should shake her hand or kiss it. He shook it and nodded. "Nice to meet you, Ms. Patching."

"Always nice to put a face with a name," she said, turning to an open doorway at the foot of the long stairway. "Dealing with people online, one can never be sure."

"Nobody knows you're a dog," he said.

"Precisely." She swept into the room where a tweedy man failed to look trendy in a pair of stacked skinny jeans and a polo shirt. He'd have been better served by shaving the comb-over and losing the pencil-thin mustache.

He extended the hand that wasn't holding the rocks glass. "Thomas," he said. "Thomas Patching." He glanced at Naomi as if he felt the need to establish that yes, he actually was somehow connected to the vision in tasteful red wool, white linen, and red stilettos.

Roger gave the twee a solid handshake and a manly nod. "Roger Mulligan."

Naomi waved them all into leather chairs around a solid coffee table. "Can I get you a drink, Mr. Mulligan?"

Roger shook his head. "I'm fine. Finished a bottle in the car and need to let it settle."

She blinked at him, as if finally tracking what he was saying.

He shook his head again. "Sorry. Joke. Poor joke." He looked back and forth between them, not liking the predatory vibe, similar to what he'd seen before in the field. Village elders thinking they have you where they want you and only looking for the right moment to slip out and——. He choked that thought off by admiring Ms. Patching's décolletage, so charmingly on display in a white silk frame with just the right hint of lace. He looked up into her eyes. "You were saying?"

She shared a glance with Tweedy-bird and then leaned forward a few degrees more. "I'm interested in your qualifications, Mr. Mulligan."

He shifted in his seat to release a little of the pressure on his qualifications. "What part of them, Ms. Patching? I understand this position is for a caretaker?"

"In a manner of speaking," she said. "You were in the military, I understand."

Roger nodded. "Three tours in Afghanistan."

Her eyebrows rose as her gaze seemed to trace the line of his shoulders. The tip of her tongue swabbed her pouty lips. "That must have been rough."

"Not a topic for discussion, ma'am."

She nodded. "We can appreciate a man who knows discretion. The situation here is rather ... delicate." She turned her head slightly and ran a finger down the side of her neck just behind her jaw.

He shifted again, glancing at the mister, who seemed more interested in his whiskey than his wife. "Perhaps if you could be more specific?"

She bit her lips together and shrugged. "It's my uncle, Mr. Mulligan."

"Your uncle?" He did not see that coming.

"Yes, Joseph Perry Shackleford. He owns this property."

"You say that like I should know the name," Roger said.

Her eyebrows rose and her smile returned with a few extra watts. "No," she said, drawing the word out. "Not at all."

The hairs on the back of Roger's neck twitched. He glanced back to see if a spider had snuck in behind him or something.

Tweedy spoke up. "He has a reputation for being somewhat— what's the word? Eccentric." He took a sip. "In certain circles."

Naomi cast him a glance that—miraculously—failed to shatter the heavy crystal glass in his hand. "We simply want you to meet Uncle Perry without any preconceived notions."

"Notions that I might have if I were familiar with the name?" Roger asked.

She blessed him with another smile. "Precisely."

Roger knew what his first online search would be just as soon as he left the house. "What—precisely—is the position?" he asked. "The agency was not particularly forthcoming." Their description of "personal assistant" had been terse to the point of being overtly cryptic. If he hadn't been so desperate, he'd probably have given it a pass.

"We need somebody to care for Uncle Perry," she said.

"Is he an invalid?" Roger wasn't keen on helping anybody dress. Even himself, if he was honest.

"Nothing like that." Naomi leaned back and shook her head before leaning forward again, a little further this time. "He's become a trifle confused."

"So, dementia," Roger said. "How old is he?"

"Honestly, I don't know his exact age," Naomi said. "Well above eighty, but we don't actually know his birthday."

3

"So, you need me to what? Babysit?" Roger began to think that the uncle in the belfry wasn't the only batty one.

Naomi glanced at Thomas and took a deep breath, which Roger greatly appreciated. "We had something more like butler in mind."

Roger looked up into her startlingly green eyes. "Wait. What?"

"Butler," she said. "Someone who can stay with him, take care of his correspondence as necessary, oversee the upkeep on the premises. That sort of thing."

"Jeeves," Roger said. "You want me to be Jeeves?"

"Well, not exactly, but—"

"Yes." Thomas leaned forward, his whiskey glass emptied along with his willingness to sit back and shut up, apparently. "Exactly. We'll provide the uniform. Pay you a stipend. You have quarters here in the house. You can use the vehicles. Just make sure the old boy doesn't do something foolish like fall down and break his neck or sell the place while he's still living here."

Roger sat back in the sumptuous leather. "Just how bad is he?"

Naomi made a good show of looking distressed, but Thomas shrugged. "Crazy as they come, I'm afraid. He thinks he's a wizard."

"Thomas," she said.

He shrugged. "The man deserves to know, Nay." He rose and crossed to the sideboard, pulled the plug on a crystal decanter, and splashed another finger or two into his glass.

"You mentioned a uniform?" Roger asked.

"Standard service dress," Naomi said.

Roger snorted. "You and I don't use that phrase the same way."

"Cutaway. Trousers," Thomas said sliding back into his chair. "Jeeves." He shrugged.

"Stipend?" Roger asked.

"Five thousand a month with the proviso that you give us one year's service," Naomi said, talking quickly as if afraid Thomas would screw the pooch.

"Why a year?"

"He's on a waiting list. Assisted living. A lovely facility in Vail," she said.

"Colorado?" Roger asked.

"Is there another?"

Roger shrugged. "Not that I know of but that's a bit of a hike from here, isn't it?"

"He grew up out west," Naomi said. "We thought it would be nice for him to go back in his twilight years."

Roger nodded, the dime finally dropping. "And it's quite a hike from here."

Thomas shrugged and Naomi looked at the perfectly polished nails on her left hand.

"Why me?" Roger asked. "I'm not exactly butler material, am I?"

"To be honest," Naomi said, telegraphing her willingness to be anything but, "we need somebody with your precise background. Army medic. Good health. Strong enough to manage him physically, if you need to."

"Is he likely to be shot? Hit by shrapnel? Explosive trauma?" Roger asked. "Those are my specialties."

"You also worked as a certified EMT for two years and can think on your feet," Naomi said.

Roger shrugged. "Yeah. That's not much use for the average dementia patient either."

"We haven't told you everything," Thomas said.

"I figured that much out on my own."

"One million dollars," he said. "If you finish the year."

"Thomas!" Naomi said.

Thomas leaned forward, ignoring her. "Bonus. In writing."

Roger blinked. "You're going to pay me five grand a month to live here and look after the nutty professor in the attic. If I make it to the end of the year, I can walk away with a mill."

Thomas nodded. "Room and board, five grand pocket money, and a cool mill at the end."

"What's the catch?" Roger asked because all the "too good to be true" alarms were going off in his head.

"No catch," Naomi said.

"You have to put up with him for a year," Thomas said. "Wear the monkey suit, keep him fed and watered."

"You make him sound like a dog," Roger said.

"More like a cat. He won't care about you unless you're feeding him and will only let you pet him when he wants it," Thomas said.

Roger raised his eyebrows. "I don't think that came out like you think it should have."

Thomas rapped his glass on the expensive table. "You know what I mean."

"There must be a thousand suckers in this town who'd jump at this," Roger said. "Why me?"

"Not that many men with your qualifications," Naomi said. "A lot of vets, sure. A lot of burned out EMTs, yes. Surprisingly few men with your qualifications."

"I find that hard to believe," Roger said.

"We've interviewed twenty," Thomas said.

"And I'm your last choice?"

Thomas shook his head. "We've got them lined up through next month, but I'm getting tired of this pussy-footing around."

"You like the scotch well enough," Naomi said.

He cast her a side-eyed glance and looked back at Roger. "You're the guy. If you want it."

Roger sat back again and folded his hands in his lap. The scent of real cowhide enveloped him. The angles didn't add up to a full circle. "What happened with the others?"

"The other who?" Thomas asked, derailed for the moment.

"The twenty guys who came before me."

"Half were alcoholics," Thomas said.

"Takes one to know one," Naomi said. "Most of the men were unsuitable for one reason or another. Alcohol, drugs. Not the right medical bona fides." Her gaze caressed his shoulders again.

"Not strong enough to wrestle the old man down?" Roger asked.

Thomas shrugged but Naomi got in first. "He can be a handful. Knowing there's somebody here who could handle him should the need arise would make me feel more secure. More confident that he'd be well cared for."

"Gimme the contract," Roger said.

Thomas's eyebrows rose but he reached down beside his chair and pulled up a portfolio.

"Don't you want to meet him first?" Naomi asked.

"No, I want to see if the contract is legit first."

"You might not like him," Naomi said.

Thomas pulled a single sheet of paper out of the portfolio and spun it around on the table, sliding it toward Roger.

"That's it?" Roger said, leaning over to look at it before reaching for it. "There's nothing here about what being a butler entails. No details about what I'm supposed to do."

"Tell you what," Thomas said. "You take that contract to whatever legal beagle you like. Add the stuff you need on it and bring it back."

"Tomorrow," Naomi said.

"Day after," Roger said. "In the morning. Today's almost over. Gimme a chance to get it done."

"Deal," Thomas said and stuck his hand out before Naomi could do more than draw breath.

Roger shook it. "Ten a.m. Thursday."

Thomas nodded. "See you then."

Naomi had that "I'm miffed but I'm not going to give you the satisfaction of showing it" look as she smiled and stood. "In that case, Mr. Mulligan, let me show you out."

He followed her to the door, where she gave him another hand-shake and peek down her blouse before the massive slab thumped closed in his face. "I think I've heard lighter vault doors," he said, looking up at the ancient pile. He shook his head and looked over the one-page contract as he followed the paving stones back to the gate and sidewalk beyond. When he pulled the gate closed behind him, he glanced up again. He half expected to see some creepy dude in a pointy hat staring down at him.

He had to admit. The house looked to be in great shape. If there was a garage someplace behind it, the lot alone had to be worth way more than the paltry million Thomas the Tweed Engine was waving under his nose. He looked at the contract again and shook his head. "There's a catch. I just can't see it."

With a shrug he fished his phone out of his pocket and started down the street toward the bus stop. Vinnie may have flunked out of BU Law, but he'd only cost a six-pack of Sam Adams. It was all he could afford at the moment—but he wasn't going to let them know that.

Vinnie tilted the bottle back and drained it. He squinted at his computer screen and sat very still for a few seconds before releasing the belch. He nodded. "Anything else?"

"What are we not seeing?" Roger asked.

Vinnie shrugged. "We've got the list of prescribed duties pretty well, I think. There's none of that 'other duties as required' shit. We specified all the things you're not going to do." He reached for the last bottle in the rack, twisted the cap off in one bony paw, and tossed it in the general direction of the wastebasket. "We added the double-indemnity clause for breach of contract. They'll kill that one, I expect. I would. What else does a butler do?"

"Combination security guard, house manager, and valet, I as-sume," Roger said, reading the document over Vinnie's shoulder.

"Just one guy in a big house? They mentioned cars?"

"Yeah. Free use of the cars."

"What d'ya suppose they got? Old Chevy Impala?"

"I'm torn between a Model-A and a '27 Silver Phantom."

"You have to wear a chauffeur's uniform?" Vinnie asked.

"I'll wear damn near anything they want if I get to drive a Rolls."

Vinnie chuckled and took a pull. "I can see it now. Drivin' Mr. Shacklebuns."

"Shackleford," Roger said. "Joseph Perry Shackleford." He took a seat at the kitchen table across from Vinnie. "That's the other thing. Man doesn't exist."

"That'll make bein' his butler pretty easy, won't it?" Vinnie nodded at his screen. "We done with this?"

Roger nodded. "Can you email it to me and maybe print a couple of copies?"

Vinnie shrugged and punched a few keys. A printer in the next room whirred into action. "What d'ya mean he doesn't exist?"

"No social media footprint. No news articles. No Wikipedia page. He's not listed in Dun and Bradstreet. Hell, he doesn't even have a LinkedIn profile."

Vinnie took a pull from his bottle and shook his head. "Even I have a LinkedIn profile. Don't use it, but keep getting notifications every damn day. Given what you've said, I'd be surprised if he's got internet."

"Yeah, that's not the same thing. His name doesn't show up. At all." Roger shook his head. "Old coot, I wouldn't expect him to have a profile himself, but a rich old coot with a reputation for being eccentric? Yeah, I'd think somebody would have snapped him on Instagram or Facebook or the society pages somewhere."

"You find the niece and nephew?"

"Yeah. Nephew is junior partner in a boutique law firm downtown. Niece is on a dozen boards around town. Banks, development corps, a couple of philanthropies."

"No job?"

"Not that I saw, but she's old money. Her father owns half the waterfront and most of the industrial zone on the other side of the loop." He shrugged. "Probably lives off the income from her portfolio and scraps from Daddy's table."

"So they're good for the mill," Vinnie said.

"Hard telling." Roger looked at his beer and, seeing the bottle empty, slid it into the middle of the dinged-up table and sighed. "Rich peepo. Stocks, bonds, futures, options, real estate, you name it, but they gotta borrow a buck for a coffee because nothing is liquid."

"Speaking of liquid." Vinnie pushed himself up from the table and shambled off to the other room. Roger heard a light switch click and the sound of Vinnie returning his share of the beer to the water table. "What's his name?" Vinnie asked, his voice echoing from the bathroom tiles.

"Who?"

"Her old man."

Roger pulled up the search on his phone as Vinnie came back, sliding the pages over to him.

"Fresh off the press," Vinnie said.

"Bruna," Roger said.

"Othello Bruna?" Vinnie asked, dropping into his chair with a thump.

Roger nodded. "Yeah. Should I know him?"

"Probably not. You don't read the finance pages. He's in court a lot these days but it's all white collar. Regulatory bullshit."

"He in trouble?" Roger eyed that million-dollar payout with a more skeptical eye.

Vinnie shrugged. "Maybe, but the kid's gotta be good for it on her own hook."

"I'd hate to drain her trust fund," Roger said, shrugging. "With that house and property in her purse, she'll earn it back ten times over."

"You think that's it?" Vinnie asked.

"Old guy won't last that much longer. Prices are only going up. Pull him out of the house. Get named guardian until they can plant him?" Roger shrugged.

"Assuming they inherit," Vinnie said. "They the only relatives?"

Roger slumped in his chair and shrugged. "They're the ones making the arrangements. Gotta figure they've got fingers in the pie somewhere and some reason to think they won't have to share."

"Sounds reasonable." Vinnie frowned and stared at the screen before slapping the laptop closed.

"You don't say that with much confidence," Roger said.

Vinnie grimaced and emptied the last of the lager down his throat. "So many things sound reasonable. Right up until you're airborne at 800 AGL with a full load-out in the dark." He tilted his head back and belched at the ceiling.

Roger snorted and stood, gathering his paperwork. "Thanks, man."

Vinnie waved him off. "If you need a groundskeeper, let me know."

"You looking for work?" Roger asked, stopping at the door. "I thought you were set up."

Vinnie shrugged and stared at his feet stretched under the table. "Never hurts to keep an eye open for new and exciting opportunities."

Roger laughed. "Keep talking like that and you'll be re-upping after all."

Vinnie flipped him the bird as Roger slipped out the door.

He skipped down the stairs to the ground floor and strode out into the chilly night. It had to be pushing midnight, but the city never slept. Car noise from the arterial filtered between the apartment houses—punctuated with the occasional downshifting semi or the revving whine of a rice burner. A cat stared at him from the alley when he walked by.

He shook his head, hunching into the navy surplus peacoat and picking up his pace. It was only a few blocks to his apartment, and he had a lot to think about. Mostly about how Vinnie was right. Too many things sounded reasonable until you found yourself hundreds of feet above ground level, falling through the night with half a ton of gear and only a nylon umbrella to keep you from becoming people-paste on the rocks.

On the flip side of that coin, he really had nothing else. The balance on his checking account lay perilously close to the red. The bastards at Mid-City Medical Transport had blacklisted him for punching out the drunk husband. Nobody wanted to hire a vet with "anger management issues." He snorted and dug his fists deeper into his coat pockets. Bastard had it coming. Drunk or not, nobody beats someone they're supposed to love like that.

He thrust the memories out of his mind, kicking an empty can so it skittered across the sidewalk before falling into the gutter with a rolling clatter.

He looked up at the moon. Nearly full. Nearly midnight. "A fucking butler," he said to the man in the moon. "Really?"

He rang the bell promptly at ten o'clock.

She must have been waiting because he didn't hear her heels before the door opened. "Mr. Mulligan. Come in." Her scarlet blazer had been replaced by a classy white bolero with gold buttons and trim. It would have looked good on a downtown doorman but her assets rounded it out nicely. He glanced down and felt mildly disappointed that she'd skipped the pumps.

"I said ten," he said, waving the folder containing his revised contract.

She smiled and held the door for him. "Let's get Thomas to look at it. I'm certain it will be fine."

He stepped in and made sure he was clear of the door. He gave it the once-over and revised his opinion of it. It thumped closed with the solid finality he'd never heard outside of a secure facility.

She led the way back to the parlor or whatever the hell the room was called.

Thomas—a tiny china cup and matching saucer on the table in front of him—looked up, his focus going to the folder like that of a dog expecting a treat.

Roger took his assigned seat and slid the folder across the varnished surface.

Thomas flipped open the cover and started reading.

"Coffee, Mr. Mulligan?" Naomi asked. "Espresso?"

"Grande mocha?" he asked. "Two shots?"

She gave him a sour look.

"Coffee. Black is fine. Thank you," he said.

She crossed to the sideboard and pumped a cup of coffee from one of those fancy restaurant-grade carafes with the lever on top. She handed him the cup and saucer before taking her place beside Thomas. "Have you given our offer more consideration?" she asked.

He took a sip and had to give her credit. It was good coffee. "I've added some conditions to the contract, but yes. If we can reach an agreement on the terms, I'd like to meet your uncle."

Her eyes widened for a moment at that. "Conditions?" she asked, glancing at Thomas.

"I learned never to trust those open-ended requirements that wind up as 'whatever we say' because, you know? I'm not going there. Been there, done that. Gave the T-shirt back because it was two sizes too small." He took another sip of the coffee. It really was quite good. "House blend?" he asked, lifting the cup.

She shrugged. "Whatever Uncle stocks."

"Who's been doing it for him?" Roger asked.

"His last butler," she said, glancing at the paperwork as Thomas flipped the fifth page.

"So, he's running low on supplies?" Roger asked.

"No, a standing order. It's delivered weekly. Staples. Meals," she said.

"He feeds himself, then?"

She frowned at him. "Of course he feeds himself." She huffed. "He bathes and dresses himself and uses the bathroom unattended. Just like a real person."

Roger let the sumptuous aromas of coffee and leather surround him as he settled back in his chair. "Real people sometimes need help with all those things, Ms. Patching. Particularly as they age."

Thomas finished reading, flipping the last page over face down. He looked up. "One question."

"One answer," Roger said.

"Authorized to hire additional help as required?"

"Plumbing, heating." Roger shrugged. "Cook, valet? Chauffeur. If Uncle Perry wants to take up polo, I'll want to hire a stable manager. Skills and tools that I don't possess. Or should I refer all those requests to you?"

"Why would he need a chauffeur, Mr. Mulligan? Can't you drive?" Naomi asked.

"I can, yes. I even have a valid driver's license, but if I didn't?"

"The household has a budget for those expenses, Mr. Mulligan," Thomas said. "If you exceed that budget, you'd have to arrange for additional funding on a case-by-case basis with either Naomi or me."

"You control his finances?" Roger asked.

Thomas glanced sideways at Naomi then shrugged. "We're concerned that Uncle not spend beyond his means."

Roger heard the message that Thomas probably didn't want him to hear. "I understand," he said.

"I found nothing objectionable in this contract," Thomas said after staring at Roger for a moment. "I'm willing to sign it if you are."

"No other quibbles? Nothing you'd like to negotiate?" Roger asked.

Thomas gave Naomi another side-eyed glance and a small smirk. "Nothing I wouldn't have added myself were I in your chair."

Naomi turned her sour look on Thomas. Roger wondered how she'd make the tweedman pay for that remark.

"I would like to meet Uncle Perry before I sign it," Roger said. "He may not like me."

Naomi's smile came back at full wattage. As fake as it looked, he began to wonder about the reality of her other assets. "I'm sure he'll hate you," she said.

Roger blinked. He had not seen that coming.

Thomas snickered. "He hates everybody. Even us."

Roger considered that for a couple of long moments, his estimation of Uncle Perry rising a little with each tick of the ornate clock on the mantel. "Fair enough. Thanks for the warning."

Naomi rose. "Shall we?"

Roger scooted forward and took one last sip of the coffee before placing the saucer on the table. "Let's," he said, standing.

Thomas picked up his espresso and leaned back. "I'll wait here," he said.

Naomi gave him the look again. "Coward."

"I just enrage him, Nay. Best I stay out of sight." He sipped his coffee, pinky raised and a smug look on his face. "Good luck, Mr. Mulligan." He raised his dinky little cup in a toast.

Roger liked the old man more and more.

"This way, Mr. Mulligan," Naomi said, leading him out of the parlor—if that was what it was called—and up the stairs to the next landing. She walked down a short corridor and opened the door near the end. "Uncle, I have someone I'd like you to meet."

She breezed into a room decked out like a library. Bookshelves, sure. Who doesn't have bookshelves built into every wall except the north one, with its big windows—no doubt "for the light." But a card catalog? One of those pedestal things, with a dictionary big enough to need it. A heavy wooden table stood in the middle of the floor with solid chairs around it. As he scanned the room, Roger picked out a cabinet with low, flat drawers and even a glass display case holding some nasty-looking old books that seemed to drip 'don't touch me or I'll crumble' vibes. The room smelled of ink and leather.

What really caught his attention was the man in the wheelchair. He had a plaid blanket over his knees and a heavy tome on his lap. He peered over his spectacles at Naomi like she'd just urped a hairball on his rug. "What now?"

She stepped to one side and made that game-show hostess gesture with her free hand. "Mr. Mulligan has agreed to be your new butler."

"That's not true," Roger said.

She rounded on him. "You said you'd sign the contract."

"I will, but only if Mr. Shackleford and I come to an understanding about my role in his household. He may decide I'm not suited, in which case I will, of course, not impose myself."

Shackleford's eyebrows rose and he started to grin but suppressed it before Naomi turned to see.

"Where's my applesauce, Maude?" Shackleford asked.

"You've upset him," Naomi said, her voice low and hissing. She turned and smiled. "I'm Naomi, Uncle. I'll get your applesauce shortly. It's almost time for luncheon, after all."

"Naomi? You can't be Naomi. She's just a small girl."

Naomi looked at Roger, one elegantly plucked eyebrow rising carefully. "Perhaps you'd like to get acquainted?" The eyebrows came together above an evil smile. "I'll just pop down to the kitchen and fetch his applesauce and cookie." With that, she swept out of the room, leaving the doors open, perhaps hoping he'd bolt to freedom.

Roger looked at the old man studying him. "She is Naomi, sir," he said.

The old man nodded and waved his right hand in the air as if dispelling the cloud of her presence or something, but the door snapped shut behind Roger. "Of course she is. Viper. What did they offer you?"

"Room and board, five thousand a month, and a million if I last the year, sir."

"You accept it?" he asked.

"Not yet. I wanted to meet you first, sir."

"Thomas downstairs, too?"

"Yes, sir."

"He doesn't know I keep the good scotch here in the library. Idiot man. Don't know what she sees in him."

"In-house counsel, perhaps, sir."

He started as if surprised and then chortled. "In-house counsel, indeed," he said. "Have a seat, man. Let's talk."

"She'll be back with the applesauce soon, sir."

He nodded with the devilish grin of a ten-year-old who knows he has a frog in his pocket but nobody else suspects. He pointed at one of the library chairs. "Sit, man."

"Thank you, sir." Roger turned one of the chairs to face the old man and sat.

"They told you I'm insane, I take it?"

"Yes, sir. Dementia, actually. A technical difference."

His eyes narrowed as he regarded Roger over the top of his wire-rimmed spectacles. "Ex-military? Army?"

"Yes, sir."

"Why do you want to be a butler?"

"I don't, but I like eating and I'm running out of funds."

"That all?" the old guy asked.

"Isn't that enough?"

The old guy just raised his eyebrows and waited.

"I got tired of people trying to kill me. It seemed like a decent career move, sir."

Naomi breezed in with a small silver tray. "Here's your apple-sauce, Uncle."

The old man exploded, all but screaming at the hapless Naomi. "Maude, how many times have I told you to knock and you know I hate applesauce. Whatever possessed you to bring me that pablum? Like I can't chew my own food? It has to be ground up for me? Take it away. Take it away. I'll ring when I need you."

"But, Uncle—"

"Take it away, I said. Get out." His color had turned ruddy and small flecks of spittle flew through the air.

She cast Roger a knowing look and backed out. "Of course, Uncle." She made good her escape and closed the door.

The old man turned back to Roger, the tip of his tongue tasting his lower lip. "Where were we?"

"My career change, sir."

He nodded, his whole upper body nodding along. "Yes, yes. Tedious woman. She told you I'm a wizard?"

"Not precisely, sir."

"What then?"

"She said you think you're a wizard."

Shackleford sat back in his chair. "Oh, that clever girl. She'd have made a vicious lawyer in her own right if she had any gumption at all."

"She seems pretty ambitious to me, sir."

He nodded. "Oh, ambition. Yes. She has ambition by the bucket but she wants somebody else to carry the pail." He paused and lowered his head, leaning forward. "I take it they started flinging money around to distract you?"

"Naomi seemed upset that Thomas mentioned the million, but yes, sir."

"Thomas has little patience for the niceties of negotiation," Shackleford said. "Miserable trait in a lawyer, but it works well enough for the bloodsuckers he works with." He shrugged. "You got anything against being a butler?"

"It's not something I've given much thought to, to be honest, sir."

"No family?" Shackleford asked.

"My parents live in the burbs but ex-army isn't the only ex- in my life, sir." Roger shrugged. "Three tours in Afghanistan. She couldn't take it. I don't blame her. She sends me a Christmas card every year."

"Quaint," the old man said. "You've met me. What d'ya think?"

Roger sized the man up, taking his time to look at him—sparse gray hair, trimmed beard. Reminded him of Sean Connery in that archaeology flick. His face and hands looked like an old man's, wrinkled, with liver spots and some arthritis in the joints. He wore a brown wool blazer over a starched white shirt and argyle vest, a perfect reverse Windsor holding the regimental tie. The toes of brown wingtips peeked out from under the hem of the blanket on his lap, polished and well cared for—save for a scuff mark on the right toe. Roger looked back into the old man's patient eyes. The eyes of a man who'd seen more than even Roger. He knew Roger was looking at him and didn't shy away from the inspection. His eyebrows twitched as he stared back, almost a dare.

"Are you a wizard?" Roger asked.

15

"Yes."

Roger paused at that, wondering if the old guy might actually be around the bend or if he defined wizard in some obscure word-game fashion known only to himself. "Does your niece know?"

"Not to my knowledge."

"Would I need to press your shirts?"

The old man's eyebrows sprang up so fast, they might have achieved orbital velocity had they been closer to the equator and not so well attached. He barked a short laugh. "No," he said.

"You know they want the house?"

"Oh, yes. More precisely the land. The house is a rotten tooth in the street's chromium smile. They want the house so they can do a little real-estate orthodontia."

Roger smiled. The old bastard was growing on him by the minute. "Do you have dementia?"

The old man nodded, his eyes seeming to turn down at the corners. "Not exactly, but it's getting worse."

"But you're a wizard?"

"Yes."

"Why do you need a butler?"

The old man tilted his head up and a little bit away, looking at Roger through the side of his spectacles. His eyes narrowed. "What makes you think I don't?"

Roger pondered that for a moment and glanced down at the scuffed toe. "I used to have a problem with my shoes in the army, sir. I'd spit-polish them until they shined so bright I could shave in them, but every once in a while, I'd catch the heel of one against the toe of the other. Left a scrape." He nodded at the old man's shoes. "Kinda like that one, sir."

"I scuffed my shoe so you think I don't need a butler?"

"No, sir."

"Explain."

"A man who can dress himself, keep track of his place in a book with print that small, and keep a pair of wingtips in shape on his own doesn't need a butler. Naomi said you feed yourself and the groceries come on schedule." Roger shook his head. "A valet, I could understand. A security guard, certainly. Somebody to talk to who's not trying to pull the rug out from under you? I can believe that, sir. A butler?"

Shackleford leaned forward, bracing his elbows on the arms of his wheelchair. "And what makes you think you didn't just describe a butler's duties?" The sly old codger's face wrinkled into a grin and his eyebrows kept asking "Huh? Huh?" as they flickered up and down.

Roger laughed. It wasn't a deep laugh or a long one but it felt damn good. He shook his head. "Got me," he said.

"Do I?" Shackleford asked. "Do I have you, Mr. Mulligan?"

"I'll sign the contract if you'll have me, sir."

Shackleford stuck out one gnarled, liver-spotted hand that trembled slightly. "If you'll have me, son."

Roger shook the man's hand, not at all startled by the strength in his grip. "When would you like me to start, sir?"

"Just as soon as you can get moved in, Mulligan." He paused. "Do you prefer Mulligan or Roger?"

"I answer to both as a rule, sir. Which would you prefer?"

"Let's go with Mulligan. It's the tradition in service."

Roger stood and gave his best impression of a butler's bow, feeling just slightly ludicrous. "Very good, sir. Will there be anything else?"

The old man leaned back in his chair and grinned at him. "Yes, Mulligan. Please settle your affairs and move in as soon as possible and get those leeches off my property."

Roger smiled and gave his little bow again. "Very good, sir. I shall do my best. With your permission, I'll attend to the paperwork?"

"Thank you, Mulligan. That will be all."

Roger got the distinct impression that the old boy was playing his role as lord and master to the hilt. He turned and headed for the door, but before he reached it, the latch released and the door swung inward. Confused, he turned to see Shackleford making an odd gesture with his right hand.

"I told you," Shackleford said, with a small nod.

Roger stepped into the hallway and the door closed behind him with a quiet click. He had to hand it to the old man. It was a pretty good trick. Probably a remote under the blanket.

CHAPTER 2

Roger grabbed his duffel bag from the Uber's trunk before the driver could get out. He'd been a little shocked to realize how little he had to show for thirty-odd years. Too many deployments. Too little time. Occasionally he'd remember something. What happened to his high school yearbook? Where were his baby pictures? Probably all in a landfill somewhere. Maybe his mother still had them. The Uber purred off down the paved alley and Roger looked up at the back of the house. He still had a couple of boxes of stuff in the apartment, but his go-bag served for his first day.

The back of the house could have been part of a country estate. Two honest-to-God oaks stood in the corners of the yard closest to the alley providing an arching entry to the property. A large-ish paved tarmac led from the alley to the garage that sat behind the house proper. The lot felt much wider in the back than in the front. Without measuring, Roger felt certain that the house itself only occupied a fraction of the land. He walked up the drive, past the four-bay garage and around the black BMW sedan. He admired the lines as he passed.

"Like what you see?"

He looked up to see Naomi waiting at an open door at the back of the house. She'd dressed down for the occasion—man-styled shirt, unbuttoned far enough to show some black lace underneath, skinny jeans, tasteful pumps. No jacket. "Yes," Roger said. "Nice lines. Too expensive for me."

She shrugged. "This time next year you'll be a millionaire. You never know."

He glanced back at the car and shrugged. "This part of the deal?"

She laughed. "That's mine."

"You drive it around town?" He stopped at the stoop. "I had you pegged for a taxi-taker. Parking must be a bitch."

She shrugged. "Some things are worth doing yourself." She tossed her careful coif as if it didn't matter. "Come on. Tour starts now. I've got an appointment downtown in two hours."

He stepped into the entry, what his mother might have called a mudroom, and pointed out a compact laundry setup. "You'll need to handle this." She arched an eyebrow. "It wasn't on your list of 'not my jobs,' was it?"

He shook his head. "No. I didn't think of it, but two of us in the house? I think I can handle it. I've got to do my own, actually. The dry cleaning bill is going to cover most of it."

She gave him a second glance.

"What? You thought I didn't know how to clean a wool suit?"

She pursed her lips and gave him a coy shrug. "Unplumbed depths," she said.

He snorted and she put a little extra sway in her walk as she headed down the corridor, pointing out various storage and staging areas. Three steps led up to the main-floor and the kitchen.

Roger whistled and updated his concept of the house from 'eccentric but charming house' to 'damned mansion.'

"How many people used to live here?" he asked.

Naomi wrinkled her nose. "No idea. Why?"

Roger took in the six-burner stovetop, the stacked ovens, a refrigerator bigger than his apartment, and enough counter and cupboard space for a regimental exercise. "No reason. Seems like overkill for a man and his butler."

Naomi shrugged it off. "It's an old house. You know how they get."

Roger didn't and wasn't sure which 'they' she might be talking about—old houses or the people who lived in mansions.

"Come on. Your quarters are just around the corner."

He followed her through a swinging door and into a wainscoted hallway, past two closed doors to one that stood open. "Bathroom," she said, pointing to the obvious. She swung the door across the hall open and ushered him in like a real-estate agent on tour. "Butler's quarters."

Roger stepped into wood and leather heaven. It wasn't large. Correction. It didn't feel large. Aged wood paneling, tongue and groove or some close facsimile, lined the walls. The furnishings were scattered tastefully around the room—a couple of leather easy chairs, end tables, a coffee table, and an ottoman. One of those old-fashioned desks with the rolling top hugged the wall, situated perfectly so light from the window fell on it. The place even had a built-in bookshelf and a small window that looked out onto the side yard and a wing of the mansion beyond. Not terribly scenic but somehow peaceful.

"Bedroom in here," she said, swinging open a narrow door.

He stepped in and nodded. A large wardrobe and a six-drawer dresser stood against the far wall. The full-sized bed, a solid-looking sleigh in some deep brown wood, took up a lot of floor space but left plenty of room for him to move around. He crossed to the wardrobe and opened the double doors, noting the mirrors inside them. He plopped his bag inside and swung the doors closed. Another nod. They should have led with this. For the first time since turning in his weapons, Roger felt like he was at home.

Naomi watched him from the doorway, not exactly in the hooker-one-leg-up-arching-her-back-to-show-off-her-breasts pose but close.

"You mentioned uniforms?" he asked.

"There's a uniform service. They're expecting you." She reached into the breast pocket of her shirt with two fingers and pulled out a business card. "I can drop you on my way downtown if you like."

He took the card. Industrial Uniforms, Inc. "Catchy name. Your company?" he asked.

She grinned and shook her head. "My father's."

"They make butlers' uniforms alongside UPS jumpsuits?"

"UPS drivers don't wear jumpsuits, but yes." She checked the jeweled timepiece on her wrist and nodded at the door. "Come on. A lot to see and I'm going to be late if we don't move it."

He waved her on, pausing for a moment at the door to look back at his new digs. Yeah. They should have led with this.

The rest of the tour became a whirlwind of this room, that room, store room, dining room, another bathroom, downstairs parlor, pantry, another bathroom, upstairs parlor, library, master suite through there, etc., etc. By the time they got to the attic, Roger had had his fill of rich and snooty. She might be fun in bed but he was never going to remember half of what she spieled off.

"I got it," he said when they'd reached the top landing.

"I haven't shown you all the rooms here."

"Attic. Probably servant quarters at some time. Now storage?"

She shrugged. "Still servant quarters. Storage is in the basement."

"Basement?"

She nodded. "I skipped it. Access is in the garage." She checked her watch again. "Probably just as well. I've got to scoot."

"Don't let me hold you up. I can find the place."

"It's right on the way," she said.

"Just give me the house keys and I'll Uber over."

"You could take one of the cars," she said over her shoulder, already heading back down the stairs. "They have free parking."

"Thanks. I'll do that." Not that he would, but she didn't need to know. "Where's my employer?"

She paused at the landing. "Uncle Perry? Master suite. He'll ring you when he wants you."

"Ring me? What? Like I have to wait downstairs or something?"

She grinned and took a small pager from her belt where it had been hidden under the tails of her shirt. "It's not all old dust and fresh wax. Here."

He took the device and looked it over. Standard electronic pager, settings for vibrate, small display screen. He made sure it was on, green light showing, and clipped it to his belt. "Thank you."

"Good luck." She tripped down the stairs, hands up for balance, looking more like a teenager than a forty-something cougar.

"Keys?" he said, calling after her.

"This way," she said, backtracking down the hallway toward the kitchen. She led him back to the butler's quarters and pointed to a key safe hidden behind the door. The safe's key stuck out of the keyhole. "Every key to every lock in the house is supposed to be in there."

"Supposed to be?" he asked.

She shrugged. "I haven't found a locked door that didn't have the key. I didn't try them all."

"Your keys?" he asked.

"My keys?"

"Yes, you have a key to the house, don't you?" He held out his hand.

"Gracious, no. Why would I?"

"How do you get in?"

She rolled her eyes and headed for the back door. He was confused when she stepped outside, afraid she was going to show him a key under a plant pot or something. She pointed to one of those "over the knob" things that real-estate agents used. "Combination is 4185."

His inner security alarm screamed at him but he smiled and nodded. "Thanks." He thrust his hands into his pockets to keep them from either grabbing the thing off the door or strangling her.

She pulled a key fob from her pocket and twee-tweeted the Beamer. "Any questions, I left contact numbers on your desk. Call if anything unusual comes up."

He nodded. "Will do. Thanks."

She pulled the door open and slid into the car in one fluid motion. He wondered if she practiced it at home in the garage where nobody could see when she slammed the door on her foot. The engine rumbled to life and, contrary to his expectation, rolled sedately down the tarmac and into the alley behind—the small sound of tires on pavement clearly audible over the quiet engine.

He released the lock box from the knob and pocketed the key. "Dumbass."

The pager vibrated on his belt. The screen had a single word. "Library." The old fellow must have been watching.

He closed the back door and threw the bolt. He'd bet his first month's pay she had a key in her pocket, but he was done with Nay and Tweed. He made his way through the maze and up the main staircase to the library. The door opened for him as he reached for it. He stepped in to find the old man sitting in his chair by the window. "You rang, sir?" he asked, without really thinking about it.

"Is she gone, Mulligan?"

"Yes, sir. I've had a tour of the house and I'm informed that I have an appointment for a uniform fitting."

"About that," he said. "Her father's establishment? Industrial Uniforms?"

"Yes, sir."

Shackleford harrumphed and shook his head. He reached into the side pocket of his jacket and withdrew a card, shook his head and put it back, drawing another. He frowned at it for a moment. "What am I doing, Mulligan?"

"I believe you're looking for a uniform company to replace Industrial Uniforms that Ms. Patching recommended, sir."

"Am I?" he asked and looked at the card in his hand. "Yes, so it seems." He took a deep breath and blinked several times, staring at the card. He nodded and handed the card to Roger. "Go here. Ask for Mrs. Pettigrew."

He took the card, a heavy stock with a street address embossed into it. "Mrs. Pettigrew, sir."

"Yes, Mulligan."

"Very good, sir. Is there anything I can get you before I go? Have you eaten today, sir? Some breakfast, perhaps?"

The old man looked up at Roger. "I haven't eaten, no." He said it as if only just realizing.

23

"It's midmorning, sir. What would you like?" He shrugged. "I don't know what's in the kitchen but I could probably handle tea and toast."

"Can you manage a bagel and coffee, Mulligan?"

"Cream cheese, sir?"

"Of course," he said. "Smoked salmon if there is any. Naomi never gives me smoked salmon."

"I'll check, sir. I'll need some time to find my way around, sir."

Shackleford smiled. "Mrs. Pettigrew."

"Yes, sir. I'll ask for her."

"Thank you, Mulligan."

"You're welcome, sir." Roger did an about face, his military training carrying him out of the room as the door latched behind him.

The path to the kitchen seemed familiar by then. On the counter he found a chromed coffee maker. He rummaged for a few minutes, lining up the requirements for coffee: whole bean, which required a grinder—also handy. Whoever laid out the kitchen knew Roger's mind, apparently. He assembled the ingredients in the machine and pressed the Brew button.

"Bagels, bagels," he said. "Where would I hide the bagels?" He spotted a four-slice toaster and flipped a mental coin as to whether bread was over or under the counter. He pulled the lower cupboard open, surprised when it turned out to be a drawer. Loaves of bread in various colors and two sleeves of bagels lay arrayed in its depths. One sleeve was cinnamon and raisin, the other onion. He pulled open the fridge to find an almost empty cavern. A quart of milk, a pound of butter, tubs of margarine and cream cheese. One crisper drawer held fresh greens; the other, carrots, celery, and mushrooms. He found a box containing cello-sleeves of smoked salmon, the expensive Nova kind, all unopened. "Sure. What else would he have?"

By the time he got a bagel toasted, schmeared, and covered in thin slices of pink fish, the coffee gave up the final gurgle. Only then did he realize that cutlery, cutting boards, and all the associated necessities had seemed to appear under his hands when he reached for them. He really had to hand it to whoever had designed the kitchen. He opened the cupboard above the coffeemaker, looking for a mug, and stopped. No mugs. His brain fought him for a moment but he realized the cupboard held cups and saucers. All matched. He pulled down a set and assembled it. "All right," he said. "Cup and saucer. I can do this." A part of his brain said, "One more dish to wash," and the other part said, "So?" He glanced down at the brushed stainless steel front of a dishwasher and shrugged.

He considered the breakfast in front of him. If it were his, he'd just eat it at the counter. Shackleford expected him to deliver it. "What would Jeeves do?" He remembered the small tray that Naomi had tried to deliver applesauce with. He frowned and looked at all the cupboards, trying to figure out where he'd store serving trays. He walked past the cook top and ovens, shaking his head. Turning, he crossed to the nearest worktable and found a collection of silver trays in various sizes slotted into a shelf under it. He picked a medium sized one and placed it on the table top. The cup and saucer fit nicely in one corner but he needed a plate for the bagel. His inner dishwasher complained again but he squelched it, pulling a small dessert plate from the cupboard.

He stared at the tray. "What else? What else?" He considered the coffee. How did the old man take it? Looking around again, he opened a cupboard beside the fridge. It contained a variety of serving dishes including those little cream pitchers they use in restaurants and some small dishes with notched covers. He took one of each, filling the little pitcher with milk—sorry, boss, no cream in stock—and placing it near the coffee on the tray. He found bulk sugar next to the bulk flour and filled the dish about half full. A silverware drawer held more silver than he'd seen outside of the mess hall. He picked a small spoon for the sugar bowl, a regular teaspoon to stir with, then grabbed a cloth napkin as he walked by. He stopped and looked at the napkin. It puzzled him but he shrugged, channeling his inner Jeeves. He arranged the accoutrements on the tray and stood back to survey his handiwork.

"What's missing?" he asked.

On a hunch he went to the back door and surveyed the tarmac again. It took him a minute to spot it, but finally saw a telltale green plastic tube beside a rather large post-box at the end of the drive. He found the day's paper rolled up inside. "At least I don't have to track it down in the bushes."

As he made his way back up the drive, he spotted a bright yellow flower beside the walk and plucked it, stripping the leaves from the lower stem and leaving a bit of green at the top. A narrow vase practically leaped from the cupboard beside the fridge and he pondered why the vase would be with the serving dishes for only a moment before garnishing the tray with paper and flower. He smiled. Not bad for the first time. He took the tray by the handles and carried it up the stairs, pausing at the library door for a moment until it opened.

"Thank you, sir. I was just wondering how I'd open it without dropping."

Shackleford smiled up from the book in his lap. "Thank you, Perkins. Just leave it on the table." He nodded at the library table at his side.

"Yes, sir. I hope this is satisfactory. I don't know how you like your coffee."

"After all these years, Perkins? Is your mind going?" Shackleford's head tilted. "That's not right." He looked at Roger. "You're not Perkins."

"No, sir."

The old man nodded and sighed. "Mulligan?"

"Yes, sir."

"Sorry, Mulligan." He offered a sheepish shrug. "The mind. A strange and terrible organ."

"Comes with age, I believe, sir."

His eyes blazed for a moment as he turned from his bagel to stare at Roger. "It's not age. This is not age." He bit each word off. Pushed them at Roger like weapons—verbal daggers, glinting in the morning sun.

"Of course, sir. Sorry, sir." Roger felt foolish and rather bad that he'd insulted, perhaps even hurt the old man. "Will there be anything else, sir?"

Shackleford assaulted one of the bagels, tearing a bite out of it before pouring a splash of milk and scooping two tiny spoons of sugar into his coffee. A quick stir with the spoon and he slurped a sip, washing the bagel down before speaking. "Not at the moment." He paused and looked up. "Mulligan. No, get your uniforms squared away. Come see me when you return."

Roger gave what he began to think of as his Jeeves bow and left the room, pausing and then pulling the door closed behind him.

The Uber driver peered out at the street numbers as he navigated the tree-lined lane. Two- and three-story brick buildings lined the narrow street. Roger keyed a tip and leaned against the window to look up at the majestic old-city architecture. The States had nothing that could compare to the ancient construction in Europe and the Middle East, but these represented some of the oldest buildings on this side of the Atlantic. In a neighborhood of old residences, Roger began to worry that the old man had slipped him the wrong card after all.

"Here ya go," the driver said, nodding at a building across the street.

Roger pressed the button to pay the man. "Thanks."

"Welcome. Have a good day."

He stepped out into the shade of one of the trees and the Uber motored off. He looked up at the two-story across the road. The number gleamed in shiny brass beside the door, but it looked like somebody's grandmother lived there. Lace curtains adorned the bay window on the ground floor. A bushy philodendron hung in the middle, long tendrils cascading out of sight. A tree blocked his view of the upper story.

Roger crossed the street and pressed the bell, checking first to see if it was really a button and not a pull. The jingling sound tinkled inside and a twenty-something young man wearing a hip-length bathrobe over some black pants answered. It took Roger a moment to recognize the robe as a smoking jacket. The floofy neckerchief made the guy look like a Hefner-bee. "Yes?" he asked.

"Mrs. Pettigrew?" Roger asked.

The man nodded and stepped back, pulling the door open to allow Roger to enter. He pointed up the stairwell. "Top of the stairs." The faint fug of actual tobacco clung to him, the sharp aroma taking Roger back to "smoke 'em if you got 'em" days. He'd have expected a different smoke, just going on the guy's looks, but books and covers, yadda yadda.

Roger climbed the narrow staircase and stopped on the landing. He rapped three times with a knuckle on the closed door.

"Just a minute." The voice gave it a sing-song cadence in a mid-alto range that made Roger grin. A chain lock rattled and the door swung wide to reveal a woman—somewhere between forty and sixty—in a smart business suit, single-breasted blazer over a sixties-era pleated skirt, both in a chocolate brown. A cream-colored blouse with a puff of lace at the throat and a pair of low-heeled shoes rounded out her outfit. A yellow cloth tape measure dangled in her free hand and a pencil stuck out of her graying hair. She gave him a quick up-and-down look. "Mulligan?" she asked.

"Yes, ma'am."

She stepped out of the doorway. "Come in." She pointed at a wooden box in the middle of the floor in an otherwise completely empty room. The bay window on this floor stood empty, the view across the street obscured by the leaves on the trees. "Stand there, please, Mr. Mulligan."

He walked into the naked apartment and stepped onto the box.

She walked around him twice, measuring him with her gaze before starting to work with the tape. She made little "huh" sounds with each measurement. Very thorough, starting at his foot and working up his leg, calf, each thigh, and stretching the tape down both left and right inseams, her warm hand close to his crotch making him look down. "Straight ahead, if you please, Mr. Mulligan."

She worked up his body—hips, waist. "Arms out, please." Chest, fingertip-to-fingertip, shoulders, cuffs, neck. "You can put them down." Apparently satisfied, she stepped back and looked him up and down again. "You're Shackleford's new man?"

"Yes, ma'am."

"You know his last man passed away in the spring."

"Perkins, ma'am?"

"You knew him?"

"No, ma'am."

A faint smile twitched her lips. "He called you Perkins?"

"Easy enough to do. Habits, ma'am."

She nodded, as if making up her mind. "You'll do." She walked behind him and he looked over his shoulder to see her opening a wardrobe tucked against the back wall, one he could have sworn wasn't there before. She pulled out a white shirt and a pair of slate gray pants. She turned to him, shirt hanging from two fingers of one hand and the trousers over her other forearm. She huffed. "Strip to your boxers, Mr. Mulligan. We've work to do."

For a moment he wondered how she knew he wore boxers but stripped down. Wasn't the first time he'd been ordered out of his clothes. At least this time he didn't have to be nuts-to-butts with some hairy grunt in front of him. She took his garments and hung them in the wardrobe before crouching in front of him, holding the pants. It felt only slightly awkward but he stepped into them, allowing her to dress him—pulling the waistband up his legs and fastening the two buttons at the top. She went behind him with the shirt and lifted it up so it hung from his shoulders.

"Button up, tuck it in, Mr. Mulligan."

He settled the shirt and ran the buttons up the front and on his cuffs before opening the front of his trousers again to settle the tails. "These fit pretty good."

She snorted. "They should." She came around him, pulling here, tugging there. She pulled his arms down to his sides and checked the cuffs. "Good." She returned to the wardrobe, emerging with a dove gray tie and black vest. She held the tie out to him. "I trust you know what to do with this?"

He took it and tied a passable Shelby without a mirror, the tail falling just shy of his waistband. He shrugged. "Near as I can do by touch."

She nodded lifting the front to check the trailing end. "Passable. Full Windsor?"

He pulled the knot out, adjusted the lay, and ran as much of a full Windsor as he could without seeing where his fingers were going.

"Keep it a little looser in the knot until it's ready to set," she said.

His fingers followed her instructions without Roger having to think about it. Again, the tie fell correctly against his waist but the knot felt a little bulkier.

"Yes. You've got the shoulders for a full Windsor and the tie's long enough to support the knot." She handed him the vest. "This is a waistcoat, not a vest. You think it's a vest. You're wrong." She held it behind him to slip on. He put his arms back and she came around the front to settle and button it. "Leave the bottom button undone. You'll want to button it. Military types always do, but this is your working uniform and it's not supposed to be buttoned."

"Yes, ma'am."

She brushed the waistcoat down, smoothing it over his stomach. She nodded and returned to the wardrobe, emerging with a black jacket. She held it for him to slip on and pulled it up over his shoulders. He shot his cuffs and buttoned the top button, feeling the jacket settle around him like armor. She tugged the back hem down and walked around, looking at the drape. "Very nice. This is your normal working uniform." She looked down. "Oh, one moment." She went back to the wardrobe and pulled out a pair of black socks and black oxfords with a simple toe-cap. "These. Put them on, please, Mr. Mulligan."

He sat on the box and put on the socks and shoes before resuming his position on the pedestal.

"Yes. Very good," Mrs. Pettigrew said, walking around him. "As I was saying, this is your normal working uniform. When in the kitchen or engaged in any activity where the jacket may be an obstacle or become soiled, you replace the jacket with an apron. Any questions, Mr. Mulligan?"

"No, ma'am."

"You'll find living and working in a jacket and tie becomes no more of a burden than your army fatigues in time. I emphasize that it takes some getting used to for most Americans, but you will adjust." She paused and nodded again. "Slip the jacket off, please."

He released the button and she pulled the garment down his arms, returning it to the wardrobe. When she came back, she carried a tailed coat in black. She held it for him to put his arms in and slid it up his back. He tugged it around and buttoned the top button again, checking his cuffs. She walked around him and he stood for her inspection, staring straight ahead. "Yes. This is for formal wear. If Mr. Shackleford needs you to officiate at a formal dinner or professional evening gathering, this is the coat you wear with the dress trousers. They'll have a satin ribbon on them." She reached into the wardrobe once more and pulled out a pair of white cloth gloves. She handed them to him with a smile. "I believe you know what these are?"

He took them and pulled them on, settling them on his fingers and tugging the cuffs to lay against his wrists.

"The gloves go with this coat. They are only for formal occasions unless Mr. Shackleford explicitly requests them." She gave him a stern look. "Do not put them—or anything else—in the outside pockets of the coat or the trousers. Am I clear?"

"Yes, ma'am." He paused. "How do I carry things?"

"What do you mean, 'things?'"

"My wallet, identification? Keys?"

She nodded. "You may place your identification in the inside left breast pocket. A card. One. Americans tend to like having their drivers' licenses, but this is largely optional since you're seldom asked to prove your identity in the house, nor do you wear this uniform when off-duty and off-premises." She reached under the right-hand side of his coat, tugging at a loop in his waistband. "You may hang a set of keys here if you must. Generally it's not required in the course of your normal duties unless you're responsible for a large house with a great deal of security." She looked up at him. "This is your first posting?"

"Yes, ma'am."

Her stern visage softened slightly. "Shackleford House is a good place to start your career. You're mature enough to understand the duties and young enough to grow into them. Mr. Shackleford has always been a kind and generous employer."

He didn't tell her it was only for a year. "Yes, ma'am."

She held her hand. "Coat, please?"

He slipped it off and handed it to her. She hung it up and came back around in front of him. She held out a gold chain with an ornate gold watch attached. "Your wrist watch is not worn when you wear a waistcoat, Mr. Mulligan. Do you know how to wear this?"

He took the watch from her, slipped the T-bar top through a buttonhole in the waistcoat and slipped the watch into the left pocket. He raised his eyebrows in her direction.

She nodded. "What time is it, Mr. Mulligan?"

He reached across and withdrew the watch from the pocket, and pressed the stem to open the cover. "Nearly noon, ma'am."

"Thank you, Mr. Mulligan," she said. "Do you have any questions?"

He closed the watch and replaced it. "No, ma'am."

"Excellent. If you'd don your street clothes again, I believe we're almost done."

As he took off each garment she put it in the wardrobe. When everything was replaced, she handed his own clothes back to him. He placed his foot on the box to tie his shoes. Straightening, he turned to find Mrs. Pettigrew standing by the door with a book in her hands.

"Some last words of advice, Mr. Mulligan," she said. "Get a notebook. Small three by five. Black. Invest in a good pen, silver. Those you may—in fact, should—keep on your person at all times. The inside breast pocket on either style of jacket. In the beginning, in particular, you'll want to write things down. Until you get the rhythm of the house and the flow of your duties, you will find yourself overwhelmed. Keeping notes as you go will help you organize your thinking."

She reminded him a little of his boot camp instructors. "Thank you, Mrs. Pettigrew. I will."

"Since this is your first posting, I would like you to take this." She held the book out to him. "The Shackleford House Butler's Bible. Anything you need to know about managing Shackleford House is described in there. This volume is specific to Shackleford House, so if you change positions, you'll need to come back to see me. Depending on where you go, there may be different requirements."

He felt his eyebrows rise as he took the leather-bound volume. The weight of it surprised him and the idea of a book outlining the duties of a specific house made his head spin. What kind of money and time went into making a unique item like that? "Thank you, Mrs. Pettigrew. I don't know what else to say."

She offered her hand and he shook it with a small bow. "I'll have your uniforms delivered shortly. Good day, Mr. Mulligan. Good luck."

"Good day, Mrs. Pettigrew."

Before he knew it, he was back on the sidewalk outside, blinking in the midday sun. He looked up at the building again, feeling like there was something he should remember. After a few moments he shrugged and pulled out his phone to summon an Uber. Judging from the weight of the book in his hand, he had a lot of reading to do. He'd feel more comfortable reading it in his quarters.

CHAPTER 3

Roger had the Uber drop him at the back of the house so he could pick up the mail on the way in. There seemed rather a lot of it, but he tucked his book under his arm and sorted out the trash from the treasures. Some pieces looked official, while others could be tossed in the bin. Probably. He looked up at the house, wondering if the old man was a coupon clipper. The idea made him snicker. He navigated the back door, remembering to throw the bolt, and made a mental note to get a notebook and silver pen so he could make an actual note to call a locksmith.

He walked through the kitchen to go to his quarters. After placing his Butler's Bible on the bookcase, he pushed the rolltop up and went to drop the mail on the surface, but held off as he surveyed the contents of the desk. Placing the mail aside on the desk's chair, Roger started exploring. Inside the rolltop were cubbies and small drawers. An elegantly shaped pen in an equally elegant stand stood to one side while on the other an antique stapler peeked out of a cubby. A bookshelf ran across the top holding a row of large, bound ledgers, each neatly labeled with dates.

"I didn't realize I was the bookkeeper, too." He kicked himself because neither he nor Vinnie had thought of it. He should have. He pulled the most current ledger from the shelf and opened it on the desk. It took him a few minutes to work out what was on the pages. The numbers and columns he understood at first glance, but it took him a moment to decipher the line items. Eventually he worked it out. The last entry was several weeks old.

He looked around his quarters for a filing cabinet or some indication of where the actual bills had been stored. Nothing jumped out at him, but there had to be something. He eyed the pile of mail. He doubted that was months' worth, although it could certainly represent several days. He replaced the ledger on its shelf and went

33

to close the rolltop, only then realizing that the bottom half of the desk was made of drawers, one of which held very modern-looking files, each tabbed and arranged in alphabetical order. The lightest touch on one of two decorative-looking knobs on a shallow drawer front to the right of center caused a writing surface, complete with blotter, to slide out from beneath the main desktop.

Every time he thought he had a handle on things, he discovered some aspect he hadn't anticipated. The whole situation began to feel more and more out of control—snowballing on him and threatening to sweep him away.

He sighed and then took another deep breath. He could do this. Roger headed to his bedroom, intent on grabbing a fresh shirt from his duffle bag, and froze in the doorway. The bag lay on its side on one of those hotel-style suitcase stands in the corner. The deep green canvas bag looked out of place in the wood and leather room. How had it gotten out of the wardrobe? "What the—"

Looking around, he spotted a small black notebook resting on the top of the dresser, a silver pen beside it. A white card stuck out of the top of the book like a bookmark. Heavy paper stock, he thought as he pulled it out.

"A gift from Mrs. Pettigrew to Roger Mulligan on the occasion of his first posting. Even the sharpest minds sometimes need help with memories. Use this to aid yours. Best wishes." The words spidered across the card in a flowing script; it was signed with an ornately flourished P.

He opened the wardrobe and blinked. The cavernous interior held clothing—the very clothing he'd been fitted for. He pulled out one of the coats and one of the white shirts. Hangers full of them took up over half the space. Long coats on the left, then the shorter. A few vests. No, waistcoats. More shirts than he'd ever owned in his life, all neatly hung. The far right held the slacks. He pulled some of them out, noting that a few had the satin stripe while most of them were plain. A tie rack on the door held a bouquet of dove gray ties. Four pairs of shoes stood lined up along the bottom of the wardrobe.

He looked around. Nothing else seemed disturbed. How was this even possible?

He opened the top drawer on the dresser and found neatly rolled black socks and a tray with the pocket watch and chain in it. The second drawer held white undershirts, the third boxers. The bottom three lay empty and he had no idea what might go in them until he glanced at his duffel bag and shrugged. "Seems legit."

He needed to report to Shackleford and realized they both needed lunch. He'd lost the morning and felt like he was wading through hip-deep muddy water into the afternoon. He stopped to pick up the pile of mail and headed for the stairs. No time like the present.

Roger knocked twice on the library door and opened it. Shackleford sat in his chair, staring into space. For a moment Roger thought the old coot had snuffed it while he was out, but he was too upright, too stiff. It took a while for corpses to stiffen up. He waited, unsure whether he should close the door and walk away or enter, possibly breaking the man's concentration.

The dilemma resolved itself when Shackleford seemed to reanimate and tilted his head to one side, staring at Roger. "What is it, Perkins?" he asked. "Sorry, Mulligan." He offered a small grin and shrug. "I beg your indulgence, Mulligan. Perkins was with me for decades."

Roger stepped into the room and shrugged. "I understand, sir. Slip of the tongue."

"Precisely," the old man said. "Did you find Mrs. Pettigrew?"

"I did, sir. It appears my new uniforms have arrived already."

"Did they? Excellent." He eyed Roger. "You're not wearing it?"

"I only just returned, sir. I have the mail and wanted to check in with you as soon as possible. I can go change, if you'd prefer?"

"Not necessary, Mulligan. Thank you." He held out his hand for the mail. "Have you sorted it?"

Roger handed it over. "No, sir. I wasn't sure how much you wanted me to. What's important and what's not."

Shackleford nodded and tossed the pile on the library table. "Sort it now and I'll see if you and I agree on what's important."

Roger crossed to the table and shuffled the advertisements, glossy magazines, and first class into three piles. He then went through the first class, weighing each in his hand and ignoring most of the 'urgent time-sensitive' come-ons. It took him only a few minutes to complete the task.

Shackleford stepped up beside Roger and nodded. "From now on, you can recycle the ads directly. Magazines go here in the library eventually, but new issues go on my bedside table. Just swap the new for the old and file the old in the appropriate box." He nodded at the neatly labeled row of file boxes on one of the library shelves. "I keep them for reference."

"Very good, sir."

The old man eyed the three stacks of first class. "You can open anything in first class, Mulligan. I've no secrets from you." He picked up one of the 'urgent time-sensitive' envelopes and ripped it open. The solicitation inside looked familiar. "Roadside service life insurance." The old man shook his head. "You can recycle anything that offers me a deal on anything. I don't deal with vendors I don't know."

"Understood, sir."

He picked up one of the envelopes marked 'invoice enclosed,' giving it the same rough treatment. He pulled it out, scanning it briefly. "Yes, you'll find bills for services rendered." He looked up at Mulligan from under his eyebrows. "You are my butler, not my laborer. It's your job to hire the people to do the work and see that it's done correctly and to your satisfaction. Not to do the work yourself. Understood?"

"Yes, sir."

"Utilities, taxes, normal bills. Simply pay them. You have signatory authorization on the house checking account. Anything that looks odd, bring it to me."

"Yes, sir."

Shackleford pointed to the last pile of envelopes. "Why did you put these in a separate pile?" he asked, looking up at Mulligan.

"They don't fit any of the other piles, sir. They're not obvious bills. They're not likely sales flyers."

Shackleford nodded. "Open them for me, please?"

Roger opened the first three—a sales offer masquerading as a letter, an invitation to a hearing aid demonstration, and a letter from a friend telling of his adventures overseas. "I'd toss the first two, sir."

Shackleford nodded again. "This one?"

Roger picked it up and put it back down. He shook his head. He picked it up again and put it back down.

"What's the matter, man? I asked you to open it." Shackleford looked at him, a mischievous grin taking the sting out of his words.

"I don't know, sir. I pick it up, try to open it, but then put it back down." He tried a couple more times. "I don't understand."

Shackleford nodded. "It's warded."

Roger stared at the old man. "What do you mean warded, sir?"

"I can open it but you won't be able to," he said. "You also can't inadvertently discard or shred it. Various messages from my colleagues around the world. They're rare but should you come across one, simply put it with those missives that require my attention."

"I understand, sir." Roger didn't really understand but couldn't deny that somehow the letter didn't want to be opened. The thought unsettled him.

"Is there anything else, Mulligan?"

"I have to be honest, sir, I don't know much about bookkeeping."

He nodded. "Neither did Perkins in the beginning." He grinned. "I don't know much either, but if you need help, hire it. You have a budget for it and if you need more, it's available."

"You mean hire a bookkeeper, sir?"

"If that's your wish. I'm not sure we have enough work to keep a full-time bookkeeper employed. You may just want to hire a consultant to teach you how to do it."

"Thank you, sir. I'll look into that. Would you like lunch?"

"I would, Mulligan. Thank you. A bit of soup would sit well."

"Very good, sir. I'll get changed and see to it."

"Thank you, Mulligan." Shackleford scooped up the recalcitrant letter and the one from his friend. He waved a hand at the rest. The junk mail disappeared, leaving only the bill resting on the table.

Roger blinked, feeling his jaw drop.

Shackleford looked up at him. "What? Did you want them for some reason?"

"No, sir. It just surprised me." He bit down on his tongue to keep from asking how the old guy had done it. "That's quite a trick."

Shackleford offered up a sly smile. "You don't believe I'm a wizard yet?"

"You're definitely a wizard, sir." He had to be the best magician Roger had ever seen. "No doubt in my mind."

Shackleford chuckled. "It's only the first day, Mulligan. It gets easier as it goes along."

Roger gave his butler bow. "Of course, sir." He turned to leave, but the old man stopped him at the door.

"A few of those little round crackers, too, Mulligan. The salt is terrible for me but a few in soup?" He shrugged, his eyes looking more like puppy-dog than wizard.

"I'll see what I can find, sir. Should I stock them?"

"Just a few, perhaps." The old man grinned.

"Very good, sir." He stepped out into the hall and realized that having that notebook right at that moment would have been a very good idea. He tried to remember what the other thing he was going to remember was and snorted when he couldn't.

He felt a little self-conscious putting on the uniform for the first time. Since it wasn't a formal occasion he took the suit pants and jacket rather than the morning coat with the fancy trousers. The mirrors in the wardrobe's doors made tying the tie pretty easy. His fingers seemed to work the knot from memory without him having to think "this goes through there" too much. He finished by slipping into the jacket and buttoning the top button. His wristwatch gleamed and he crossed to the dresser, sliding the top drawer open to get at the tray. The bulky wrist chronometer found a home there and he pulled out the pocket watch. Fastening the chain, he checked the time against the wristwatch. One of them was off by a minute, but he didn't try to correct either.

He pulled the pager off his belt and held it in his fingers, wondering where to put it. No pockets allowed. Finally he clipped it to the waistband of his trousers near the key-ring loop on his hip. The device was barely bigger than a pack of matches and didn't break the line of his coat.

He picked up the notebook from the top of the dresser and pulled off the elastic cord holding it closed. The pen was a simple retractable ballpoint, a few grades above your basic Bic, and it wrote in black ink, of course. He jotted down a quick note about oyster crackers and another about calling a locksmith to change the locks on the outside doors. Then he made a note to look in the garage to see what vehicles it held. After thinking for a moment, he added one about inventorying the house and hiring a bookkeeper to help him make sense of the household finances.

He clicked the pen again and closed his notebook, slipping the elastic around it and clipping the pen in the handy loop. The whole thing slid into his inner pocket like it had been made for it. Given the source, it probably had.

He checked himself in the mirror again, frowning at the shadow on his jaw. He'd need to pay a little more attention to the morning shave, apparently. He shrugged and headed for the kitchen, his new shoes clicking on the parquet floor.

He glanced around looking for something. What was it Pettigrew had said? Apron. He didn't have one. Did he?

He opened what he thought was a broom closet only to find a full pantry behind the door. Yes, there was a broom and dustpan in spring clips. Beside them, a black apron hung on a peg. He slipped his jacket off, swapping it with the apron. He looped the top strap over his head and pulled the buckled belt around his back. The two ends clicked together with a snap.

It took him some looking and poking but he found the soup and crackers. Soup went into the microwave and he co-opted a sugar bowl sans lid for the crackers. The two bowls looked rather lonesome on the tray, so he added a glass of sparkling water, a small side-salad of greens he found in the fridge, and a china ramekin which he filled with a ranch dressing he'd found with the rest of the condiments. The old guy must like it. Satisfied with the luncheon tray, he swapped his apron for the jacket once more and took the tray up to Shackleford.

The old man barely looked up when Roger swapped the lunch tray for the breakfast one that still sat on the table, nothing but crumbs and an empty mug left on it.

"Lunch, sir."

"Thank you, Perkins," he said without looking up. "Just leave it on the table."

"Yes, sir." He turned and left the room, pulling the door closed behind him. He wondered what was so important to the man that he spent days studying that book.

Tray returned and breakfast dishes in the dishwasher, he retired to his quarters to call a locksmith. Time to get the security under control.

Roger always rose early. At 5 a.m., he rolled out of his new, comfortable bed and did his morning twenty-five—pushups, jumping jacks, and sit-ups. Twenty-five each. A far cry from his army days, but it got his blood moving. He changed into his jogging clothes and headed for the back door. He'd need to find the right path in his new neighborhood but felt confident that in the upscale, gentrified environs he'd find plenty of paths.

His dawn patrol took him out the back door, down the tarmac, and around the alley. The backs of the townhouses lining the alley all looked the same, each with its fenced-in yard, some with parking lots, most with just a stockade privacy fence and trash-bag gate. Almost all had the same dumpster in a sedate green with a white triangle logo. The alley itself seemed remarkably clear of gang tags or loose litter. The occasional plastic bag fluttered in a corner, but those things went wherever the wind blew. It wouldn't surprise him to find them in the Sahara.

The alley continued across several cross streets, the gentrified row houses seemingly unending. He jogged three blocks down and turned up to the main street to jog back. He dodged a few early dog-walkers by stepping off the sidewalk to run in the gutter. The overnight parking bans appeared to be strictly enforced since he didn't have to run around vehicles. The repetitive warning signs with their red zero-slash ticked by him so often he wondered which councilman's son had the franchise on producing them. He jogged past the front of the house, glancing up at it and feeling a pang that the edifice might be gone in a year, erased in favor of the monotonous stone, brick, chrome, and wood façades of yet another two or three "modern townhouse condominiums starting at the low 1Ms." He snorted, startling a forty-something in trendy cross-trainers, capri-length leggings and an oversized Miskatonic U. Athletics hoodie as she walked her mutt along the brick-paved sidewalk. She scowled at him and he gave her a smile, a nod, and a wide berth as he passed. At the next cross-street he turned down to complete his loop by jogging up the alley to the tarmac. He paused to walk the last bit, giving himself a bit of cooldown. It hadn't been much of a run but it would do until he had more time to find his way.

Back in his quarters, he slipped into a pair of jeans to walk across the hall to the bath and take a shower. When he returned to his rooms, he took the notebook from the top of his dresser, flipping it open. He'd crossed off the locksmith note as soon as the locks had new keys. The locksmith made short work of the front and back doors, presenting Roger with four keys for each. He made sure one hung in the key safe but also left one out on his desk.

He checked the remaining items on the list as he changed into his uniform of the day. Roger wasn't sure what time Shackleford got up. He went to the kitchen and prepared one of his own favorite breakfasts—a pair of poached eggs with well-buttered toast and coffee. It took only a few minutes, and he ate in the kitchen, leaning against the counter near the sink.

He put his dishes in the washer and went to the key safe in his quarters to retrieve the key marked 'Garage' in big letters. On his way down the tarmac to pick up the morning paper, he swung by the garage. Flipping the switch inside the door kicked on a row of fluorescent tubes down the length of the barnlike structure. Three cars, each parked nose out, gleamed side by side in a row. A mechanic's work bench held tools he'd seen before but had only limited experience with. The concrete floor looked clean enough to eat off.

First in line, a classic black limousine from sometime in the fifties, maybe. Long nose, short trunk. It looked European, like something from a diplomatic newsreel. He strolled past the nose, where a Bentley badge above the grille held a B with wings. He peeked in at the leather interior but felt nervous about even looking at it.

Next a black Cadillac limo from the 60s, judging from the design. Compared to the sleek Bentley beside it, it looked like a box with fins but the wide stance and longer wheelbase probably made it a good choice for a longer ride.

A red MG convertible perched last in line. The boxy shape, curved doors, and gleaming chrome made him smile. It had to be from the forties or fifties. Older than Roger's mother. He glanced back up the line. Probably they all were. He couldn't imagine how much money the three vehicles might fetch from a classic car buyer. The thought made him swallow hard at the idea that—at some point—he might have to drive one of them.

The last bay stood empty. A few faint tire tracks on the concrete made him think it hadn't always been that way. Perhaps the late Perkins had kept a vehicle there. He shrugged and walked back up the line around the backs of the cars. Each was as inspiring from the back as the front. Cars had never been Roger's passion, but gazing at the collection in the old man's garage, he could see why some people might love them.

He flicked off the lights and made sure the door locked behind him before picking up the morning paper and a fresh flower for Shackleford's breakfast tray.

The house kept surprising him, but what did he expect for his first actual day on the job? There were whole rooms he hadn't been in and had no clear idea what the daily routine might be.

He dropped the paper on the counter in the kitchen and went back to replace the garage key in the safe in his quarters. The lone book on the shelf caught his eye. He took it back to the kitchen with him, wondering what he'd find in the Shackleford House Butler's Bible. If the information was half as good as Pettigrew's work on his uniform, he looked forward to digging in.

The morning light gave the kitchen a warm glow and he pulled one of the tall stools over to the work table. He poured a fresh cup of coffee and settled with the book. He flipped the cover open, skipped the few opening pages and found a table of contents. The topics Uniform Expectations and Daily Routines caught his immediate attention, while farther down the list he found Building and Grounds Maintenance and Financial Responsibilities. He eyed the chapter headings of Staff Management and Vehicle Protocols. Given that he was a staff of one and pretty used to managing himself, he ignored that while filing the vehicle one away for the moment.

As he scanned down the long, long list—flipping to the next page to see even more—he began to consider that a year wouldn't be enough time for him to figure the whole thing out.

He sat back and sipped his coffee, surprised at the sense of regret that the gig would be over in a year even though he'd be rich. Looking around at the opulent kitchen and picturing the location of the house on the street, he recalibrated that thought to "well, richer." He put the coffee cup back into its saucer and flipped back to the Daily Routine entry. "Page forty-seven," he said, grabbing a few pages and flipping the book open to the right page on the first try.

He dug into the chapter and immersed himself in the minutiae. Each day of the week had a routine but the variations all fit within an overall structure. Mr. Shackleford rose at 8 a.m., sharply. He carried out his morning ablutions privately and was not to be disturbed. He enjoyed his breakfast in the library at 8:30 a.m., imparting daily orders to the staff. See Meal Preferences and Variations, Appendix M, page 921. Roger blinked at that but checked the time on his pocket watch—only 7:30—and the day of the week on the front page of the paper. Thursday. He nodded and dug back into the daily routines. It seemed Mr. Shackleford enjoyed lunch on the balcony when the weather was fine ("see Map Inset"), preferring to stay in the library during the colder months or in inclement weather.

Roger sat back, intrigued. The old man had a balcony off the back of the house in a room taking up the corner opposite his suite. He remembered seeing the sunny corner room on the running tour that Naomi gave him—was that just yesterday? He'd have to check it out. Summer in the city wasn't a good time to be out at noon, but if the balcony had some shade, it might be pleasant enough.

Each day had some housekeeping chores besides meals. While some had schedules—changing linens on Monday, trash pickup on Wednesday, and a dry cleaning service that picked up and delivered on Thursday afternoon—some appeared to be required daily. He hadn't done any of them yet but took out his notebook and opened to a blank page, marking it with the ribbon. He jotted down the four things he needed to do before noon, which included picking up the paper and seeing to Shackleford's breakfast, already done of course, but also "service the master suite" and "deposit outgoing correspondence." All of them made sense to him and soothed his military sense of required order and cleanliness. He finished his notes, closed the notebook, and slipped it back into his pocket.

Looking ahead to the afternoon, he saw that afternoons were dedicated to a specific task. It seemed he had his choice of Saturday or Sunday off. His years in the army had inured him to working 24/7, and his EMT days were the civilian version of watch-standing, so he hadn't really had a regular day off for most of his adult life. He wondered what he'd do for a few moments before giving himself a little shake and looking back at the book. Somewhere there was an Appendix M with meal preferences. He found the reference to page 921 and flipped to the back of the book.

He checked the page number and realized he'd hit it the first time. "All right, Mr. S. What do you like for brekkie?"

Roger gave his uniform the once-over and nodded before taking the tray with two poached eggs on a single slice of buttered wheat toast, coffee with cream and sugar, the flower he'd picked in the garden in a familiar square vase, and the morning paper. According to the Bible, he'd inadvertently committed a faux pas by serving without a full setting of silver, which he'd corrected this morning.

At 8:29 he climbed the stairs to the library and knocked twice on the door with his knuckle, a tricky maneuver until he learned to balance the tray on his left hand, only using the right to steady it as he walked. The door latch clicked and the door swung inward.

"Breakfast, sir."

"Thank you, Mulligan. I see you're finding your way." Shackleford sat in his usual place beside the window, but the chair no longer had wheels and he held no book. "Put it on the table, please."

"Yes, sir. Mrs. Pettigrew's guidance has been invaluable." Roger heard the words coming out of his mouth and felt both pleased and puzzled. The suit must have come with a thesaurus.

Shackleford smiled and nodded. "Thought she might be. Do you have any questions?"

"One, sir. I took the liberty of touring the garage this morning and noticed the empty bay."

The old man stood and walked to the table, taking a seat in front of his breakfast tray.

"Yes, Perkins had a vehicle he used for jaunts on his day off. His estate claimed it when he passed away." He glanced up from his poached egg. "You did this, Mulligan?"

"Yes, sir. I'm not known for my cooking skills but I can boil water and cook an egg."

"Thank you, Mulligan. I appreciate your efforts." He finished stirring his coffee and took a sip. "If you have a vehicle, you're welcome to park it in the garage if you like. Comes with the job."

"I'm without a vehicle at the moment. It never seemed to be worthwhile in the city."

Shackleford nodded. "The offer stands. You're welcome to use any of the cars there should you have need."

Roger shook his head. "Thank you, sir. I'd be afraid someone would hit me. I wouldn't want to be responsible for something happening to one of them."

"The cars are safe in the garage, Mulligan, but being safe in the garage is not what cars are for. Isn't that the saying?" the old man asked with a grin.

"I believe it's ships are safe in harbor, sir, but I take your point."

He tilted his head to one side and nodded, turning to address his breakfast. "Probably so. Thank you, Parsons. Carry on."

Roger gave his little bow. "Thank you, sir."

He left the library, pulling the door closed behind himself and turning to the master suite at the end of the short hall. Double doors opened to a large corner room, windows on two sides. It shared a wall with the library, and a door in the other wall opened to an en suite bathroom. The room had a light and airy feeling in spite of heavy drapes and a lot of dark wood. A king-sized four-poster held pride of place, and some familiar-looking wardrobes and dressers stood at attention around the room. A cozy reading nook with chair, ottoman, reading lamp, and side table occupied the corner between the windows. He set about putting the room in order, collecting clothing and making the bed. He'd have to find the linen closet to get sheets to change it and procure some fresh towels. He pulled out his notebook and jotted down a reminder before he forgot. Shackleford's robe hung on a hook behind the bathroom door; his pajamas lay in a heap beside the surprisingly modern chrome and granite tile shower. Roger picked up the pajamas and gave them a shake, folded them neatly, and placed them on the vanity. He really wasn't sure what to do with the room beyond basic straightening. At some point he'd need to do a cleaning pass on the bathroom and run a vacuum over the rugs in the bedroom proper. He'd need to wipe down the lateral surfaces. His Bible probably had guidance that he'd overlooked but, putting on his barracks inspection hat, he mentally checked off the points he'd look at in that situation. It felt overwhelming for a moment. He shrugged it off.

A few minutes' work had the room in order, if not inspection ready. Even barracks don't get inspected every day.

He nodded to himself and left, closing the doors behind him. He sighed. He had a lot to do.

CHAPTER 4

Roger started carrying his bible with him as he went around the house. If nothing else, the map insets aided in his navigation. The linen closet turned out to be on the third floor, so the laundry on the first floor meant carrying the linens down to be cleaned but back up for storage. It seemed an inefficient arrangement but he worked with it, promising himself not to change anything until he discovered the reason it existed.

By the end of the second week, Roger had a daily routine down. His exercise in the morning, the uniform of the day, his duties varying within a framework of meals and cleaning. He'd used his day off to move out of his apartment—donating whatever he didn't want to the local thrift and storing the rest in a storage locker. Bookkeeping remained a mystery process that he went through based on the handbook's step-by-step instructions. It made him uneasy that he didn't understand it. A few pages gave him what he needed to know about managing the master suite and the old man seemed happy—or at least didn't complain—about the state of his rooms. Shackleford seldom left the library, leaving the rest of the house to Roger to prowl alone. He'd even become comfortable in his uniform—cycling the clothes through the dry cleaning pickup and delivery along with Shackleford's suits.

He'd just finished paying the latest utility bill at the desk in his quarters when he heard and felt the old man fall.

He bolted from his chair and took the stairs two at a time. Bursting through the library door, he found Shackleford collapsed on the rug. A quick visual pass revealed no obvious injury, no limbs misplaced or bleeding. He located the old man's pulse—steady but a bit weak. His skin felt normal and his color, while pale, didn't indicate any extreme condition. Roger sat back on his heels to consider the options. By the time he'd made up his mind to call 911—probably a full minute later—the old man stirred on his own.

"Blast," he said, stretching his limbs and rolling over on his back. "Mulligan. Help me up, if you please." He held out an arm.

Roger pulled him to his feet, surprised by the strength in the old man's grip. In fact, his arm—his whole body—displayed much more strength as he stood than Roger would have expected from a man who spent so much time in a wheelchair with a blanket on his lap. "Are you all right, sir?" He pulled a chair out from the library table and turned it so Shackleford could sit.

Shackleford took the chair and nodded. "Nothing to be concerned about. If you could get me some water?"

Roger went into the master suite and returned with a tumbler of water from the sink there.

The old man took it and upended the glass, pulling the water in with deep gulps before giving the glass back. "I do this to myself," he said. "Dehydrated. Stood up too fast."

"Is this why you use the wheelchair?" Roger asked.

Shackleford shrugged. "Partly. Another?" He nodded at the glass.

Roger refilled the glass and returned it to him. "Should I keep a pitcher here, sir?"

"That shouldn't be necessary," he said, then shrugged. "It couldn't hurt, but I'm normally not this—" He paused and glanced up at Roger. "This weakened." He took a few swallows of water.

"Should I consult your doctor, sir?"

Shackleford seemed to consider it for a moment but shook his head. "Fusty old pill-pusher. He'll just tell me to drink more water."

Roger nodded. "Very well, sir. Is there anything I can do for you?"

"There is one thing, Mulligan."

"Yes, sir?"

"The pixies are complaining that you're doing their jobs."

"The pixies, sir?"

He nodded and offered a sheepish shrug. "I should have mentioned it sooner. You don't need to be quite so diligent with the dusting and cleaning."

"Because that's the pixies' job, sir?"

"Yes, Mulligan. I know it sounds mad, but the house gives them shelter and they repay it by keeping it clean."

"So, you're saying I don't need to dust? Sweep the floors?"

"Correct, Mulligan." He smiled. "You haven't noticed that things don't get particularly dusty? Even in rooms we seldom use?"

Roger shook his head. "No, sir. I haven't."

"They've taken to leaving the kitchen and your quarters to you. It's a protest of sorts. They still look after my room and here in the library, of course."

Roger glanced around. "Of course, sir."

"I'd hoped you'd understand," Shackleford said, taking a few more swallows of water before placing the glass on a nearby coaster. "How are you adjusting, Mulligan? I know this position is not one you're trained for."

"Aside from the pixies, sir?"

Shackleford smiled. "They can be a bit of a handful at times, I know. If they give you any trouble, splash a little whiskey in a saucer and leave it on the counter overnight. Not too much. A few teaspoons or they'll drink themselves silly."

"Anything else I should be aware of, sir?"

"The fairies maintain the gardens. I don't know if that's in the Bible," he said.

"Fairies, sir?" Roger said.

He nodded. "They keep the lawns and gardens in shape. Surely, you've noticed that the lawns haven't needed mowing since you've been here."

Roger hadn't but he'd been so engaged in learning his indoor duties he hadn't given it much thought. "I see, sir. Thank you for the explanation."

"Any time, Mulligan." He looked around the room and pointed to a book on the floor near his chair. "If you could pick that up for me, Mulligan?"

Roger stooped and picked it up, recognizing it as the heavy tome that Shackleford seemed to have chained to his wrist. The title embossed on the cover meant nothing to him. Gibberish in a foreign language he didn't recognize. The weight of the book surprised him, but he knew how much thin sheets of paper seemed to weigh when bound in lots of over a thousand. He handed the book to Shackleford, who easily one-handed it onto the table behind him.

"Thank you, Mulligan. Carry on."

"Thank you, sir. Do you have any preferences for dinner tonight?"

Shackleford gave the matter much more thought than Roger expected. "Dim sum, Perkins. I believe dim sum."

"I'm not sure I have the necessary skills to prepare dim sum, sir."

The old man waved the objection away. "Of course not, Perkins. Didn't expect you to. Call the Dragon's Pearl for delivery."

"The Dragon's Pearl, sir?"

"Yes, Perkins. Do we ever order dim sum anywhere else, man?" Shackleford frowned at Roger for a split second before his expression changed. "Oh. You're not Perkins. Do I know you?"

"Yes, sir. I'm Mulligan. The new butler."

"Mulligan," Shackleford repeated.

"Yes, sir."

Shackleford stared into Roger's face, his gaze seeming to search for something between his eyes. "Of course. Mulligan. Roger Mulligan."

"Yes, sir."

"Sorry, Mulligan." He sighed. "It seems to be getting worse, doesn't it?"

"I'm in no position to say, sir."

Shackleford nodded a few times, looking down at the carpet, the tip of his tongue tasting his bottom lip. "It's getting worse," he said, almost to himself. "There must be an answer." He glanced up at Roger. "Thank you, Mulligan. That will be all."

"About the dim sum, sir?" Roger asked.

Shackleford grinned. "Excellent idea, Mulligan. Call the Dragon's Pearl. They deliver."

"Of course, sir. Would you like anything with your dim sum?"

"An order of moo shu pork? Yes, that would be lovely," he said. "Their pancakes are to die for. Order some for yourself, Mulligan. You won't regret it."

"Very good, sir. I'll make arrangements."

"Thank you, Mulligan."

Roger left Shackleford staring at the rug, his brow furrowed and his eyes narrowed. Something percolated in that old brain of his, but Roger wasn't sure what it might actually be. He walked down the stairs to the foyer and—on a whim—went into the parlor. The room hadn't been on his housekeeping route yet and had been unused since the last time he'd seen Naomi Patching. He walked around, looking at the table tops and other lateral surfaces. He ran a finger across the side table. It left a faint streak but no trail. He tried the top of the window sash on the front windows overlooking the yard and street. Same result. Not a hint of dust on his fingertip. The place either had one hell of an air filtration system or very little dust filtered in from outside.

He stood there for a few moments staring out at the grass, no taller than it had been on his first walk up the stone path. He shook his head. There had to be another explanation. A yard service that tended the yard with eco-friendly electric mowers might have snuck in while Roger was busy at the back of the house. They'd send a bill at the end of the month.

He shook his head and chuckled. "Pixies." He shook his head again. "And I fell for it."

He checked the time. Nearly three. The dry cleaner should be arriving soon and Roger still needed to collect the soiled garments. He found it somewhat wasteful, but his handbook said to rotate the jackets and keep Mr. Shackleford's clothing in top condition at all times.

For room and board plus five grand a month, Roger was more than willing to spend the old man's money keeping things in order.

He stepped out into the foyer and pulled the door shut behind him after one last glance around the room. "Pixies," he said again, and chuckled.

One of the things that Roger found a trifle frustrating was the prohibition of using personal phones for house business. The Bible had a whole chapter on it. The rationale made little sense to him but he followed the regulations for Shackleford House the same way he'd followed the regs in the army. The phone prohibition didn't extend to his personal use, so he saw no reason to break it. The frustration came from having to go to where the phone was and use the rotary dial. The first time he saw it, he didn't believe it would still work, but the manual had not steered him wrong yet.

His immediate problem was finding the number for the Dragon's Pearl restaurant.

He contemplated looking it up on his cell phone and then dialing, but that felt like cheating. What would Jeeves do?

Roger went to the phone extension in the kitchen. It had its own little cubby near the back door. The black beauty rested on a small table with a single drawer. He pulled the drawer open and pulled out a current phone directory. "Huh." He thumbed through the pages, found Dragon's Pearl and dialed the number, sliding the directory back in its drawer and pushing it closed with his thigh.

The call picked up on the first ring. "Dragon's Pearl." The voice on the other end fired the words down the line like bullets, so fast Roger barely understood.

"I'd like to place an order."

"Pick up or delivery?"

"Delivery."

"Address?"

Roger gave the street address.

The pause felt longer than might be suggested by writing the address down. "Is this Shackleford House?"

"Yes."

"You're not Perkins."

"No, Mr. Perkins no longer works here."

The pause ran longer than the last. "What's your name?"

"Mulligan."

"Please hang up, Mr. Mulligan. We will call you back."

Roger hung up and waited only a few heartbeats before the harsh jangle beat from the phone. He picked up the receiver and answered. "Shackleford House."

"Mr. Pelican?"

"Mulligan."

"Huh. Very well, Mr. Mulligan. What would you like this evening? Dim sum and moo shu pork?"

"Yes, please."

"And for you?"

"For me?" Roger asked.

"That was for Mr. Shackleford. What would you like?"

"I'll have the same, I guess," Roger said.

"Thank you, Mr. Mulligan. We'll have it there in time for dinner."

"Thank you," Roger said and the line went dead.

He hung up the phone and stared at it for several long moments, before his brain caught up with the situation. In a few minutes—perhaps half an hour—some delivery guy was going to show up at the back door with two orders of dim sum and moo shu pork. Was he supposed to write a check? Did people still accept checks?

He went to the bible in his quarters and scanned the table of contents. "Payments for Deliveries. Page 823." It appeared under the Financial Management chapter heading. Whoever put the book together had done one hell of a job.

He flipped to page 823, finding it the first time he opened to the back of the book. "Use the petty cash box for small denomination deliveries (key 71). Find the box in the drawer under the worktable, opposite the serving trays. Take the cash needed and place the receipt in the box." Seemed simple enough.

Roger found key 71 in the key safe and took it to the kitchen. The drawer hid under the end of the prep table, just out of sight. He pulled it open and lifted out a flat metal box. Inside, the cash—three twenties, a ten, four fives, and ten ones. He counted it twice—exactly $100.

"Gotta love a well-run household," Roger said, replacing the box in its drawer. He slipped the key into his waistcoat pocket before checking the time.

He pulled out a serving tray and began arranging it for Shackleford's dinner. His cleanup would be easy tonight. As he worked, he pondered the pixie issue. The old man really sold it. Roger could believe that Shackleford seriously thought that pixies cleaned the house and fairies inhabited the garden. Who shoveled the drive in winter? Dwarves?

He chuckled to himself but the thought sent him back to the handbook to check the section on property maintenance. The table of contents had nothing on either lawn and garden care or winter snow removal. He checked it twice. Everything else he could think of was covered. Interior maintenance—straightening the rooms, making the beds, refilling the decanters. The kitchen had its own section on restocking the pantry (standing order with Barthmore & Co., delivered weekly, billed monthly), a menu suggestion guide for various meals. Each suggestion had enough variation that Shackleford could eat a different breakfast, lunch, and dinner every day for two weeks without repeating.

Curious.

Were these his favorites or just the forty-odd meals the grocery order supported? His respect for the menu planner notched up a few levels as he considered what kind of effort that must have taken.

The back doorbell jingled, and Roger put the bible back on the shelf. Something to consider later.

He strode to the back door to find a red-haired delivery driver in a black motorcycle jacket with wide lapels and a side zipper, leather pants, and heavy boots. She carried a padded case emblazoned with a glowing golden dragon on a red background. She looked to be about twenty. One of those little econo-cars stood at the end of the tarmac. "Mr. Mulligan?"

"Yes, thank you. Come in." He took her through the short corridor and into the kitchen. She seemed to know her way and placed the carrier on the work table while he pulled the petty cash box from its drawer and unlocked it. "What do we owe you?"

"Fifty-seven dollars." She pulled a folded receipt from a pocket in the top of the bag, placing it on the table beside Roger, and unzipped the large flap around the front. She pulled a cardboard tray from the carrier, sliding it onto the table and zipped the carrier up again.

Roger glanced at the bill and counted out sixty-five dollars.

She took the bills and grinned. "Thanks." She folded the money and tucked the carrier under her arm. "Enjoy your dinner." She headed for the back door and Roger followed to secure the deadbolt behind her.

He pulled out his pen and marked "Tip: $8" on the receipt before tucking it into the box and securing it once more in its drawer. From a security standpoint, the process made him a trifle uneasy.

A stranger had come inside the perimeter, seen where the cash box was hidden, and had drawn him away from it before he'd had time to secure it. He considered how he might change that to make the house more secure in the future. The aroma wafting from the folded containers made him forget all that as he finished dishing up Shackleford's meal. He placed a small teapot full of fresh tea on the dinner-sized tray and kicked himself for not changing to his apron. Seeing no telltale spills on his clothing, he breathed a sigh of relief.

He took the tray up to the library and paused outside the door to knock and enter. Shackleford looked up from his book and his face lit up. "Ah. What a treat."

The old man's obvious delight made Roger smile. He seemed almost childlike in his glee. "Dinner is prepared, sir."

"I see that, Mulligan." He closed his book and slid it down the table, patting the now-empty space in front of him. "And you made tea to go with it. Good man. It's just not the same without tea."

Roger slid the tray in front of the old man. "There you go, sir. I have to admit it smells delicious."

Shackleford nodded, leaning over his plate to inhale the aromas. "This is the best place I've found for moo shu this side of Baotou." He looked up at Roger. "You know the traditional dish isn't served with these little wrappers. Just rice. I've grown fond of them and the Pearl does them right."

"I'm looking forward to trying it myself, sir."

"Don't let me keep you from your meal. Carry on, Mulligan." He nodded and addressed his meal, pouring a bit of tea from the pot and taking a sip, before taking fork in hand.

Roger left him digging into his dinner. As he walked down the stairs toward his own meal, he wondered if the old boy got lonely up there. He never left the house, at least not since Roger had come. He never came downstairs. He spent his days reading the same book. Granted, the book had to have a million pages. The old man might be a slow reader, but always that one book. What could possibly be so interesting?

Thoughts of the old man's reading habits evaporated at the aroma of the garlic and spices filling the kitchen. Roger grabbed a plate from the cupboard, scooped a helping of pork and mushroom ambrosia from the paper box, and added a few of the still-warm pancakes before settling onto one of the tall work stools at the table and digging in. The food drove all thoughts from his mind as his mouth and nose explored the various flavors and textures.

His plate emptied almost before he'd realized it and he sat back, savoring the after-tastes and debating on going back for another helping. He shook his head and wiped his mouth with a napkin, folding it beside his plate. He started to clear the leftovers, but he stopped to change into his apron. "Proper equipment for the job," he said.

As he put the leftovers in the fridge, his mind wandered back to the old man eating alone in the library. Did he like it? Was he lonely? The train of thought soon came around to Roger himself.

He rinsed his dirty dishes before stacking them in the dishwasher. Since taking the job, he'd eaten every meal alone. It hadn't been that big a shift for him since turning civilian again. He'd have to use both hands to count the number of meals he'd shared since leaving the army but it wouldn't take all the fingers if he ignored those meals grabbed on the fly with the ambulance crew. Was he lonely? He shrugged and made a last inspection of the kitchen before changing back to his jacket, leaving the apron hanging in the pantry. On a hunch he ran a finger over one of the shelves and saw the trail it left in the dust.

He felt the frown building on his face and looked around the oversize closet. Perhaps this space wasn't on the regular schedule. He'd done little more than use the pantry since he'd been on the job. He went out to the kitchen and ran a finger through the dust on the shelf under the work table. It wasn't a lot, but there was some. He checked the phone niche, lifting the black behemoth off its stand and looking at the outline of its base on the surface. The rectangular shape stood out against the surface dust. Again, not a lot, but enough to notice. He replaced the phone and walked down to the mudroom. He traced across the top of the windowsill and saw no trail in the dust. He tried the storage shelf above the laundry units. No trail. Everywhere he tested, he found no dust.

The old man's words came back to him. The kitchen and his quarters. He strode back to his rooms and did a fast inspection of the lateral surfaces. He found traces of dust everywhere. He grabbed the key for the cook's quarters and went in there. He had no idea how long the house had been without a cook but surely there would be dust aplenty in a locked room.

The cook's quarters occupied a slightly smaller footprint than Roger's but it was all one room, laid out in a logical manner with a full-sized bed, a sitting nook in one corner and its own window onto the garden. He ran his finger down the windowsill and across the top edge of the sash. No dust. None on the top edges of the sleigh bed, or the top rail of the wainscoting. None on the empty bookshelves. No dust anywhere. The room looked as clean and fresh as any inspection-ready barracks he'd ever seen, barring the unmade mattress on the bed. He slapped the mattress hard, watching the ray of light shining in from the window. No poof of dust.

A chill slid down his back and he felt the hairs on the back of his neck standing up. That sense of being watched that used to happen in the villages sometimes. Out in the mountains where there was too much cover for snipers to hide in and not enough for him to use. He felt his heart rate notching up and heard his own breathing rasping in and out of his chest. He took a breath and held it for a four-count before letting it out again.

Not enough evidence. The room had been closed and locked for months. He shook his head and left, locking the door behind him.

He tucked the key away in the safe and considered what the old man had said about whiskey. He shook his head and checked the time before heading up to the library to get the old man's tray and see if he needed anything before bed. He checked the railings and even the top of the wainscoting as he passed from the ground floor up to the library. No dust anywhere. He shook his head, trying to find some rational explanation for the evidence. Could there really be pixies?

"What the hell is a pixie?" he asked, finding that he only had the word but no real concept. He had a better idea of a leprechaun from folklore. Not for the first time, he wished the house had internet access. He stopped outside the library and took a cleansing breath, putting the notions of pixies and fairies and leprechauns out of his mind. He tapped twice and swung the door open, stepping into the room.

"If you're through with dinner, sir?" he asked.

The old man looked up. "Yes, thank you, Perkins. You may clear. What did you think of the moo shu?"

"Delicious, sir. A nice break from my own cooking. Thank you for the treat, sir."

He waved the comment away. "Quite welcome, quite welcome." He turned back to the book—the same book as always—that lay splayed open on the table.

Roger took the tray and paused at the door. "Is there anything else, sir?"

Shackleford shook his head, not looking up from the book but placing a fingertip on the page. "I'll take a hot chocolate at 10, if you please, Perkins."

"A hot chocolate, sir?"

The old man looked up from his book. "Yes, Perkins. If it's not too much trouble?"

Roger gave his butler bow. "Not at all, sir."

"Thank you, Perkins."

Roger left and went to the kitchen to find a recipe for hot chocolate. The last time he'd made it, he put a couple spoons of powder in a mug and poured boiling water on it. He felt certain that Shackleford wanted something a little more than powdered gratification. He felt sorry for the old geezer; his confusion level seemed to be mounting. Roger knew there was little he could do about it except to make him as comfortable as possible.

CHAPTER 5

Roger came in from his run and tossed the paper and the morning's flower onto the counter before locating a vase. He put a little water into it and stood the blossom—pale yellow petals with a black center—in the slender milk-glass container. While he was there, he ground the coffee and filled the pot with water. Setting it to brew, he headed for the shower, stripping off his T-shirt as he went.

Under the steamy spray, he considered his hot cocoa skills. The old man hadn't seemed bothered by the cup he'd gotten, but Roger couldn't help but think he could have done better. He'd have to pursue that. He'd tried a little himself and found it just a bit unsatisfying.

He shut off the shower and scooted across the hallway to his quarters as he finished drying his hair.

Something smelled funny but he couldn't place it. Almost like pickles. He checked his deodorant but that wasn't it. He shrugged and pulled on the uniform, making sure to put the watch in his pocket. He stopped to make a note about cocoa recipes before slipping the notebook and pen into their proper place.

He caught another whiff. Definitely pickle-smelling.

He followed his nose out into the hallway and out to the kitchen where the pickle smell nearly overwhelmed him. It wasn't quite pickle. It had just a hint of coffee.

Frowning, he went to the coffee maker and pulled the pot from under the spigot. He held the glass container up to the light. It looked fine, but when he stuck his nose near the spout, the vinegar smell caught him right between the eyes.

He pushed the pot away, flipping the lid and pouring it down the drain.

"What the hell?"

He rinsed the pot with hot water, smelling it and rinsing a few more times before the pickle smell dissipated. He pulled the filter full of pickled grounds from the basket and dumped it into the trash, before rinsing the gold basket clean.

He looked at the faucet and at the vase with the flower in it. He picked it up, pulled the flower out and sniffed the water. Just water. He replaced the flower and put the vase back on the table.

Next he flipped the top open on the coffeemaker and sniffed inside. The vinegar smell lingered but he still couldn't figure out where it came from. With a shrug, he refilled the reservoir with fresh cold water and set the machine to cycle. It took him three cycles but he finally got the hot water coming out without the vinegar smell.

He checked the time and set about making the first pot of the day. With luck, he'd get it done in time to take Shackleford's breakfast up.

The whole time he worked on breakfast, he kept an eye on the coffee maker. The fresh brew smelled fine and tasted like coffee.

He shook his head. "What the hell?"

Roger delivered breakfast at the usual hour: a ham and cheese omelet, one slice of buttered toast, a small glass of orange juice, and the old man's single cup of coffee.

Shackleford looked up at his entrance. "Good morning, Mulligan."

"Good morning, sir. Did you sleep well?"

"Passable, Mulligan. Passable." He put the book down and examined the tray. "This looks delicious, Mulligan. Branching out in your culinary endeavors?"

"Just trying to keep mealtime interesting, sir."

The old man smiled. "Excellent work. Thank you, Mulligan."

"Is there anything else, sir?"

Shackleton paused. "There is one thing, Mulligan."

"Yes, sir?"

"It's the pixies."

"The pixies, sir?"

Shackleford nodded. "They are becoming more upset. They didn't appreciate having their work critiqued."

"Critiqued, sir?"

"Yes. Apparently you inspected their handiwork?"

"I don't follow, sir."

"They believe you were checking up on them, Mulligan. The front parlor. Cook's quarters."

Roger struggled to keep his surprise from showing on his face. "They are concerned, sir?"

"Yes, Mulligan. It appears they disapprove of your standard of housekeeping in the areas you've taken over and wish to resume their work."

"I see, sir." Roger swallowed. The old boy had lost it. "What would you suggest, sir?"

Shackleford pursed his lips and stared at his breakfast for a few moments. "A thimbleful of whiskey."

"For me, sir?"

He laughed. "It wouldn't hurt, Mulligan, but no. For them. Leave a bit of whiskey in a saucer on the counter in the kitchen. Think of it as a libation." He frowned slightly. "I had a cook who did it on a regular basis, actually. Back when Shackleford House had a full staff. Mrs. Chapman, I believe. Lovely lady." He looked up at Mulligan. "She claimed it kept them happy and out of her flour crock."

"Flour crock?"

"She claimed they hunted the weevils in it." Shackleford laughed. "Preposterous idea, but that's what she claimed."

"That the pixies hunted weevils in her flour?" Roger asked.

"Precisely, Mulligan. We have no weevils in the flour for them to hunt." He shook his head, a smile playing around his mouth. "She claimed they left their floury footprints on her counters."

"I see, sir."

Shackleford chuckled and shook his head before addressing his breakfast. "If you'd see to that little matter? Tonight if possible?"

"Of course, sir. Any particular whiskey the pixies favor?"

"Use the cheap stuff in the front parlor. They don't have particularly refined palates. It's mostly the thought that counts with them. They like being acknowledged for their service. Best do it before they start playing pranks on you."

Roger nodded. "Of course, sir."

"Carry on, Mulligan." Shackleford dug into breakfast.

"Thank you, sir," Roger said and left the library to straighten out the master suite. He'd done it so often he hardly had to think about it at all. That gave him plenty of time to think about what the old man had said, and he didn't like it. Clearly his dementia was advancing, but a couple of his comments struck a nerve. Shackleford knew that he'd been in the cook's quarters. For a man who never left the sanctuary of the second floor, how had he known? He sighed, giving the suite a last once-over before gathering the dirty clothing for the laundry. He'd do it, of course. Put out the whiskey.

He'd had much stranger orders from superiors and he knew enough to follow them.

He also resolved to do some research on dementia to see if there might be something he could do to help make the old man's life less confusing.

In the meantime, he had laundry to do and the grocery delivery should be arriving at midmorning. He wondered what life at Shackleford House had been like with a full staff. Who lived here? It seemed incomprehensible that the old man would have a full staff. If he was honest with himself, Roger knew there wasn't enough work for him to do as full-time butler as it was.

He shrugged and got on with the morning routine. "Five grand a month with a million-dollar chaser," he said. He could put up with a lot for that kind of money.

His afternoon routine was thrown into disarray by the front doorbell. He closed the ledger and put it back on its shelf before answering the summons. On the stoop stood a tiny old woman smiling up at him. Wearing a fetching shirtdress in a navy blue that made her eyes shine like jewels, an open-weave shawl around her shoulders that matched her shock-white hair, and stylish but sensible black flats, she barely came up to Roger's shoulders. "May I help you?" he asked.

"Good afternoon. You must be the new butler," she said. "I was so sorry to hear about Perkins."

"Yes, ma'am. May I help you?"

"I've come to visit Joseph. May I come in?"

"Of course, ma'am." Roger stepped back, holding the door open.

She breezed through the entry and paused long enough for him to close and bolt the door behind her.

"I'll see if Mr. Shackleford is accepting callers. May I say who's calling, ma'am?"

"Of course. My card." She pulled a heavily embossed calling card from her purse and presented it to him. It read "Fidelia Necket."

Roger took it and indicated the parlor with an open palm. "Would you care to wait in the parlor, ma'am?"

"Thank you, Mulligan. That would be lovely." She sailed into the room and took a seat in one of the overstuffed chairs, crossing her legs and relaxing into it as if it were her own.

"I'll only be a moment, ma'am."

Roger left her peering about the parlor. He couldn't remember seeing anybody so completely at home in their own skin. The

60

woman had to be pushing seventy but she moved with the grace of a thirty-year-old. Her face might be wrinkled and her hair white, but there was nothing old about her.

He knocked on the library door and entered. "Excuse me, sir. You have a caller." He handed him the card.

He took the card and glanced at it, a grin exploding onto his face. "Delia? Here?"

"In the front parlor, sir."

"Oh, how marvelous. Show her up, Mulligan. Show her up."

Roger nodded. "At once, sir."

Returning to the parlor, he found the woman where he'd left her. She looked up when he appeared in the door. "Mr. Shackleford is in, ma'am. May I show you to the library?"

She stood and nodded. "Thank you, Mulligan."

He started toward the stairs and stopped at the foot, offering his arm. "May I offer my assistance, ma'am?"

She gave him a smile and hooked her wrist over his elbow. "I'm always happy to walk on the arm of a handsome man," she said. "But I just got back from the base camp at K-2 so I'm fairly certain I can navigate the stairs."

Roger couldn't suppress the surprise. "I'm impressed, ma'am."

"Don't be," she said. "It's a long walk that's been spoiled by too many hikers." She paused as they turned at the landing. "You believe me?"

"Of course, ma'am. Why would I doubt you?"

She gave a delicate shrug. "Oh, possibly because I'm old and frail? You'd be surprised how many people believe old means weak."

Roger smiled. "I would never presume to comment on a lady's age, ma'am."

"Yet you offered your arm," she said. "Thank you, Mulligan."

"My distinct pleasure, ma'am." He started up the next short flight.

She disentangled herself at the top of the stairs and waited until Roger introduced her. "Ms. Fidelia Necket, sir."

He stepped aside so she could enter and was astonished at the speed with which Shackleford crossed the room and enveloped the woman in a bearlike hug. "Delia, my stars. How was Xinjiang?" he asked, breaking the clinch and holding her at arm's length, gazing at her. "I can't believe you're here."

"It was elevating," she said, with a girlish laugh. "Although the trails are in dreadful condition."

"Come in, come in. Sit." He pressed her into one of the comfy chairs and took the one across from her. "Can I offer you some refreshment? Tea? Sherry?"

"A sherry would be welcome, Joseph. Thank you."

"Perkins, the Palo Cordato Chipiona? There should still be a bottle or two in the cellar."

The woman shot Shackleford a raised eyebrow before looking at Roger. She pursed her lips and her eyes tightened.

"I'll look, sir. It may take me a few moments to find it."

Shackleford waved him off. "We've a lot to catch up on. Thank you, Perkins."

Roger gave a small bow and left, pulling the library door closed behind him. He went to the kitchen and checked the small cellar there. He'd not given it more than a cursory glance before. None of the menu items in his bible mentioned wine. Other than the occasional whiskey that the old man poured himself from the decanter in the library, he didn't think the old boy drank. It took only a moment for him to find two sherries among the thirty or so bottles; neither was Palo anything.

He went to the key safe and pulled keys for the garage, cellar, and one marked "wine storage" for good measure.

It took him only a few moments to open the cellar door and go down the stairs. He flicked the light switch and blinked at the cavernous space. Ceramic tiles covered the floor, reminding him of the black and white subway tiles he'd seen in New York City. Wood panels covered the walls. A workbench against the near wall held woodworking and mechanic's tools. Arched brick passages led out of the cellar's entryway. He took the first one and came to a heavy wooden door with a padlock and hasp. The "wine storage" key fit the lock, which snapped open with a click. He pulled the lock and hasp, hooking the open padlock into the freed hasp and locking it. The door swung open on silent hinges revealing the kind of wine cellar that he'd only seen in movies.

He stepped in, marveling at the racks—mostly full of bottles. The place had a very faint aromatic tint in the air and the temperature dropped enough that he was glad he wore his uniform. It wasn't cold, exactly, but definitely chilly. He started scanning the racks, noting that each had one or more labels. He strolled through the racks and finally found a rack devoted to ports which led him to another with sherries. He rifled through the bottles, disturbing them as little as possible before finding a heavy brown one with "Palo Cortado" in a flourishing script and the word "Chipiona" in heavy block print on the label.

He pulled it from the bin and tucked it under his arm. He had no idea what the price of such a bottle might be, but knowing the old man, it was probably a really good sherry. The guy didn't do anything in half measures.

He retraced his steps, securing each lock as he passed. As he switched off the light, Roger looked back at the cellar. He probably should take one of his afternoons and do a tour down here to learn the layout. He had a feeling there was much to be discovered.

Back in the kitchen, he found a decanter and sherry glasses in the glassware closet. He wasn't sure of the appropriateness of actually decanting it, though, stopping at the last moment and satisfying himself by pulling the seal off the neck of the bottle and loosening the rimmed cork. He set the bottle and two glasses on a serving tray and walked it up the stairs. He should brush up on the actual etiquette for entertaining guests. Pretzels were almost certainly inappropriate, and he didn't have a clue as to what cheese or fruit might be well matched. He gave a mental shrug and knocked on the door before opening.

They sat smiling up at him as he entered.

"Ah, excellent. You found it. Thank you, Mulligan," Shackleford said.

"Sorry for the delay. I had to go down to the cellar to find it. I took the liberty of loosening the cork but thought you'd prefer the sherry sooner than in a decanter." He settled the tray on the table.

"Thank you, Mulligan," he said, again. "That's fine." He reached for the bottle himself and pulled the cork, giving it a cursory glance before pouring the small glasses half full. Even at the distance, the heady aroma filled Roger's nose. "That will be all for now, Mulligan," he said, placing the bottle back on the tray and lifting a glass. "If we need anything more, I'll ring you."

Roger nodded and gave his best Jeeves bow before leaving them to enjoy each other's company.

The house had two dining rooms. Three, if he counted the servants' table. Mulligan inspected the smallest—a cozy room with a neutral wallpaper above the wainscoting. Windows let in daylight and several paintings hung on the walls, mostly pastoral scenes with the occasional portrait. The oval table seated ten, but stood without its extra leaves with six chairs; the other four had their positions, one on each side of the sideboard, and two more flanking the window opposite. He consulted his bible on guests for dinner. Something told him Ms. Necket would be joining them.

It took him a few wrong turns but he found the linens in the sideboard and the silver chests in a closet in the kitchen. The bible offered suggestions on which setting to use—from simple, clean modern lines in stainless steel to the most decorative silver with baroque flourishes on the handles. Some of the sets had place settings for eighty people in full kit and filled several chests, while the smallest could handle ten. He hadn't been aware that the everyday flatware he had used so far was stainless steel and part of a larger set.

Having done his homework, he straightened his uniform and took a deep breath before knocking on the library door. He waited a few moments before entering, not wishing to interrupt anything too intimate. The door latch clicked and the door swung open on its own, something that hadn't happened in days.

"I beg pardon, sir. Will Ms. Necket be staying for dinner?"

"Splendid idea, Perkins." Shackleford looked at her. "Delia, my dear? Can you stay?"

She sighed and shook her head. "Sadly, no. I'm meeting Lilly to go over the arrangement for this year's Fête d'Étoile. They're quite put out with me for being in Pakistan last season and would never forgive me for not carrying my end this year."

"How is dear Lilly?" Shackleford asked. "I haven't seen her in ages. Is she still seeing that Adkins fellow?"

"I believe Ned threw her over for a younger woman sometime in the spring."

Shackleford's eyebrows shot up. "Anyone we know?"

"I don't believe so," she said, glancing at Mulligan.

Shackleford took the hint and nodded to Roger. "Thank you, Perkins. Carry on."

Roger bowed and backed from the room, closing the door behind himself. He felt a modicum of disappointment at not having a guest for dinner, but was also somewhat relieved that he wouldn't have to practice his untried skills just yet. He pulled out his notebook and jotted a reminder to look into some culinary training. Perhaps there was a course he could take. He added a note to speak with Shackleford about getting internet in the house as well. He felt like he'd stepped back twenty years. He hadn't had it on deployment, but he missed the ability to just look something up online. The limited access he had through his phone simply wasn't the same.

At four, Roger's pager beeped and he went up to the library.

"You rang, sir?" Every time he said it, Roger couldn't help but hear a deep, sepulchral voice in his head.

"Ms. Necket is ready to leave, Perkins." They both stood and Shackleton took her hand. "Thank you for calling, Delia. Please don't be a stranger while you're in town."

"It's lovely to see you, Joseph. I'll call again soon and fill you in on all the details."

Roger escorted Ms. Necket down the stairs to the front door. She paused, putting her palm to the wood, holding it shut. "He's getting worse."

"I'm not at liberty to discuss Mr. Shackleford's health, ma'am."

"You're not discussing it, Mulligan. I am. He called you Perkins more than once."

"Old habits die hard, ma'am."

"Ned Adkins died some time ago," she said. "Joseph attended the funeral."

Roger felt his eyebrows rise. "And the younger woman?"

"The year before he passed away," she shrugged. "It seemed kinder than correcting him. Lilly Granger is happily married to her third husband. She's Lilly Pennington now. He attended the wedding."

"It comes with age for some people, ma'am."

Her face clouded in a fierce frown. "This isn't age. This is—" she paused, glancing up the stairs toward the library. "This is something else."

"I'm sure I don't know what you mean, ma'am."

"How well do you know your employer, Mulligan?"

"The Patchings employ me to look after Mr. Shackleford, ma'am."

"That pair?" She scoffed. "They're probably afraid he'll have the place declared a historical landmark to keep it out of their clutches."

"I couldn't comment on that, ma'am."

She stared into his face, her eyes narrowing. "Did they tell you about him before you agreed to work here?"

"They made me aware of his diminished capacity, ma'am, yes. I was not hired under false pretenses, if that's your question."

"They told you he was ... different?"

"They told me that he had a diminished capacity, ma'am," Roger said, repeating himself. "I met him, talked with him, before I signed the contract."

"How are you getting along with the pixies?" she asked, tilting her head to the side and staring into his eyes.

Roger blinked as his mind struggled to make the conversational turn. "Pixies, ma'am?"

"Yes, Mulligan, the pixies. New man in the house. The adjustment period is often challenging."

Roger glanced up toward the library and looked back to find Ms. Fidelia Necket's knowing smile.

"I thought not," she said. "A word of advice, Mulligan. Put out the whiskey before they start playing pranks."

"I'll take that under advisement, ma'am."

She sighed and shook her head. "Are all men pig-headed fools?" Her delivery turned what might have been a bitter insult into a quiet plea.

"I suspect most of us are, yes, ma'am."

She pulled her hand from the door and stood back so he could open it. He swung it open for her but she paused at the threshold, one hand on the doorjamb, and looked back. "It's not dementia, Mulligan. It's that damned amulet. I fear it's stealing his mind, one piece at a time." She was down the steps before Roger could respond. She didn't look back, simply walked to the street and slipped behind the wheel of an older model Taurus parked at the curb. He watched her pull out into traffic and drive away.

"What amulet?" he asked the empty yard.

"Thank you, Mulligan," Shackleford said, when Roger returned to the library for the tray and glasses. "If you'd decant that and bring it back? I'd forgotten how much I enjoyed it."

"Of course, sir."

"What did you think of Ms. Necket?" he asked, settling himself back in his usual chair with the book open in front of him.

"A lovely woman, sir. Quite adventurous."

"You have no idea, Mulligan. No idea. She's a real mountain climber, you know. When she was younger she was one of the first women to climb Aconcagua. Terrible climb, her last big one, I believe. She still likes to travel to the base camps as she's able."

"She seems quite able, sir."

He nodded and stared off into the distance. "Oh, she's more than able, Mulligan. More than able. Brilliant mind. Stronger than she looks." He sighed and shook his head. "Quite a looker in her youth." He shrugged and gave him a sad smile. "Alas, not for the likes of men like me."

"She seems a staunch friend, sir."

"She worries about me. I'm getting up there in age."

"We all aspire to that height, sir."

He chuckled. "Well said. Well said." He turned back to his book. "It's good to see her back."

Roger took the tray and exited, taking the tray and glassware back to the kitchen. He didn't know quite what to make of Fidelia Necket. She seemed overly concerned with his employment status, to say nothing of this amulet. What kind of amulet could steal anything, let alone memories? Stuff of fantasy. He frowned as he placed the tray on the work table.

Like pixies.

"Twice is coincidence," he said. He pulled an empty decanter out of the cupboard and snagged a funnel from the utility drawer. He glanced at the cupboard that held the cups and saucers but shook himself. Silliness. Pixies, indeed.

Placing the funnel in the decanter, he pulled out his cell phone—the jacket had two inside pockets, one on each side, and he used them both, regardless of what Pettigrew said—and turned on the flashlight, laying it flat on the table to shine up through the neck of the bottle. The how-to article he'd read on his phone mentioned a strong light and it was the strongest portable he had. Sadly, the bible gave explicit instructions on some things but assumed he knew basic skills when it gave instructions on running the house.

Perhaps next year he'd go to butler school. Compared to combat and life as an EMT, it seemed a relatively safe occupation. Even with the long hours and limited privacy, seeing the house in order soothed him.

The sediment started to show in the neck of the bottle so he backed off, letting it settle a bit more. He glanced at the cupboard again. What would it hurt to put a little whiskey in a saucer? He'd heard of sillier superstitions, and it might give the old guy a little peace.

When evening came, he made his usual check of the household, making sure the doors and windows were locked and the house in order. His gaze fell on the coffee maker on the counter as a faint whiff of vinegar tickled his nose.

"Pranks," he said. It wasn't possible.

Was it?

Feeling a bit foolish, he pulled a saucer out of the cupboard and placed it on the counter between the coffee maker and the sink. He fetched the whiskey decanter from the front parlor, dribbled some of the amber liquid onto the saucer, and poured a finger for himself in the bottom of a glass. It might be the cheap stuff to Shackleford, but it was still a cut above his usual.

Roger went through his morning routine—calisthenics, run, and shower—before checking out the saucer in the kitchen. He fully expected to find it, at most, tacky from evaporation overnight. What he found was a perfectly clean dish. He touched it with his fingertip. Perhaps the film was too fine to see. Nothing. He held it up to the light, letting the overheads reflect on it. It looked like it had just come out of the dishwasher, except for his fingerprint.

Was the old man messing with his head?

He opened the dishwasher and deposited the saucer. He'd emptied it the night before, so the saucer was the only dish there.

"He could have rinsed it and just put it back," he said. The clock reminded him he wanted to make steel cut oats for breakfast. They were on the approved menu and he'd always wanted to try them himself, anyway. No time like the present. He put on his apron, gathered the ingredients, and followed the recipe in the bible; it called for adding apple juice and dried cranberries along with cinnamon and ginger. The bible warned him that they took some time to cook and needed to be stirred occasionally. He brought his coffee to the stove and sipped while he worked.

The recipe went together smoothly and he had a quiet half hour, eyeing the clock and scanning the headlines on Shackleford's paper. He really didn't follow the financial news so most of it meant nothing to him. What the various markets did and who got caught with his hand in some cookie jar didn't really interest him. Every so often a mention of Naomi Patching's father, Othello Bruna, showed up. Weird name, but the one picture he'd seen showed a man staring at the photographer with the same supercilious sneer that Naomi used.

The oatmeal came out very nicely. He'd never been an oatmeal guy before. Give him a couple eggs over easy, some fried potatoes, and a few rashers of bacon and he was happy. Judging by the way his mouth watered at the aromas wafting up from the oatmeal, he might have been short-changing himself. He split the pot between two bowls, being careful with Shackleford's presentation. He consulted the bible while he ate his breakfast over the sink, thoroughly amazed at the textures and flavors. For Shackleford the Bible suggested a toasted English muffin with some marmalade and coffee, but no juice. The garden yielded a pretty yellow flower with a brown center for the morning tray. There always seemed to be at least one for him to pluck on his way back from his run.

The fairies seemed to be doing a good job with the grounds because, while nothing looked overgrown or out of place, it also didn't look like a garden. It looked more like the house—huge as it was—merely sprouted from the lot in primordial times and the lawns and landscaping grew around it.

He chuckled at the thought and made sure Shackleford's tray had everything it was supposed to before changing out of his apron and slipping into his jacket.

He took the tray up to the library and knocked before entering. As was his habit, Shackleford sat in his normal chair, book before him. "Good morning, sir." Roger placed the tray on the table.

Nathan Lowell

"Good morning, Mulligan. What have you for me this morning?"

"Steel cut oats, sir."

"Oh, perfect. I generally prefer them during the winter months,
but I was just thinking about them this morning."

"I'm glad, sir. If there's something in particular you'd like, I'd
be happy to try to prepare it for you."

Shackleford looked up at him. "Thank you, Mulligan." He
paused for a moment as if trying to remember something, his eyes
rolling around in their sockets. "It is Mulligan, yes?"

"Yes, sir. Mulligan is correct."

He sighed. "I keep calling you Perkins, don't I."

"Yes, sir, you do. Parsons, at least once."

The old guy's white eyebrows rose at that. "Parsons? Oh, my.
That's distressing."

"Why, sir? Parsons, Perkins. They sound alike."

"Parsons was my father's valet. I haven't thought of him in
decades."

"Did they live here when you were young, sir?"

Shackleford nodded. "One of the first houses built when the city
housed immigrants from the old country. Stories have it that the
original Shackleford took quite the ribbing for moving so far out
into the woods, fully five miles from the coast." He smiled. "Urban
sprawl overtook the place within half a century and now people on
the west side see us as being way over on the eastern side of the
city." He shook his head. "I think it was originally built in the
late 1600s but it's been upgraded several times. Once by fire." He
grinned. "Nothing like burning a city to the foundations to get
them to improve building codes, eh?"

Roger laughed. "I can see how that might make an impression,
sir."

"Tell me, Mulligan. How do you like it? Working here, I mean."

"I find it quite soothing, sir."

"Not as exciting as riding an ambulance?" Shackleford offered
a grin. "Is there anything you need?"

"Well, sir, since you brought it up ..." Roger paused, unsure of
how to broach the subject.

Shackleford nodded. "Go ahead, man."

"I would like to get better as a cook, sir. My skills in the kitchen
have been limited to frying eggs and boiling water, for the most part.
The bible lists several meals that I might prepare, but I have no
idea how to make them. Ms. Necket's visit made me consider that
I lack the skills and knowledge to put on even an informal dinner,
let alone prepare dishes for a festive occasion or formal dinner."

Shackleford nodded again. "For the record, your service has been exemplary over the short time you've been here. You think you'd like to continue in service, then? After your year is up with me?"

"It has crossed my mind, sir."

He sat back in his chair and stared into the middle distance for a few moments. "Two distinct problems, isn't it?"

"Yes, sir. Running the household and becoming better in the kitchen. I have a suggestion for remedial cooking, sir, but I'm afraid I don't know where to start on becoming a better butler."

Shackleford's eyes widened. "I'm listening."

"Well, sir, there's the matter of the internet."

"What of it?"

"With access to the net, I could watch cooking videos and look up how to prepare some of those dishes that I don't know."

"The internet? Here in Shackleford House?" He tilted his head and gazed into the distance for several long moments. "Do you have any idea how to do that without disturbing the pixies?"

"I don't, sir, but I could find out what's involved."

"I'm not opposed, Mulligan. At least not on principle. Never saw the need for it myself." He glanced around the room, his gaze seeming to caress the spines arrayed on the shelves. "Put together a proposal. Let's see what we can do."

Roger nodded. "Yes, sir. Thank you."

"You're welcome, Mulligan."

"Will there be anything else, sir?"

Shackleford turned to his breakfast and shook his head. "Thank you, Perkins. That will be all for now. I'd like a copy of the Fête d'Étoile guest list by end of day, if that's possible. And don't forget to add a case of caviar to the grocery order for next week's Circle meeting."

Roger paused, unsure how to respond in the moment. "Of course, sir," he said, and left the library.

Perhaps the Bible had some guidance on these events. He turned to the morning routine after making a note to check for references on both the Fête and a weekly Circle meeting. The old guy probably got confused by the visit and the reminder of the Fête, whatever it was. Christmas celebration, maybe? Months away, but it sounded like something that took months in the planning. He sighed and stripped the bedding, collecting the sheets and towels in a bundle to take to the laundry, and straightened the room.

The internet was good news but he pondered how to approach the issue of the pixies. He needed a consultant. No one came immediately to mind for the pixie problem, but for the internet? Luckily, he knew just the woman for the job.

At the stroke of one, the front doorbell rang. Roger opened it to find Samantha Bicker staring wide-eyed at him. "Rog?"

"Sam, thank you for coming." He stepped out of the doorway and ushered her into the house.

"Vinnie said you got a job as a butler, but I thought he was kidding." She glanced around the foyer before giving Roger the once-over. "Look at you." She grinned. "Monkey suit and all."

Roger shrugged. "A uniform is a uniform. It's just that this one doesn't represent Uncle Sam." He nodded toward the back of the house. "Come into the kitchen and I'll explain what we need to do."

She followed him down the short passageway and whistled at the kitchen. "You know how to cook now, too?"

He laughed. "No, and that's the problem. I need to learn and I don't have the time to go to school."

"Ah," she said, drawing out the single syllable. "Hence the internet and the wonders of instructional videos."

He nodded. "I don't expect to become a chef, but I need to be able to do more than fry an egg and boil water."

She pulled a tablet out of her shoulder bag and fired it up. "What do you need?"

"First, we need high-speed access. The house has never had television, even, let alone cable. We'll need a line run, and I'm thinking wireless from a hub in the basement."

She made a few notes. "The basement?"

"No drilling," Roger said.

She bit her lip but nodded. "We can do that. I assume the place has electricity?" She glanced up at the overhead lights.

"And indoor plumbing," Roger said with a laugh.

"How big is this place? Will you want the whole house covered?"

"It's massive. The east and west wings are closed off. Mr. Shackleford keeps mostly to his rooms and the library at the top of the stairs. You want coffee?"

"Love a cup. You want internet access up there?"

Roger pulled down two cups with saucers and poured coffee. "My quarters, primarily. Need cream and sugar?"

She shook her head. "Black's fine. Show me?"

He slid the saucer over to her and picked up his own. "This way." He'd become inured to his rooms but the look of wonder on Sam's face reminded him of the first time he'd seen them.

"Holy shit," she said. "You're kidding me." Her head swiveled back and forth taking it in. "How much do they charge you for this?"

"Comes with the job," he said, waving her to the cozy conversational grouping in the corner.

Samantha put her cup down on the coffee table and settled into the chair, running her hand along the arm. "This is real leather."

Roger sat across from her. "Everything in this house is real. Wood, leather. Crystal. Silver."

"Man." She kept looking around at the room. She nodded at the still mostly empty bookcase. "Not a big reader?"

He held up his phone. "Ebooks. This is my only connection to the outer world."

She nodded and pulled up her tablet again. "Okay. Where do you want your terminal?"

He turned to look at the rolltop desk. "I was thinking there, but I don't know. I hate to block the access to the desk."

She nodded and looked around the baseboards. "You need an electrical outlet."

He frowned and followed the cord from the lamp on the end table back to the wall. "There's one behind my chair." Between them, they found four in the two rooms.

"No drilling," she said after they'd completed the survey. "Absolute requirement?"

He nodded. "The pixies wouldn't like it."

She froze in place and stared at him. "The pixies?"

He laughed. "Long story."

She shrugged and eyed the top of the dresser. "What about there?"

"What about there?" he asked.

"I'm guessing you won't want a lot of exposed cables and wires?"

He nodded. "Yeah. I didn't think this through."

"That's why you hired me," she said, with a grin. "And I'm doubling my usual rate for this gig."

He laughed. "I have to get it approved before we do it."

She shrugged. "What about a laptop?"

"What about a laptop?" he asked.

"Put it here to charge it up." She slapped the top of the dresser. "Take it to your desk when you want to use it. Put it back here when done. Something in a black or steel gray case? Closed, it wouldn't stand out in the room. Plug it in down there." She pointed to the outlet between the wardrobe and dresser. "I'm guessing you're not going to have a lot of time to surf the net?"

He pursed his lips and shrugged. "Probably not."

"Laptop, you could take it to the kitchen while you're working on new recipes," she said. "Decent machine is good for hours on battery."

He blinked. "That would be really useful."

She shrugged. "Where's the basement?"

He stopped at the key safe and pulled the relevant keys before leading her out to the garage. "Don't mind the cars," he said, grinning at her over his shoulder and opening the door.

"Are you kidding me, Mulligan?" She froze inside the door, staring at the lineup of vehicles. "What's that? A million dollars on twelve tires?"

"I have no idea."

"Do you drive them?" she asked, her eyes widening as she looked at him.

He shook his head. "I could. Mr. Shackleford gave me permission, but can you imagine parking one of these anywhere in the city?"

"What if you got hit?" she asked.

"Exactly," Roger said. "I can't imagine taking one of these out in public." He unlocked the basement door and opened it. "Come on. Basement's down here."

She eyed the construction leading down. "No drilling? How do you think you're going to get the cable down here?"

"I don't know. Air gap under the door plate? Maybe over the top of the door?"

She looked around the cellar's entry, then peered down one of the arches. "What's down there?"

"Wine cellar."

She looked at him. "Of course. I should have known."

He shrugged.

"Does it have to be down here?" she asked.

"You're the expert. You tell me."

He followed her back up the stairs.

"This butts up against the house, right?" Sam slapped the end wall.

"Yeah. There's a small gap but that's all."

"Is the kitchen through there?"

"One of the pantries, I think."

"Even better," she said. "If we mount the access point here, we can broadcast to a repeater inside and build off that. Can I see the pantry?"

"Sure." Roger secured the doors and led her back inside, paying attention to the geometry of their turns back through the laundry and mudroom. He took her to the back corner and opened the door to a closet. "Without a measuring tape or a floor plan, I think that back wall is where the garage sits." The room had been rough storage for odds and ends, apparently. A few open shelves lined the far wall and a bucket held a bouquet of clean mops and brooms. Other than that, the room was pristine.

"Electrical outlet?" she asked.

"In a closet?" he asked, but leaned over to peer around the baseboards.

"Bingo," Sam said, pointing to the bucket of cleaning gear.

Roger slid the bucket to one side and revealed the socket.

"So. Repeater on that shelf broadcasting to the house. We can use little modular relays that plug into outlets to tailor the coverage. You won't have gigabit service, but you're the only one using the bandwidth. Should be fine."

"Can you give me a work plan with estimates of the costs and who we need to do the work? I take it the cable company will need to install the line from somewhere in the neighborhood."

"Yeah. Air gap under the garage door should be fine to get the line into the house. As long as the pixies don't mind the equipment being screwed to the wall out there ...?" She paused and raised an eyebrow in his direction.

"I'm pretty sure that would be alright. I'll have to get the work approved by Mr. Shackleford."

"I can email you the work order this evening."

"I have no way to print it," he said.

She closed her eyes and sighed. "Of course not." She shrugged. "Sorry."

"You can just mail it to Shackleford House. I open the mail."

She laughed. "I'll swing by tomorrow and drop it off. That will give me time to check with my guy at the cable company to see when they can schedule it."

"Thanks. I really appreciate it." He nodded toward his quarters. "Got time to finish that coffee?"

She nodded. "Probably gone cold by now but I'd take a warmup."

Roger grinned. "I know the butler."

She chuckled. "So do I, now." She paused. "I do have one question."

"Only one?" Roger asked, leading the way down the corridor.

"Well, no. More than one, but pixies?"

Roger shrugged. "I shouldn't have mentioned that. Mr. Shackleford insists that pixies take care of the routine maintenance of the house. He claimed they were upset with my interfering with their work."

"What were you doing?" she asked, settling into the leather chair like she wanted to move in.

"Routine cleaning. Dusting. That kind of thing."

"You're responsible for this whole building?" she asked, her eyes growing wider.

"Yes. Technically, but as I said before the east and west wings are closed off. There's no need for anything but the main house with just two of us."

"You had me going there for a minute," Sam said, sipping her coffee. "Whatever did they use that much space for?"

Roger frowned. "I don't know. It's been the family seat for centuries. As far as I know, Mr. Shackleford has no children so I guess the line ends here."

"As far as you know," Sam said.

"He's never mentioned any. Never mentioned any wife. No pictures." His brain halted on that and he froze mid sip.

"What?" Sam asked.

"There are no pictures. Of anybody. Just the paintings."

"Think he's a vampire?" she asked with a grin.

"No," he said, shaking his head. "He's up during the day. Sits in the sun."

Sam stared at him. "I was kidding."

Roger laughed. "Of course. I knew that." He was pretty sure, anyway. He shook his head. "But there are no photographs anywhere in the house."

"Have you seen the whole house?" Sam asked. "I thought the east and west wings were closed off."

He nodded. "They are and you're right, I haven't."

"It's just the two of you here in this magnificent house?" she asked. "Well, and the pixies, obviously." She laughed.

"The fairies care for the yards," he said.

"Fairies?"

He shrugged. "That's what he claims. They tend the gardens. The pixies tend the house."

"Is this guy around the bend?"

Roger bit his lip and looked into his coffee cup.

Sam paled and set her cup into the saucer. "My God. He is."

Roger shrugged. "I'm not at liberty to discuss Mr. Shackleford's health."

She narrowed her eyes and lowered her head. "You're going to run this work order past the old man?"

"Well, of course. It's his house."

"The old man who thinks there's pixies in the woodwork and fairies in the gardens."

"Yes." He shrugged. "That's why I was hired."

"What if he rejects it for being anathema to the chi in the house?"

"Then we don't do it. I find some other way."

"Just like that?" Sam stared at him with her mouth half open.

"It's not like this is forever. My contract is up next summer."

She sat back in her chair and shook her head. "You're going to all this trouble for a job you're only going to have for a few months?"

He shrugged. "So it would seem."

She looked around the room. "You're going to give up this place?"

He shrugged again. "Won't have much choice, but yeah." As he looked around, he realized how much he'd come to enjoy living in the house.

CHAPTER 6

Roger delivered breakfast at the appointed hour. Shackleford stood at the window, staring out at the dismal, rainy morning, hands clasped behind his back. "Breakfast, sir."

"Thank you, Mulligan. Did you run this morning?"

"Yes, sir."

He turned to face Roger. "Admirable. What do you do in the winter?"

Roger placed the tray in its usual spot. "I run when I can. The temperature's less an issue than the footing, sir."

He nodded. "Did I mention that the pixies appreciated your libation?"

"No, sir. Thank you for letting me know."

Shackleford sighed. "It's so hard keeping track of everything, Mulligan. I forget what I've said. Forget that I've said it before or think that I've said it and I haven't."

"If there's anything I can do to help, sir?"

"Thank you, Mulligan, but no. This is something I brought on myself and I need to find my own way back." He took his seat in front of the tray. "Looks marvelous, Mulligan."

"Thank you, sir. Blueberry pancakes. Some bacon. Simple recipe."

Shackleford looked up at him. "How are you doing on the internet project?"

"A friend in the business surveyed the house yesterday, sir. She'll get me a project plan and estimate for your approval."

The old man blinked. "My approval?"

"Yes, sir. I thought you might like to know what's being done to Shackleford House. I can't judge what might upset the status quo, sir."

"Like the pixies?" Shackleford asked, a smile tickling his lips.

"Or the fairies, sir."

"I told you about them, did I?"

"Yes, sir. I don't know what other sprites might be affronted so I thought it best that I get the proposed work order for your approval before anything unfortunate happens."

Shackleford chuckled and took a sip of coffee. "Did you mention the pixies to your friend the consultant?"

Roger paused for a moment, debating the wisdom of admitting the truth. "I may have overstepped my bounds, sir. I did. And the fairies."

"Did she believe you?"

"No, sir."

"But accepted the work anyway?"

"Yes, sir."

Shackleford nodded. "I'd like to meet her."

"Shall I bring her up when she returns with the work order, sir?"

"If it's not inconvenient," he said.

"Of course, sir. Would there be anything else, sir?"

"Have you done an inspection of the wings, Mulligan?"

"No, sir. Ms. Patching said they were closed off and I shouldn't bother with them."

"Do me a favor and just take a quick look around. Make sure none of the windows are broken? No leaks in the roof?" He nodded at the window. "Rainy day. Best time to check."

"Of course, sir. Will there be anything else, sir?"

"Thank you, no, Mulligan. Carry on."

Roger bowed and headed off on his morning routine. In just a few short weeks, the pattern had become as automatic as breathing. Each morning's tasks varied slightly but none of them were overly taxing. He did find it strange that the old man would pick today to mention the wings. Perhaps the rain triggered something. The first heavy rain since he'd come to Shackleford House—that idea made sense. He finished the master suite and tossed the linens into the washer.

"No time like the present," he said.

Armed with a fistful of keys from the safe, he set off into the eastern wing. A pair of doors on the ground floor opened into a ballroom. Roger's laughter echoed around the room. The place looked like it could host a basketball tournament. Two immense crystal chandeliers hung from a white pressed-tin ceiling. Windows along the south wall let the gray morning light in through gauzy curtains bracketed by heavier drapes. The parquet flooring from the foyer continued through the room; his footsteps echoed in the space. Dark wainscoting ran around the perimeter. Flowered print wallpaper graced the gap between chair-rail and ceiling, giving the room a rosy glow even in the rainy light.

A pair of wide doors opened to the north and another to the east. The north doors opened onto a windowed gallery that looked out onto the gardens behind the house. Draped furniture huddled in conversational groups along the inside wall, canvas ghosts engaged in their own tête-à-têtes. French doors at either end opened onto a flagstone patio. He could almost smell the perfume and cigarette smoke lingering in the air.

The east doors opened into a storage space filled with folded tables and chairs that would have looked at home in any hotel conference center in the city. A closet held table linens and place settings for what looked like four hundred people. He didn't count them but gulped at the thought of being responsible for any event that hosted that many.

Another pair of doors on the east wall opened opposite the first pair. They hid a service area of stainless steel tables and racks. Warming ovens and refrigerators lined one wall. Glassware from crystal goblets to water glasses, and china from coffee cups and saucers to plates in various sizes stood on open shelves. A huge machine stood nearby, all copper and chrome with sliding doors, one on each side. It took him a moment to recognize the elder cousin of the dishwashers he'd seen in army mess halls. Wooden racks stood on their sides under each end of the beast.

"What in the world ...?" Roger stared, overwhelmed by the sheer expense of having a complete conference facility in your house. "What kind of conference would need this?"

Another pair of double doors opened on the north wall to reveal a small loading dock and parking lot tucked away behind a tall hedge. It didn't look big enough for a semi, but any of the large delivery vans would have little trouble. "Catering. Duh." Still, the scope of the installation boggled him.

He retraced his steps back through the house, closing and locking the doors as he went. He went up the main staircase and around the corner to the double doors on the east side. He didn't quite know what to expect—but after the ground floor, he braced himself against what he might find. He swung the door open to a corridor and felt foolish. He found the light panel inside the door and flipped all the switches. A string of wall sconces down each side illuminated a corridor punctuated by facing doors. The house theme of paper above wainscoting carried over up here with a lightly stained wood below and a textured paper in sand above.

He strolled down the hall, looking up at more pressed-tin tiles on the ceilings. The white paint appeared unblemished by water—or even time. The doors had numbers on them—odd on the right, even on the left—of some silvery metal, maybe pewter. The first door opened to his touch into what turned out to be a three-room suite: a common area with bookcases, a pair of desks, and a conversational grouping for four under draped canvas, with bedrooms on either side. Each bedroom held a wardrobe, a dresser, and a lamp on a night table beside a single bed, its mattress draped in canvas like everything else.

The door across the hall opened into what looked like a class-room, complete with almost a dozen old-style wooden desks with holes in the upper right corner for something. Inkwells? One wall held a single sheet of slate. It took him a minute to recognize it as a blackboard, complete with chalk tray along the bottom edge.

He kept an eye on the ceilings and sniffed for mold or mildew as he worked down the hall, but the place seemed tight. At the end he turned and looked back. Six suites on the street side, but only four classrooms across the hall, along with a couple of bathrooms, one on each side near the middle of the wing. The other two doors were for supply closets with empty shelves. He had no clue if they'd originally held linens or school supplies. From what he'd found, either seemed equally likely.

He shook his head and crossed the landing to the west wing. The ubiquitous double doors opened onto a parlor with enough room for a dozen easy chairs, a few low tables, and what appeared to be a card table in one corner. The light switch turned on a few standing lamps around the room. The wallpaper in this room—twining ivy leaves—gave the walls a pleasant greenish blush, while the pressed-tin ceiling tiles had a faint blue tinge. It made the room feel almost like it was outside.

A narrow corridor led toward the street side of the house. He found six large one-bedroom suites similar to the ones in the east wing with windows facing the street to the south but with double beds and a little more elbow room. The corridor wrapped around the end of the wing revealing a view of the trees outside and not much of the apartment building just on the other side of it. A metal fire escape hung on the side of the house just outside the window. He found a linen closet with towels and bedding. He didn't count but the piles filled the closet.

The corridor ended in a locked door that yielded its secrets with the application of a key. The hallway beyond mirrored the one before, with a linen closet and a fire escape outside the window. He continued around the upper floor corridors, finding rooms that looked less like office spaces and more like bedrooms. All told, he counted enough bedrooms for a family of ten and two more bathrooms off this corridor. His spatial sense told him there was a void of some kind in the middle—a space as wide as the parlor, running the length of the wing minus the linen closets.

Returning to the parlor, he found no door leading in that direction either. "Curious," he said.

He shrugged and secured the doors before going to the lower floor. Opening the double doors there revealed a fairy land of trees and gardens. He paused, stepping back into the main house again, just to make sure he knew where he was. He shook his head and re-entered the garden, following a stone path between benches and low plantings to where the rain beat down on the glass roof two stories above. "An atrium," he said. "My God." He looked around at the trees planted, some with trunks thicker than his chest but only reaching up to the glass roof at their tallest, but all still looking like healthy trees. He spotted at least four or five different kinds. Here a small birch grove, there a pine. A blue spruce contributed its spicy scent to the blend of loam and leaf, flower and tree. An odd tree with huge leaves stood tucked half under the overhang from the rooms above. It took him a moment to recognize it as a magnolia.

Eventually he completed his circuit of the ground floor and made his way back to the main house. He locked the door and checked the time. His tour had taken most of the morning. It wasn't at all what he expected, although he hadn't really known what to expect. He headed to the mud room to swap the laundry and fold the clean clothing before lunch.

Something light. A soup and sandwich, perhaps.

He wanted to ask Shackleford about the house's history but perhaps the Bible would be a better first stop.

Roger served a lobster bisque—canned but tasty—with a salad of summer greens. The warm soup felt right. He was proud of himself for whisking up the balsamic vinaigrette with only one side trip to a recipe on his phone. "Lunch, sir."

"Thank you, Mulligan." He looked up from his book. "What did you find?"

"No damage, sir. Everything seems dry and secure."

A smile grew slowly on the old man's face. "Good news, but what did you find, Mulligan?"

"I don't know, sir. The ballroom in the east wing was a surprise. The sheer size of it."

"What else?"

"Classrooms? Dormitory? Family quarters? Perhaps, faculty quarters?"

His eyebrows rose a bit. "What did you think of the atrium?"

"Astonishing, sir."

"No plants that needed insects or wind for pollination. The trees. All special dwarfed cultivars."

"Why is it closed off, sir?"

He shrugged. "Easier than answering questions about how an old man in a wheelchair and his butler can manage it."

Roger blinked, letting that statement echo in his head for a few long moments.

Shackleford watched him, spoon raised to taste the bisque—almost as if he expected Roger to ask.

Roger looked around the library. He saw no wheelchair. He couldn't remember seeing a wheelchair in the old man's room. His mouth went dry and he wriggled his tongue around in his mouth to try to work up enough spit to swallow. "The only time you're in a wheelchair is when Ms. Patching is in the house."

Shackleford stuck the spoonful of soup into his mouth and nodded. "Not entirely. I've kept it around for you until we had a chance to get acquainted. There are a couple others who seem to think they know what's best for me. It amuses me to make them think I'm less than I am."

"The fairies," Roger said.

Shackleford nodded.

"The pixies," Roger said.

Shackleford nodded again.

"It's not possible," Roger said.

Shackleford shrugged. "Lots of things aren't possible. Impossible things happen every day. What makes them impossible, Mulligan?"

"They can't happen," he said, knowing that his answer was wrong.

"Close," Shackleford said, taking another spoonful of bisque.

"People think they can't happen," Roger said.

"That's the right path," the old man said, rolling back from the table in a wheelchair. "Now think, Mulligan. What didn't you find in your tour this morning?"

Roger swallowed hard. "Dust, sir."

Shackleford nodded. "Still want to work in Shackleford House?"

Roger looked around the room, trying to spot a camera. It had to be some kind of prank. A joke. Even as he looked, he knew that he couldn't spot it. Cameras can be hidden almost anywhere.

"Well, Mulligan?"

"What happens if I don't, sir?"

The old man settled back into his wheelchair and shrugged. "For you? Nothing. I'll pay off your year's salary and give you the million that Naomi offered. You're free to go." He paused, tilting his head and seeming to weigh Roger with his eyes. "Do you want to leave?"

Roger's brain kept slipping its clutch, running a million miles an hour in circles and seizing up for a moment, only to start spinning again. "I—I—." He shook his head, forcing himself into combat mode. Assess the situation. "What if I want to stay?"

"You'd make an old man grateful," Shackleford said. "You'll still be paid well for your work. You get to live here." He looked around the room. "While it lasts, anyway."

"Is any of it real?" Roger asked.

Shackleford chuckled. "Define real."

"That chair?" Roger asked, trying to find some ground to stand on.

"Oh, quite real. The wheels are the illusion. These days it's harder to maintain."

"Pixies? Fairies?" Roger asked.

"You know the answer to that," Shackleford said. "You've examined the evidence yourself. Can you explain the atrium some other way? The lack of dust built up in the wings? You've lived here a month now. Have you ever seen a yard crew working the lawns? Housekeepers stopping by to dust and wax the floors?"

Roger shook his head. "No, sir."

"The world is magical, my boy. Always has been. We put names to things we don't understand and tend to avoid the things with no names. It makes them no less real because we don't believe in them."

"So pixies are what? Tiny invisible people?"

Shackleford shrugged. "If that's how you choose to visualize them, sure. Fairies are human-shaped dragonflies, if you like. Invisible to those who lack the sight, and—sadly—too few have the vision."

"You can see them?" Roger asked.

Shackleford shook his head. "Not my skill. I know they exist. I can see their effect. I can't see them."

"Like electricity," Roger said.

Shackleford smiled and nodded. "An apt metaphor. Magic and technology are sometimes seen as the two sides of a coin."

Roger took a deep breath and looked around the library again. "Your dementia?"

"Very real," Shackleford said. "I'm having what might be called 'a good day' in certain circles. I'm quite aware when I'm here. It's when I'm not that I run into problems."

"But it's not age related," Roger said.

Shackleford's eyebrows rose slowly. "What are you saying, Mulligan?"

"You've never lied to me, that I know of."

Shackleford nodded. "I've never knowingly lied to you." He shrugged. "I can't be sure I haven't inadvertently done so. Nor can anyone."

"You said it wasn't age. You became rather distressed."

"Did I?" Shackleford said, his face closing in a frown. "Hm. Well, it's true."

"It's the amulet," Roger said.

Shackleford's eyes grew round. "Where did you hear that?"

Roger shook his head. "Not important. What's going on here, sir? If I'm going to stay in the fight, I'd like to know the rules of engagement."

"Are you, Mulligan? Are you going to stay in the fight?"

"I need to know what I'm up against."

Shackleford nodded. "That's fair. Let me finish my soup. Come back in an hour. I'll answer all your questions then."

"All of them, sir?"

"All of them, Mulligan." He shrugged and grinned. "Although I reserve the right to say 'I don't know' if I need to."

Roger gave his Jeeves bow. "Very well, sir. Enjoy your lunch, sir."

"Thank you, Mulligan. I shall."

The front bell rang just as Roger reached the ground floor. He swung the door open, expecting to see Samantha Bicker. Instead he was met with Naomi Patching's scowling face. "You changed the locks."

"You said you didn't have a key, ma'am." Roger shrugged. "It's my responsibility to keep the property secured. It starts with the doors, ma'am."

"May I come in?" she asked, the peevish tone clear in each word.

"Of course, ma'am." Roger stepped back from the doorway, holding the heavy door open for her. "May I inquire as to the purpose of your visit?"

"It's been a month. I've come to check up on him."

"Mr. Shackleford is eating his lunch at the moment, ma'am. He's asked not to be disturbed."

"My, my," she said. "Really getting into the role, are we?"

"I've found that I quite enjoy the position, ma'am."

"Performance art? I had no idea you were more than a pretty face on a sturdy frame."

Roger nodded. "As you say, ma'am."

"So what's happened in the last month? Any visitors?"

"I'm not at liberty to discuss Mr. Shackleford's affairs, ma'am."

Her frown came back with a crash. "I'm your employer, mister. Not him. I have a question, you answer it. Capisce?"

"Capisco, ma'am, but you hired me to be the Shackleford House butler, not to be your spy on Mr. Shackleford."

She grimaced. "Damn barracks lawyer. Don't pull that crap with me or you'll be out of here before you knew you were leaving."

"I'm sorry you find my service unsatisfactory, ma'am. Might I suggest you take it up with Mr. Shackleford."

"Do you want to get paid?" she asked. "Or do you want to get fired?"

"As you remember, ma'am, I have a copy of the employment contract which explicitly states that our arrangement is not 'at-will.' You cannot fire me except for just cause. Since none of the duties listed in that contract involve me spying on your uncle, I am under no obligation to answer those questions which involve him. If you'd like to litigate it in court, I'd be happy to oblige."

"Fine. How's the house?" she asked.

"The house is in good repair, ma'am. The facilities all work properly."

"You're not finding your duties too onerous? Caring for the house and one old man?"

"I'll confess I felt a bit overwhelmed the first few days, ma'am, but I hope I'm settling in well." He indicated the parlor. "If you'd care to wait, ma'am. Mr. Shackleford should be done with his luncheon shortly. May I offer you coffee? Tea? Some lunch for yourself?"

"Coffee would be fine, thank you." Her fulminating tone backed down to a simmer and she crossed to the parlor.

"One moment, ma'am." He half expected her to make a dash for the library as soon as his back was turned. He found her lounging comfortably in one of the armchairs when he returned with a tray containing coffee, creamer, sugar, and a small dish with a few shortbread cookies. He placed it on the coffee table in easy reach. "I'll be back shortly, ma'am."

"Stay a moment, Roger, if you would." She seemed to have calmed down a great deal in the few minutes he'd been gone.

"How may I assist you, ma'am?"

"Tell me about the change," she said.

"Change?" Roger asked.

She finished amending her coffee with cream and sugar, stirring them together—the metal making quiet tings on the cup's sides. "You've changed from the angry man who applied for the job a month ago."

"I've found the house to be a settling influence, ma'am. Seeing it functioning as it should satisfies my desire for order."

"You like the control," she said.

Roger let that idea roll around in his head for a moment. "I used to think so, ma'am. Control is everything in the military, but without order, control becomes an impossibility." He smiled. "I find it mildly ironic that the order I chafed against in military service should be revealed as the key ingredient to my contentment now that I'm out."

"Without control, how can you have order?" she asked sipping the coffee.

"A good question, ma'am. I'm not sure. I think order depends more on preparation than control."

"But don't you need control to be able to say what the order should be?"

"Perhaps, ma'am."

"So you like controlling the house?"

He gave a short laugh. "I don't control the house any more than I control the sidewalks out front. True, I guard its entrances and care for the inhabitants, but I serve the house."

"So it controls you?" she asked, a smirk growing on her lips.

He recognized the jab behind the question but nodded. "In a way, yes, ma'am."

She sipped her coffee again and took up a cookie. "You have changed."

"It's the uniform, ma'am." Roger gave his Jeeves bow. "If there's nothing else, ma'am?"

"Thank you, Mulligan. You may go."

He returned to the kitchen and cleaned up from lunch, wiping down the counters and settling the dishes in the dishwasher. He'd no sooner paused to look around when the beeper went off. Its message read "Bring her up."

Returning to the parlor, he found Naomi sipping coffee and reading something on her phone. "Mr. Shackleford will see you now."

She sighed and stood, tucking the phone in her bag and smoothing the front of her skirt. "Thank you, Mulligan."

He led her up the stairs and knocked before entering. "Ms. Patching, sir."

Shackleford looked up from his lunch tray, blinking as if just waking up. "Ah, Naomi. Lovely to see you, my girl. Come in. Sit down. Entertain an old man." He waved her into one of the easy chairs and rolled across to park opposite. "Would you like some tea? Coffee? A sherry, perhaps?"

"Nothing, thank you, Uncle." She crossed her legs at the ankle and settled into the chair. "I just came to see how you're doing."

Shackleford looked at Mulligan. "Thank you, Perkins. If you'd check to see that my tux is ready for this evening?"

"This evening, sir?" Roger asked.

The old man wheeled the chair around to face him, putting his back to Naomi. He winked. "This evening, Perkins. The banquet? Surely you remember."

"Of course, sir. I'll make sure all the preparations are in order, sir."

Shackleford grinned before straightening his expression and turning back to Naomi. "Thank you, Perkins. Carry on."

Roger bowed and took the used lunch tray from the table. "Of course, sir." He caught the raised "I warned you" eyebrow from Naomi before he closed the library door and retreated to the kitchen. He took the opportunity to review the evening's menu from the Bible. It listed meals that interested him, but he lacked the basic tools even to understand which ones he might attempt. He'd served Shackleford most of the easiest ones—those he could confidently prepare with a skillet and saucepan—but what exactly was coq au vin? Chicken in wine? He hadn't known what lobster bisque was until he opened the can delivered by standing order. He paused that thought, wondering how much of "standing order" involved some mechanism of communication he just didn't know about. Could the old man be ordering stuff telepathically?

He took out his notebook and started jotting questions on a fresh page. The longer he wrote, the more intrigued he became by the idea that magic—real magic, not the sleight-of-hand, rabbit-out-of-my-hat kind—existed in the world.

He stopped, pen poised. Did it really? Or was it some con the old man had pulled on him?

He couldn't explain the lack of dust or the garden in the atrium. On a whim, he stepped into the telephone nook and lifted the device off its table. The table gleamed, dust free. He placed the phone back down and flipped his notebook closed, tucking it and the pen away.

He'd learned to trust his eyes and ears in the field. If he could see it, hear it, smell it, it was real. The trampled brush meant something. Somebody left footprints in the sand. He hadn't cleaned the dust off the table but it was gone. Somebody did it. Either the old man was messing with him or something else happened. Pixies? Possibly. Giving it a name—even a frivolous one—gave him an anchor.

The pager went off, summoning him to the library again. He shook himself to center his thinking and climbed the stairs. He knocked before entering. Shackleford still sat in his wheelchair across from his niece. "You rang, sir?"

"Yes, Perkins. Ms. Patching is leaving."

Naomi rose from the chair and sighed. "Please think it over, Uncle."

Roger stood out of the doorway to allow her to pass. She breezed past him without even looking in his direction.

"When she's gone, please come back, Perkins."

"Of course, sir."

He followed Naomi down the stairs and opened the door for her. "Good day, Ms. Patching."

"You're not fooling me, you know," she said, making no move to actually leave.

"Fooling you, ma'am?"

"This butler act."

"I don't know what you mean, ma'am."

"He's much worse," she said. "I have the right to know about his condition."

"You seem to have ascertained his condition, ma'am."

"You could have saved me a great deal of trouble if you'd just told me."

"I'm not at liberty to discuss the happenings within Shackleford House, ma'am. Especially not where Mr. Shackleford is concerned. You've seen him yourself. You've made your judgment."

"We'll see about that," she said and strode from the house and down the steps.

Roger closed the door behind her and set the bolt before returning to the library.

"She's got her hair on fire over something," Shackleford said. "Any idea what it might be, Mulligan?"

"She was most interested in any visitors you may have had, sir."

"Was she now?" Shackleford's eyebrows levitated up his forehead. "What did you tell her?"

"That I was not at liberty to discuss the matter with her."

Shackleford snorted. "Oh, that went over well, I'm sure."

"I enjoyed it, sir. Ms. Patching seemed less enthusiastic."

"Did she threaten to fire you?"

"She did, sir."

"You don't seem upset by that, Mulligan."

"She needs cause, sir. The amendments I made to the draft contract negate the default at-will employment. We both signed the contract. It should be binding. If she defaults, she has to pay double."

"You know she'd fight you on that?" Shackleford asked, leaning forward slightly in his chair.

"I'd expect nothing less, sir."

"If she does, I'll hire you. Same terms," Shackleford said. "She can fight me on that. I've got better lawyers than her father and more money than both of them combined."

"If I may be so bold, sir?"

"Yes, Mulligan?"

"Why did she hire me, sir? Why didn't you?"

"When Perkins passed away, she volunteered. I let her. They had a regular parade through the house for weeks. Tedious."

"What did you do without a butler, sir?"

"Well, I can feed myself, after all, Mulligan." His eyes twinkled with mirth.

"The wheelchair, sir? There are no ramps."

"I don't need one, Mulligan, remember? I'm perfectly capable of climbing the stairs."

"But the ruse, sir?"

"Oh, that? Pfft. The door won't open if I don't want it to."

"You know she had a key, sir?"

"Oh, yes. I expect she has duplicates. You changed the locks on the first day. Smart move. Good initiative, Perkins." He caught himself. "Sorry. Mulligan. It slips out."

"For a man with dementia, you seem fairly present, sir."

"It's the moon's phase. New moon protects me from the worst of it."

"I see, sir," Roger said, schooling his features.

Shackleford laughed. "You didn't believe the pixies and fairies either, did you?"

"To be honest, sir, I'm not sure I believe now. I just don't have an alternative hypothesis."

"Fair enough," Shackleford said. "Now, I promised you answers." Roger pulled his notebook out and the old man's eyebrows rose. "You wrote them down?"

"So I wouldn't forget, sir."

"Carry on, then."

"You're a wizard?"

"Yes. In the vernacular. Wizard is as good a term as any other. I pay a price for bending the universe to my will."

"You know other wizards?"

"Yes."

"If I guess who they are, will you tell me if I'm right?"

"No. By now you should be able to spot them. If you can't, then you're not paying attention and I won't reveal their secrets to you."

"They live in the city?"

"Some. I have rather a broad network, as my correspondence will have told you."

Roger nodded. "What's the amulet?"

Shackleford's eyes widened slightly. "Fidelia," he said. "Had to be."

Roger waited.

The old man pulled his tie loose and unbuttoned the collar of his shirt. He reached in and pulled out a chain with a flat disk attached like a locket. The chain and disk looked like the same dark metal. "This is the amulet.

"In my youth, I did my own share of adventuring, my boy. Wizard's downfall, really. Needing to know more. Discover the next lost artifact. Pull back the veil on reality to see the infinite clockwork behind." He shrugged. "I was no better than the rest. Always wanting more." He snorted and looked up at Roger. "I grew up in the Southwest, out in the desert and mountains. The indigenous peoples had magic beyond measure. Many of them still do but have to hide it from—well—from people like me." He paused. "You know the legend of Kokopelli?"

"Only the image," Roger said. "Trickster god. Coyote."

"Music and fertility," Shackleford said. "There's a reason they're together in Kokopelli. His flute had the power to attract people and to seduce them, hence the trickster. We still have music like that today. Music that moves us to passion." Shackleford sighed.

"You went looking for his flute?"

Shackleford chuckled. "Well, I was young and randy. Full of myself and needing to drain it off. What better magic than sex magic, eh?"

"Not something I've considered, sir."

"Anyway. Down in the Four Corners region, Kokopelli is everywhere. Carved in petroglyphs, ancient paintings. The cultural appropriation started in the 1900s, Put him on real-estate signs and jewelry, T-shirts and lawn ornaments. When I was a lad, he was the local equivalent of Pan and Bacchus rolled into one. It's impossible to find the truth about him anymore. It was even then." Shackelford's gaze turned inward. "That didn't stop me from looking."

"You found that?" Roger asked.

Nathan Lowell

"One of the things I discovered was that the Navaho had a word that we translate as 'canyon.' It's literal meaning is more like 'inside the rock.' There's a national park in northeast Arizona called Canyon de Chelly which reads as 'canyon inside the rock.'" He shrugged. "It set me looking for caves. I found this in one of them." He paused. "Rather, it found me."

"That's what's causing your dementia?" Roger asked, trying to move the conversation along.

Shackleford nodded. "When I found this, I found the spirit behind Kokopelli. Something ancient. Primordial in the truest sense. A being so old it predated language and communicated in pictures and signs. So powerful it shaped and reshaped rocks."

"Sounds like water," Roger said.

"Not a bad metaphor," Shackleford said. "Anyway, I found this cave in the Chuska Mountains. Wasn't the first to find it, either. Firepits around the mouth. Some animal signs inside. I'd seen a hundred like it before, but this one was the first to speak to me."

"Speak?"

"Communicate. In my head. It promised—" He sighed. "It promised everything. Money. Power. Fame. Anything I wanted. All of it. No three-wishes limits."

"The price?" Roger asked, guessing where the story headed.

"Not my soul, if that's what you're thinking," Shackleford said, grinning at Roger. "Although that might have been a better deal."

"What then?"

"My mind," Shackleford said. "It wants my mind. One piece at a time."

"So, you get worldly rewards but go crazy?"

"Baldly put, yes. It sent me out into the world and granted me amazing gifts. Wealth through foresight and intuition. Magical resources to call on, almost without limit. Women. Men. Whatever I wanted." He paused and shook his head. "Until I turned seventy. On my birthday, it started taking my mind and has been for over a decade."

"Did you know?" Roger asked.

Shackleford nodded. "Oh, yes. I was young and dumb and full of ... myself. I didn't really think I'd live to 70, let alone 80."

"Can't you just take it off?"

"I can," he said. "But I'll die. That's the deal. I've worn this thing for something like half a century."

"How do you know you can't take it off if you've never done it?"

Shackleford's haunted gaze met Roger's. "Because I found it beside the corpse of the last man to wear it. It was in his hand."

91

"So your choice is to let this thing take away your memories or commit suicide?"

"In a nutshell, yes."

"What happens if somebody else puts it on?"

"If they're magical, the deal is struck anew. The spirit wasn't in the cave. It's in the necklace." Shackleford tucked it back under his shirt and rebuttoned his collar. "It's been handed down from wizard to mage for eons."

"So that's what you meant. It's dementia but not age," Roger said.

Shackleford nodded. He finished restoring his clothing and shrugged. "In another year, my grabby niece will probably succeed in her plot to have me declared incompetent and put in a home far away."

"Vail," Roger said.

"You knew?" Shackleford asked.

"It was their rationale for the yearlong contract and the million-dollar payout."

"Cheeky of her. To actually tell you that."

"Is she magical?" Roger asked.

Shackleford's lips twisted to one side. "I said I wouldn't tell you if you guessed. You already know."

"My guess is that the only thing she has going for her is sex appeal and a rich daddy."

"Close," the old man said. "She's got her own money. Trust fund on her mother's side. She was a Shackleford, my sister. May she find the peace in death that she never saw in life." He sighed. "What Naomi sees in Thomas, I'll never know, but maybe he's got assets that crazy Uncle Perry doesn't know about." He looked up. "Any more questions in that book?"

"Just one. What is this place?"

"What was it, you mean?" Shackleford asked. "Back in the 1700s, it was an orphanage. Charity being a godly virtue and all. Rich women with embarrassing babies could leave them here, with the appropriate donation, of course."

"Of course," Roger said.

"It was a good racket until the fire, apparently. Too many unanswered questions about who the children really were." He looked around. "In the 1800s it became a boarding school. Much more fashionable, don't you know. Very private. Very elite. You had to know somebody to get in. Later you had to know somebody who had attended to get in. The place got renovated a few times. The ballroom used to be the chapel. Godliness is next to godliness, I suppose. That went away in the 40s, if I remember."

"Now you live here alone," Roger said.

Shackleford shrugged. "Perkins and I took up residence about thirty years ago. My father, Oliver Franklin Shackleford, left it to me. Much as you see it here."

"Was he magical?"

"You know the answer to that," Shackleford said.

"I can guess," Roger said.

"I inherited more than the house," the old man said, and shrugged.

"What happened to the boarding school?"

Shackleford shook his head. "First World War, I think. Money shifted hands. Power shifted seats. The prestige survived. Still survives. It just went to other places and neither my father nor grandfather seemed inclined to pursue it."

"Who inherits it next?" Roger asked.

"The Shackleford Foundation." Shackleford grinned. "At the moment, it's a shell company. Not-for-profit corporation that's going to put the house and grounds into the National Register as a historic treasure." He glanced around the library. "Not exactly Monticello, but it does predate it. It's the oldest continuously occupied dwelling in the state—even if the dwelling itself has been rebuilt a couple of times."

"And Naomi can't have it razed," Roger said. "The land alone must be worth a fortune."

"A lot this size in this city? Millions. She wants the money more than the land." Shackleford shrugged. "She's been angling for it since she was a girl."

"Why do you care?" Roger asked.

"Is that one of your questions?"

Roger shook his head. "Just seemed like an important idea. You'll be gone. Are there any more Shacklefords to pass it on to?"

The old man paused. "None in the direct line."

"Any of the cousins who might appreciate the pixies and fairies?"

The old man's head started shaking back and forth, slowly at first but building up speed. "All of my nearest relations passed away and by the time I came to the point of needing to designate an heir, I was the only one left."

"That you knew of," Roger said.

He nodded. "That I knew of. I've employed an agency to carry on the search but no luck so far."

The front doorbell tinkled. Roger snapped his notebook shut. "Thank you, sir. Most illuminating."

"Thank you, Mulligan." The old man seemed lost in thought as Roger closed the library door.

CHAPTER 7

Sam Bicker smiled as she handed Roger the envelope. "Everything's there."

"Any surprises?" he asked.

She shook her head. "Plug and play. Off-the-shelf components. The only pricey piece is the wireless rig to get through the wall."

"The old man wants to meet you, if you've got the time."

"Really? Why?"

"You took the job even after hearing about the pixies and fairies."

She shrugged. "If he's that far gone in dementia ..."

"You up for it?"

"Meeting him? Now?" she asked.

Roger nodded.

She glanced at her watch and nodded. "I've got a few minutes."

"Come on, then." Roger led her up the stairs and tapped on the library door before entering. "Ms. Samantha Bicker, sir. She's just dropped off the estimate for the installation of internet services." He stepped aside so Sam could enter.

Shackleford stood from the table and met her halfway with an outstretched hand. "Ms. Bicker. Thank you for meeting me."

"Call me Sam," she said, taking the old man's hand in a quick shake.

"Come in. Have a seat," he said, waving at the easy chairs in the corner. "I understand you heard about the pixies and fairies?"

She perched on the front of the chair and stared at the old man. "Roger mentioned them. The work order specifically avoids drilling any holes in the house."

"That's probably for the best. They can be a bit territorial, I fear."

"I wouldn't know, sir," she said.

"Yet you took the job even after finding out that I'm a bit touched in the head," Shackleford said. "Why?"

Sam smiled. "If I refused work from everybody I thought might be crazy, I'd have no customers at all."

"Do you think I'm crazy, Sam?"

"My grandmother had conversations with ghosts. My uncle lived according to the instructions he got from some spirit in a Ouija board." She shrugged. "I don't really know what's crazy and what's not. I just try to do my job the best I can and not worry about what my clients might think or say or do. Long as you pay your bill on time, I'll give you the best service I can."

Shackleford nodded. "Pragmatic as well as smart. What do you think of Mulligan's idea of installing internet here?"

She glanced at Roger. "Well, he's right. If his duties require him to be on premises almost full time, then the internet will give him access to the instructional materials he wants when he wants them."

"You know I'm a bit old-school?" Shackleford said, waving a hand at the substantial collection of books.

"Nothin' wrong with old-school, Mr. Shackleford," she said.

He grinned at her. "How would you add internet to this room?"

"Here?" She looked around and blew out a slow breath. "Once the router's connected, it would be pretty easy to put in a terminal. We might need a repeater, but as long as you've got the electrical outlet, it's not difficult." She paused.

"What is it, Ms. Bicker?" Shackleford asked.

"Won't it feel—I don't know—out of place? Modern technology in this room?"

Shackleford shrugged. "At one point, books were considered modern technology."

"I'm thinking aesthetic," Sam said. She bit her lower lip for a moment. "Pardon my asking, but can you type?"

Shackleford looked down at his hands. "They're a bit less flexible than they used to be, but I can still hunt and peck with them."

She shrugged. "I can add that to the work order. It'll cost a bit more but the biggest expense is the first terminal. After that, it's really how much you want to spend for each incremental access point."

"You may have suspected, money isn't really a concern," Shackleford said, a smile on his lips. "What would you recommend?"

Sam gazed around the room. "You've not got a lot of wall space. Does that dictionary pedestal move?"

Shackleford glanced at it. "Yes. It can go away as far as I'm concerned. The dictionary is probably a century out of date. I leave it because I never had a reason to remove it."

Sam pulled a tape measure from her bag and held it up. "May I?"

Shackleford waved a hand. "Whatever you need."

Sam measured the gap between the shelves and peered down behind the pedestal. "It'll need an outlet back here somewhere."

"I can manage that," Shackleford said. "I can have a desk built into that place. Anything Roger needs to know about specifications?"

She looked at Roger. "Height? Holes for cables?"

Roger nodded. "We can manage that. You're thinking a full workstation?"

She looked at the place and squinted for a moment before looking around the room. "I am. I know of some custom workers that could make it fit here. May take them a while."

Shackleford shrugged. "I'm a patient man."

She shrugged. "Add another four thousand to the order. That'll include the machine and extra network repeaters. You'll handle the desk."

"Excellent," Shackleford said. He looked at Roger. "Thank you, Mulligan. I'll trust you to make the paperwork right?"

"Of course, sir."

Shackleford extended a hand to Sam. "Thank you for your time, Ms. Bicker."

"Thank you for the order, sir."

"I'm looking forward to seeing this internet in action," Shackleford said. "I haven't needed it before but something tells me Shackleford House might just benefit from it."

Roger held the door for Sam as they left the library but didn't speak until they returned to the kitchen. He pulled the contract from its envelope and used his pen to add the new terms in the margin on both copies. "You're sure about this?"

"The custom machine? Oh, yeah. I know a few makers who do the whole steampunk keyboard monitor thing. Wood and brass. It'll feel right at home in the library up there."

"Why didn't you suggest that for me?"

She grinned. "If you'd had a space for it, I would have. I get a better cut on custom work."

He grinned back and signed both copies of the amended contract, initialing the changes.

"I have to say, he's not what I expected," she said.

"Tell me about it."

"I thought you said he has dementia," she said. "I've seen forty-somethings with less on the ball than him."

"He has good days and bad. This has been a pretty good day for him. I think he's only called me Perkins twice."

"That why you're signing the contract instead of him?"

Roger shook his head. "The house is my responsibility. He directs me and I get it done. Not exactly power of attorney. If there's a problem, he takes it out of my hide. If I don't pay, you come after me."

She nodded. "That's a lot of responsibility. Can you afford it?"

He grinned. "Personally, no. Not right now." He looked at the totals on the page. "I could in another couple of months. I won't need to. I keep the books for the house and this is petty cash."

"He's really that wealthy?"

Roger laughed. "You know how much this place costs? Just the taxes on the property run into six figures."

"And he has it?"

"So it would seem. The city isn't here dunning him for it."

"How did you luck into such a sweet deal?" she asked. "I mean other than the whole monkey suit thing."

Roger spun the paperwork around and handed Sam his pen. "Luck of the draw and a willingness to take the chance on working for a madman."

She took the pen, initialing the amendments and signing at the bottom of each. She handed the pen back. "You're loving it, aren't you?"

Roger shrugged. "It's just a job."

"No," Sam said, tilting her head to one side. "You've changed."

"Just because of the suit," he said.

"No," she said again. "Pardon my saying so, but you were a mess when that EMT thing blew up."

Roger sighed and took his copy of the contract back. "My own fault. I shouldn't have punched the guy."

"The way I understood it, he'd beaten that woman half to death," she said.

Roger nodded. "Still no reason for me to return the favor."

"You've changed," she said again. "You actually like waiting on the old guy."

He shrugged and looked away. "It's ... complicated."

"Tell me," she said, leaning forward on the work table.

"It's the house," he said.

"You know this place has a pretty checkered past, right?" she asked. "I checked it out."

"Like how checkered?"

"Orphanage until it burned down. Half the kids died," she said.

Roger felt a jolt like a punch in the gut. "I knew it had been an orphanage. I didn't know the kids died."

Sam shrugged. "The wonder was that more of them didn't, I suppose. Not like the city had fire codes then." She paused. "Did you know it was a boarding school for rich people's kids?"

"Yeah, closed down after the First World War." He looked at her. "Some scandal there, too?"

"Not that I know of," she said. "Just felt kinda squicky when I found out."

"Now?" he asked.

She looked around as if weighing the house. "I have to admit the pixies and fairies thing is a biasing factor."

"Because you believe they're real or because you believe they're not?" Roger asked.

She shrugged. "The old man certainly seems to believe in them."

"He does." Roger bit back a further comment. No need to get Sam biased against him, too.

Sam glanced at her watch again and straightened up. "I need to get going. I want to see a man about a computer before he closes up shop for the day."

"Mine?" he asked.

She gave him a sour look. "Yours is coming from a big box catalog." She nodded toward the library. "His will take some finesse."

Roger led her to the front door. "Thanks for this, Sam. It'll be nice to be connected to the world again."

"You know there are people who use their smart phones for this stuff, right?"

He shrugged. "I need the bigger screen."

She gave him a side-eyed look. "What kind of videos are you planning on watching, again?"

He laughed.

"Can he get that desk built?" she asked.

"Money opens many doors," Roger said. "He probably has some ancient friend who did cabinet work for Nixon in the 70s or something."

"Holler if you need a referral. I know a few people who do that kind of work."

"Thanks. I'll do that." Roger held the door for her. "Any idea when the outside work will get done?"

"Cable company," she shrugged. "I'll call and get a date and time for you. Whether they make it in that window? Your guess is as good as mine."

"Not like I won't be at home," Roger said.

"Do you get any time off?" she asked.

"I do. One day a week. I picked Saturday. Why? You interested?"

She laughed. "Just curious. Nothing personal."

"I don't usually stray very far from the house," he said. "It's funny. I have almost no interaction with the outside world. Not a single TV in the place. Not even a radio. We get a newspaper delivered in the morning. That's it."

"What'd you do with your record collection?" she asked. "You were a big stereo nut when you got out."

He shrugged. "Sold the gear. Boxed the records. They're in my mother's attic."

"CDs would have been easier to store," she said.

He shrugged again. "Not the same."

She gave him a long look. "You've changed."

"You keep saying that."

"You seem calmer. More centered."

He snorted. "No, I'm not taking up yoga or meditation or anything woo-woo."

"It's the pixies," she said. "Must be."

He laughed as she sashayed out the door and down the walk.

"I'll call you when I have the install date," she said over her shoulder.

He swung the door closed behind her and threw the bolt. Had he changed so much? He checked the time and reviewed the tasks he'd not accomplished yet. His schedule had gotten off track with all the visitors. Time to fix it.

The carpenter came to the back door. Roger had expected an old man in overalls and a tool box. He got a guy that looked to be around his own age with a walrus mustache, cargo pants, and a T-shirt with a breast pocket. His work boots had sawdust caught in the seams. A late-model cargo van stood parked in front of the garage.

"Afta-noon," the guy said. "You the new butlah?"

"Yes. You are?"

"Enoch. Enoch Cahtwright. The old man's expecting me?"

Roger stood back from the doorway, holding the door for him. "He is. Thank you, Mr. Cartwright."

"I love workin' on this ole place." He clomped in and waited for Roger to close and lock the door behind him. "Not another like it in a hundred miles."

"This way, sir," Roger said, leading the way through the kitchen and up to the library. He knocked before entering.

Shackleford looked up from his book.

"Mr. Cartwright, sir." Roger stepped into the library and off to the side.

Enoch clomped in and grinned at the old man, holding out his hand. "Mr. Shacklefud. What kinda mess you need me to make today?"

"Enoch, my boy. Thank you for coming on short notice." Shackleford stood and shook Enoch's hand. "I need a little remodeling done."

Enoch nodded. "Fig-yud. What's the what?"

Shackleford pointed to the dictionary stand. "That needs to be a computer desk."

Enoch's eyebrows shot up. "Seriously? Ya bringing the old barn up to this century?"

Shackleford laughed and shrugged. "I don't know about that, but Mulligan here needs it and I thought I might be able to use it for some of my research."

Enoch nodded, his gaze on the niche. "You want me to take that out or will you do it?"

"I can get it out. I need you to put in the desk so it matches the rest of the woodwork."

Enoch nodded again. "Yeah. I can handle that. You want it today?"

"If you can," Shackleford said. "A man with your talents probably has work lined up around the block."

Enoch chuckled. "Happens I'm between right now. Finished a big job yestahday. New one tomorrow. If you can clear that space I can do it right now." He paused and wrinkled his nose. "You know what you want?"

Shackleford shook his head. "Not my area of expertise. Mulligan?"

Enoch looked at Roger. "Any pref'rences?"

Roger shrugged and looked around the room. "Can you do a rolltop to hide the computer when it's not in use? Maybe a keyboard tray that tucks out of sight?"

Enoch squinted at the dictionary stand and nodded slowly. "Yeah. I can see that. Cable run down the back?"

"Yes," Roger said.

"You gonna put a printer in here?"

"Hadn't thought of that," Roger said. "We've got a color laser coming for the house. Is there room?"

"Oh, yah. Cabinet underneath. Probably room for an inkjet or a small laser." He glanced at Shackleford. "You okay with that?"

"I leave it in your capable hands, Enoch."

Enoch nodded. "All right." He fished in one of the cargo pockets and pulled out a steel tape, took a few measurements, and nodded. "Nice size." He stepped back. "If you'll get that moved, I'll have the new desk ready by this afternoon."

Shackleford smiled. "Thank you, Enoch. That would be splendid."

Enoch gave the old man a salute with his index finger. "My pleasure, as always, Mr. Shackleford."

Enoch took his leave, and Roger led him to the back door.

"You can get that done today?" Roger asked.

"Oh, yah. Most uv it anyway. Rolltop's the tricky part. I'll have ta go back ta the shop for that." He shrugged. "Shouldn't be any problem."

Roger had his doubts that Enoch could get the stain dry in that amount of time, but he'd worked on the house before. He must know what he was doing.

"Should be back around three," Enoch said, nodding as he strode across the tarmac. The van rumbled to life and backed around before driving out into the alley.

Roger closed the door and sighed. "Stranger and stranger," he said, before climbing the stairs to the library. That dictionary and pedestal needed to be out of the way before Enoch returned. The library door opened as he approached it. He entered to find Shackleford standing in the gap where the dictionary had been.

"Ah, come in, Mulligan. I need your help."

Roger looked around the room but saw no sign of the dictionary or its pedestal. "Yes, sir?"

"How many outlets? Two? Four?"

"I don't understand, sir."

"For the computer," Shackleford said. "How many plugs need to get plugged in?"

"Generally, one, sir. Best practice calls for a surge suppressor. That plugs into the wall and the gear plugs into that."

Shackleford pursed his lips and bent over to look at the baseboard. "Like that?"

Roger crossed the room to see whatever the old man was looking at. "Yes, sir. Looks like a standard outlet." He frowned. "I didn't think there was one there before."

Shackleford shrugged. "Pixies."

"Do I want to know where the dictionary went?"

"Storage in the basement," the old man said. "We may find a use for it." He looked at Roger, as if waiting for him to ask.

"I see, sir."

"You see what, Mulligan?"

"I see that you can do a great deal more than turn straight chairs into wheelchairs."

Shackleford nodded, a sad smile on his lips. "I used to be able to do more, but I've forgotten."

"Why didn't you just build the desk yourself?"

"Oddly enough, I never had any affinity for it," Shackleford said. "This way is better. Enoch's a true craftsman."

"He seemed to know the place pretty well."

"He's done work for me before, if that's what you're asking."

Roger nodded. "Is there anything else, sir?"

"Do you think I'll be able to figure it out, Mulligan?" he asked, staring into the empty space.

"The computer, sir? Yes, sir."

Shackleford looked at Roger. "Even with my memories being scooped out?"

"It's not a memory yet, sir."

Shackleford snorted. "Pragmatic view as always, Mulligan. You give me hope."

"Hope, sir?"

"Hope that I'll find a solution." He paused. "Or an heir."

"I hope so, too, sir."

The old man nodded and waved a hand, settling himself in his chair and taking up the book. "Carry on, Mulligan."

"Thank you, sir."

Roger left the room and allowed his inner child to celebrate for a few minutes. He struggled with conflicting beliefs about magic. It couldn't exist and yet he'd seen more than one instance with no other explanation. That electrical outlet had not existed before. The dictionary had. He toyed with the idea of exploring the storage room in the basement, just to see if it was really there, but his morning schedule called for changing the linens in the master suite. Not a big job, but one that needed doing before he satisfied his curiosity. "Pixies," he said, shaking his head.

Enoch returned at the stroke of three. He'd parked his van at the back door and swung the doors wide. "Mulligan, en it?"

Roger nodded. "Or Roger. Mr. Shackleford calls me Mulligan, among other things." He grinned.

"It's probably not in your job description, but if you'd give me a hand lugging this stuff?"

"Of course," Roger said. "Glad to help."

The first piece—a base unit—went up easily. The smooth finish surprised Roger. Enoch had only been gone a few hours, yet the rich wood tone matched as if he'd spent days staining and sealing the wood. When they slotted it into place, not only did it fit perfectly, but Roger wouldn't have suspected it was new construction.

The second piece—the rolltop—went up a little harder. "It's heavy," Enoch warned. "An' awkward as a pregnant cow climbing a ladder."

Roger snickered at the image, but the carpenter had been right. The bulky piece kept trying to twist out of Roger's hands as they maneuvered it down the halls, up the stairs, and into the library. Once there, it fit solidly into its designated place. Enoch fiddled with some pieces under the desk's surface before stepping back and shaking the top. It didn't budge.

"Locked tight," he said. "Doors and shelves and that's it."

One more trip had the various components in the library. Enoch hung the doors on the front and showed Roger and Shackleford how to adjust the shelving units using a handful of pegs and the corresponding holes in the unit. The keyboard tray had its own flat shelf that pulled out, similar to the writing desk in Roger's quarters.

"Once you've got the parts," Enoch said, "you can adjust the shelves to where you want 'em. The keyboard should be in the right place." He pulled the rolltop down. "When you're done, this'll hide the beast away."

Shackleford nodded. "Excellent work, Enoch. Thank you. Send me the bill?"

"Of course," Enoch said. "Labor and materials. Installation's free." He grinned.

Shackleford nodded and Roger showed Enoch back out to the tarmac.

"Thank you, Mr. Cartwright. That was astonishing work."

Enoch closed the loading doors on his van and shrugged. "Been doin' it since I was a lad and I'm olda than I look." He squinted at Roger. "You're new. How're you and Shackleford getting along?"

"I find the position both challenging and rewarding."

Enoch gave him a lopsided grin. "He's the real deal, that one."

"So I'm learning."

"His last butlah, Perkins. Good man. Been with the old guy for decades. Shackleford took it hard. I wonder'd if he'd ever get a new fella."

"I was hired by his niece."

Enoch frowned. "Naomi? She's a piece o' work, that one. Watch your back with her."

"So I'm learning."

Enoch held out his hand. "Nice to meetcha, Roger. Hope ya stay around for a while. He needs somebody stable."

Roger shook, noting the calluses and strength in Enoch's grip. "Thank you for the work. It's much appreciated."

"Don't thank me yet. I haven't sent the bill." He laughed and clambered into the van, cranking it over before the door slammed shut.

The routine fell into place once more. The morning schedule, the weekly tasks in the afternoons. On a Saturday in August, Roger grabbed a library card from the local branch—which happened to be only a few blocks from Shackleford House, just in a direction he didn't normally frequent. He intended to read up on cooking but stumbled on The Butler's Guide, written by a real butler. He started reading it and soon became engrossed. There wasn't much time to read during the day, but over the course of a week he worked through the slim volume and ordered a hardcover for his personal library as a reference work. It was just a handbook on how to do things, but he glimpsed a fascinating history between the lines. While Shackleford House wasn't exactly a castle, he found the writing style comforting and the content intriguing.

He also picked up a few cooking books from names he didn't recognize but which the librarian recommended, chief among them Julia Child—who he vaguely remembered for being a comedic personality in his childhood. Who knew?

Thus armed, he settled in after dinner most evenings with the Pettigrew Bible and his other books. He lost himself in the stories and the food. He often padded through the kitchen in the night, looking at the equipment and examining the larders. The spice rack—which had seemed overwhelming in the beginning—proved to be almost as enchanting as the freezers full of meats and fish. Game hens became his favorite poultry because they were essentially little single-serving chickens—each a delightful portion alongside a brown rice pilaf and a side of steamed vegetables.

He practiced his sauté work with dried beans in a skillet. Getting the pan-shake just right meant he didn't spill navy beans all over the work table. The effort took several evenings. He almost gave up before he found the right combination of shake and flip to roll the beans around and around. For several minutes he grinned and flipped steadily, before he lost it all and beans went everywhere.

The cable company hooked up the router in the garage near the end of August, one of the hottest days of the year.

Noon in the city wasn't usually too bad, but in August it could feel like a steam bath. Of course, that was when the cable company showed up and rang the back doorbell.

Roger found the guy with a computer tablet in his hand, a smile on his face, and a lanyard around his neck with an ID photo facing the wrong way.

"You're the butler?" the guy asked, more out of surprise than a need to confirm Roger's identity.

"Yes, sir. How can I help you?"

The guy lifted the lanyard to flash the ID card at Roger before looking down at his clipboard. "Says you want cable installed in the garage?" He glanced at the garage.

"Internet service, yes," Roger said. "No drilling."

The guy frowned. "I saw that on the work order. What do you mean 'no drilling?'"

"When you run the cable into the garage, route it under one of the doors, sir."

"You realize that's crazy, right?"

"I realize that the request sounds odd to you, yes, sir."

"The cable will be exposed to the elements. Weather. The door opening and closing on it."

"The same cable that will be buried approximately six inches underground from the nearest hub?" Roger asked.

The guy gave a short laugh. "Well. Of course."

"And it survives just fine there? All through the seasons? Rain? Snow? Ground freezing and thawing?"

"You got it, buddy. But the ground protects it, buffers the extremes. Leaving it out like that will age it fast. Degrade your service."

"Thank you for informing us, sir."

"No drilling." The guy said it as if confirming the fact.

"Correct, sir."

"Well, all right." He shrugged. "Where do you want this connection made?"

"One moment. I'll fetch the key, sir." Roger closed the door and retrieved the key from the key safe in his quarters. The installation tech waited patiently on the back stoop. "This way, sir."

The guy followed behind Roger as he opened the door and flipped on the lights. He stopped cold as soon as he got into the garage and saw the cars. "Holy sh—" He bit off the word but Roger knew the feeling. "Are those real?"

"No, sir. Holograms." Roger kept his face as straight as he could.

The guy looked at Roger, one eyebrow raised. "You just make a joke?"

"Yes, sir. They are quite real."

The guy gave a soft whistle and shook himself. "Where you want the box?"

Roger indicated the wall beside the cellar door with a broad gesture. "Anywhere in that section of wall will be fine."

"You know we can install it in the house itself," the guy said.

"Without drilling, sir?" Roger asked.

"Well, we need to get the connection inside the house somehow."

"Yes, sir. We're aware of that, but drilling through the wall is not permitted."

"So? Are you going to be setting up a terminal out here?" He looked around as if trying to figure out where there might be a desk. "Gets drafty in the winter, I bet."

"Hot in the summer, too, sir."

"You're not going to tell me, are you?" he asked.

"Are you familiar with the concept of 'need to know,' sir?"

"Like for security clearances?" The guy's eyes widened ever so slightly.

"Yes, sir."

"Well, sure. Everybody knows that."

"Then you'll not take offense when I suggest that you do not have a need to know, sir."

The guy frowned. "Okay, okay. I got it. Top secret. Forget I asked." He pulled out his smart phone and took a picture of the wall. "Right there?"

"Yes, sir."

"All right. I'll go look up the nearest hub. Can you leave the garage unlocked?"

"No, sir." Roger looked at the vehicles parked in the bay. "Would you?"

The guy paused a moment, glancing at the cars before shaking his head. "No. No, I wouldn't."

"I'll stand by if you need me, sir."

"It'll be a few minutes."

"I understand, sir. Ring the bell again when you need my assistance."

The guy went out to his van and pulled a well-provisioned tool belt from the back, strapping it around his hips and checking the pockets before shouldering a big coil of black coax. He walked down the tarmac and turned right at the alley. Roger closed and locked the garage door. The wet heat wrapped around him until he got back inside Shackleford House. He wasn't sure how far the guy would have to go but he felt pretty certain that coil of coax wasn't going back in the van.

He put a pitcher of ice water and a tumbler on a tray in preparation for the worker's return. Hydration was so important.

Almost thirty minutes passed before the back doorbell rang again. Roger poured the tumbler full of ice water and took the tray to the back door. The neatly dressed cable installer looked a bit the worse for wear. A stream of sweat flowed down one cheek on his reddened face. His uniform showed damp patches at the armpits.

Roger offered the ice water. "Some water, sir?"

The guy looked at Roger and then the tray. He took the tumbler and poured it down his throat, gulping loudly. "Oh, man. Thank you," he said, gasping before placing the glass back on the tray.

"My pleasure, sir. One moment." Roger placed the tray on the laundry table. He went back outside. "Did you find your junction box, sir?"

"Yeah. About a quarter mile down the road." He went to the far corner of the garage, where the last few turns of cable lay on the tarmac. "I laid it out on the grass in as straight a line as I could get but used up almost the whole coil."

"I'll just open this door for you, sir." Roger went into the garage and pressed the door opener for the empty bay at the end. The motor whined and lifted the door, letting the afternoon sun in to wash out the competition from the overheads.

The installer brought the cable in tight around the door frame and popped a staple into the inner wall near the floor. "That should hold it," he said, straightening and looking down the length of the garage. "I'm gonna need to get another coil."

Roger nodded. "Of course, sir. Would you like more water?"

He wiped his forehead with a sleeve and nodded. "Yeah. That would be terrific."

"I'll be right back, sir." Roger went into the house and took the pitcher to the sink to refill while he grabbed a tray stand. When he returned, he found the tech staring at the cars. "Beautiful, aren't they, sir?" he asked, setting the stand up by the door and placing the tray on it.

"Incredible. Blast from the past."

"Indeed, sir."

The tech shook himself and headed for his van, and came back with some boxes and another coil of cable. "This should do it," he said, placing the boxes near the wall and spooling out the cable along the front wall of the garage. "This would be a lot easier if I could just put a hole in the wall back there. Less cable inside."

"Drilling is a problem, sir. Not the exposed cable."

The guy shot Roger a look, but shrugged. "Your house."

Roger had to admire the speed and efficiency of the man as he added connectors and joined the two cables together. He secured the line against the wall, running it up beside the door frame and across the top, threading it over all the garage door rails to staple it neatly to the wall near the ceiling line. Clearly a man with a great deal of practice.

It took next to no time for the technician to secure the box to the wall after getting a final nod from Roger on the placement. A few moments later, he had attached a handheld unit to the wired and powered box.

"I just need to make sure you're on the network at this end and we're done here. You can hang pretty much anything you want on this port." He consulted his device and nodded. "That's got it." He shut off the device, collected his tools, and policed the area for trash. "You know, this thing has wireless access. You'll need to secure it so the neighbors don't steal your Wi-Fi."

Roger nodded. "I've got a contractor to handle that. She'll be here in the morning, sir."

"Really? It's simple, you just need a password. I could lock it for you."

Roger reached over and pressed the power switch. "Seems secure enough for the night, sir."

The tech laughed. "Can't argue that." He took himself and his gear out to the van while Roger closed and locked the garage. "The crew will be here in a couple of days to bury that cable," he said.

"Not necessary, sir. The groundskeepers will see to it."

"Groundskeepers?" he asked, glancing up at the house. "You have groundskeepers, too?"

"Yes, sir."

The guy slammed the back doors on the van and turned to Roger with the tablet. "If you'd just sign here to certify that I've done the installation as required? I can't test the connectivity for you because ... well, you know."

"Of course, sir." Roger took the tablet and used his fingertip to scrawl his signature in the box.

The guy took it and nodded. "Thanks." He paused. "Can I ask you a question?"

"Of course, sir."

"You're really a butler?"

"Yes, sir."

"Why a butler? Isn't it ... I don't know ... kinda boring?"

Roger shrugged. "After three tours in Afghanistan and two years as an EMT here in the city, I find that my capacity for excitement has been filled, sir. At Shackleford House, I have a good boss, good pay, a safe place to sleep, plenty to eat, and nobody trying to kill me. Why wouldn't I be a butler, sir?"

The tech smiled. "Hooah." He patted the back of his van. "This is my Humvee now. As rough as some of the neighborhoods claim to be, I've never worried about IEDs in it." He thrust out a hand. "Nice to meet you, Mulligan."

Roger shook the man's hand. "Thank you for your service, sir."

The tech laughed and climbed into the van, started it up and pulled it out of the drive to idle in the shaded alley.

Roger watched him for a moment, replaying the conversation in his head. He realized, for perhaps the first time, that he did not want to see Shackleford House be bulldozed. Not that he hadn't had the thought before, but shaking the man's hand—explaining to a fellow vet? Something clicked inside him. He looked up at the house and down at his uniform. Sure, the old guy wasn't insane. The house had pixies. He was pretty sure that the fairies would bury the cable. He wasn't sure what would happen at the end of the year, but he was damn certain that he'd do everything in his power to prevent Naomi Patching and her money-grubbing husband from getting control of the place.

"Hooah," he said, for the last time, and remembered to fetch the tray and stand from the garage before going back into the kitchen. It was nearly time to prepare dinner, and he needed to call Sam about the extra printer and an installation date.

"Other than he really wanted to drill a hole?" Roger shook his head. "I wasn't going to allow it and he didn't want to go back to the barn without the install done." He didn't mention the cable crew who couldn't find the cable to bury.

"Let's get this done, then," she said, holding up a box. "Got the wireless link. Garage locked?"

"Oh, yes. Let me get the key." Roger walked back to the key safe and pulled the garage key from its hook. His morning routine would wait for this.

When he let Sam into the garage, she took a moment to admire the vehicles again before focusing on the equipment on the wall. She stripped the link from its packaging and held it up to the wall beside the modem. "Yes. This will work." She handed him the device and rummaged in the packing material, pulling out a plastic mounting bracket and a zip-top bag of screws. "These are okay, I hope?"

"I suspect so," Roger said. "I haven't had any complaints about the modem."

She pulled a screwdriver from her bag and mounted the bracket beside the modem.

"You've done this before," Roger said.

She grinned at him, thrusting the screwdriver back in her bag. "Not this setup but yeah. Enough times that I always carry a screwdriver." She took the link from him and snapped it into the bracket with a loud click. She rummaged in the box again and pulled out a piece of cable and a small white pasteboard container. The cable plugged into a socket on the bottom of the link and into the modem. The container held a small power supply and cord. She got everything all wired and took a half step back, looking it all over. "I think that's got it." She reached over and turned on the modem, waiting for the lights to stop flashing. "You ever used one of these?"

Roger shook his head. "Not this model. I'm a 'plug it in and hope it works' kind of guy."

"This takes the cable signal, breaks out the data channels from the TV stuff, and feeds it into this ethernet port for distribution to the local network in the house." She pushed all the loose bits of cardboard and packing material back into the box and tucked it under her arm. "Let's go get the other side connected."

She went out to the van and pulled out the mate to the box in her hand, leaving the empty behind. "You okay leaving the garage unlocked for a few minutes?" she asked.

Roger shook his head. "Not really." He shrugged and locked the garage behind them. He led her into the house and through the kitchen to the broom closet.

She pulled the link from its packaging and set it on the shelf. A minute later she had the power cord plugged in and turned the device on. "Okay. We need to secure both ends of this link," she said. "If we're lucky, we can get it to do it auto-magically." She pointed to a slow-flashing yellow indicator. "It's polling, looking for its mate." She pointed to a button on the top edge. "If you press and hold that button, it'll look for another device that's also polling. We don't want it to find just any device in the neighborhood, only the one in the garage. What I want you do to is go out there, then press this button on that unit and hold it until the light turns solid green or I come out."

"Press the button. Hold it until the light turns green."

She nodded. "If it turns green, meet me at the van."

"If?" he asked.

She shrugged. "Never know. Usually it works. Sometimes not." She raised her eyebrows. "Good?"

"Good," he said. He left the closet, made his way into the garage, and pressed the button, holding it down. Nothing happened for several long moments. The yellow light just kept up its slow blink, blink, blink. Then the green blinked and stayed. He released the button and headed for the van.

Just as he reached the back of the vehicle Sam showed up and pulled the back doors open. Roger spotted a collection of boxes: a few commercial packages with bright printing and pictures, and a couple of brown corrugated pieces.

"Lemme lock the barn," he said.

She nodded and continued lining up the boxes at the doors of the van.

He glanced down at the cars, just to make sure they hadn't transformed into cardboard cutouts or something. He chuckled to himself and locked the garage. "The cable guy said we needed to secure the router, too."

"Yeah. We'll do that from the inside so we're not locked out ourselves. Here." She thrust four smallish boxes into his hands before pulling out a computer bag and looping it over her shoulder. She grabbed a flat box with the picture of a sleek, black laptop on it. "I figured we could start in the kitchen and make sure the network comes up. There's more room there than in your quarters. Once we have the network, you can fire up your own machine and work through the set-up process while we get Mr. Shackleford's unit installed."

Roger nodded and held up the boxes. "What are these?"

"Network repeaters. Plug them into an outlet within twenty feet or so of the access point in the closet or each other and any authorized device can link to the network."

Sam knew her business. Within ten minutes she had established network access to the ground floor. She walked around with her small laptop open, checking the signal strength from the front parlor back through Roger's quarters and all through the kitchen. She stopped at the kitchen prep table again. "Okay. We have network. I'll set the firewalls while you boot up that bad boy." She nodded at the laptop box.

He recognized the brand and model well enough to know that he'd never have been able to afford it. The specs on the end label just reinforced the idea. He slipped the machine out of its packaging, the smell of foam and plastic filling the kitchen. A mouse and power cord came nested in the foam cradle. It took him less than a minute to plug them both in and fire up the computer.

"It's a bit oversize," Sam said. "I went for the seventeen because it'll be your only device and you're not going to be lugging it around town."

"It's gorgeous." He found the power button and pressed it. A familiar loading screen came up and asked for credentials. He started down the set-up tree.

"What do you want the network name to be?" Sam asked. "Sixteen characters. Shouldn't be the house or the address. We can hide it but still shouldn't be something traceable."

"FBI Surveillance Van?" he asked.

She snorted. "Not my first choice."

"How about capital P, Parsons 1900."

She looked at him and blinked. "That mean something?"

"Parsons was Shackleford's father's butler back at the beginning of the last century."

She typed it in. "Password?"

"Capital P, Pixie, capital D, Dung, 2020."

"Not dust?" she asked.

He shrugged. "If you were guessing, would you guess dust or dung?"

"Fair enough," she said. "A special character?"

He looked over at her. "Interrobang before the numbers."

"Interrobang?"

"Technically a question mark superimposed on an exclamation point? Use question-exclamation?" he asked.

"I know what it is. I thought you weren't a computer geek," she said.

"I've a thing for funny glyph names. Like that pound sign thing? The hash mark?"

"Yeah?" she asked.

"Octothorpe." He shrugged. "I ran across interrobang somewhere. It's not a glyph but it stuck with me."

She rattled a few more keys. "I'll leave the access point visible for now. When we have the machines hooked in, we can hide it from the public."

Roger nodded. "This is hooked in. Going through its setup."

"Let's get the machine installed in the library, then. I can't wait to see it in place."

"Ah, about that?" Roger said.

She stopped halfway to the back door and turned to look at him.

"Remember the last time you were here? He was having a good day?"

Her face clouded. "Not so much today?"

He shook his head. "Just go with it. I have no idea what we'll find. If he's too bad, we'll just stage the boxes in the upstairs parlor. I can probably figure out how to plug them together when he's doing better or asleep or something."

"Thanks for the warning," she said.

He shrugged. "Just wanted to make sure you were prepared if we go in there and he starts swearing at Perkins or something."

"Perkins?"

"His last butler." Roger shrugged. "Occasionally he thinks I'm Perkins."

She shook her head. "That's got to be hard."

"It's usually not much of a problem. I'll answer to anything except late to supper and since I'm also the cook? I eat first." He grinned. "Let's get the machine up there and see where we are."

Roger took the awkward box while Sam took a pile of smaller ones. Outside the library door he paused to put his down. "Lemme just check."

She nodded.

He knocked on the door and entered. "Your computer is ready, sir."

Shackleford looked up from his book—the wrong book. Roger braced himself. "Excellent. And the delightful Ms. Bitters?"

"Bicker, sir. She's here to do the installation."

"Of course. Ms. Bicker. My apologies. Show her in, Mulligan."

Roger stepped back into the hall to usher Sam in.

She smiled at him in passing and grinned at Shackleford. "Good morning, Mr. Shackleford."

Nathan Lowell

He rose from his chair, holding the book in one hand, his place marked with his finger between the pages. "Ms. Bicker. Lovely to see you again." He swept the room with his free hand. "Please, don't let me get in the way of progress."

She nodded. "May I use the end of the table, sir?"

"Of course, of course. Would you like me to leave the room while you work your magic?" He practically beamed at her.

"Not necessary, sir." She looked at the new desk. "That looks like it had always been there."

"Carpenter is a miracle worker," Shackleford said. "Cartwright by name. Third or fourth generation. Knows his business."

She nodded and rolled the top up while Roger brought in the awkward corrugated box from the hall. "That's your monitor, sir. I had it custom designed for this room."

"You build them, too?" Shackleford asked.

She laughed and shook her head. "No, sir. I know some crafts-men around town who take stock components and dress them up. One of them made these pieces." She pulled the top open on the awkward box and reached in, pulling out a large monitor dressed in brass. The base consisted of a slab of greenish stone. Brass arms reached up to hold the sides of the display with broad brass knobs on each side. "I knew we couldn't match the wood so I asked for a brass look." She placed it on the table. "It tilts to adjust for your preference. Just tighten the knobs to hold it at the angle you prefer."

Roger marveled at the monitor but Shackleford seemed entranced by it.

"It's beautiful," the old man said, reaching out to stroke the top of the frame. "How clever."

"Wait until you see it set up," she said, taking the monitor to the desk. She adjusted the shelf to the correct height and placed the monitor on it, stepping back to gauge her work. Nodding, she fished in the box again, pulling out two cables—a power cord and a thick video cable. She finished wiring the monitor and turned to the smallest of the three packages she'd brought up. "This is the actual computer unit," she said. She held up a wooden box with brass hinges on the back and a brass key plate on the front. It looked like a mahogany jewelry box. A line of sockets ran along the back, just under the hinges. "We'll plug everything in here." She pointed to the back and looked at Roger.

He nodded. "Got it."

Sam pulled the power cable out of its packaging. She plugged that into the base unit, fed the plug end down the hole, and slid the box into the gap formed between the monitor shelf and the desk

117

after connecting the video cable. Then, she pulled a small key from her pocket, placing it in the keyhole in the front. Ducking under the table, she plugged the two power cords into the power strip mounted under the back edge of the desktop.

She packed all the loose material back in the cardboard box and set it aside in favor of the wide, flat box she'd carried. "This is your keyboard and mouse. Same guy did the work on the monitor, and I'm stupidly pleased. If you don't like these, I'll take them back." She pulled out a brass-and-leather-bound keyboard that looked like an early typewriter on steroids.

Shackleford's eyes widened. "That's a work of art, isn't it."

The mouse looked like a solid brass puck with its three buttons fitted so closely the seams hardly showed. Sam flipped over the keyboard and mouse to show Roger the battery hatches on the bottom. "It's all wireless but the lifetime on them is really good. Weeks if not months." She placed them on the desk in the appropriate places and stepped back.

Shackleford walked over and gazed at the setup. "So this is a computer," he said. "I never imagined that we'd see the likes in the house. Or believed we might need it." He glanced at Bicker. "I've heard tales."

She smiled at him. "Turn it on with the key." She pointed to the key in the base unit.

He reached forward and gave the key a twist. A faint whir sounded and the monitor flickered once, then flipped up to an image of the house itself, taken from a height.

Roger stepped forward and looked at the picture. "Where'd you get that?"

"Drone image. I took it myself." She grinned. "Why?"

"Just curious. Looked like the kind of thing you'd see on a real-estate brochure."

The computer finished booting and a small window opened asking for username and password.

"What do I put?" Shackleford asked, sitting down at the keyboard, his two index fingers hooked in the air.

"We set it up for you as jpshack for the username and 1wizard as the password," she said. "I tried to make it as simple as I could for you to get started, sir."

He glanced up at her and nodded. "Thank you, Ms. Bicker. Very thoughtful." He pecked his way through the login, painfully slowly from Roger's perspective but his face brightened in delight when he pressed the enter key and the image of Shackleford House was replaced by a browser screen. "Now what?"

"Type what you want to see in the little slot at the top, sir." Sam pointed to the address bar. "Hit enter and you'll be given a list of things available on that topic."

He started to type but nothing happened. "I've missed a step," he said.

"Use the mouse, sir," Sam said. "Put your hand on it and you can move that little arrow up until it points to the slot. Use your index finger and press the button."

Shackleford put his hand on the mouse and looked back and forth between the screen and his hand several times before managing to push the mouse into the correct position.

"Now click, sir," Sam said.

He clicked and the vertical blinking line came up.

"Type what you want to see."

"Anything?" Shackleford asked, looking up at her.

"Well, pretty much anything. Lots of things you probably don't want to see, but just because you don't want to see them, doesn't mean nobody else does." She shrugged. "It's still a more or less free internet."

He focused on his keyboard and pecked out "genealogy."

"Press enter, sir," Sam said.

"Oh, yes. Of course." He nodded and pressed the key. The screen immediately filled with suggested genealogical resources. He looked up. "Now what?"

Sam gave him a brief rundown on the various features on the page, particularly how to identify links and advertisements. She had him click a link and use the back button to move backward. "Experiment, sir. Try things. You can't break it. You just need to be careful not to take anything at face value. The internet is infested with scammers, many of them criminal."

The old man frowned. "That sounds less than optimal, Ms. Bitter."

"It is, sir, but we've installed some powerful protections. On the machine and in the network itself. It's as safe as we can make it. Some simple rules. Don't tell anybody your password—which is why you should change it because we all know it now."

He nodded.

"Don't tell anybody your credit card, Social Security, or Medicare number." She looked at Roger and glanced at Shackleford.

Roger nodded. He didn't know if Shackleford was on Medicare or eligible for Social Security. He pulled his notebook out and made a note.

"That seems logical," Shackleford said. "Treat everybody as if they're just looking for a way to pick your pocket."

"Until you establish their bona fides, yes, sir," she said. "There are millions of reputable players out there. You can always ask Mulligan if you have any questions." She looked at Roger. "Right, Mulligan?"

"Of course, sir."

Shackleford sat back in his chair. "So this is like a library."

"Yes, sir. A library of digital materials. Also a catalog of items for sale. If it's for sale anywhere, you can find it here."

"Anything?" Shackleford asked, raising his eyebrows.

"Almost. There are some legal limits, even online, but it's a global network. Things that might be illegal in the US aren't always illegal in other countries. You could probably order them, but whether or not they would be delivered? That's a different problem."

He nodded, pursing his lips. "Yes, Ms. Bicker. I take your point." He glanced at the last box. "And that?"

She grinned. "A printer. If you find something you'd like to keep a record of, you can print a copy. It's not as pretty as the rest."

He stood and stepped back. "I'll get out of your way."

The printer was a standard black plastic inkjet model that tucked neatly onto the shelf under the desk. She plugged it in and turned it on, waiting for the machine to cycle through and ping. "No paper in it," she said. "You have to keep supplying it with ink and blank paper, but it'll print anything you want in gray scale. I've got a larger color printer that Mulligan will care for."

"Sounds complicated," Shackleford said.

"It's only different," she said. "By this time next year, you'll wonder how you got by without it."

Shackleford glanced at Roger, one eyebrow raised.

"I'm familiar with the technology, sir."

He nodded. "Very well. Is there anything else you need to do here, Ms. Bicker?"

"No, sir. We need some paper for your printer, but we can clear out the trash and leave you to it. Do you have any questions for me?"

"I'm sure I will as soon as you leave the room," he said, smiling.

"That's generally the way it goes, sir."

Roger helped her bundle up the empty boxes and loose packing material. Most of it went into the monitor's box. He paused with the load in his arms. "Will there be anything else, sir?"

"Not at the moment, Mulligan. Thank you. And thank you again, Ms. Bicker. I look forward to entering the digital age."

"You're welcome, sir," she said.

Roger followed Sam into the hall and pulled the library door shut. He went down the stairs and into the kitchen, sliding the packaging into the corner by the back door. "I'll get that broken down later," he said. "We have a big printer?"

"Well, bigger. The color laser is a pretty hefty beast compared to that inkjet. Also noisier. It's in the van along with a case of paper, spare ink for his printer, and a spare cartridge for the laser. All of it's wireless. Can you link his printer into the network?"

Roger shrugged. "Probably. If I run into trouble, I can always look it up on the internet."

She laughed. "True."

"That's a pretty sweet rig you got for him."

"The guy does great work. It's not going to win any prizes as a gaming rig, but as a general office machine, it'll do the job."

"I don't think we'll be hosting any LAN parties," Roger said. He remembered the ballroom. "At least not right away."

Sam frowned. "What was that look?"

He shook his head. "The house has a lot of surprises. The ballroom is a conference center. One of the wings is set up as classrooms."

"You know this place used to be an orphanage and a boarding school?" Sam asked.

"Didn't we have that conversation already?" Roger asked. "I'm more concerned that he won't still be here a year from now."

Sam's eyebrows rose at that. "Is he sick? Beyond the dementia?"

Roger shook his head. "Seems healthy as a horse. Has no trouble dressing himself and getting around when he wants to. I should be so healthy at his age."

"Does he ever come downstairs?" she asked.

Roger shrugged. "He hasn't as long as I've been here. I serve his meals in the library. He's pretty focused on his research."

"You know, getting him out more might help his mental condition. A little exercise? Some mental stimulation."

"You a doctor now?" Roger asked, smiling at her.

She laughed and shook her head. "No. My grandmother had to deal with Gramp for his last few years. She always claimed he was better after his walk around the block in the morning."

Roger nodded, thinking he had a lot more than recipes to research now that he had internet.

"Well, let's get this printer set up and I'll get out of your hair," Sam said, glancing at the clock. "I suspect you've got luncheon to prepare."

"I've got it mostly taken care of already. It's soup and salad day. I just need to warm the soup and whip up a little dressing. Only take a few minutes."

"What kind of soup?" Sam asked.

"A minestrone today."

"Did you make it?"

He laughed and shook his head. "Canned. I think I'd like to try my hand at it, though. One of the reasons I wanted to get internet."

"Not just porn, then?" she asked.

He laughed. "No, not just porn."

"You know, big houses like this usually had a cook and house-keeper."

"To take care of a whole family, sure. One old man?" Roger asked.

"Yeah. I take your point. Come on. I'll grab the paper if you'll lug the printer."

Roger followed her out to the van and dragged the last of the equipment in. It only took a few minutes to set up and load the laser printer. Sam used her laptop to trigger a test page to make sure it was communicating on the network and closed down her gear. They added the detritus to the pile of trash by the door.

"That's it, then," Sam said. "I'll send the bill by snail mail but you might set up a Shackleford House email address now that you can handle it. Almost all business is being done digitally these days."

"Not a bad idea," Roger said. "I'll look into online banking, too. Maybe I can get some of the recurring bills on auto-pay."

"I'll leave you to it," she said. "Call if you need help with anything."

"Thanks, Sam. I really appreciate the extra steps you took here." He held out his hand.

She shook his hand and nodded. "You're welcome. It was a fun project and nice not to have to low-ball everything to meet an unreasonable budget."

"I'll let you know how it works out."

She waved and took her bags back to the van, placed them inside, and closed the cargo doors before climbing into the cab and driving away.

Roger watched her go, wondering if she might like to have dinner some night. He shook his head and went to break down the extra packaging for the trash pickup. Shackleford House might have entered the digital age, but his duties remained significantly analog.

———————————————

Roger hated it when Naomi Patching came to call. Sure, she looked good, but she had the heart of a killer. He'd met enough of them to know. It wasn't that they had dead eyes. It was what made their eyes light up. Getting away from those eyes was one of the reasons he declined re-enlistment. Her showing up reminded him that not all the killers wore uniforms, even if most of the uniforms didn't contain them.

"Are you going to let me in?" she asked, when he'd stood too long in the front doorway.

"Of course, ma'am. My apologies." He stepped back and held the door open.

"I presume I'm not interrupting meal time or—perhaps—nap time," she said, the caustic tone making clear that she remembered being kept waiting.

"I'll see if Mr. Shackleford is receiving visitors, ma'am. If you'd care to wait in the parlor?"

"I'm not a visitor, Mulligan. I'm a relative, in case you've lost sight of that."

"Of course, ma'am. If you'd care to wait in the parlor, I'll see if your uncle is receiving relatives."

"What are you hiding, Mulligan?" she asked, eyes narrowing.

"Hiding, ma'am?"

"Why this charade of checking with him? Are you afraid of what I'll see if I arrive unannounced?"

"Not at all, ma'am. One of my duties as butler is to make certain Mr. Shackleford is not disturbed." His beeper vibrated and he checked the message. It read "Show her up." He nodded. "Mr. Shackleford will see you now, ma'am."

She harrumphed but followed him up the stairs to the library. Roger knocked before entering. "Ms. Patching, sir."

Shackleford sat in his usual wheelchair, appearing much frailer than normal. A wan smile on his lips and the sunlight streaming in behind him shining on a few strands of hair combed over his scalp. "Thank you, Mulligan."

Roger stepped out of the doorway and Naomi swept in. "Uncle. How are you feeling?"

"Passable," he said. "Quite passable. Come in. Have a seat. Can I offer you tea? Coffee?"

She lowered herself onto the front edge of one of the easy chairs and shook her head. "No, thank you, Uncle. I can't stay very long. I just came to see how you were. When was the last time you had a physical examination?"

Shackleford stared daggers at her. "I fail to see how that's any of your business."

Naomi gave him a serpent's smile and glanced at Roger. "You may go, Mulligan."

Roger looked to the old man who gave him a short nod.

"Thank you, Perkins. Carry on."

Roger nodded and left the room, closing the door behind him. Although tempted to listen outside the door, he went back to the laundry to finish folding the towels. He should have anticipated the physical. Naomi wanted her uncle declared incompetent; establishing his physical disability would feed that narrative if it came to a hearing. He felt pretty sure that it would.

The question remained as to who would conduct the examination and under what conditions. Naomi wouldn't stand for a family doctor, would she?

He finished the laundry and tossed a freshener capsule into the washer to clean it while he ran the towels up to the third floor linen closet. In the beginning he thought the setup to be inefficient, but the truth was that starting with the clean at the top meant all the laundry flowed downhill and only had to be carried up the stairs when clean again. For one man—two, counting himself—it seemed over the top, but then having the entire mansion for the two of them did, too.

Roger stopped outside the door on his way back down. He paused for a moment before knocking and entering. Naomi looked at him with a sour scowl. Shackleford smiled at him.

"Perkins, thank you. Would you show my niece out?"

"Of course, sir." Roger stood away from the door and gave a small bow. "Ms. Patching?"

She turned to Shackleford. "Uncle. You're being unreasonable."

"You're being tedious, Naomi. You want a physical. I'll get a physical. I'll use my own physician, thank you." He shrugged. "Who better than to give me a checkup than the man who knows me best?"

"But he'll just report what you want him to say," Naomi said.

Shackleford snorted. "And yours would do the same for you. I'm sorry, Naomi, but I'm not playing this game. If you'd like to have my records reviewed? Fine. Get a second opinion, but if I'm to suffer the indignity, at least let it be on my own terms."

Naomi stood, arms rigid at her sides with fingers splayed like she wanted to keep them from clenching into fists. "This is not over, Uncle."

"Good day, Naomi." He looked at Roger. "Be careful she doesn't fall down the stairs, Perkins. She's not seeing very well right now."

"Of course, sir."

Naomi growled and stomped out of the room.

Roger followed her and pulled the door closed behind him.

"You see what I'm up against?" Naomi said, striding down the stairs. "The man is impossible."

"As you say, ma'am."

"He needs a physical. Man his age? He could have all kinds of things failing on him left and right. Not just his mind."

"You make a good case, ma'am. I get an annual myself and I'm not even half his age."

"He wants to go to that quack. Man never finds a thing wrong with Uncle Perry." She stopped at the door and Roger opened it. "That can't be right. Not even high blood pressure?"

"He seems to be in relatively good health, ma'am."

"Then why is he in a wheelchair?" she asked. "Answer me that."

"I'm not at liberty to discuss Mr. Sha—"

"Oh, shut it," she snapped. "I'll subpoena the bastard if I have to. Discuss that." She turned and continued her progress out the door and down the steps.

He watched to make sure she didn't catch a heel between the pavers. The way she drove them into the stone, she'd have stuck for certain. When she cleared the gate, he closed the door and returned to the library.

"She gone?"

"Yes, sir."

"Do you know what she's planning, Mulligan?"

"No, sir. Beyond getting you committed to the assisted living facility in Vail? No."

Shackleford nodded and walked over to his desk, pushing up the rolltop. "What do you know of this DNA test thing?" He pointed to the screen.

"They claim to be able to match up people according to their lineage, sir."

"How do they sample it?"

"I'm not sure, sir. Perhaps a swab of the inside of the cheek. Saliva would do it."

"They require payment," Shackleford said, grimacing.

"Most people do, sir."

"Yes, but they require a credit card," Shackleford said, thrusting his hands into his trouser pockets and scowling at the screen.

"You have one or two, don't you sir? I keep getting statements."

"I do, but I'm damned if I'll give the number to them."

Roger nodded. "Might I suggest a prepaid card, sir? Put the amount you need on the card and use that?"

Shackleford looked at him. "That would work," he said. "Limit the downside exposure. Do they have those now?"

"Yes, sir. They're fairly common."

"Can you get me one, Mulligan? With perhaps a hundred dollars on it?"

"Of course, sir." Roger paused. "May I ask why you're looking into this DNA test?"

Shackleford shrugged. "Probably a long shot, but the Shackleford line goes back to the 1600s here. I know I'm the eldest of the main line, but there must be other Shacklefords. Married women. Pioneers who moved west and disappeared. If I can find some likely heir, then Shackleford House doesn't need to go the foundation."

"Somebody who wouldn't turn around and sell it to Naomi as soon as they get their hands on the title, sir?" Roger asked. "You realize that the heir would have to have submitted their DNA as well."

Shackleford nodded. "Yes, Mulligan. That's a limitation on the strategy, but I've spent thousands on private investigators and researchers. Every Shackleford I've found is either from a different branch or came much later."

"This won't rule them out, sir."

Shackleford nodded again. "Yes, but I believe it's the best I can do now."

Roger realized what the old man sought. "You're looking for another wizard, sir?"

Shackleford glanced at him and shrugged. "You reminded me, Mulligan. The pixies."

"You realize you may have found one or two already, sir?"

"No, Mulligan. Like calls to like. If any of them had the skill, we'd have both known it."

"Is there anything I can do, sir?"

"Get me one of those prepaid cards, Mulligan. Something that can't be traced back to me."

"Tomorrow's Saturday, sir. I'll pick one up while I'm out."

"Thank you, Mulligan."

"What are you going to do about the physical, sir? Can I make a call for you?"

Shackleford shook his head. "I was bluffing. My doctor died three years back. I need to find a new one. Somebody who makes house calls."

"May I suggest that will be a hard order to fill, sir?"

Shackleford grunted. "The right doctor could earn a good living just giving me my annual physical, Mulligan." He stared at me. "Any ideas?"

"Pettigrew, sir?" I asked.

"She's good but she's not a doctor, Mulligan."

"She may know one who has the right skill set, sir."

Shackleford blinked and shook his head. "Of course. I'll write her tonight."

"Sir, if you'd like me to, I could deliver the message for you. I'll be out and about tomorrow anyway."

He nodded. "Excellent. Thank you, Mulligan. I'll have it ready by breakfast."

"Anything else, sir?"

"No, thank you, Per—" He stopped and sighed. "No, thank you, Mulligan."

"You're welcome, sir."

Roger left him staring at the screen and tapping his lips with the fingers of his left hand. Would an heir solve the problem or merely complicate it?

He sighed and returned to polishing the silver. The butler book recommended it be done every week. He didn't have that kind of time or the staff to help him do it, so he just did the best he could and rotated through the various cutlery drawers each week.

As he rubbed each piece with the well-used polishing cloth, he let the idea of a revitalized Shackleford House play in his mind.

CHAPTER 9

Roger stopped outside the building and looked up at Pettigrew's apartment, Shackleford's letter in his jacket pocket. The old man hadn't said anything but he was pretty sure that going to any old physician wasn't in the cards for him. He climbed the four steps to the stoop and pressed the bell.

The same Hefner-bee opened the door. He had the pipe and smoking jacket schtick down cold, but he didn't have the right vibe. "Yes?"

"I have a message for Mrs. Pettigrew."

The guy gave him a squinty-eyed stare before stepping out of the doorway. "You know the way."

Roger nodded his thanks and climbed the stairs to the landing. He knocked twice and waited.

The door opened just as he was about to knock again. Mrs. Pettigrew peered out at him, her head cocked just a bit to the right. "Mulligan," she said.

"Sorry to disturb you, Mrs. Pettigrew. I have a message from Mr. Shackleford." He reached into his jacket and withdrew the envelope, offering it to her.

"He could have mailed it," she said, not taking it.

"The matter is somewhat urgent and I volunteered to deliver it, since today is my day off, ma'am."

Her face tightened around the eyes and lips as she stared at him. "I see," she said. She took the envelope and held the door open. "Come in, Mulligan."

He stepped into the apartment, which was just as bare as the last time he'd been there.

She closed the door and ripped open the envelope, pulling the single sheet from it. "You know what this is about?"

"Yes, ma'am."

She glanced up at him. "How are you adjusting to service, Mulligan?"

"I find it peaceful," he said. "At once soothing and gratifying."

She nodded, just the tiniest of motions. "This Patching woman is a problem."

"So it would seem, ma'am."

"When you get back to Shackleford House, check your bible under Medical Assistance," she said. "You should find whatever you need there."

Roger felt a flush of embarrassment. "My apologies for disturbing you, ma'am. I should have checked there first."

She waved a dismissive hand. "Not necessary. I take it you've found the volume helpful?"

"Invaluable, ma'am. Astonishing in its detail." He paused. "Thank you for your time, ma'am."

She opened the door and smiled. "Not at all, Mulligan. I'm happy to be of assistance."

He left the apartment and turned at the landing. "Good day, Mrs. Pettigrew."

"Good day, Mulligan. Keep up the good work." She smiled and closed the door.

All the way down the stairs, he kept kicking himself. Medical assistance. He couldn't remember seeing such a heading but if Pettigrew said it was there, it was there. On the street outside, he glanced up once more and wondered how long it had been there.

He spent a quiet afternoon at the library looking at more cookbooks. While watching videos on the internet had helped, he still struggled with some fundamental knowledge. Like how did a cook know what kind of whisk to use, or did it even matter if it was a whisk? He understood most of the words but felt like he didn't have a good handle on the meaning. Add a sprinkle of this or that? How much is a sprinkle? The library shelves had plenty of choices—and he'd read several of them—but he really didn't have a clue which to choose.

He walked out of the place without a book, and pulled out his phone. A last resort, but some things you needed to do. He pulled up the dialer and thumbed in a number. It rang three times before someone picked up.

"Hello," she said.

"Hi, Mom."

"Roger?"

"Yes. How are you?"

"Roger!" She spoke away from the phone. "Ed? It's Roger."

"Jeez, Mom. It's not like I've disappeared. I'm out of the army, remember?"

She sniffed. "Well, I wouldn't know, would I? I think you called more on deployment than since you've been home."

"Roger?" His father's voice came over the line.

"Hi, Pop."

"You all right, son?"

Roger stepped out of the middle of the path and took a seat on the stone steps. "Never better, actually."

"You should come to dinner," his mother said.

Roger laughed. "Tonight?"

"Tonight?" his mother asked. "Can you come tonight?"

"Saturday's my day off," he said.

"You're working?" his father asked.

"Yeah. Had the job for a few weeks, actually."

"What are you doing?" his mother asked, a hint of suspicion in her voice.

"I'll tell you about it tonight," he said. He glanced at the clock on the library tower. "I can be there in half an hour."

"Seriously?" his mother asked.

"Is that a good time?"

"Of course," his father said. "Whenever you can get here. We can catch up."

"I've got one more errand to run and I'll be along shortly."

"I'll put the coffee on," his mother said.

"See you soon," Roger said and broke the connection. For a moment he sat there and looked at the people walking past. If they only knew.

He snorted and pushed up from the stone, brushing the seat of his jeans off with his free hand. He needed to find a prepaid debit card before calling an Uber.

You'd have thought Roger hadn't been home in years, given his mother's glistening-eyed welcome and the way his father hugged him. They still lived in the modest bungalow in the burbs. He hadn't grown up there, but he still admired the house for its cozy feel whenever he visited. They ushered him into the kitchen and plied him with coffee. The meaty aroma of pot roast with onions filled the house, and he felt himself unwind as he settled into one of the wooden kitchen chairs.

His mother sat across from him while his father took the head of the table, each with their own coffee mug.

"So, what's this mysterious job?" his father asked.

"You'll laugh," Roger said, suddenly shy about what he was about to say.

His father grinned. "What? You a barista or something?"

Roger shrugged. "Close. Butler."

His father's eyes opened wide and his mother's jaw dropped.

"Butler?" she asked. "Did you say butler?"

"Yes, ma'am."

"You couldn't keep your room clean for more than twenty seconds as a boy and now you're a butler?"

"Yes, ma'am."

"Where?" his father asked.

"Here. In the city. Shackleford House. Over on the North Side." Roger sipped his coffee and waited.

His parents shared a look—half confusion, half concern.

"How in the world did that happen?" his mother asked, leaning forward over the table. "Was it something you wanted?"

Roger shrugged. "You know I was having trouble after the EMT thing."

They both nodded.

"I signed up with an employment agency and they matched me with this job. Well, a bunch of jobs, really, but none of them worked out. A couple of months ago they sent me out to this job and I got it."

"You don't have any qualifications to be a butler, Rog," his father said.

"Well, it seems that I had the qualifications they wanted. The old man lives in the house alone. His niece and nephew have him on a waiting list for assisted living in Colorado but needed somebody to look after him and the house until his name comes up on the list. They didn't need a butler as much as somebody who could look out for him and make sure he ate and stuff." Roger shrugged.

"Assisted living?" his father asked, one eyebrow raised. "What exactly are you doing for this guy?"

"Mostly just making sure the house stays in order, laundry, making meals."

"Why does he need assisted living?" his mother asked.

"Dementia. He's sometimes confused about where or when he is." Roger shrugged. "He sometimes calls me Perkins. That was his last butler."

His mother smiled. "That's not dementia. Half the time I called you Ed and him Roger."

Roger smiled. "He's a nice guy. I met him before I signed the contract. It's only for a year, and the pay is good." He shrugged. "That's why I'm here, actually."

"Oh?" his mother asked.

"I need to learn to cook."

His father gave a short bark of laughter while his mother's eyes shot open wide.

"You can cook," she said.

"No, I mean I need to know how to cook better."

She shook her head and looked to his father for a moment. "What do you mean by better?"

"I can make the few things I learned here, but I need to expand my menu a little. I've been reading books and watching videos but it seems all disjointed."

She pursed her lips and frowned. "You want to be what? A chef?"

"Maybe," Roger said, glancing at his father.

"What do you need to know?" she asked.

"That's the thing," he said, leaning over his mug. "I don't know what I need to know. I need some fundamental kind of text or instruction or something." He shook his head.

"What about this butler thing?" his father asked. "I didn't think butlers cooked."

Roger shrugged. "It's just the two of us. A big house would have a full staff and the butler's job would be to oversee it. I get to do all of the jobs."

"All of them?" his mother asked. "That's a lot of work even if you're the only one there."

"Well, we have help with the routine dusting and such. A yard crew." He swallowed back the temptation to explain exactly what that help consisted of. "I don't have much to do with them or them with me. Long as the job's done."

His father nodded. "So you're more like cook and bottle washer?"

"Mostly. I have a uniform. I tend to Mr. Shackleford's clothing. Make sure his suits get cleaned. He dresses himself." He addressed that last to his mother. "I handle the pantry and the cooking. I have a schedule of chores to do every day. It took me a while to get up to speed on the how and why of it, but I kinda like it."

His father smiled at him. "You seem a lot less frazzled than the last time we saw you."

Roger nodded. "It's been a while."

"But you want to know how to cook, now?" his mother asked.

"Yes, ma'am."

"There are whole schools for that, you know," his father said.

"I know, and I might look into one of them when Mr. Shackleford no longer needs me."

His father sat back in his chair and tilted his head to one side. "Good for you. It makes me happy that you're thinking of the future again." The tone of approval warmed him.

"On Cooking," his mother said. "That's the text you want."

"That's the title?" Roger asked. "On Cooking?"

"Yeah. That was the text I had in school," she said.

"You studied cooking in school?" he asked.

"Don't look at me like that," she said. "I studied a lot of things in school."

"I didn't mean anything by it," Roger said, grinning. "I just thought you studied mostly business and economics."

"That, too, but I had to have some non-core credits. You know how that works."

Roger didn't. He'd enlisted a year after high school, anxious to leave the nest and at a loss as to what to do. It wasn't the worst decision he'd ever made, but in hindsight, he'd probably have been better off doing almost anything besides learning how to kill people at long distance.

"Hey," his mother said, staring into his face. "None of that."

"What?" he asked.

"That staring off at nothing stuff. Focus. You need that book." She slapped the table beside her cup.

Roger pulled out his phone and opened the search function. He thumbed in the title and found a text with that title online. He turned the phone to his mother. "That one?"

She leaned in to look at his screen. "Yeah. That's the one. Different cover, it's a new edition. Publishers have to make their money somehow."

He flipped the phone around and ordered it, choosing the expedited delivery. "Done. I'll have it Tuesday."

"You could probably have found it locally," his father said.

"Yeah, but I don't have another day off to look until next week."

"That's a lot of hours. They paying you for them?" he asked, not suspicious, exactly.

"Room, board, five thousand a month, and a stipend for expenses." Roger felt uncomfortable mentioning the bonus at the end. He wasn't convinced he'd ever see that money.

"So, you live free and they pay you besides?" his mother asked.

"And the pay's a lot better than the army," Roger said.

"You like it," his father said.

"I do."

"You like it and can afford it? Nothing wrong with that," he said, settling the matter.

"Who's ready for dinner?" his mother asked. "That pot roast has to be done by now."

"Smells heavenly," Roger said. "Can I help set the table?"

His mother's eyebrows shot up. "Yeah. I suppose."

His father grinned. "Show off."

Roger shrugged and stood. "I don't get to set many tables. Mr. Shackleford takes his meals on a tray."

"Don't be making fun of him, Ed," his mother said. "I'm not one to turn down help in the kitchen. Or the dining room."

His father held up his hands, palms out. "Nothing of the kind," he said but he grinned and winked at Roger.

Roger picked up the now-empty mugs and took them to the sink, rinsing them and stacking them in the dishwasher before washing his hands and heading for the cupboards.

"When you're done with that, come over here and I'll show you how I make gravy," his mother said.

Roger grinned and started dealing out plates and water glasses, the pictures from his butler book playing like a slideshow in his mind. "It'll be just a moment." His parents didn't have the range of cutlery or china that Shackleford House used, but that didn't stop him from laying them out as neatly as if they were Wallace Silversmiths and Noritake.

Replete with his mother's cooking, he waved good-bye from the sidewalk as his Uber pulled to a stop. His parents waved back from the door and he slipped into the car. The ride back to Shackleford House went without incident. Roger took the time to review his book order. The cost would have made him balk before. Nearly $150 for a single book. It included the expedited shipping, but still, it would have been an unconscionable amount. He smiled and looked at the nighttime streets scrolling past his window. He keyed a generous tip and left a positive feedback in the app when the driver turned onto his block.

He directed the driver to the alley and driveway at the back. The guy gave him an odd look but followed the directions. Roger got out and walked up the tarmac toward the darkened house, the only light in the upper window that marked the library.

Roger let himself into the house and strolled through the kitchen to his quarters. Without giving it much thought, he changed into his uniform and hung up his civvies. The jacket and tie had become second nature to him; the jeans and polo were now something odd.

His trainers went into the base of the wardrobe and he tied on his oxfords. He felt the calm settle on him as he checked his tie and the drape of his jacket in the mirror. He removed his wristwatch, replacing it in the dresser drawer when he got out the pocket watch.

He checked the time and picked up the debit card from where he'd dropped it on the dresser. There was time to see if Mr. Shackleford needed anything.

He knocked twice before entering. Shackleford looked back over his shoulder from the computer chair.

"Ah, Mulligan. Excellent, but this is your day off."

"Thank you, sir. I visited my parents for dinner." He held up the card. "I also got this for you and delivered the message to Mrs. Pettigrew."

"You did, did you? What did she say?"

"I'm embarrassed to say that she advised me to look in the book she provided for me. That I would find the information there."

Shackleford nodded and took the card from Roger's hand. "Don't let that bother you," he said. "She's a remarkable woman." He looked up at Roger from under lowered brows. "I suspect you knew that already."

"I found her to be so, yes, sir."

"Thank you for this, Mulligan." He waved the card. "I've been doing some more research. This internet is a marvel."

"I'm happy you're finding it useful, sir. Is there anything I can get you, since I'm back?"

"No, thank you, Mulligan. I had a light dinner earlier and stashed the dishes in the washing machine. I'll have a nightcap shortly and call it a night."

"Pardon my saying so, sir, but you seem quite focused tonight."

Shackleford looked up at him, nodding. "Tomorrow you may find me swinging from the chandelier in the foyer wearing nothing but my boxers and a towel around my neck as a cape, Mulligan." He shrugged. "I'm always better during a new moon. Worse during the full. None of my research has come up with any rationale for either."

"If you're sure, sir."

"Quite sure, Mulligan. If something changes, I'll ring you."

"Thank you, sir."

Roger turned to go but Shackleford spoke again. "Your parents, you say?"

"Yes, sir. I have been neglecting them of late."

"Did they have a comment on your new position?"

"They seemed rather surprised by it, sir. My father's opinion was that if I liked it and could afford it, then it was good enough for him."

"And do you, Mulligan? Like it?"

"I do, sir. Much more than I expected I would."

Shackleford smiled. "Applies to much of life, I've found. Sometimes the things you like the most start out as things you'd never imagine actually doing." He nodded. "Thank you, Mulligan. Good night."

"Good night, sir."

Roger left the library and pulled the door closed behind himself. The latch clicked and he wondered for a moment if he should practice the silent door trick he'd read about in the butler book. He shook his head and went to the kitchen, helping himself to a cup of tea and a cookie before retiring to his quarters. Settling in at his desk, he picked up his Bible and scanned the table of contents for "medical." It was halfway down the second page. "Page 699," he said and flipped to page 699 on the first try.

He frowned. He'd never had to search for a page when using the Bible.

He closed the book, reopening to the table of contents. He ran his finger down the column of entries to "Banquets and Parties" on the list. "Page 271," he said and flipped the book open to page 271 without trying. He sat back in his chair, a little thrill running up his spine, his suspicion about the woman confirmed. Mrs. Pettigrew was a powerful wizard in her own right. For a moment or two, he wondered how many other wizards might exist in the city alone. He shook the thought out of his head. Did no good to speculate.

Back in the section on medical assistance, he noted that Mr. Shackleford's previous doctor had a notation beside his name saying "deceased." Several names and addresses were printed below as possible replacements. He wasn't sure what the order indicated—they were not alphabetical—but he made a note to call on Monday to find a new physician for the old man. He'd bet dollars to donuts that all of them were wizards. He closed the book with a snap, placing it on his desk.

He settled back in his chair and fired up the laptop. He had a new video about sauté work to watch before calling it a night himself and there was nothing else left for him to do for the day.

A woman joined Roger on his morning run, the next morning, a situation that surprised him. She came up from behind and started pacing alongside. "Hi," she said.

"Morning," Roger said, glancing over. Her chestnut hair pulled back in a pony tail, she wore a purple, sports bra top and matching shorts with a pair of Asics running shoes. Also purple. She looked to be about Roger's age, maybe a little younger.

"I see you out here every morning," she said, running easily on his left. "Clockwork."

"I try to run before work," he said.

"Me, too. Mind if I run with you?" she asked.

"Free country," he said.

"So I've heard," she said. "You're at Shackleford House, right?"

"Yes," Roger said, his security buttons beginning to light up.

"I have the condo next door. I'm Molly. Molly Flint." She held up a hand for an awkward handshake.

"Roger Mulligan."

She nodded. "Nice to meet you, Roger."

He focused on his breathing and kept his pace even, letting the morning and the zen of running carry him forward. Sure, she was pretty and in good shape, but she probably had a jealous husband waiting at home.

They ran his usual loop, down a block and across to the running path through the park. Roger always saw a lot of joggers, nodded to those he recognized. Some of them nodded back. Most said nothing because they had ear buds in or just looked too focused, barely acknowledging his existence. As they came around to the alley again, Roger slowed to a cool-down walk, Molly following suit.

She'd worked up a sweat, but neither of them had to pant. "Good run," she said. "Thanks."

He shrugged. "No problem."

She stopped at the back gate by the condo next to Shackleford House. "Seriously. Thanks. I hate running alone."

"Well, you're welcome to join me. I go out at the same time, almost every day."

She nodded. "Yes. Clockwork. I've noticed."

"I haven't seen you running."

She shook her head. "I've been using the treadmill for the last few weeks. I had a ..." She paused and shrugged. "A situation. With another runner."

"A guy?" Roger asked.

"Yeah." She shrugged again. "Treadmill just isn't the same."

Roger nodded. "I know the feeling." He left her standing at the gate. A few moments later he heard it open and close.

Monday morning, after breakfast service, Roger called the four doctors on the list. He got through to none of them directly, but left a name and number and short message with each service.

He all but forgot about it until right after lunch when the first one called back.

"Shackleford House," he said.

"Dr. Jane Littlefield's office calling for Roger Mulligan." A woman's voice.

"Speaking."

"One moment, sir."

Less than a moment later another woman's voice came on the line. "Mr. Mulligan, Dr. Littlefield. How is Mr. Shackleford?"

"That's what we'd like to know, Doctor," Roger said. "He's probably overdue for a checkup."

The pause lasted so long Roger started to think the connection had dropped before the woman spoke again. "I see," she said. "I need to put you on hold for one moment."

The line clicked and a rather uninspiring string quartet started playing, somewhere in the middle of the tune. Roger waited, imagining some kind of hurried conversation behind the scenes.

The line clicked again. "Mr. Mulligan, would you be able to bring Mr. Shackleford in for a new patient interview tomorrow?" The first woman's voice.

"Mr. Shackleford was hoping for a house call," Roger said.

"I'm sorry, Mr. Mulligan. That's quite impossible."

"What time tomorrow?" Roger asked.

"Dr. Littlefield has an opening at 2:30."

Roger made a note in his notebook. "I'll have to check with Mr. Shackleford and get back to you."

After a short pause, the woman asked, "Would it be possible to speak with Mr. Shackleford directly?"

Roger frowned, trying to remember if he'd seen a phone extension on the upper floor. "I need to see if he's available. Can you hold?"

"Yes."

"One moment." Roger laid the receiver down beside the phone and headed up the stairs. He knocked at the door and entered to find Shackleford in his usual chair.

"Yes, Mulligan?"

"Sir, I have a Dr. Littlefield's office on the phone and they'd like to speak to you in person."

Shackleford nodded. "Figured." He stood and placed the book on the side table. Roger followed him out of the library and next door to the upstairs parlor, where Shackleford picked up the telephone tucked into an out-of-the-way alcove that Roger hadn't noticed in his previous—and brief—forays into the room. "Shackleford." He listened for a few moments. "Yes, I understand." He nodded a couple of times. "Very well. Good-bye." He looked at Roger. "You'll want to make sure the Bentley will start. We're going for a drive tomorrow."

"I have calls in to three other doctors, sir."

Shackleford shook his head. "It'll be Littlefield. I know her already. Solid physician. Good doctor. Well connected when it comes to the politics and I trust her."

"The Bentley, sir?"

"Yes. Why? You have a driver's license, I presume?"

"I do, sir, but I confess to being intimidated by taking any of those vehicles out. They're classics, sir."

Shackleford gave a short laugh. "They're just vehicles, Mulligan. Nice cars. Old cars, but ultimately merely something to use. Tools. They'll be fine."

Roger gave him a short bow. "Very good, sir."

Shackleford nodded. "Good man."

"Anything else, sir?"

Shackleford shook his head. "Carry on, Mulligan."

Roger went back downstairs and hung up the receiver there before heading for the key safe to retrieve the Bentley's keys. It was one thing to know a quarter-million dollars' worth of vehicles sat parked in the garage, and quite another to consider taking one of the museum pieces out onto the rough streets of the city. Still, the old man had a point. A car is just a tool—even if an expensive one.

He went into the garage and opened the bay door in front of the Bentley. The car itself sat unlocked. Roger slid into the lush leather interior and slipped the key into the ignition. He kept trying to convince himself it was just a car, but he had a sense of surrealism about the situation—sitting in a classic wearing a butler's uniform and turning the key.

The engine caught on the first spin and rumbled to life. Roger checked the controls and let the engine warm up a little. He pressed his foot on the brake, pulled the emergency brake off, and pushed the gear-shift into drive. The heavy vehicle rolled out into the afternoon sunlight. He had often heard of cars being described as boats but had never driven a large vehicle before. The Bentley felt like an ocean liner compared to the midsize cars he'd driven.

He stopped the car, shifted it into park, and took a deep breath. "Just a car." He shook his hands in the air in an attempt to relax the tension in his wrists, then shut the vehicle off, taking the key. Looking around the cabin, he spotted a very modern-looking small plastic box clipped to the dash. He pressed the only button and in the rearview mirror saw the garage door lower. He got out of the car, locking the door behind him, and went back into the house.

He knocked on the library door before entering. "Mr. Shackleford?"

"Yes, Mulligan?"

"I'd like to take the Bentley for a quick spin around the block to familiarize myself with the vehicle. Will you need anything while I'm gone, sir?"

Shackleford shook his head. "Excellent idea. I'll be fine, Mulligan. Carry on."

Roger left him, closing the door and returning to the car. He walked all around it, looking it over for any dings or scratches in the paint. He saw no flaws in the perfect finish and wondered if the pixies cared for the vehicle or if there was some other kind of sprite that dealt with the vehicles.

He took his place behind the wheel and fired the engine. "Just a car," he said, putting it in gear. The vehicle rolled down the tarmac, the power steering making it feel a little floaty until Roger adjusted to its assistance. He turned into the alley, letting the engine's idle speed carry it to the first intersection. He stopped and looked both ways before pulling out onto the street, overcompensating a bit on the turn but going slowly enough that it didn't matter. He rolled up to the next stop sign and took another right onto the street that ran in front of Shackleford House. Midday traffic was not particularly heavy but he still had to deal with other vehicles—both parked and moving. He forced himself to relax his grip, letting the heavy engine roll the car along at a comfortably sedate city speed.

He drove several blocks along the street, practicing his stops at each of the intersections, before making another right onto a side street and picking up the alley once more to close the loop. By the time he got back to the tarmac behind the house, he felt much more at ease. He pressed the button and maneuvered the car to back into the garage while the door rose. The overactive power steering still made the car feel like it was floating, so occasionally he overcompensated, but he managed to get the thing backed into place without hitting the garage. He shut it off and took a deep breath.

"I can do this," he said.

He got out, closed the garage door, and returned the keys to the safe, and then checked in with Shackleford.

"I'm back, sir."

"How'd it go, Mulligan?"

"I'm glad I gave it a spin, sir. It handles a little differently than my recent vehicles."

Shackleford nodded. "Perkins hated that car. I think that's why he kept one of his own."

"It's a lovely vehicle, sir. A work of art."

Shackleford shrugged. "In its own way, I suppose. Tell me, Mulligan, what would you suggest?"

"As a vehicle, sir?"

"Yes. It does little good to have these museum pieces when I could have something a bit more practical and still travel in comfort." He looked up at the ceiling for a moment before looking back at Roger. "If you had your choice of car to drive me around in, what would it be?"

Roger pondered for a moment. "I'd pick something inconspicuous, sir. Something with a bit of weight to it but not a car people would notice in traffic. A midsize sedan. Even a modern luxury car would blend in more than those classic vehicles, sir."

"Do some research, Mulligan. Bring me three choices. Something you'd be more comfortable driving."

Roger gave his Jeeves bow. "Of course, sir. Would there be anything else, sir?"

Shackleford shook his head, his attention already falling back to his book. "Not at the moment, Perkins."

Roger left and headed back to his afternoon routine for a Monday—collecting the dry cleaning in preparation for Tuesday's pickup.

Roger had just finished his warm up stretches when Molly jogged up to the foot of the tarmac.

"Ready?" she asked.

He joined her in an easy lope and they headed down the alley. The previous day's weather had deteriorated to a dull overcast, threatening rain or at least a drizzle. Neither of them spoke. Roger's kept imagining all the ways the Bentley could come to an unfortunate end at his hands, leaving him to wonder what kind of vehicle he might recommend.

At the halfway mark, Molly broke the silence. "Heavy thoughts this morning?"

"Car trouble," Roger said.

"That sucks. Broken down?"

Roger laughed. "Embarrassment of riches, rather. I have to recommend a new car for my boss."

"What's he drive?" she asked.

"Nothing. It's for his chauffeur to drive him in."

"Terrible problem to have." She laughed.

"I'm probably making too much of it. A new car to him is petty cash."

"So, your basic Lincoln? Cadillac?" she asked.

"He's got a classic Cadillac limo. One of the old ones from the 60s. I'm thinking something a little less conspicuous."

"Have you noticed how many luxury cars are out there? You could blend in with a Beemer these days."

"I'll do some more research," he said.

"What do you do, anyway?" she asked. "Besides buy new cars for your boss?"

He glanced at her out of the corners of his eyes, suddenly a bit self-conscious about his position. "You'll laugh."

"You say that like it's a bad thing," she said, grinning at him.

"I'm a butler."

She gave him a quick glance, her eyes wide. "No shit?"

"Yeah. I work at Shackleford House."

"Why would I laugh at that?" she asked.

"How many butlers do you know?"

"Just you, now, but it's awesome. Do you have a cutaway and everything?"

He chuckled. "Yeah, but I just wear a suit, mostly. The fancy dress is for special occasions. Every house has its own rules. Mr. Shackleford is not the most demanding."

"So you take care of the house and manage the staff and polish the silver and 'Dinner is served' and all that?" The questions tumbled out of her and the grin stretched all the way across her face.

"Well, I'm the only staff. It's just Mr. Shackleford and me. I do polish the silver, but I also serve as cook and chauffeur and all that."

"So you have to pick a new car for you to drive? Instead of the Caddy? What's wrong with the Caddy?"

"It's a classic. Probably worth more than I am, even with my life insurance. I'd feel terrible if anything happened to it, running him to the bank or something."

She shrugged. "I can see that. A new car wouldn't be the same? How much you worth?"

He laughed. "I could get a new car repaired. Take it to the dealer and have done with it. The Caddy? Maybe. The Bentley? Not a chance."

"Oh, shut up. A Bentley?"

Roger came to the sudden realization that he'd said too much. "Yeah."

She shook her head. "I can see why you want something less ostentatious."

"What do you do?" he asked, trying to turn the conversation around.

"Photography," she said, giving him a sideways glance. "Portraits mostly."

"Not a starving artist, then?" he asked.

She snorted. "It's hardly a garret, but no. If I had to support myself with my camera, it'd be a hard row to hoe. Revenue from investments." She glanced at him. "You can laugh. It's okay."

"Why would I laugh?"

"Cliché? Rich girl playing at artist?"

"Are you rich?" He asked, glancing at her.

"I'm not Bentley rich, if that's what you're asking," she said, grinning back at him. "It's an expensive condo, but it's still a condo."

"None of my business," he said. "Sorry."

"Naw. 'S okay. I started it." They ran for a few more yards. "In real life I'm a CNA."

"Not photographer?" Roger asked.

"CNA is what I do for pocket money. Photographer is my dream."

Roger grinned. "I can understand that."

The threatening skies released a heavy mist that collected on their faces and turned their clothing soggy. Roger focused on his running.

"Do you like it?" she asked. "Being a butler?" She glanced at him. "You don't have to answer. I'm just trying not to think about being wet."

He chuckled. "I've only been doing it for a few months, but yeah. I like it. You like taking pictures?"

She sighed. "I like taking pictures but ..." She glanced at him. "Honestly, I just fool around with it. My parents keep sending me rich friends who want me to take family photos. Boring, line them up in their designer clothes against some mansion in the burbs, photos. Or hubby wants a 'bedroom shoot' of his wife. Or ... fill in the blank. Every lame-ass excuse you can think of."

"Why do it?" he asked.

"Well, it pays for my equipment. Keeps my parents happy that I'm doing something 'arty.'"

"You're a CNA. That's not good enough?"

She shrugged."

"What would you want to do if you could do anything?"

She wiped the water from her face with a swipe of her hand. "I don't know," she said. "Hell of a thing, huh? Thirty-five, still drifting?"

Roger snorted. "Join the club."

"You've got a job," she said. "What did you do before?"

"Unemployed for a few months. Hitting the bottom of my reserves when the butler thing happened." He sighed. "EMT before that. Army before that."

"You don't have to answer my nosy questions."

"It's fine," he said, shaking some of the water out of his eyes. "I'll need to find a new job in a few months. My contract is only for a year."

"Any plans?" she asked.

"Nope. I kinda like the butler gig, but how many butler jobs are there?"

She shrugged. "Maybe more than you think. It's a rather specialized skill."

"I looked up butler schools," he said.

"No shit? There are butler schools?"

"Yeah. Mostly they look for people with hospitality management degrees."

"Oh, that makes sense," she said. "Would you be interested in that? EMT doesn't quite match."

"I'm better at biology than table settings, but I'm finding it relaxing in an odd way." He shrugged. "Might not find it quite so attractive in a full house."

"Can't you renew your contract?"

"It was only for a year." He paused, pondering how much he should say.

"What's going to happen to Mr. Shackleford?"

"What makes you think something's going to happen?"

"Logic. You have a short-term contract to take care of a single person. He's probably old, clearly rich, and you're being cagey." She shrugged.

"Maybe nothing," Roger said. "Maybe I'll continue on with him but my contract is up next June."

She snorted. "We're a pair." She glanced at him. "Come on. Sprint for the gate. Stretch it out, butler boy." She took off running full out, the soles of her running shoes flinging water into the air.

He swallowed a laugh and tried to catch her but couldn't make up the distance until she stopped at her gate, hands on hips and walking in circles to cool down.

"Good run," she said, panting a little, a smile on her lips and water matting her hair against her head.

"Good run. See ya tomorrow."

She turned to her gate as he walked by. "Street photographer," she said.

"What's stopping you?" he asked.

She shook her head and slipped through the gate, pulling it closed behind her, the latch snapping shut.

He shrugged and headed for the back door and his shower. He still had to make breakfast and come up with three new car suggestions for Shackleford. Perhaps while he cooked breakfast he'd do a little online car shopping.

CHAPTER 10

By the time Roger got Shackleford's breakfast tray assembled, including going above and beyond by drying out the soggy paper with a clothes iron on Low, he had three solid choices for a new car. He knocked on the library door before entering. "Breakfast, sir."

Shackleford looked up from his book—the wrong book again. Well, the other book. "Thank you, Perkins. Just leave it on the table." He picked the book up again and started reading, or at least staring at the page.

"Is there anything else, sir?" He scanned the room, looking for anything out of place. The rolltop hid the computer. Shackleford's primary reading material—the thick book with thin pages and tiny print—was nowhere to be seen.

Shackleford didn't take his eyes off the page. "Mm? No. Nothing. Carry on, Perkins."

Roger sighed and left the breakfast in its usual spot. He scanned again, spying the old man's book tucked under one of the throw pillows in an easy chair. He left it there and went on with his morning routine—making Shackleford's bed, picking up and hanging clothes that needed hanging, gathering any loose laundry and linens from the bath. He'd done it a hundred times before and found nothing out of place, yet the room seemed somehow wrong.

"Imagination," he said, tucking the laundry under his arm in a tidy bundle. He'd dropped a stray sock on the stairs one morning and was embarrassed to find it when he returned for the breakfast tray later. He would have been mortified if Naomi Patching—or, worse, Fidelia Necket—had called and found it. He laughed at himself as he sorted the load into the washing machine, bemused by his own change in outlook since coming to Shackleford House. He piled the leftover laundry into a waiting basket, measured the detergent, and started the machine.

He went to the kitchen for a second cup of coffee while he waited for the appropriate hour to pick up the breakfast tray. His laptop still rested on the work table, so he opened it up and looked up the address for the doctor's appointment. He wrote the street address in his notebook, and realized that he'd nearly filled it with various notes and tasks. He'd need a new one soon. That done, he pulled up the map and got directions to the office. The app found the street and address for him. "Modern technology," he said. He zoomed in on the location and realized it was in a medical park on the west side of the city. The map provided names and specialties of other physicians in the area: a rheumatologist, an ophthalmologist, several dentists, and a collection of medical office buildings with names like "West Side Medical Group" and "West View Center for Internal Medicine." He'd half expected to find Dr. Littlefield operating out of one of the classier brick townhouses along the "Ritzy Row" on the north end.

A mystery for another time. Roger noted the hour and closed his laptop. He tucked it under his arm and took it back to his quarters to recharge while he continued with the morning.

He found Shackleford still engrossed in his book, the breakfast tray untouched. "Sir? Was there something wrong with your breakfast?"

The old man looked up. "What? Oh, no, Perkins. Lovely, thank you for the bacon." He stuck his nose back in the book.

Roger looked down at the bacon still on the plate. "You haven't eaten a thing, sir. Aren't you hungry?"

Shackleford shook his head without looking up. "Not right now, Perkins, thank you. Carry on."

"Sir, I should remind you that you have a doctor's appointment this afternoon at 2:30. We'll need to leave by 1:45 to arrive on time."

"Yes. Thank you, Perkins. Fetch me when it's time to go, would you?"

"Sir—"

Shackleford's head jerked up and he glared at Roger. "What is it now, Perkins? I'm really rather busy." He bit the words off, one at a time.

"Would you care for some breakfast, sir?" Roger asked.

"I've had my breakfast, Perkins. Thank you. It was delicious." He paused and tilted his head just the tiniest of fractions to the side. "Now, if you don't mind, I really need to finish my research."

Roger gave his little bow. "Of course, sir." Roger picked up the tray and left. In the kitchen he scraped the plate into the trash and took care of the dirty dishes by stacking them in the dishwasher.

He closed the dishwasher a little too hard and scowled. He didn't know what to do about any of it—the room, his flare-up, and an imminent doctor appointment.

The laundry dingled and he pressed everything to the back of his mind. "At least I can handle that," he said.

The door to the library stood ajar when Roger returned with a luncheon tray. According to his schedule, he was a bit early, but he was sure that after not eating all morning, Shackleford had to be feeling hungry. Roger pushed into the room but the old man wasn't there. "Oh, shit."

He placed the tray in its customary position and fled toward the master suite. He knocked twice and entered, his gaze raking the room and freezing at the closed bathroom door. He felt his heart pound in his chest and held his breath, the indecision driving the air from his lungs. Should he? What if the old guy had fallen?

The toilet flushed and Roger breathed a sigh of relief, stepping back out of the suite and pulling the door closed behind him. That would have been embarrassing for all concerned.

He stepped back into the library and looked for the books. The wrong book, as he'd come to think of it, lay in Shackleford's normal chair while the other still peeked out from under the cushion in the armchair. He picked both up, placing them side by side on the library table. As he started to look inside, Shackleford returned.

"Ah, Mulligan. Lunch, excellent. I seem to be more peckish than usual today."

"My pleasure, sir. You didn't eat much breakfast today."

Shackleford stopped halfway down into the chair before lowering himself slowly to the seat. "Did I eat any?" he asked, looking at Roger.

"No, sir."

He sighed. "Was I myself?"

"Not precisely, sir. No."

Shackleford glanced at the two books, frowning. "That's ... strange." He looked at Roger. "Where'd you find these?"

"The brown covered volume was in your chair, sir. The green one under a cushion over there." Roger nodded at the armchair.

Shackleford pulled his napkin from the tray, shook it open, and laid it on his lap before taking up his spoon and tucking into the soup. He nodded. "The green has been the most useful in illuminating my current predicament." With his free hand, he stroked the cover of the brown one. "This one." He shook his head. "You say I've been reading it?"

"Yes, sir. Generally when you're least yourself, sir."

Shackleford looked up at Roger. "Really?"

"Yes, sir."

"Interesting. We have a doctor's appointment this afternoon, don't we?"

"Yes, sir. We'll need to leave in about two hours."

"Did you find a replacement for the Bentley?"

"I have three suggestions, sir. All current models. All luxury sedans that will blend in with modern traffic, sir."

"Blending in is important?" Shackleford asked.

"Unless you're trying to be noticed, yes, sir."

"All that you'd be comfortable driving, Mulligan?"

"Yes, sir. At least if something happened to any one of them, repairs would not require a specialist or parts that are no longer available."

Shackleford scraped the last of the soup out of his bowl and nodded. "I suppose we'll need to test drive them?"

"Do you have a budget in mind, sir?"

Shackleford shook his head. "Petty cash. Anything under a quarter million. We can move the other cars into secure storage with the rest. They'll make a good addition to the estate." He paused. "You should find something you're willing to drive yourself. I'll buy it and tie it to the position. You shouldn't have to pay for running my errands from your pocket."

"That's not necessary, sir."

Shackleford shook his head. "It is, Mulligan. I'm going to need you to run more errands as Naomi ramps up her attempts to get me committed. I don't want you relying on some ride-for-hire service or taxi." He turned a dark eye on Roger. "You don't know the influence she has."

"Her or her father?" Roger asked, leaping to the obvious conclusion.

"Does it matter?" Shackleford asked, looking up with a frown.

"No, sir. I suppose not."

"Now, we have an appointment this afternoon. What do you know about the physician?"

"She came from Pettigrew's book, sir." Roger paused. "We spoke to her before."

Shackleford sighed and shook his head. "Sorry. That one's my brain," he said. "Littlefield, right?"

"Yes, sir."

"Of course. Good doctor. Thank you, Mulligan. Remind me to get ready. I'll need half an hour."

"Of course, sir."

"Carry on, Mulligan."

Roger left the library, his head spinning. How did rich people buy cars? It probably wasn't by visiting the lots around town. Send the chauffeur? He sighed and headed for his quarters. He'd check with the Bible before he did anything rash.

He looked up the Secured Storage Facility first. It seemed that Shackleford owned a couple of warehouses in the old port district, well away from the gentrified sections closer to town. He pulled up a map on his laptop and noted the locations. Some street-level photos showed old-style brick warehouses surrounded by fencing. One of the photos showed a loading ramp and another a rolling garage door. Secured Storage, check.

He flipped to the table of contents again and looked up Purchasing. He'd seen that section before but hadn't checked all the way down the list of things that might be purchased. Vehicles showed up near the bottom. He flipped to the page and discovered one Nehemiah Midgeley, purchasing agent, with a contact number. He took the Bible to the phone alcove and dialed the number.

"Midgeley Autos. Randolf speaking. What can I sell you today?"

"Good afternoon. May I speak to Nehemiah Midgeley?" Roger asked.

"Nehemiah?" Randolf asked. "Who did you say was calling?" The voice got quiet and almost suspicious.

"I'm Roger Mulligan. I work for Mr. Joseph Shackleford."

"One minute. I'll get him."

The line went to music, a cheap midi jingle that repeated itself every fifteen seconds. Three cycles passed before the line picked up again.

"Midgeley. Can I help you?"

"Mr. Midgeley, I'm Roger Mulligan, Joseph Shackleford's new butler."

"Can you confirm that?" Midgeley asked.

"You have the number for Shackleford House, I presume?" Roger asked.

"I do."

"If you could call me back, would that convince you?"

Midgeley grunted. "Fair enough."

The line went dead and Roger hung up. Seconds later the phone rang and Roger picked up. "Shackleford House."

"Okay. I guess it's you. How can I help you—Mulligan, was it?"

"Yes, sir. Roger Mulligan. Mr. Shackleford is in need of two new cars. A modern-day replacement for one in his classic collection and a late-model compact for me to run errands in."

"What? You don't want to use the MG?" Midgeley's voice carried the hint of a smile, even over the phone line.

"To be honest, Mr. Midgeley, I'd love to use it, but I'm afraid something would happen to it while I did. I couldn't bear the thought."

Midgeley chuckled. "Yeah. I understand. They're just cars, but it's hard not to think of them as works of art."

"I've done some research into vehicles," Roger said. "You are a purchasing agent for Shackleford House and I trust your judgment. Do you have any suggestions?"

"You don't know me. How can you trust me?"

"Because it's Shackleford House, Mr. Midgeley."

The line was quiet for a bit longer than Roger expected. "Parameters?" Midgeley asked.

"Late model, not necessarily new, luxury sedan. A limousine that doesn't look like a limousine, if you know what I mean."

"Something you can ferry Mr. Shackleford around in without feeling like you're painting a target on your back?" Midgeley asked.

"Precisely, sir."

"Fer instance?"

"Mercedes, Audi, maybe a Lincoln?" Roger said. "I'm less concerned with damaging a late-model vehicle, even an expensive one, when I can get it repaired with off-the-shelf parts."

"Logical. You married to any of those brands?"

"No, sir. Just preliminary research."

"Timeline?" Midgeley asked.

"Within the next month, I should think."

Midgeley laughed. "I was thinking within the next week."

"That would be acceptable, sir. I wasn't sure how soon you could find suitable vehicles."

"I could have them this afternoon, but I'll look around just to see if there's anything I've missed. Budget?"

"It's Shackleford House, sir."

Midgeley snorted. "Fair enough. What about the compact?"

"I need something to run errands with. Nothing fancy."

"Van? Crossover?"

"Anything we'd need a van or truck for, we'd hire out. I was thinking more like Fusion or Jetta. Something I can park," Roger said.

Midgeley snorted again. "Yeah. Dime a dozen there." Midgeley paused. "Tell ya what. I'll swing by tomorrow in the afternoon with the first runabout. See what you think. I've got an idea for the other but I need to see if it's still available. I could bring that by next Monday."

"Thank you, Mr. Midgeley. That would be excellent."

"See you tomorrow," Midgeley said and rang off.

The storage facility listing had no information beyond the fact that it existed and the address. He made a note to ask Shackleford about the procedure for getting the vehicles moved and checked the time.

"Get a move on," he said and went to get the Bentley's keys.

For all his concerns, the ride from Shackleford House to Littlefield and Gosling, MDs, turned into a nonevent. Roger soon adjusted to the floaty power steering and the overly long front end. At least he didn't hit anything even if the ride felt like a crawl through the streets rather than the stately cruise he'd imagined. Nobody honked at them for their pokey progress; in fact, only a few people seemed to notice the vehicle at all, let alone stop and stare.

Shackleford, for his part, rode in silence, gazing out at the passing scenery.

The medical park looked like any of the modern campus facilities that sprang up in the periphery of the city. Two largish, three-story buildings of glass and brick marked the hub of the park while smaller, single-story duplex and singleton bungalows circled the outer edges among tree-shaded parking lots. Roger found the office without difficulty thanks to the GPS on his phone and parked the car in a "Patients Only" spot near the front.

He secured the vehicle and went back to open the door for Shackleford.

"Thank you, Mulligan. Accompany me, please?"

"Of course, sir." He fell into step, half a pace ahead of Shackleford and opened the doors as they passed.

The airlock outer entrance opened to a comfortable-looking lobby in whites and pastels with a reception desk facing the door. The place smelled like new carpet and fresh paint. A receptionist smiled up from his terminal. "Good afternoon, gentlemen. How may I assist you?"

Roger stepped back to give Shackleford some privacy.

"Shackleford. I have an appointment with Dr. Littlefield."

The receptionist tapped a few keys and nodded. "Of course, Mr. Shackleford. If you'd take a seat? We'll be with you momentarily." He held a hand palm up to indicate a waiting room to one side.

Shackleford nodded and Roger led the way, finding only a single patient waiting—a middle-aged woman, maybe 40-something, dressed in a stylish navy business suit—thumbing through a glossy magazine. She looked up at Shackleford and nodded.

153

Shackleford smiled and nodded back before lowering himself into the stiff chair.

"Magazine, sir?" Roger asked, indicating the pile of reading material to the side.

Shackleford shook his head.

An inner door opened and a young woman in scrubs stepped into the waiting room, nodding to the woman. "The doctor will see you now."

The woman rose and sailed through the open door. The nurse smiled and nodded at Shackleford. "Be right back," she said, and followed her.

"Is there anything you'd like me to do, sir?"

"Hold the fort, Mulligan. This shouldn't take long."

Roger had his doubts but kept them to himself.

As good as her word, the nurse returned within a couple of minutes. "Your turn, Mr. Shackleford," she said.

The old man rose and went through the door.

Roger pulled out his phone and picked up the book he'd been reading about French cooking. The chapters on egg dishes seemed a little weird. Like adding cream to stop scrambled eggs from cooking? Heat-transfer issue, maybe. On the other hand, he got some interesting insights into souffles.

After a relatively short time, the nurse returned and looked at Roger. "Mr. Mulligan? If you could come back, please?"

A cold flash of foreboding zipped down his back but he stood and put his phone away, following her back to a conference room. A gray-haired woman in a white smock smiled as he entered and waved at the chair beside Shackleford before extending her hand across the table. "Mr. Mulligan. I'm Dr. Littlefield."

"Nice to meet you, Doctor." He glanced at Shackleford.

"I've asked her to fill you in, Mulligan. Your memory is better than mine." He gave a slight shrug.

"Of course, sir." He took out his notebook and flipped to the next blank page. "How can I help, Doctor?"

"Mr. Shackleford has some heart issues that we'll need to look into further. It's been some time since his last checkup." She gave Shackleford a mildly reproving glance. "We've taken some blood work and will get the results back probably tomorrow. In the meantime, we need to keep an eye on his physical conditioning."

Roger made notes on the key points and looked up at that last. "More exercise?"

"Specifically balance. He tells me he sits a lot."

Roger nodded. "I see. Do you have some recommendations?"

"I do. Can I email them to you?"

"Of course." Roger gave her his email address.

"And can you work with him to start getting these going?"

Roger looked at Shackleford. "I can, if you're willing, sir."

He nodded. "I thought I'd prefer that to bringing in a physical therapist or personal trainer, Mulligan. I know it's not in your contract, but I'd prefer the devil I know." He grinned.

"Of course, sir."

"I understand you have some medical training, Mr. Mulligan," the doctor said.

"Army medic. Civilian EMT certified," he said.

She nodded. "The exercises are simple and low impact. Just watch for signs of over-exertion, shortness of breath, that kind of thing."

He nodded. "I know the signs."

"Do you have a defibrillator in the house?" she asked.

Roger raised his eyebrows at that. "Not that I know of."

Shackleford shook his head. "Basic first aid only, I believe."

"Do I need one?" Roger asked.

The doctor shrugged. "You're certified on them, aren't you?"

"Yes. Emergency use only."

She shrugged again. "If you need it, it'll be an emergency. You can get an automated home unit for a reasonable amount these days."

Roger made a note. The idea that the old man might actually need one had him taking it more seriously than he might otherwise have.

"Depending on the blood work, I may be sending some prescriptions to your preferred pharmacy. His blood pressure is a bit high, but I'm taking a wait-and-see stance on that. Do you have a cuff?"

"I know where to get one," Roger said.

"If you could monitor his blood pressure. Before and after his exercise sessions, just to make sure we're not putting too much stress on him?"

"Should I get him a wearable monitor?"

"Couldn't hurt," she said.

Shackleford harrumphed. "I'm old. I expected to be resting in my dotage."

Dr. Littlefield grinned at him. "We'd like you to continue that dotage for at least another decade. This could help and won't hurt."

Shackleford smiled back at her. "That's a bit of an intimidating thought."

She shrugged. "I'd suggest some kind of meditation. Even a few minutes a day of mindfulness exercise for your mental capacity.

Perhaps taking up yoga or tai chi for balance when you get a bit stronger."

"At my age? It seems too late for that."

She shook her head. "I've got centenarians who will probably see their 110th birthday."

Roger's eyes widened.

"Don't look so surprised," she said. "It's more common than you think." She looked back at Shackleford. "Many of them didn't start until late in life. As long as you're not stressing your body, giving it something to do will keep it healthier."

Shackleford grimaced and shrugged.

"Anything else, Doctor?" Roger asked.

"Yes. Diet."

"He's overweight?"

"Under a bit. I need to see his blood work to get a better feel for it, but he needs a bit more protein, perhaps a little less fat. I'd prefer he not load up with unnecessary carbs, but you're also the cook?"

Roger nodded. "Yes, Doctor."

"Generic advice, but go with whole grains, get a mix of colors in the veg, lean cuts—although he doesn't need to lose the weight, cholesterol is almost always a concern. Some fatty fish every week."

Roger nodded again. "So basic doctor advice."

She grinned. "Pretty much." She looked at Shackleford. "You're a pretty remarkable man, Mr. Shackleford. I'd like to keep you as a patient for as long as I can."

"Thank you, Doctor," Shackleford said. "I need to keep going for at least a little longer." He paused. "I suspect you'll be pulled into this competency foolishness."

"Doctor-patient privilege," she said. "I can only be compelled to reveal what you allow me to."

"That's the thing," Shackleford said. "I want you to defend me."

"I can attest to your physical health, but if you want my advice, find a psychiatrist or a geriatric physician specializing in dementia."

"Do you have any recommendations?" Shackleford asked.

She pursed her lips. "Possibly." She gave a quick glance in Roger's direction before raising an eyebrow at the old man.

"He knows," Shackleford said.

The doctor seemed to relax a bit, her shoulders losing some of the tension. "Let me get the blood work back and see where we are. I'll make some inquiries."

"Fair enough," Shackleford said.

The doctor rose as the nurse re-entered the room. "Winnie will show you out. I'll send that information to your email, Mr. Mulligan. I'm holding you responsible for him." She smiled at him.

"I'll do my best, Doctor," Roger said.

"Winnie, show them out and give Mr. Shackleford a callback for six months. We may need to see him sooner, but I'd like to check on his progress then."

The nurse nodded. "Of course, Doctor." She stood aside from the doorway and ushered them into the hall. "Right this way, gentlemen."

It took only a few minutes for them to get back to the Bentley. Roger pulled the car out into traffic and headed back for Shackleford House before Shackleford spoke. "Thank you, Mulligan."

"You're welcome, sir. Dr. Littlefield seems quite competent."

"More than, Mulligan. Very much more than." Shackleford cleared his throat and looked out the window. "Any luck on the vehicles?"

"Midgeley will have something for us by the end of the week. I meant to ask what the procedure is for getting the current vehicles into your warehouse, sir."

"We can drive them over," Shackleford said. "One at a time. I'll have to go with you to unlock the doors."

"Even the MG, sir?"

Shackleford laughed. "That used to be my car. Technically still is, but I'm not allowed to drive anymore."

"I'm sorry, sir."

"Eh, don't be. I lost too many points for traffic violations and the state took the license away when I was 50."

Roger glanced at him in the rearview mirror only to see him nodding at him with a grin on his face.

"I was young and foolish," Shackleford said.

Roger thought about that for a while, finding the Bentley felt less like the Queen Mary as he got used to the size and steering.

"We could take the Bentley now, if you like," Shackleford said.

"Sir?"

"To the warehouse. We've got the car out already. You know where it is?"

"Roughly, sir."

"Let's take care of this one at least."

"Of course, sir."

Roger adjusted his course a bit and took the northern arterial to the right part of town. He wasn't sure how they'd get back to the house, but Shackleford didn't seem bothered by it.

"What did you think of Dr. Littlefield?" Shackleford asked.

"She seemed very competent, sir." He glanced at Shackleford in the mirror again. As usual, the old man stared out at the passing scenery.

"More than, Mulligan. Quite astonishing, really."

Roger let the sigh die in his chest and checked the side mirrors.

"You're going to make me exercise, Mulligan?" Shackleford asked.

"No, sir. I'm going to help you exercise, sir."

"You know it's probably for naught, right?"

"How so, sir?"

"Naomi will win and I'll be tucked away in Aspen."

"Vail, sir, but I'm not betting against you."

"Not yet, eh?" Shackleford asked.

"Not ever, sir."

Shackleford laughed.

Roger found the cross-street, turned into the short driveway and stopped at the front gate in the chain-link fence. A ramp beyond it led to a roll-up garage door. "We're here, sir."

Shackleford leaned forward to peer out the windshield. The gate swung to one side and the garage door started rolling up. "You can go in. There should be a place to park on the left."

"Yes, sir." Roger eased the car through the gate and started up the ramp. As he drove into the dimness of the structure, he saw the gate swing shut behind them in his rearview mirror. The ceiling felt low. A series of lights flickered to life as the Bentley made its way down a row of cars. He didn't get a good look at any of them, but he thought one might have been a Model-A and he definitely spotted what looked like several vehicles from the 20s and 30s with their bug-eyed headlights and flaring fenders. The last car in line looked like something from the 40s. Roger eased up, angling the front of the Bentley toward the opposite wall to get the right position to back in beside it. He guided the car back into the stall and shut it down. The sudden quiet sounded odd.

"Humber Limousine," Shackleford said.

"Sir?" Roger turned to look at him.

Shackleford nodded at the car next to them. "Humber. My grandfather's, I think. They used them in the war over there."

Roger flashed on Humvee for a moment but blinked the image away. "You've got quite a collection here, sir."

Shackleford nodded. "Indeed. Take the keys."

Roger pulled the keys from the ignition and set the emergency brake. He had no idea how long the car might sit there and hoped it would release when the time came. He got out and walked around to open the door for Shackleford.

The old man got out and struck off across the aisle, back toward the front of the building. Roger followed along. "There's a key safe here by the door. You can hang the keys there." He glanced over. "The tag's still on them, right?"

"Yes, sir."

As they approached the open door, it began to roll closed with a dull rumble, blocking off the outside brilliance and giving Roger a better look at the vehicles lined up along the row. He swallowed hard as he realized just how much automotive history stood waiting in this place.

"I'll get the supervisor to mothball them when we get them all over here. He'll make sure they're all in good shape." Shackleford glanced at Roger. "You thought I might just leave it parked there?"

Roger shrugged. "It crossed my mind, sir."

Shackleford smiled. "I try not to use magic when I can use mechanics."

Roger glanced at him but the old man stared straight ahead, a tiny smile playing on his face.

A huge metal key safe hung on the wall beside the garage door rails, a hooded light over it shining down on the metal cover. Shackleford reached up and flipped the door open, revealing a booklike structure of metal pages with extrusions in rows as hooks. He flipped two pages and pointed to the next hook on the row. The top of the page held the word "CARS" stenciled across the top. "Not all of them took keys," Shackleford said.

Roger hung the key on the indicated hook and Shackleford swung the safe closed. "One down."

Roger glanced around as the old man took off again, heading along the wall toward a person-sized metal door at the corner of the building. As he opened the door the light inside came on and the overheads went out in the garage. A set of concrete stairs led down to the basement and another metal door. The knob turned at Shackleford's touch, and he led the way into another cellar. Roger closed the door behind himself and stepped into the cellar at Shackleford House. He froze for a moment, then looked at Shackleford's grinning face.

"Shocker, eh?" the old man said.

They'd come out of one of the arches into the cellar's entry. Roger recognized the flooring and looked toward the arch that held the wine cellar. "I wondered how we were going to get back, sir."

Shackleford laughed. "Stout man, Mulligan. Stout man." He headed for the stairs up to the garage.

"I didn't bring the key, sir."

Shackleford kept climbing the stairs. "It's my house, Mulligan. You think there's a door that won't open for me?" He reached the top and turned the knob, swinging the door open and stepping out onto the concrete. He turned and smiled.

Roger followed him into the garage. It felt empty without the Bentley. His footsteps echoed oddly.

"This where the internet comes in?" Shackleford asked, walking over to the blinking boxes on the wall.

"Yes, sir. I had the technician run the cable in under the last door down there."

Shackleford's gaze traveled up and along the ceiling. "Nicely done, Mulligan."

"Thank you, sir."

A car door slammed outside the garage.

"Are we expecting anyone, Mulligan?"

"Not that I know of, sir."

Shackleford frowned and crossed to stand by the door. "I'll open it. You go out."

Roger nodded.

The door clicked free of its latch and Roger pulled it open, stepping out into the afternoon sun. Naomi's BMW stood on the tarmac and she stood at the back door, key ring in her hand. "Good afternoon, Ms. Patching. Can I help you?"

She whirled to face him. "Mulligan. What are you doing out there? Are you the chauffeur now?"

"And the cook, ma'am. Can I help you?" he asked again.

"I've come to see my uncle."

"I'll see if he's receiving, ma'am." Roger pulled the garage door closed behind him and walked toward the house, hoping that Shackleford could open the door for him. He needn't have worried. As soon as he touched the latch, the door popped open under his hand. He swung it wide for Naomi and ushered her in. He walked her through to the front parlor. "Just one moment, if you'd care to wait?"

"I would not care to wait, Mulligan. I want to see my uncle and I want to see him now."

"I'm sorry, ma'am. I need to check with Mr. Shackleford." His pager buzzed at his belt. He checked the message. It read "Bring her up."

"Mr. Shackleford will see you now," he said.

"I should think so." Naomi stormed out of the parlor and up the stairs, walking fast and ahead of Roger, as if she was racing him to the library. She got to the door first and swung it open, entering the room without being announced and leaving Roger to follow after. "Uncle."

"Mildred?" Shackleford asked. "Mildred? What a surprise. I thought you were still on the continent. How was Paris?"

"Uncle Perry? It's me, Naomi." She crossed to his wheelchair and crouched beside it, hand on the arm. "Uncle?"

Shackleford blinked and shook his head. "Naomi? You can't be Naomi. She's just a girl."

Naomi stood, a triumphant smile on her face. "I'm so sorry, Uncle."

"Perkins," Shackleford said.

"Here, sir." Roger took a step forward.

"Tea, Perkins."

"Of course, sir."

"That won't be necessary, Mulligan," Naomi said. "I won't be staying."

"Of course, you'll stay, Mildred," Shackleford said. "It's been so long since I've seen you. You haven't told me how you found Paris. Please, sit. Keep an old man company."

Naomi shook her head and left the library, her sharp heels tapping on the wooden floors.

"I'll be right back, sir," Roger said, following her out. He caught up to her at the back door, holding it for her as she left.

"He needs to get a physical, Mulligan."

"He's had one. Dr. Littlefield will send you a copy of her report."

She stopped, midstride. "He what?"

"He's had a physical exam. I have some exercise and diet recommendations from his doctor, ma'am."

"What did she say?"

"I'm not privy to the results beyond some small details, ma'am. I suggest you wait for the doctor's report."

"What did she say about his dementia?"

"She recommended he see a specialist in geriatrics. She is making some inquiries among her colleagues, ma'am."

Naomi's predatory smile raised unpleasant associations in Roger's mind. "Thank you, Mulligan."

"Your key won't work, ma'am," Roger said. "I had the locks changed."

"I know that, Mulligan."

"Very well, ma'am. Good afternoon, Ms. Patching."

She turned on her heel and strode to her car, giving him one last grin before sliding in and rolling away.

He closed the door and threw the deadbolt before going back to the library. "She's gone, sir."

"Nicely done, Mulligan."

"Thank you, sir. Is there anything I can get you, sir?"

Shackleford stood and crossed to the rolltop, sliding it up and turning the key on his computer. "A cup of coffee and perhaps a cookie if there are any in the pantry?"

"I'll see, sir."

"Thank you, Mulligan." The old man looked back at Roger over his shoulder. "Seriously. Thank you."

Roger gave his butler bow. "It's my pleasure, sir." As he left the library he realized that it was true.

Midgeley—good as his word—rang the back doorbell just after lunch the next day. When Roger opened the door, a bulky guy, made larger by a tweed coat and heavy woolen pants, stuck out a blocky hand. "Mulligan?" Certainly overdressed for an autumn afternoon, but he seemed unaffected by the warm sun. A dark blue Prius waited on the tarmac.

Roger shook the hand and nodded. "Mr. Midgeley, I presume."

The man beamed and nodded. "In the flesh." He turned and waved a hand at the car. "What d'ya think?"

"A Prius, sir?"

Midgeley nodded. "You're looking for something inconspicuous? Small enough to run errands in? Cheap enough that you're not gonna feel bad if it gets hit or scratched?" He shrugged. "There ya go. Hatchback for groceries. Hybrid. Probably run all year on a tank of gas."

Roger nodded and walked out to look the vehicle over. "New?" he asked.

Midgeley shook his head. "This year's model, but used. Got it from a college student. Was a gift from his parents but he didn't like the looks he got when he drove it on campus."

Roger looked at Midgeley. "Really?"

"Ya have ta admit," Midgeley said. "It's not exactly a panty-dropper." He shrugged. "He traded it for an older Mustang. Key's in it if you want to take it for a spin."

Roger shook his head. "Not necessary, Mr. Midgeley."

"You sure?" Midgeley looked almost offended.

"It's perfect, sir. Small, economical, and—as you pointed out—cheap." He eyed the vehicle. "Well, cheaper than anything in the garage at the moment. I trust your judgment on the fitness of the vehicle."

Midgeley nodded. "All right then." He opened the driver's door and pulled the key fob, tossing it to Roger. "It's yours. We'll settle the paperwork when I bring the sedan next week."

Roger caught the fob. "Thank you, Mr. Midgeley."

Midgeley grinned and gave him a jaunty two-finger salute. "Appreciate the business, Mr. Mulligan. Have fun with it." He struck off down the tarmac and jumped into a car waiting at the curb. It rolled away, leaving Roger standing there with the key fob. He looked at it for a moment, realizing that he didn't really know how to deal with keyless entry. He pressed the lock button and went back to the house to get the garage door key—and to see if he could find a video online.

How hard could it be?

The phone rang as he walked back through the house, interrupting his plans.

"Shackleford House."

"Mr. Mulligan? I'm Winnie, Dr. Littlefield's assistant."

"Yes, ma'am."

"Please hold for Dr. Littlefield."

"Of course."

The line clicked and Dr. Littlefield came on the line. "Mr. Mulligan. I have a referral for Mr. Shackleford. One of my colleagues specializes in dementia and he's an expert witness on the topic. I can give you his information."

Roger pulled out his pen and notebook. "I'm ready, Doctor."

She gave him the name—Dr. Edgar Cuttle—and a number. "His office should be calling you within the next couple of days to set up an appointment," she said.

"Thank you, Doctor. I'll wait for the call." He hung up the phone and took some small satisfaction from having thwarted Naomi Patching, if only for a little while.

CHAPTER 11

Before the end of the week, Roger drove the other two vehicles to the warehouse in the company of Shackleford. The old guy grinned like a boy all the way there in the MG, even when Roger fumbled the shift. He had to admit, the low-slung vehicle made him happy as well. Something about the old car, the rag top, and the closeness of the road. Still he was glad to have it parked safely in the dimness and away from harm.

The Prius looked lonely in the last bay of the garage, a tiny bug lost in what had seemed a cozy home for vehicles when the other cars had been there.

Monday morning, Dr. Cuttle's office called to make arrangements for an evaluation of Mr. Shackleford's mental acuity later in the week. As soon as he hung up the phone, it dawned on him that the Prius was still the only car in the garage. He gave a small laugh at the thought of Shackleford riding with him in the tiny cabin of the hybrid.

Roger took Shackleford's lunch up at the stroke of noon and found him hunched over his keyboard, peering into the monitor. "Lunch, sir."

"Mulligan! Astonishing. I might have found her." He grinned at Roger over his shoulder.

"Her, sir?"

"Descendant, Mulligan. My DNA match turned up a number of potential relatives but this one looks particularly promising."

Roger placed the tray on the table. "Something in particular, sir?"

"According to her family tree, she's a direct line from a mutual great-great-grandparent back in England. Aldus Gideon. He used the old spelling of the surname, EL instead of LE, but he had two sons that came to the new world. My great-great-grandfather

165

Henry James came over in the late 1600s, but according to this his younger brother, Barnabus Franklin, followed at the turn of the century. This woman, Barbara Griffin, is a direct descendant on her mother's side."

"Sounds promising, sir. How would you like to proceed?"

Shackleford sat back in his chair and shook his head. "I need to think about that, Mulligan. I don't know anything about this woman other than her name. I don't know if she'd be any better than Naomi." He frowned and his lips twisted into a grimace. "Check in Perkins's rolodex for Featherstone. First name Amos. Call him and tell him I may have a job for him."

Roger took out his notebook and wrote the name down. "I'll do that directly, sir."

"Thank you, Mulligan."

"The specialist called, sir. Dr. Cuttle would like to meet you later this week."

"Ah, the head doctor?"

"Yes, sir. Geriatrics specialist, focused on dementia."

Shackleford laughed and moved to the table for his lunch. "Was a time I'd have resented needing a geriatric specialist." He peered up at Roger. "Seems rather comforting from this vantage point."

Roger nodded. "I can see why, sir. Can I get you anything else?"

"No, thank you, Mulligan. You'll let me know when Midgeley comes up with the new car? I'd like to see it before we buy it."

"Of course, sir."

Roger left him working on his soup and went to find the rolodex in his desk. He'd seen it there but had never had cause to look through it. Without knowing the people the names belonged to, it seemed a wasted effort. Featherstone's card held the phone number and the additional information that he was a licensed investigator. Roger jotted the number into his notebook and stopped at his laptop to order a replacement. After only a few months, his was already almost filled.

He placed the call immediately and got Featherstone himself on the second ring.

"Featherstone. Can I help you?" The man's voice sounded pleasant enough. Roger felt mildly disappointed it wasn't the noir detective growl.

"Mr. Featherstone. I'm Joseph Shackleford's butler, Roger Mulligan. Mr. Shackleford asked me to call. He may have work for you."

"Mulligan," he said. "He has another relative to track down?"

"Something like that, sir. Could you come speak to Mr. Shackleford? He can explain what he wants."

"Sure. My calendar's clear tomorrow morning. Say 10 a.m.?"

"I'll notify Mr. Shackleford, sir. Thank you."

Featherstone rang off and Roger hung up the phone. After weeks of steady routine, the pace around Shackleford House seemed to be picking up.

Midgeley rang the back bell at 2 p.m., just as Roger wondered if he'd show up. The black Mercedes in the yard drew him like a magnet as soon as he opened the door.

"Maybach," Midgeley said. "Ritzy. Pricey. May not have the same cachet as a Bentley, but it's a Mercedes."

Roger walked around the vehicle and nodded. "Mr. Shackleford would like to see it before he makes up his mind."

"Or before you make up his mind for him?" Midgeley asked, grinning.

Roger chuckled and nodded. "This one's on him, sir. I can't spend that kind of money on my own."

Midgeley nodded. "I hear you on that."

"I'll get him," Roger said. "One moment."

Midgeley nodded and took up station beside the back door. "I'll just stand here and look at it for a while."

Roger walked up to the library and knocked. "Sir, Mr. Midgeley has a vehicle for you to look at."

Shackleford stood to look out the window and down at the tarmac below. "A Mercedes? Interesting. Nice looking car. New?"

"Mr. Midgeley has the details, sir."

Shackleford grinned at Roger. "You like the looks of it."

"I do, sir, but it's a bit intimidating."

"Why?"

"I'm not used to that kind of luxury in my life, sir."

Shackleford shrugged. "Let's go take it for a spin, shall we?"

Roger led the way down the stairs and back to the waiting car.

Shackleford took a moment to shake Midgeley's hand. "Thank you for this, Nehemiah. I appreciate the service."

"My pleasure, Mr. S. I love satisfied customers." He looked at the vehicle. "Doesn't hurt my feelings to get to work with a vehicle like this either."

"Details?" Shackleford asked.

"Mercedes Maybach 650. Brand new. Just came off the train from an assembly plant down south. Wood and leather interior. Same market sector as Rolls. It's classy and distinctive but easily overlooked as just another luxury car. I think it's a solid investment, but it's all a matter of how the dice roll. It's got enough muscle to move when it needs to and enough metal to stand up under stress."

Shackleford nodded and walked around the vehicle. "Shall we take it for a ride?" He looked at Roger.

"Key's in it," Midgeley said.

"Let me lock up, sir."

Shackleford nodded.

Roger grabbed the back door and garage keys from the safe and made sure he had his driver's license. He locked the house and opened the rear door for Shackleford. The old man slid into the car easily enough. The door closed with a solid thunk. "Mr. Midgeley? Front seat or back?"

"I'll take the front," Midgeley said, helping himself to the door before Roger could react.

Roger went around to the driver side and lowered himself into the seat. He closed the door and found himself in a world of wood, leather, and silence. Midgeley walked him through the controls and sat back in his seat, clicking the seatbelt. Roger swallowed and started it up. The engine rumbled to life and settled into a low growl, barely audible in the cabin.

"It's a heavy beast," Midgeley said.

Roger nodded, put a hand on the wheel, a foot on the brake, and shifted it into drive.

After the old Bentley, the Mercedes felt like a dream. He rolled down the tarmac, taking the alley to the street and moved out into city traffic. The car moved with precision. The turn radius felt long, because it was, but Roger adapted to it quickly. The heavier vehicle took a little more stopping distance for a smooth stop but the brakes had enough grab that the one time he needed to stop short, he could. Yes. It still felt like a bit of a boat but it was a really nice boat. He returned to the house after a jaunt around the neighborhood.

"You don't want to take it out on the interstate?" Midgeley asked.

"My biggest concerns are driving in town traffic," Roger said, looking back at Shackleford. "Sir?"

Shackleford shook his head. "You're my driver, Mulligan. If you're happy with the vehicle, I'm certainly comfortable enough back here."

"Thank you, sir," Roger said. "Is it too much car?"

Shackleford laughed. "I've a reputation to uphold, Mulligan. This will do nicely, as far as I'm concerned." He snickered. "I'm rather looking forward to Naomi seeing it."

"So? That's a yes?" Midgeley asked.

"Yes, Nehemiah," Shackleford said. "That's a yes. Thank you. Send the bill and we'll arrange transfer."

Roger got out of the car and went around to open Shackleford's door. Midgeley beat him to it and they shook hands all around.

"I think you're going to like this," Midgeley said. "I'll settle the tags and title for you. You can drive on my dealer plates if you need it in the meantime."

"Thank you, Nehemiah," Shackleford said.

Midgeley grinned and gave his two-finger salute. "Your business is my pleasure." He strode down the drive and a car started up in the alley, pulling up to the end of the drive as Midgeley approached. He jumped in and they drove off.

Shackleford looked at Roger. "Concerns, Mulligan?"

"Perhaps a bit ostentatious?," Roger asked.

"It's time Shackleford House stepped up to the times, Mulligan."

Roger looked at him, a bubble of surprise bursting in his brain.

Shackleford turned and looked up at the mansion looming over them. "It's been an icon of the past for a long time. Even the cars. Antiques. Old money. Boarding school." He shook his head. "I've been dealing with this little problem of mine for so long, I've left the world behind." He looked at Roger. "You've helped me more in the last four months than Perkins did in the four years before he died."

"I'm just muddling along, sir, but you seem better."

Shackleford shrugged. "It comes and goes. I feel like it's taking more of my memories every day." He smiled. "I have a lot of memories and not all of them good. It's not all bad."

Roger stopped himself from thinking about his own memories by focusing on the immediate issues of getting Shackleford back inside and the car into the garage before Naomi drove up.

"Mr. Featherstone will be by tomorrow morning, sir."

Shackleford looked at him, eyes blank for a moment. "Oh. Featherstone, yes." He shrugged. "Sorry. For a moment I thought I'd lost that one, too." He grinned. "Sometimes, it's hard to tell the difference."

"I should put the car in the garage, sir."

"Carry on, Mulligan. I'd like a cup of coffee and a cookie when you get a moment." The old man shambled into the house without pausing at the locked back door.

Roger wished he could do that and pulled out the garage door key.

When Roger opened the door the next morning, he decided that Amos Featherstone looked like a 50-something accountant. He stood there in a navy blue wool-blend suit with a white shirt and badly knotted tie, blinking at Roger through tortoise-shell glasses that distorted his eyes. "Mulligan? I'm Featherstone."

"Good day, Mr. Featherstone. Please come in." Roger stood back and led Featherstone up to the library. "Mr. Shackleford is expecting you."

The man followed along behind, seeming uninterested in his surroundings.

At the library, Roger knocked twice and entered. "Mr. Featherstone has arrived, sir."

Shackleford stood and met Featherstone as he entered, holding a hand out in greeting. "Amos. Thank you for coming. Again."

Amos shook Shackleford's hand and smiled. "You found another lead, I take it?"

"I have. DNA testing. Amazing stuff." Shackleford's normally laconic delivery took on new excitement with Featherstone. "Would you like some coffee?"

"Yes, please. That would be lovely."

"Mulligan, a tray if you please?"

"Of course, sir." Roger bowed himself out of the room and headed for the tray in the kitchen. He'd anticipated the request and had it waiting. By the time he got back, Shackleford and Featherstone had their heads together in front of the computer monitor. "Coffee, sirs." He put the tray on the table.

"So you see, Amos? She could be the one." Shackleford pointed to some detail on the screen.

Featherstone nodded. "Yeah. I never would have found her." He paused and looked at Shackleford. "You sure you want me to look into this?"

Shackleford sat back in his chair. "Why wouldn't I?"

Featherstone shrugged. "Money does funny things to people."

Shackleford nodded. "Just get me some background on her, Amos. Find out what kind of woman she is."

"All right. Usual fees."

"After all these years, you know I'm good for it," Shackleford said with a grin.

Featherstone chuckled and turned to the coffee. "Never a question, Joe."

"Will there be anything else, sir?" Roger asked.

"Thank you, Mulligan. No. I think we're fine for the moment."

Roger nodded and left them there. Featherstone seemed to be a shrewd operator and apparently knew what the old man needed.

Or at least wanted. Roger returned to his morning routine and wondered what he'd do if some distant relative offered to pluck him from obscurity the way Shackleford seemed to be considering for this Barbara Griffin woman. Looking around at the house, he chuckled. Naomi Patching wasn't a relative but her influence had certainly pulled Roger into a world he never knew existed. He wondered, not for the first time, if she knew that Shackleford was indeed a wizard.

The thought that she might know left him disturbed but he forced himself to shrug it off and work through the weekly grocery order. Regardless of what Patching knew or didn't, they still had to eat and Shackleford relied on him to make sure the pantry stayed stocked.

Shackleford called him to the library to show Featherstone out about half an hour later.

"I look forward to your findings, Amos."

Featherstone shook the old man's hand. "Don't get your hopes up, Joe. How many times have we done this so far?"

Shackleford shook his head. "No idea. A lot."

"And it always starts with 'I think this is the one,' doesn't it?"

Shackleford laughed. "Yes, well. You have to admit, this one is different."

Amos shook his head. "I don't have to admit anything." He grinned. "But maybe she's the one you're looking for. I'll know more in a few days."

"Thank you, Amos."

Featherstone nodded and Roger escorted him back to the front door.

"Don't let him get too excited, Mulligan," Featherstone said as he left. "He's looking for something very rare."

"I know, sir. I'll do my best."

Featherstone shot him a sharp glance. "Do you really?"

"He's looking for a descendant who shares his particular gift, sir."

The man's eyes narrowed behind the oversized lenses. "And do you share that gift, Mulligan?"

"No, sir."

Featherstone nodded. "I'll be in touch, Mulligan. Thanks for the coffee."

"My pleasure, sir. Good day."

Dr. Cuttle's office turned out to be in the same medical complex as Dr. Littlefield's, just diagonally across the park. It boasted the same utilitarian architecture, same fresh paint smell, and the same relentlessly cheerful air.

Roger found a seat in the waiting room while the assistant took Shackleford back for the examination. He made himself comfy in an easy chair and pulled up a science-fiction novel on his phone. He'd rediscovered a love for reading in the quiet of Shackleford House, although he avoided adventures. The authors never got the mechanics right and they reminded him too much of things he'd rather forget. He sank into the story and let time pass unremarked.

The assistant returned for him just as the story turned an interesting corner. He put the phone back in his pocket and followed her to a consultation room.

Cuttle stood and shook his hand. The doctor turned out to be one of those whip-thin, white-haired gentlemen who slouched around in cowboy boots and string-ties. He wore a smock around the office but left the stethoscope-wielding to his staff. "Roger, is it?"

"Yes, Doctor."

"Have a seat." They sat, Roger and Shackleford on one side of the table and Cuttle on the other. "Joe here says you're his primary caregiver?"

"I'm his butler, sir."

"So you take care of him and the house," Cuttle said.

"Yes, Doctor."

"He ever seem irrational to you?"

Roger glanced at Shackleford who shrugged in return.

"He's seemed confused at times, yes."

"You think he has dementia?" Cuttle leaned back in his chair, lacing his fingers together over his chest.

"Honestly, I don't know if I'd recognize dementia if I saw it."

Cuttle's bushy gray eyebrows rose a fraction. "Why do you say that? Doesn't everybody know it when they see it?"

"I know there are some common beliefs about it, Doctor, but I'm pretty sure it's not just being forgetful."

Cuttle smiled. "Good. Joe here has given me permission to share the preliminary findings with you. I believe him competent enough to give me that permission. Do you understand what that means?"

"Not precisely, Doctor, no."

"It means that his memory is a bit scratchy in places but—in my opinion—he's not dealing with dementia. At least not yet."

"That's good news, isn't it?" Roger asked.

Shackleford nodded but Cuttle shrugged. "He tells me there's a hostile family situation. Do you know anything about it?"

Nathan Lowell

"I know his niece said she wants to move him into an assisted living facility in Colorado."

"Is she hostile?" Cuttle asked.

"Butter wouldn't melt in her mouth," Roger said.

Cuttle grimaced. "Your opinion on the relationship between Joe and his niece?"

"I believe she wants the property, Doctor, and knows she isn't in line to get it. She's working to get him declared incompetent in order to either get control of it after moving him to assisted living or through probate after he passes away."

"That's just your opinion?" Cuttle asked, a note of incredulity in his voice.

"Well, some of it she told me. Some of it I've extrapolated, sir."

"He's not incompetent. He aced his MMSE and seems particularly cogent for a man of sixty. Given that he's got a couple of decades more than that on him, that's damn good in my book."

Roger nodded.

Shackleford leaned forward. "I wanted you to hear this, Mulligan. Direct from the good doctor's mouth."

"Honestly, I think you're doing better, sir. You hardly ever call me Perkins anymore."

"Who's Perkins?" Cuttle asked.

"My late butler. He was with me for nearly forty years," Shackleford said. "Old habits die hard."

"I'll happily certify him as rational," Cuttle said. "I should be so sane. I don't know what else I can tell you."

"Thank you, Doctor," Shackleford said. "I may be back to you on that, depending on how this all shakes loose in the end."

Cuttle nodded and rose. "I've got another patient to get to. Nice to meet you, Joe. Roger." He paused to shake hands before leaving the room.

"We seem to be getting the pieces together, sir."

Shackleford nodded. "It won't satisfy her, but it's a foundation we can build on."

A medical assistant opened the door. "This way, gentlemen."

Shackleford stayed quiet the whole way back to Shackleford House, gazing out the window as he always did.

Roger rolled onto the tarmac behind the house to find Naomi waiting in her BMW. He pulled to a stop and looked back at Shackleford. "Suggestions?"

"It's probably too late to leave," the old man said with a chuckle. "There's a wheelchair in the trunk if you need it. Let me see if I can make her angry enough to leave before it comes to that. Pull up so I can talk to her through the window."

The Wizard's Butler

Roger maneuvered the Mercedes around in a loop and stopped. Shackleford rolled down the window to Naomi's astonished stare. Her window dropped. "What are you doing?" she asked.

"Just got back from my checkup," Shackleford said. "To what do I owe the pleasure of your visit?"

"Checkup? What checkup?"

"Geriatrics specialist in dementia. Recommendation from my regular doctor. Isn't that what you wanted?"

"That is not what I wanted," Naomi said.

Shackleford chuckled. "No, I suspect you wanted me to go to one of your pet doctors who already has the diagnosis on file."

"Uncle, you're not yourself." She leaned out to look at the Mercedes. "And what is this car? Where's the Bentley?"

"The Bentley is safe," Shackleford said. "This is my new car. Mulligan's suggestion, actually."

"Mulligan?" Naomi asked. "That's not part of the deal, Mulligan."

Roger turned his head to look at her. "Ma'am?"

"You were supposed to keep him from doing stupid things like this."

"You hired me to take care of him and the house. Using the old cars—taking them out of the garage where they may have become irreparably damaged—would have been reckless."

"So you spent how much money to buy this?" she asked. "He's not competent to be making that kind of decision and you know it."

"I'm right here, Naomi," Shackleford said. "I'd appreciate it if you'd go back to sniping behind my back and not talk about me while I'm in the room. For your information, according to the specialist, there's nothing wrong with my mind. The decision to safeguard the antiques and get a modern vehicle with better safety features and readily available repairs makes a great deal of sense."

"How much did that cost?" she asked, narrowing her eyes.

"That's none of your business," Shackleford said. He paused. "What do you want, Naomi?"

"I just wanted to see how you were doing, Uncle."

Shackleford nodded. "As you can see, I'm doing very well. Now, I'm tired and I want my nap. I suggest you piss off." He pressed the button to roll the window up.

"Think she'll leave, sir?" Roger asked.

Shackleford shrugged and stared straight ahead. "Let's give her a few moments, Mulligan."

Naomi fulminated in her seat for a few moments. She spoke occasionally, the sound of her voice making its way into the car but

174

not the actual shape of her words. She paused and then Roger's phone rang.

He slipped it from his pocket. "It's her, sir."

"May as well see what she has to say," Shackleford said.

Roger pressed the answer key. "Yes, Ms. Patching?"

"I have no idea what game you think you're playing, Mulligan, but this will cease. Am I clear?"

"No, ma'am. You are not clear. You hired me to keep Mr. Shackleford safe and to take care of the building. I am doing that."

"Don't play the fool with me, Mulligan. What's the idea of getting rid of the Bentley and buying that thing?"

"As Mr. Shackleford explained, ma'am. The Bentley is a priceless antique. Since you have insisted that he venture out of the house for medical purposes, Mr. Shackleford has retired the classic cars and obtained a late-model vehicle to replace them."

"He's spent a quarter of a million on a damn car, Mulligan. That's not rational."

"If you say so, ma'am."

She paused and Roger thought he could hear her teeth grinding over the phone. "What did they say? The doctors?"

"One moment, ma'am." Roger put the call on hold. "She wishes to know what the doctors said, sir."

Shackleford rolled his window down and peered out at her. "They said I'm in good health and sane, Naomi."

She hung up her phone and glared. "Of course they did. It's what you paid them for."

"Any of yours will find the same thing, unless you're paying them to say differently," Shackleford said. "It's over, Naomi."

"What's over?" she asked, her face going blank.

"Your meddling," Shackleford said.

"Meddling, Uncle?" Her voice rose an octave. "I only want what's best for you. You're not a young man—"

"Enough," Shackleford said. He didn't raise his voice but the word snapped across the short distance like a ruler on her knuckles.

She winced and her jaw clamped shut with a click of teeth.

"You're not welcome in my home as long as you persist, Naomi." Shackleford's gaze seemed to burn into the woman and she wilted back from the pressure. "If you want to visit, set up the date and time with Mulligan in advance. Do you understand?"

Naomi's eyes could have shot lightning at him based on the storm on her face. "This is not over." She bit each word off and spit it at the old man. She cranked the BMW over and slammed it into gear, pulling off of the tarmac with a little pop of rubber and disappearing down the alley with a growl of abused engine noise.

"Thank you, Mulligan," Shackleford said. "I'll get out here while you take care of the car."

Roger got out to hold the door for the old man and watched him cross the short distance to the house. His back seemed a bit straighter, his gait steadier. He didn't bother with the door knob, just gestured with his left hand and walked through the open door. It swung closed behind him, and Roger shut the door on the Mercedes.

The exchange gave him a lot to think about. What would Naomi try next? He felt certain that she wasn't done and the property represented too much money—and too much ego—for her to let the old man win. He'd seen that look before on tribal warlords. It never boded well for anybody. He keyed the garage door open and backed the Mercedes into place. The rules of engagement here were different, but he felt sure that Shackleford had just gone to war.

Featherstone showed up at the front door unannounced. "Sorry, Mulligan. Is the old man in?" His suit looked rumpled, but he seemed otherwise calm and collected.

Roger held the door open. "Come in, sir. He's just finishing his breakfast. If you'd care to wait in the parlor, I'll see if he's taking visitors."

Featherstone nodded and took a seat in the parlor while Roger went upstairs.

Roger knocked twice on the door and entered.

Shackleford looked up from his paper, coffee cup lifted halfway to his mouth.

"Sorry, sir. Mr. Featherstone just arrived, asking to see you."

The old man put the cup back on his tray and nodded. "Show him up, Mulligan, and bring some more coffee."

"Of course, sir." Roger returned to the parlor and collected Featherstone, taking him up to the library. "Would you care for some breakfast, sir?"

Featherstone shook his head. "I've eaten, thank you."

Roger opened the library door and ushered Featherstone in before heading down to the kitchen for a carafe and an extra cup. By the time he returned, Featherstone and Shackleford had their heads together, Featherstone with an odd smile on his face and the old man staring into the middle distance with a frown. "Coffee, sir."

"Thank you, Mulligan," Shackleford said. "Just leave it."

Roger arranged the cups and coffee on the low table between their chairs and retreated from the room. He still had the master suite to clear and the morning's chores to do. As much as he wanted to be a fly on that wall, duty called. It wasn't the first time he'd been shut out of a meeting, nor would it be the last.

The two men stayed closeted for nearly an hour before Roger's pager called him back to the library. He knocked and entered as Featherstone stood from his seat and shook hands with Shackleford. "I'll have a full report later today, Joe."

"Thank you for the preliminary, Amos. I'll look forward to the detail. You really think she's not the one?"

Featherstone shrugged. "I'll be honest. She seems like the real deal. She's definitely a Shackleford somewhere back along, but ..." He paused and glanced at Roger. "But I don't know," he said, looking back at the old man.

"I appreciate your insights, Amos. I'm still tracking through the DNA data. New names come up but none as close as this Griffin woman."

Featherstone nodded. "I'll leave you to it. I've got a report to write." He followed Roger down to the front door. "Thank you, Mulligan."

Roger gave him a little bow. "Thank you, Mr. Featherstone."

Featherstone paused at the stoop and looked up at the house before striking off down the path.

Roger returned to the library to clear away the breakfast.

"Oh, Mulligan. Good," Shackleford said. "Featherstone says she's unlikely to want to give up her life and her business to move here."

"The Griffin woman, sir?"

Shackleford nodded and crossed to his computer terminal to turn the key. He looked at Roger as the machine booted up. "She has a business, it seems."

Roger gathered the used cups and the empty carafe onto the breakfast tray. "What kind of business, sir?"

Shackleford chuckled. "That's why Featherstone's a bit leery." He tapped on the keyboard, his gnarled index fingers pecking their way around until he hit enter. A website painted itself on the screen with a wash of text and individual images blinking into the blanks. A banner across the top of the page showed a woman staring over the top of a crystal ball. She wore a blue turban with a white jewel in the front. The text underneath read "Madam Dionysia Knows."

"It seems she's a fortune-teller," Shackleford said, grinning at Roger, his eyebrows working up and down.

A thin shiver shook the skin between Roger's shoulder blades as he looked between the two faces—the woman stared from the screen with Shackleford's eyes. They may not have been as old or as wrinkled around the edges but the shape and the icy green depths matched perfectly.

"You see it, too, Mulligan?" Shackleford asked, turning to look at the screen again.

"Yes, sir."

"So did Amos," Shackleford said. "Do you think she'd give up that charade to come live here?"

"What makes you think it's a charade, sir?"

Shackleford spun around to stare at Roger. "Telling fortunes isn't magic, Mulligan. It's make-believe. It's not one of the arts."

Roger picked up the tray. "If you say so, sir. I thought it was all make-believe not long ago." He glanced at the eyes on the screen. "What if she's using the psychic bit as a cover for what she's really doing, sir?"

Shackleford's confident stare faded and he turned to look at the screen again, the tip of his tongue tasting his lower lip. "A good question, Perkins. A very good question."

Roger left him gazing into the screen and took care of the dirty dishes. The speculation wouldn't be resolved any time soon. He felt pretty sure that he'd get a chance to take the Mercedes out for a spin on the interstate sooner rather than later. Whatever Barbara Griffin was doing, whether she was a wizard or not, she had the old man's eyes, not those of a thirty-something charlatan.

CHAPTER 12

The phone rang in the middle of the night, its jangle pulling Roger from a sound sleep around 3 a.m. He went to the alcove off the kitchen—cursing whoever had called, while afraid of what might be the reason. "Shackleford House."

"Mr. Shackleford?" A man's voice came over the line, almost buried in the sounds of shouts and engines in the background.

"No, sir. I'm Mulligan, the butler."

"Wake him. His warehouse is on fire."

A splash of cold water seemed to drench Roger's spine. "One moment." He put the phone down and raced up the stairs to the master suite where he found Shackleford already vertical and belting on a robe.

The old man looked up as Roger entered. "Telephone?" he asked.

"Yes, sir." He held the door for Shackleford and followed him to the upstairs parlor.

He picked up the receiver and spoke into it. "Shackleford." He stood there for several long moments, nodding occasionally but saying nothing. "Thank you, Hedgecock. Does the fire chief need me there?"

Roger didn't hear the reply but Shackleford nodded. "I'll expect him in the morning, then." He listened for a few more moments. "Keep me apprised and good work." He hung up and looked at Roger. "Looks like Naomi's peeved."

"The cars?" Roger asked.

"Different warehouse. Mostly old furniture and household goods." Shackleford headed for his bedroom. "Nothing we can do tonight. Fire chief and arson investigators will be here in the morning. Make sure to keep a pot of coffee on."

"Of course, sir."

179

Roger settled back into his bed but lay there staring at the ceiling until morning. He strapped on his running gear and headed out, Molly Flint joining him halfway down the alley.

"Something wrong?" she asked.

"Sorry. I'm a bit distracted this morning. A fire in one of Mr. Shackleford's warehouses last night."

"I saw the news. That was his?" she asked.

"Yeah. We got the call around three."

"It was a wonder they saved the building," she said.

Roger glanced at her. "I haven't seen the news."

"The brickwork got scorched pretty good but the flames didn't get inside." Molly shrugged. "Pictures on the news this morning. Lotta smoke but it didn't even burn through the doors."

"Lucky break, I guess," Roger said.

"That and the night watchman found it almost immediately and called 911." She looked at him. "You didn't know this?"

Roger shook his head. "I'm just the butler and we don't have TV at the house. Mr. Shackleford took the call."

The morning sun promised a nice day, and the trees along the path glowed with autumn colors, occasionally crunching underfoot as they ran. They never talked much once the running started in earnest, so the morning progressed normally. Molly peeled off to cool down at her gate and Roger continued on to Shackleford House. The whole way he pondered how much of the lack of damage had to do with the lucky night watchman and how much of it was some kind of magical protection.

He got through his shower and poured the first cup of coffee before the front doorbell rang, but only barely. On the stoop he found a tired looking pair smelling of smoke.

The woman held up a badge. "Chief Bray. This is Inspector Tinker from the State Fire Marshall's Office. Can we come in?"

"Of course, Chief. Mr. Shackleford is expecting you." Roger stepped back and ushered them in. "You can wait in the parlor while I see if he's awake. Would you care for coffee?"

"You're the butler?" Tinker asked.

"Yes, sir."

"Were you here all night?"

"Yes, sir."

"Was he?"

"Yes, sir."

"Adrian." The chief cast a glance at the shorter inspector. "Thank you, Mulligan, is it?"

"Yes, ma'am. Roger Mulligan. Mr. Shackleford and I were in all night."

"We're a bit smoked up, Mr. Mulligan. We can wait here," she said. "Save the furniture."

"It's not an issue, ma'am, but wherever you're most comfortable. I'll be just a moment."

Roger went up the stairs to the master suite and knocked before entering.

Shackleford exited the bathroom, tying a flannel robe around his pajamas. "They're here already, Mulligan?"

"Yes, sir."

The old man scrubbed a hand over his face. "Give me a moment to find some trousers. I'm sure they have questions. Can you lay on coffee and pastry in the small dining room?"

"Of course, sir."

"Five minutes, Mulligan."

"I'll tell them, sir."

Roger closed the doors to the suite and returned to the ground floor. "Mr. Shackleford is dressing and will be with you shortly. If you'd come this way?" He led them back to the small dining room off the kitchen, where he opened the drapes to let in the morning light. "Please, make yourselves comfortable while I get some coffee for you."

"Thank you, Mr. Mulligan," the chief said.

Roger slipped through to the kitchen and pulled a tray together with cups, creamer, sugar, and a full carafe of coffee. He set the next pot to brew while he took the tray back to the dining room, placing it on the sideboard. "Coffee," he said. "Would either of you prefer tea?"

"Coffee's fine with me, thanks," the chief said, crossing to the sideboard to help herself.

"I'll be right back," Roger said, going back into the kitchen to rustle up a few breakfast sweets from the pantry and arrange them on another tray with some dishes. He added some napkins and cutlery, returning just moments before Shackleford entered from the other end. He placed the tray beside the coffee and stepped back out of the way.

"Good morning," Shackleford said. "Sorry to keep you waiting."

The chief and inspector introduced themselves, and Shackleford took a seat at the head of the table. "Coffee, please, Mulligan."

Roger collected the carafe and a cup and saucer, placing the cup down before filling it for him. "A pastry, sir?"

"Not yet, thank you." Shackleford nodded to the visitors. "Please. Sit. You've got better things to do than be here, I'm sure."

The inspector took a seat immediately to Shackleford's right, the chief beside him. "Your man here says you were in all night."

Shackleford sipped his coffee and nodded. "I don't get out much these days, particularly at night. Old bones."

"And your butler was here all night as well?"

Shackleford nodded. "As far as I know. It's possible that neither of us stayed in. We live in separate parts of the house. I'm afraid we don't have much by way of alibis."

The chief shook her head. "Neither of you is under suspicion, Mr. Shackleford."

The inspector gave her a sour look which she looked past. "Do you know anybody who would want to burn your warehouse?"

"I'm currently feuding with my niece over the disposition of my estate," Shackleford said. "We had an argument about my vehicles recently."

"Your vehicles?" the inspector asked.

"I retired my old fleet in favor of a more up-to-date model," Shackleford said, taking another sip. "My niece objected to the expense."

"What's her name? This niece?" the inspector asked, taking a notepad from his pocket.

"Patching," Shackleford said. "Naomi Patching."

"Would she firebomb your warehouse?" the chief asked.

"Personally?" Shackleford shook his head. "She wouldn't get her hands dirty."

"But she might get somebody else to do it?" the inspector asked, leaning forward.

"Speculation on my part, Inspector. She's the only person that I'm aware of that has a beef with me."

"I'm interested in the fire suppression system," the chief said. "Those doors stood up to three direct hits with Molotov cocktails."

"I'm pleased," Shackleford said. "But they're nothing special as far as I know."

"The night watchman seemed to think you had something special done," the inspector said.

"I brought the facility up to code about a decade ago," Shackleford said. "I couldn't tell you what that code standard is—or was then—but Shackleford House has been burned down a few times over the ages. I'm particularly cognizant of the risks. I take it as my obligation to keep it from happening again if I can."

"Would you object to me giving it an inspection, sir?" the chief asked. "Just a courtesy check to see if it's still up to code?"

"Not at all," Shackleford said. "Welcome it, actually. I'd only ask that you arrange it with the facilities management people on site and keep me in the loop on it."

"When you say she wouldn't get her hands dirty, do you have any reason to suspect she might hire it done?" the inspector asked.

"She's a headstrong young woman," Shackleford said. "I try not to speculate on what others might do, particularly where money is concerned."

"Do you have a valuation on how much that warehouse is worth, sir?" the chief asked.

"The building? At least half a million. The lot itself is probably worth almost that much," Shackleford said.

"And the contents?" she asked.

"Insurance estimates it at between five and ten million."

The chief and inspector both froze in their seats.

"That's a lot of household goods and furniture," the inspector said.

"Much of it is antiques going back to the late 1600s and early 1700s," Shackleford said. "Some artwork from pre-colonial days. It's being held for a restoration project after my death."

"That's a lot of money to have in a warehouse," the inspector said.

"It is, and I pay well to have it protected. Some things can't be replaced by money."

"You say you retired your vehicles?" the inspector said. "What did you mean by that?"

"I kept some classic cars in the garage. I venture out so rarely, I never saw the need to replace them."

"But recently you did?" the inspector asked.

"Yes. Mulligan here convinced me that I would be better served by a modern vehicle that could be repaired more easily should something happen."

The inspector looked at Roger. "You convinced him?"

"I'm also the driver, sir. I felt uncomfortable driving an antique through the city streets on routine tasks."

"What happened to the old cars?" the inspector asked, looking at Shackleford again.

"Storage," the old man said. "Different warehouse."

"How many do you have?" the inspector asked.

"What? Cars or warehouses?"

"Warehouses, sir," the inspector said.

"Three," Shackleford said. "One is currently empty, I believe. I should probably sell it."

The inspector asked for the addresses and Shackleford gave them to him. He wrote them all down in his notebook.

"Anything else that might shed light on this?" the chief asked.

"Anarchists?" Shackleford said. "Random violence?"

"Arson's not generally random," the inspector said. "We don't have a firebug in the city. At least not that we know of. This could be the beginning of a pattern." He shrugged and hunched over his coffee.

"But you don't think so," Shackleford said.

"No, sir. Somebody threw five bottles of gasoline at that door. Two fell short, three hit and coated the front of that building with flammable liquid."

"Is that a normal pattern?" Shackleford asked.

The chief looked at the inspector, her eyebrows raised. "Adrian?"

"No, sir. It's not. Molotov cocktails aren't particularly effective. Most arson I've investigated has been inside the building where the fire can do some damage. Pour some incendiary liquids and poof."

"But they couldn't get in," Shackleford said.

"Anybody can get in if they want to badly enough," the inspector said.

"So they just wanted to send me a message," Shackleford said, placing his cup into the saucer with a click.

The inspector shrugged. "Until we find who did it, it's all speculation."

"Will you find them?" Shackleford asked.

The inspector shrugged again. "Unless somebody saw something, it's unlikely."

"Cameras?" Shackleford asked.

"Do you have any on your building, sir?" the chief asked. "We didn't see any on the outside."

Shackleford shook his head. "No. The warehouse was built sometime in the 50s, as I remember. I updated the sprinklers and added some internal doors at the request of the insurance people, but no cameras."

"Who's your insurance agent?" the inspector asked.

Shackleford gave him the name and agency. "Mulligan can give you their contact address."

"He was on site this morning," the chief said. "I have his card."

"Is there anything else?" Shackleford asked.

"Will you be visiting the site, sir?" the chief asked.

"Would you like me to?"

"If it's possible, sir. Most people want to see the damage for themselves." She smiled.

Shackleford nodded. "Is the area secured?"

The chief nodded. "The fire is out. It's all taped off and the fire marshal has people there."

"Give me a couple of hours? I'll come over around eleven?"

"That would be fine, sir," the chief said.

Shackleford stood, drawing the chief and inspector to their feet as well. "Thank you for coming," he said.

The inspector grunted and stuffed his notebook into a coat pocket. "I'll be at the site later."

The chief shook his hand. "Thank you, sir. Sorry to start your morning on the wrong foot."

Shackleford smiled. "I've been wrong-footed before. Nobody was hurt. Nothing was seriously damaged. Mulligan will show you out."

They followed Roger to the door and he held it open for them.

"How long you worked here?" the inspector asked.

"Four months, sir."

"What did you do before that?"

"I was unemployed for several months, sir. An EMT before that. Army medic before that."

"Butlering isn't that common. Why'd you take the job?" he asked.

"I needed the job, sir. I've found I quite like it. The hours are long, but I'm paid well and my duties are not too taxing."

"How'd he find you?" the inspector asked.

"His niece placed an ad with an employment agency. The agency sent me over. My EMT background appealed to them, sir."

"The same niece that has a beef with the old man?" he asked.

"Yes, sir."

"You know about the beef going in?"

"She wants this property, sir. I don't actually remember if she said so in so many words, but her intentions are clear."

"What are those intentions?" the inspector asked.

"She wants me to make sure Mr. Shackleford survives until she can place him in an assisted living home and have him declared incompetent, sir."

The inspector's eyebrows shot up. "That seems pretty specific."

"Yes, sir."

"That doesn't jibe with trying to burn down the warehouse," the chief said.

"Yeah, what's with the cars?" the inspector asked.

"Mr. Shackleford recently purchased a new Mercedes to replace three antique model vehicles. Those vehicles are in a storage warehouse. Ms. Patching learned of those two facts recently. She became quite upset that Mr. Shackleford had spent that amount of money."

"I understand if she wants the estate for herself but why try to destroy them?" the inspector asked. "Wouldn't she want to keep them safe to sell them later?"

"I don't know that she did, sir."

"What would you call five firebombs in the middle of the night?" he asked.

"Perhaps a message, sir."

"A message?"

"Yes, sir. That she knows where Mr. Shackleford's warehouse is. At least one of them. It wasn't the one with the vehicles in it."

"Seems kinda thuggish," the inspector said. "Stupid, even."

"Speculation, sir. It might not have been her idea. It might not even be related. Coincidences happen."

The inspector nodded. "Thank you for your time."

Roger gave his little bow and they left. When he turned back, he saw Shackleford standing in the corridor that led to the dining room.

"He really wanted to pin that on me, you know," he said.

Roger nodded. "I suspect you're correct, sir. He's just following the money. If it burns, then your insurance would pay you."

"Pennies on the dollar, Mulligan."

"True, sir, but that depends on the actual value of the contents. Burning old picnic tables instead of antique furniture?"

Shackleford laughed. "I take your point. But the inspector raised an interesting question."

"Why did they firebomb it, sir?"

"No, Mulligan. If not Naomi, then who?"

"We may never know, sir."

Shackleford nodded. "True, but if I were going to wager, I'd bet on her father."

"Seems farfetched, sir."

"Maybe not as much as you think, Mulligan. He's been trying to get this property for much longer than Naomi has. Ever since Evelyn's death."

"Evelyn, sir?"

"My sister. Naomi's mother. Cancer, twenty years ago. Bruna got her inheritance but it didn't include Shackleford House. He fought it in probate but got laughed out of court."

"How does burning the warehouse help him, sir?"

"If he can't have it, he doesn't want anybody to have it."

"Even Naomi?"

Shackleford shrugged. "I'm not sure he'd factor that in."

"What now, sir?"

"Now, I'm going to get cleaned up and have some real breakfast, if you'd be so kind, Mulligan?"

"Of course, sir."

Nathan Lowell

"Then we'll take a ride over to the warehouse and show the inspector and the chief what it was that almost burned."

"Was it in any real danger, sir?"

Shackleford shrugged. "Everything's a risk, Mulligan. I'd like to think that the building and contents would be safe from random acts of violence, but the very nature of random acts makes them difficult to guard against. It's why I pay insurance premiums. Money can't replace the irreplaceable, but it provides a foundation to build a recovery on." He shrugged again. "One of the lessons from the earlier Shackleford House burnings." He started up the stairs.

"I'll have your breakfast ready by the time you're out of the shower, sir."

"Thank you, Mulligan."

The fire left Roger feeling unsettled. He felt certain he'd over-looked something; some detail in the report didn't add up. His hind brain snagged on it but couldn't tell his fore brain what it was. He hated that feeling.

Roger pulled the Mercedes to the curb near the gated warehouse. A police cruiser and a lone fire department utility van blocked the entrance. Yellow crime scene tape festooned the area at the front of the building. Black scorch marks ran up the façade. Roger got out and went around to hold the door for Shackleford. The smell of gasoline and smoke still wafted on the morning breeze.

Shackleford slid out of the car and looked up at the building, then over at the vehicles. A uniformed cop stood sentry at the gate and watched them. "With me, Mulligan, if you please."

"Of course, sir."

Shackleford paced off the few steps to the officer. "I'm Shackleford, the owner. The fire inspector is expecting me."

"Got some ID, Mr. Shackleford?"

The old man pulled a wallet from the inside of his jacket and flipped out a passport. "This do?"

The officer opened it and compared the picture to the man. "Yes, sir. Thank you. One moment." He mumbled something into his shoulder radio and it squawked back. "He'll be right here, sir."

A moment later the door opened and the inspector came out followed by a burly, bow-legged man, wearing a brown cloth coat and a flat cap. The inspector frowned at the ground, picking his way across the yard while the man with him scowled at his back.

"Shackleford," the inspector said. "Your man Hedgecock here has been giving me the tour."

"Sorry, Mr. Shackleford. He insisted," Hedgecock said.

187

"Quite right, Mr. Hedgecock. He's just doing his job," Shackleford said.

"You've got a lot of junk in there," the inspector said. "What makes it worth so much?"

Shackleford shrugged. "You'd be surprised what an old piece of Shaker furniture goes for. What you call junk, collectors call 'lost treasures.'"

"You wanna show me what you've done to upgrade the fire suppression system?" the inspector asked. "Your man here wasn't sure."

"Of course. Mr. Hedgecock took the position after I did the upgrades. There's no reason he could know." He nodded at the yard. "Is it all right to walk through?"

"The forensics people got what they needed," the officer said. "There's still a lot of glass."

The inspector nodded at the door. "Come on."

They went single file, the inspector leading the way along a scuffed path in the fire-stained paving. Roger had seen a lot of gasoline firebombs and his eyes traced the subtle shadings and shadows on the tar. The morning light glittered on the glass fragments scattered on the ground; a few were even embedded in the wooden door. The door itself, while singed and stained, hadn't really caught fire at all.

"Solid door," the inspector said.

"Doesn't look like the fire did much damage," Shackleford said.

The inspector nodded, then shrugged. "Curious that. The bricks, sure. The door, though? There should have been enough heat to burn that. At least catch on the edges." He eyed Shackleford with an eyebrow raised.

"Maybe the bottles were small," Roger said.

The inspector turned his gaze on Roger. "Less gasoline?"

Roger nodded. "Less gas, more vapor. Flash over fast and die out fast."

The inspector took a half step back and looked the door over. "That's possible." He glanced at Roger. "Why do you think that?"

"Three tours in Afghanistan."

The inspector nodded and looked at the door again. "We've collected enough glass to reconstruct the bottles. We should know soon."

Shackleford pushed past the inspector and into the warehouse. The lights already illuminated the first floor. A wide passage, big enough for a truck, led the way into the building. Partitions broke up the interior space into corrals for mostly wooden furniture. They walked down the central aisle toward the back of the building.

Roger saw several different styles of furniture, pieces ranging from some simple chairs and tables to herds of ornately carved four-poster beds, their frames strung with ropes.

"Some of this is European," Shackleford said, pointing at the beds. "Those came over as prized possessions in the early 1700s. They survived the fires more than once, which is a miracle in itself."

"Valuable enough to keep?" the inspector asked.

"Oh, yes. They should probably be in a museum, but the warehouse is climate controlled. It's very close to museum grade." He led them down a side passage that Roger would have walked by. "In here." He opened a metal door and flipped on a light, revealing a room filled with red, metal cylinders against the far wall, all connected to a manifold above them. An electronic control box stood beside them with what looked like a thousand green lights arranged in a grid. "Waterless extinguishing. State-of-the-art sensor network." He shrugged. "What was state of the art as of the turn of the century." He looked at the inspector. "This century, not the last."

The inspector surveyed the room and walked over to peer at the labels on the bottles. "This is museum grade." He turned to look at Shackleford. "In this building? It must have cost a fortune."

"Money isn't that big a concern when you're protecting something that's priceless," Shackleford said with a shrug. "I have plenty of money."

"Who else knows about this?" the inspector asked.

"The company that installed it. Mr. Hedgecock here. You, now."

"Your niece?" the inspector asked.

"I don't know. I doubt it. It's not exactly a secret, but it's not a subject that comes up around the dinner table, now is it?"

The inspector ran his hand over his mouth as if rubbing away a bad taste on his lips. "I suppose not." He looked down at his feet, frowning at the floor.

"Any other questions, Inspector Tinker?" Shackleford asked.

Tinker shook his head. "No, sir. I think I've got all I'm going to get."

Shackleford nodded and stood by the door, his hand on the light switch. "In that case ...?"

The inspector walked out, eyeing the furniture with a level of curiosity he hadn't had coming in.

"Hedgecock, walk with us, if you would?"

The man nodded and lingered with Shackleford. Roger brought up the rear.

"Any problems?" Shackleford asked, keeping an eye on the inspector ahead of them.

"None, sir."

"How long did it take you to get here?"

"Two minutes, tops. The fire was still burning but it died out within like five minutes."

"You didn't see anything?"

Hedgecock shook his head. "I heard a truck leaving when I came around the block, but I didn't see anything."

"You tell that to the inspector."

"Yes, sir. Told them everything."

"Any problems with access?"

"No, sir."

"They give you any guff about getting the alarm?"

"Never questioned it, sir."

Shackleford nodded. "When they've cleared the scene, hire some people to clean up the glass. Let me know."

"Will do, sir." He paused. "Think they'll be back?"

Shackleford stepped out into the sun and looked around before shaking his head. "Message sent. Message received."

"Any idea who it is, sir?"

"I have suspicions, but none I'd hang a hat on."

Hedgecock nodded.

"Let me know when the cleanup's done," Shackleford said again.

"Yes, sir. Be at least a couple days, based on what the cop's been sayin'."

"I figured as much," Shackleford said. He put a hand on Hedgecock's shoulder and stared into the man's face. "No heroics, Stanley. You hear me?"

"Yes, sir."

"I'm serious. I'd rather the place burn down than you get in the way and get hurt."

"You think it'll come to that, sir?"

"No, but I don't take those kinds of chances and I won't stand for it if you do."

Hedgecock nodded once, a sharp downward jerk of his chin. "Understood, sir."

Shackleford clapped the man's shoulder twice and then started back across the yard toward the gate with Roger on his heels.

"You're not planning on leaving town, are you?" Tinker asked as they passed.

"No, Inspector. I'm not planning on it. Why?" Shackleford asked.

"I just want to know where to find you if I have any more questions."

Shackleford nodded. "If something comes up, I'll have Mulligan notify you. Will that do?"

"Yes, sir."

Roger opened the door to the Mercedes and Shackleford slid into the seat. Roger took his place in the driver's seat and looked at Shackleford in the mirror. "Home, sir?"

Shackleford looked out at the scorched building, rolling his tongue around in his mouth. "Yes, Mulligan. Something doesn't smell right here, but I can't put my finger on it."

"You have wards up on the building, don't you?" Roger asked.

Shackleford's eyebrows did a little dance on his forehead. "Wards?"

"Some kind of protective magic, sir. Like you do on the other buildings?"

Shackleford seemed to consider his response for a few moments too long. "Yes, Mulligan. I do."

"What message do you think Naomi's father is trying to send?" Roger asked.

Shackleford shook his head. "I think he's just trying to rattle my cage a little."

"So you think it's Bruna, sir?"

"He's a thug. Always been a thug. This is just exactly the kind of thing I'd expect from him." Shackleford glanced at the building for a moment before catching Roger's eyes in the mirror again. "You be careful on your morning runs. It wouldn't surprise me to have him send a message through you as well."

Roger nodded. "I'll keep an eye open, sir."

"Then let's get home. I suspect we'll hear from Naomi by midafternoon," Shackleford said. "Bet she doesn't call for an appointment, either."

"I'm not much for gambling, sir." Roger started the car and pulled it out into the street, cruising past the warehouse before taking a cross-street to get back on the road to Shackleford House.

CHAPTER 13

The phone rang as soon as Roger walked through the back door.

"Shackleford House."

"Is this Mr. Shackleford?" A woman's voice.

"No, ma'am. I'm Mulligan, Mr. Shackleford's butler."

"I'd like to speak with Mr. Shackleford, please."

"May I ask who's calling?"

"This is Dr. Littlefield's office calling."

"One moment, ma'am."

Roger placed the phone on the small table and went up to the library, knocking before entering. "Dr. Littlefield's office on the phone for you, sir."

Shackleford snorted and headed for the upstairs parlor phone. Roger considered how difficult it might be to get a phone installed in the library—or at least a cordless model in the parlor that he could carry to wherever the old man might be. It seemed a small enough upgrade that it shouldn't upset the pixies and enough of a convenience that Shackleford might go for it. They'd had more calls in the last two weeks than the first three months of his employment.

He followed after Shackleford, giving the man room to have a private phone call while still remaining within earshot in case Shackleford needed him. He paused outside the parlor door, waiting.

Shackleford said something that Roger couldn't understand and hung up the phone, the heavy receiver making a distinctive rattle on its cradle. Shackleford came out of the parlor, a frown on his face and his mouth screwed into a grimace. "Ah, Mulligan. Dr. Littlefield wants me to start taking some medications and adjust my diet."

"How can I help, sir?"

"High blood pressure and cholesterol," he said. "I need you to call them back with the information on the pharmacy so they can place the prescriptions."

"And diet?" Roger asked.

"Typical stuff. Same thing she said before. Less red meat, fewer saturated fats. More whole grains and green vegetables."

Roger processed that for a moment, rolling the menus over in his head. "That's going to be difficult, sir. Your diet includes very little red meat already."

Shackleford nodded. "I know. I'll leave it up to you, Mulligan. I don't really notice food, to be honest." He patted his chest. "This keeps stealing my attention away."

"You've been doing much better, sir."

Shackleford shook his head. "I'm not sure about that. I've had these periods in the past. I always pay for them in the end." He sighed.

"I'll call the doctor's office, sir."

Shackleford nodded. "Thank you, Mulligan. Carry on."

"Sir? About the telephone?"

"What about it?"

"There are wireless handsets. If we installed one here in the parlor, you wouldn't need to come here to answer it. I could bring the phone to you."

Shackleford's eyes widened. "That's a good idea, Mulligan. See to it."

"Will it bother the pixies, sir?"

Shackleford shook his head. "I doubt it, but we can always bribe them with a little whiskey." He grinned. "Probably wouldn't hurt to give them a little treat anyway, now that I think of it."

Roger nodded. "I'll see to it this evening, sir."

"Thank you, Mulligan. Carry on." The old man went back into the library. The door closed behind him with a snap of the latch.

Roger went to his Bible and looked up the information for the preferred pharmacy. He took the book to the phone alcove and dialed the number for Dr. Littlefield's office, waiting for the menu to push him through to a person.

"Dr. Littlefield's office. May I help you?"

"I'm calling for Joseph Shackleford, one of Dr. Littlefield's patients. I have the pharmacy information you requested."

"Of course, sir. One moment." The line clicked onto hold music before a new voice came on the line. "Mr. Mulligan?"

"Yes."

"What's the pharmacy?"

Roger read the information off the page.

"Thank you, and can you hold for one moment? Dr. Littlefield would like to speak to you."

"Of course, ma'am."

The doctor must have been waiting because she came on the line almost immediately. "Mr. Mulligan? Dr. Littlefield here."

"Yes, Doctor."

"Have you ordered that defibrillator yet?"

"Not yet, Doctor."

"You should consider doing that," she said.

"Is there something that I need to know, Doctor?"

Her sigh came through clearly. "Nothing specific, Mr. Mulligan. Call it a hunch. He's got some markers that I'm not happy about seeing in a man his age. Add the stress of his ..." She paused for a heartbeat. "The stress of his condition," she said. "I'm worried about his heart. You know what having that device at hand could mean in terms of survival, probably as well as I do."

"Yes, Doctor. I'll order one right away."

"Thank you, Mr. Mulligan."

"Thank you, Doctor."

"The pharmacy will call when the prescriptions are ready. Do you have any questions about his dietary changes?"

"He eats very little red meat already, doctor. Other than eggs, are there any foods I need to watch out for?"

"Any saturated fats like cheese and full-fat dairy products. Any trans-fats like most commercial vegetable oils. You can find a lot of information online if you have access."

"We do, and I'll look. Thank you, Doctor."

"You're welcome, Mr. Mulligan. Good-bye." The doctor rang off and Roger hung up the phone.

He had some electronics to buy. He went back to his quarters and began researching defibrillators. If the doctor thought he'd need it, he was more than willing to spend a few of the old man's dollars to get it and get it fast. With luck, he could get it and the phone on expedited shipping within a couple of days.

Naomi rang the front doorbell just as Roger dropped off Shackleford's lunch tray in the kitchen. She breezed in as soon as he opened the door. "Is he receiving visitors today, Mulligan? Or should I make an appointment?"

"He's expecting you, ma'am."

She blinked hard a couple of times. "Expecting me?"

"Yes, ma'am," Roger said. "Just this morning, he predicted he'd see you by midafternoon."

"Did he say why?"

"No, ma'am. If you'd follow me, I'll take you right up."

Naomi walked beside him, casting him sideways glances all the way up the stairs.

Roger knocked twice and opened the door. "Ms. Patching, sir."

"Who?" Shackleford rolled out from behind his table.

"Ms. Patching, sir. Your niece." He stepped out of the doorway and Naomi walked in.

"My niece is twelve years old. Who is this woman, Perkins?" Shackleford asked, peering at Naomi above his glasses.

"Uncle, it's me. Naomi," she said, glancing at Roger with a satisfied gleam in her eyes. "Don't you remember me?"

Shackleford paused, sitting more upright in his wheelchair. "Naomi? My gracious. Is it you?"

"Yes, Uncle." She swept across the room to kneel beside his chair and take one of his hands in both of hers. "Yes, it's me."

He stared at her for several long moments. "You look like your mother. How is she?"

Naomi swallowed hard and blinked several times. "She's ... she's well, Uncle. She misses you."

Shackleford nodded. "I miss her, too." He looked up at Roger. "Perkins, put a note on my calendar. We'll go by the house and visit her. Next week?" He looked at Naomi. "Would that be acceptable?"

"I'm sure she'd like that, Uncle."

Shackleford nodded, more a tremble than a full nod. "Yes, then that's what we'll do." He looked at Naomi again. "What brings you to an old man's side, my dear?"

"I had a premonition that you might be lonely, Uncle. It's been just ages since I've seen you."

"Well, I'm happy to see you. Would you care for a cup of tea?" He looked at Mulligan. "Perkins, tea and some of those shortbread cookies."

"No, Uncle. That's not necessary." Naomi drew his attention back to her. "Please. I can only stay a few moments. I just wanted to check up on you. Make sure you were doing well."

"Are you sure?" he asked. "Perkins can just pop down to the kitchen—"

"I'm sure, Uncle," she said. She released his hand and stood, leaning over to kiss his balding pate. "You just rest and take it easy."

The old man nodded. "If you're sure. It would only take a moment."

"I'm sure, Uncle," she said again. "I have an appointment to show a house in the neighborhood in a few minutes."

He smiled up at her and nodded. "Well, don't let me hold up commerce, my dear. I hope they love it."

"I'm sure they will, Uncle." She patted his shoulder. "You rest now."

Shackleford nodded. "Yes. I think I'll take a nap. That sounds rather good. I didn't get a good night's sleep, did I?"

"Probably not, Uncle." She turned and smiled at Roger on her way out the door.

"I'll be right back, sir," Roger said.

Shackleford waved a hand and spun the chair around. "I'd still like a cup of tea."

"I'll get it, sir."

"Thank you, Perkins."

Roger caught up with her on the stairs.

"His geriatrics specialist didn't see that side of him, I wager," she said with the kind of smirk that Roger longed to slap off her face.

"No, ma'am," he said.

"He smelled smoky. Has he taken up the pipe again?"

"No, ma'am. We were called to a fire at one of his properties this morning."

She froze, midstride, and lowered her foot to the floor before turning to him. "A fire?"

"Warehouse. Firebombed. The fire chief and arson inspector woke him."

"That was when he thought he'd hear from me," she said, almost to herself. "Was he like this?" She waved a hand up the stairs.

"No, ma'am. It comes and goes rather quickly on occasion."

She frowned. "What did the inspector have to say?"

"Only wanted to know if he had any enemies and why the warehouse didn't burn."

Her eyebrows shot up as her eyes went wide. "It didn't burn?"

"No, ma'am. Fire inspector supposes that it was some kind of warning. A message, I believe he called it."

"Did he say why?"

"No, ma'am."

Naomi's eyes focused somewhere off to the side. "Why did he go?"

"To the warehouse, ma'am?"

"Yes."

"The fire inspector wanted him to point out the upgraded fire control systems."

Her eyes narrowed. "Upgraded systems?"

"Yes, ma'am."

She shook her head and checked the dainty jeweled timepiece on her wrist. "I've got to go. You know he's not all there, right?"

"I know he has good days and bad days, ma'am."

"We still have a few months before we can ship him off to Colorado." She said it almost to herself, before turning to Roger. "Keep him safe. You hear me?"

"Of course, ma'am."

Roger held the door for her while she stormed out, feeling sorry for the client she was going to meet. He closed and bolted the door behind her before going back to the library.

He knocked before entering, but Shackleford wasn't there. On a hunch, Roger went to the master suite and gave a softer than normal knock before peeking in. The old man had apparently crawled into bed, making good on his threatened nap. Roger didn't blame him. It sounded like a good idea. He froze when he saw the wheelchair beside the bed.

Roger spent most of the afternoon researching dementia. Treatments and medications seemed to have some efficacy. Still, he questioned how much of Shackleford's trouble was dementia and how much was that damned amulet around his neck. The thought rocked him back in his chair, and he stared at the ceiling.

A few months ago, the idea that he'd be weighing the implications of a magical curse on a patient would have had him considering his own grip on reality. It wasn't like he could see magic or do magic, but he could see the results. The whiskey didn't evaporate. The dust didn't blow away on its own. He had no idea what it might really be, no alternative hypothesis to explain what he'd seen.

Other than he might be delusional himself. He snorted. It was not an outrageous assumption.

Pettigrew and her magic wardrobe. The wheelchair that wasn't. Although that might have been another illusion, since he'd just seen it parked beside the old man's bed.

The Shackleford House Butler's Bible caught his eye. Another artifact that appeared to operate on a magical plane, even if he couldn't do magic himself. What was the old science-fiction quote about sufficiently advanced technology? Was it better to think the old man and Pettigrew were aliens?

Did it matter?

He looked back at the screen open on his desk. This thing did not seem like dementia. Sure, good days and bad days, but the occasions on which Shackleford had exhibited signs of dementia without Naomi in the room had been few. He had to force himself to take a deep breath and question his assumption about the wheelchair. He honestly didn't know if Shackleford's behavior had been just an act. Closing his laptop, he checked his notebook. He had chores to do before preparing dinner.

Chores. That would distract him from the growing concern that Naomi was going to win, that the necklace would steal so much of the old man's mind that the result would be indistinguishable from dementia.

By dinner time, Roger had calmed himself by falling back on routine. He couldn't control much, so he worked on what he could—caring for the house, dealing with the evening meal, and setting aside a decanter of whiskey for later.

He took the tray up to the library at the usual hour. Shackleford sat in his usual seat and looked up from reading the usual book. "Ah, Mulligan."

"Dinner, sir."

"Excellent. Something the good doctor would approve of, I hope?" He grinned.

"Chicken Marsala, sir. Whole grain rice. Green beans. I've a pie in the kitchen for dessert."

"Your cooking lessons paying off, are they?" Shackleford said, crossing to the table on his own two feet and taking his seat.

"They are, sir."

Shackleford leaned over the plate and took a deep whiff. "Smells delightful, Mulligan. Thank you."

"You're welcome, sir." Roger started for the door but Shackleford spoke again.

"Mulligan? Did something happen this afternoon?"

Roger stopped, turning back to see Shackleford looking up at him, a frown on his face. "Your niece stopped by, sir. She didn't stay long."

Shackleford's gaze seemed to be focused somewhere in midair. "I ... I don't remember."

"She came in, found you in your wheelchair, sir. You spoke briefly and she left. By the time I got back, you'd gone for a nap."

"A nap?"

"Yes, sir."

Shackleford sighed. "How did I seem? When Naomi was here?"

"Rather confused, sir. She left believing that you were quite far gone, mentally."

"And was I, Mulligan? Quite far gone?"

"I didn't think so at the time, sir. Your behavior around your niece is frequently indicative of dementia."

"Later?" Shackleford asked.

"When I came back, I looked in on you, sir. The wheelchair was parked beside the bed."

Shackleford's eyebrows rose. "Really." He tilted his head a bit sideways and stared at the tabletop for a few moments. "That's ... unexpected." He looked back at Roger. "I don't remember leaving my bed and returning here. Would you check to see if it's still there?"

Roger nodded. "Of course, sir." He went down the hall to the master suite and found the room much as he'd have expected to see it. He made a circuit of the room and straightened the bedclothes in passing before returning to the library. "Nothing out of the ordinary that I could see, sir. Your bed looked like you'd slept in it."

Shackleford nodded. "Thank you, Mulligan."

"You're welcome, sir."

Roger left him sitting there, picking at the food and staring into the distance. Clearly the old man was getting worse and there was damn all he could do about it.

Halfway through the morning run, Molly nudged Roger with an elbow as they made the turn back toward home. "Earth to Roger. Come in, Roger."

Roger laughed. "Sorry."

"Deep thoughts this morning," she said. "You haven't said three words since we started."

Roger shrugged. "Nothing I can really talk about."

"Something about that fire the other day?"

"Yeah. We went over to show the fire inspector around."

"That part of butler duties?" she asked, swiping an arm over her forehead.

"I'm a one-man band. What can I say?"

"You still like it? Being a butler?"

"I do. When this gig ends, I'm thinking of going to butler school."

"When it ends?"

"One-year contract. It's up next summer and I don't know if it'll get renewed."

"Why wouldn't it?" she asked. "You stealing the silver?"

Roger laughed. "No. Nothing like that. Mr. Shackleford is old. His family is worried about him living in the house with just a butler."

She cast him a side-eyed glance. "Uh huh," she said. "Lemme guess. They've found a nice assisted living facility for him where he'll be much happier?"

Roger shrugged but didn't comment.

"It's more common than you think," Molly said. "I see it all the time."

"You never said where you work," Roger said.

"CNA at Bridge House."

The name meant nothing to Roger. He shook his head.

"Assisted living facility. West side, out past the industrial park," she said. "Not the most glamorous but it keeps me from feeling like a leech on society."

"You get many people there who don't want to be there?" Roger asked.

"I don't know if anybody wants to be there," she said. "Some need to be there. We can take care of them. Make sure they take care of themselves as much as possible. A few of them get pushed there, either by relatives or by conditions." She shook her head. "Getting old is not for the faint of heart."

"How do you know?" Roger asked. "Who needs to be there, I mean?"

She shook her head. "Some people just fade away before their bodies are ready to quit," she said. "That's what scares me the most. The ones who don't remember themselves. Some have real trouble with short-term memory. Don't remember they just had lunch ten minutes ago, let alone whether or not they took their medications in the morning. Some have physical issues with muscle control. The hardest cases are when they know what's going on and can't do anything about it. There's not a lot of dignity there."

The images she painted in Roger's head did not make him feel any better about Naomi's scheming.

"You have to dress him?" Molly asked. "Mr. Shackleford?"

"No. He's not going to be running any marathons but he's able to feed and dress himself. Showers by himself. Just had a physical and the doctor's given me some exercises to do with him for strength and balance."

"Are you doing them?" she asked. "That's actually huge."

"We haven't worked it into the daily routine yet," Roger said.

"Tai chi," she said.

"Really?" Roger asked.

"Yeah. Moving meditation. Wouldn't hurt you either." She grinned at him.

He snorted and glanced over at her. "You think I need more exercise?"

She shook her head. "Different muscles. It's kinda like yoga in that it's as much about thinking about moving as moving." She shook her head. "More like training yourself to move without thinking."

"Muscle memory," Roger said.

She nodded. "You probably trained that way in the army. Do it until you didn't have to think about it?"

Roger nodded.

"We have a couple of patients who can't pick their spouses out of a lineup but they get up every morning and do their tai chi in the rec center. Long forms. I don't know what they're called but they get out and do that same set of moves every day." She shook her head. "Their bodies are much stronger, better muscle tone. They both have better balance than I do." She laughed. "I should learn myself, I guess."

"You do yoga? Meditate?" Roger asked.

"I used to do yoga. Fell out of the practice when I started working at the Bridge." She shrugged and shook her head. "Hard to work it in when you're working shifts."

"You manage to make it out here often enough," Roger said.

"Timing is right. Doesn't matter what shift I'm on, I can usually get this time slot. At least for now. We're coming up on the quarterly schedule shift and I'll be just getting home about this time for three months."

"You shift every quarter? Not every month?"

"Yeah. Company policy. They say it helps if the patients see the same people for longer periods of time, so we don't rotate every few days like some facilities." She shrugged. "It is what it is."

Roger nodded, rolling the ideas around in his head. The open expanse of the ballroom suggested itself as a likely location for some better workouts.

"Is he fading?" she asked, her voice low—barely louder than their footsteps on the trail or the birds waking in the bushes around them.

Roger started to answer but his inner guardian shut him down. "I'm not at liberty to say."

"For some people, it's really a good choice," she said. "Assisted living. Even those with pushy relatives. I suspect it's the hardest on those closest. Trying to make that kind of decision for somebody else? I think the only harder one might be whether or not to discontinue life support."

Roger shook the memories of broken bodies from his mind, or tried to. "Yeah. That's a tough one." He swallowed hard. "Tai chi?" he asked, his desperate mind scrambling for some other topic.

"There are some studios here in the city," she said. "Google can find them for you." She grinned.

He nodded. "Any good exercises for dementia?"

She shrugged. "Textbooks say 'keep the mind active by learning new things,' which is well and good but finding something new to learn? I don't know."

"Why's that?" he asked.

"Well, think about it. You go to school in the beginning because you have to, right? You're a kid. No agency. No say in what or where. Just 'go there and get good grades.'"

"Yeah," Roger said.

"Later you have to go to get certified so you can get a job." She shrugged. "There's a certain amount of agency involved, but for people without the financial resources, it becomes impossible to get ahead of it. Even for some with limited resources."

"I never went beyond high school," Roger said. "Army got me as soon as I graduated."

"You got your EMT certification, though, right? Didn't you tell me that?"

Roger nodded. "After the army training, it wasn't that hard."

"Didn't you have to take some classes, though?"

"Yeah."

She shrugged. "But you wanted to take them. You had a reason for those particular classes? You're thinking of butler school?"

"Well, probably I'd need to do some preliminary work. Apparently they like their students to have a background in hospitality management."

She gave him a look. "You've done your homework."

He shrugged.

"Point being most people have reasons for learning something aside from 'I should learn something to keep my brain active.' They're either going because they don't have the agency to say no, or they're trying to achieve some end."

"I can see that," Roger said.

"So if I told you, 'Go learn something. Anything. It doesn't matter what,' what would you do?"

Roger shook his head. "I don't know."

"Nothing," she said. "You might look around for something you always wanted to know, but without a use for that knowledge, without engaging your mind in it, it's useless. It's not exercising the parts of the brain that it needs to, to get the benefit. People just give up when it doesn't keep their attention, or doesn't seem as interesting as it might have been."

Roger nodded. "I could see that. Suggestions?"

"Hobbies are good. Learn a skill that you can apply. Something that doesn't require you to do something you can't actually do. A lot of our patients take up art. Sketching, painting. There's enough technique to learn that it keeps them mentally limber, but the physical requirements are generally within reach. A surprising number of people like bird watching but by the time they get to assisted living, they have trouble getting out into the places where they're likely to see birds." She shrugged. "We have a small group of birders. Some of them need wheelchairs to get around, but we organize field trips to accessible parks. Nothing too far away but at least they can get out. That little extra stimulation seems to help."

"Change of scenery," Roger said.

"Yeah," she said, pulling up to start the cool-down walk back to the gate. "You worried about him?"

Roger sighed and thought about it. "Yes," he said. "He's a crusty old guy. I kinda like him."

She nodded. "It's hard not to get attached, but nobody gets out alive." She offered him a sad smile.

Roger left her at her gate and headed for his shower. He knew Shackleford studied that one book for clues about the necklace and wondered if it was enough. The guy might be a wizard, but his body was human. Roger didn't think you could reverse dementia. Shackleford's magical mental state didn't seem to follow the rules. He pulled the morning paper from its slot and plucked the day's flower—a delicate, white petaled blossom with a tiny green center and golden stamens.

Molly had given him a lot to think about. He pulled out his notebook to make some notes while he cooked breakfast—some oatmeal with fruit. Magical or not, when it came to the court hearing—and Roger felt confident that it would, eventually—being able to prove the old man had been looking out for his brain could only help his case.

Roger added the old man's exercises to the morning routine.

"I don't see why I need to do this," Shackleford said.

"Doctor's orders, sir. It will only take a few minutes and, who knows, it might make you feel better."

"I don't feel bad now."

"Come on, sir. I'll do them with you." Roger stood behind one of the solid wooden chairs and placed a hand on the back for balance. He waited until Shackleford put his book down and stood with him at the next chair. Roger led him through a series of lifts and stretches ending with some squats. After the last set, Shackleford flopped into his favorite chair and picked up a book while Roger poured him a glass of water from the waiting pitcher. "Hydrate, sir."

Shackleford took the glass with a poisonous glance at Roger. "Do I strike you as the kind of person that hydrates, Mulligan?"

"You strike me as the kind of person who might live to a hundred and twenty if he'd just pay as much attention to his body as his mind, sir."

Shackleford tilted the glass back and swigged it down, handing it empty back to Roger. "I'm not going to have a mind much longer and that niece is going to have the house, unless I can find a way around the damned amulet."

"These exercises will help, sir. Improved blood flow, better strength."

Shackleford scowled and took up his book again. "I'm humoring you, Perkins. Don't push it."

"Of course, sir." Roger took the used breakfast tray back to the kitchen. He'd been tracking the old man's mental state against the phases of the moon. There definitely seemed to be a correlation. The closer they were to new moon, the fewer mental slips, while the full moon could be something else altogether. At the worst, Shackleford had periods of perfect lucidity interspersed with absolute confusion about basic things like his own name.

Roger sighed and focused on his duties. Shackleford House may have its pixies and fairies, but it still needed him to manage the more mundane moving parts like laundry, cooking, and keeping track of Shackleford's schedule of medications and exercise.

A wet and rainy fall rolled into early winter with a snow storm in November that put an end to outdoor exercise for Roger for a few days until the city cleared the snow and ice from the streets and sidewalks. He still found it uncanny that snow didn't build up on the sidewalks and drive of Shackleford House. He watched the snow falling from the back door but it melted as soon as it hit the tarmac, leaving the surface wet but never frozen, never snow-covered even as the white stuff piled up on the grass and gardens. If he hadn't been convinced by then, the snow would have provided the final argument.

The gray weather continued through Thanksgiving, leaving Roger feeling cooped up and jumpy, even after Shackleford sent him off to have turkey dinner with his folks.

"Are you sure, sir?" Roger asked.

"Go, Mulligan. I've never been one for these holidays. Once you get to be my age, they turn into maudlin affairs as you remember all the people who've passed away." He shrugged. "Go. Enjoy your family gathering."

Roger left a turkey dinner in the fridge for the old man—some sliced turkey, mashed potatoes, and a mound of peas and carrots alongside a pumpkin pie—trusting that he'd find it and feed himself. He took the Prius out to his parents' home, basking in the warmth of family in a way he hadn't for a very, very long time.

He helped clear the table and do the dishes with his mother while his father and sister retreated to the living room to fall asleep over a football game.

"You seem happy," his mother said, rinsing a plate and propping it in the drainer. "You found somebody?"

Roger chuckled and shook his head, running the dish towel around a water glass before placing it in the cupboard. "No, Mom. I like the job."

She grinned at him. "You seem to be adapting. Why is that?"

"I don't know what you mean," Roger said, although he knew that was a lie as soon as he said it.

"You've always been an adrenaline junkie. Army, then EMT. You never seemed happy unless you were out there on the edge." She rinsed and stacked another plate. "Scared me almost to death more than once."

Roger sighed and worked through the plates, drying them and putting them up into the cupboard. "Maybe I just got tired of it," he said.

"That's a big jump," she said. "War zone to pantry." She glanced at him. "You don't find it too tame?"

"Too boring, you mean?" he asked.

She chuckled. "I suppose I do."

"There's always something to learn," he said. "I'm trying to help the old guy with his physical and mental conditioning. Which means I need to learn about things that could help."

"Is he really out of it?" she asked.

"No, Mom. He's mostly there most of the time. He has spells where he's pretty confused but they've been few and far between."

She sighed and nodded. "But he's getting worse," she said.

"It's hard to tell," Roger said. "I don't know how much of it is him getting worse or me getting more attuned to it."

"You think he's going to go to the assisted living facility?" she asked.

"Maybe one day," he said. "I don't know if you can reverse that kind of thing."

"Well, they're doing a lot of research. Maybe they'll come up with some kind of magic bullet for it."

Roger fought the urge to laugh. "That's what I'm hoping, but anything I can do to help him slow down the memory loss—well, just seems like something I should do."

His mother finished the last of the dishes and wrung her dishcloth out before swabbing down the counter. "There's only so much you can do, Roger."

"I know, Mom. I know." He wiped the last dish and placed it in the correct cupboard. "But I feel better knowing I'm doing what I can."

She nodded and gave him a one-armed hug. "You're a good man, Rog. You make me proud." She looked up at him, her eyes suspiciously shiny.

He gave her a hug back. "Now, don't go getting all sappy on me."

"When do you have to get back?" she asked.

Roger glanced at the clock over the sink. "I don't have to be back at any given hour, but I hate thinking of him in that big house by himself."

"You still get days off, don't you?"

"Oh, yes. Every Saturday."

"Come to dinner?"

Roger shrugged. "Not this week but next? Sure."

"What are you doing this week?"

"Looking into gym memberships," he said. "I can't run outside through the winter."

"Why not?"

"Well, I could but I'd prefer not. It's dark in the morning to begin with and I don't really need to risk slipping and falling."

She nodded. "I can see that. Can you get away for that amount of time?"

Roger sighed. "I've been running for half an hour in the morning before he gets up, but you're right. I'll need to think about that."

She nodded again and gave him another hug. "Well, you go if you need to. It's just lovely having you home again. I've seen more of you in the last few months than the previous few years." She grinned at him. "Can't help it if I like it."

He hugged her back. "Thanks, Mom."

Roger circulated through the living room, giving everybody hugs and saying his good-byes. He drove away with a warm sense of fulfillment in his core but the uneasy feeling that he needed to be back at Shackleford House. He couldn't shake the feeling and didn't breathe easy until he'd parked the Prius and got back inside. He took his time putting on his uniform but checked in with Shackleford as soon as he was appropriately dressed.

He knocked on the library door and entered, finding Shackleford slumped over in his chair. Alarm bells went off in Roger's head and he crouched beside the old man's chair just as he snored loud enough to wake himself.

Roger stood while Shackleford blinked himself awake and straightened in his seat. "Good afternoon, sir."

Shackleford looked up and nodded. "Perkins. Good, you're back. I'm feeling a bit peckish. A cup of tea and some of those shortbread cookies?"

"Of course, sir. Anything else?"

"That'll do for now, Perkins." Shackleford picked up the book that lay open on his lap: the brown one again.

Roger bit his lip and nodded. "Very good, sir. I'll be just a moment."

"Thank you, Perkins."

Roger organized the tea and found the turkey dinner still wrapped in film in the fridge. He slipped it into the microwave and nuked it for a couple of minutes while he added a small plate of shortbread cookies to the tray. He pondered the significance of the brown leather-bound book. Whenever Shackleford went walkabout in his head, he picked up the brown book. Was it because the demon in the necklace made him take it? Or was it because something in his head recognized that the brown would be more useful even when his focus seemed to go elsewhere?

The tea timer and microwave dinged at about the same time, and he finished assembling the tray.

When he returned to the library, he placed the tray on the table in its usual spot. "Luncheon is served, sir. I thought you might enjoy a bit of turkey dinner today. It is Thanksgiving, after all."

Shackleford perked up and smiled. "Thank you, Perkins. That was thoughtful. It's Thanksgiving?"

"Yes, sir."

"Shouldn't you be with your family today?"

"Thank you, sir. I spent the morning with my family. We had a lovely meal together. I've just returned."

"Did you?" he asked. He shook his head and lifted the book. "I've been absorbed in this and didn't notice."

"I've noticed you reading that volume many times, sir. Is it interesting?" Roger held the chair in invitation for Shackleford, hoping to get him to the food before it got cold.

The old man took the hint and placed a ribbon in the book before placing it on the table beside his chair. "Fascinating, Perkins. Simply fascinating. It's an examination of certain myths—specifically creation myths—from the Mesoamerican people. Olmec forward, as it were. Simply fascinating." He crossed to his meal and took his seat. "So much we've lost, Perkins. So much."

"I see, sir." Roger spotted the green book on a chair across the room. "What about that one, sir? With the green cover."

Shackleford looked up from his meal, a bite of turkey on his fork. "Interesting enough work on cursed artifacts. Fascinating in its own way, but lacking in scope, depth." He shook his head and ate the turkey.

"Thank you, sir. Quite enlightening."

"Feel free to borrow them if you wish, Perkins. Anything in the library, for that matter. You know that."

"Yes, sir. I appreciate the offer, sir." He gave a small nod and left the library, closing the door behind him. He felt no clearer about why one book over the other seemed to gravitate to the old man's hands, but at least he seemed to have a reliable indicator of Shackleford's mental state. He had no idea about what to do with that knowledge, but it was a step.

Now if he could only figure out a way to get the necklace off the old man without killing him.

CHAPTER 14

The front doorbell drew Roger out of the laundry to find Amos
Featherstone on the stoop. "Good morning, Mr. Featherstone.
Please come in."

He nodded and stepped inside. "Is Mr. Shackleford available?"

"I'll check, sir. If you'd care to wait in the parlor?"

Featherstone made his way in and sat on the front edge of one
of the easy chairs. He rested his elbows on his knees and clasped his
hands together. His frown made Roger step a little more quickly
than normal.

At the library door, he knocked twice and opened the door.

Shackleford looked up from the brown covered book. "Yes, Mulligan?"

"Sorry to disturb you, sir. Mr. Featherstone would like to speak
with you. He's in the parlor."

"Show him up, please, Mulligan. And some coffee might be in
order."

"Of course, sir."

Roger returned to the parlor and collected the detective. "Mr.
Shackleford will see you, sir."

Featherstone nodded and followed him, a half step behind and
to one side. "How's he doing?"

"I'm not at liberty to discuss Mr. Shackleford's health, sir."

Featherstone snorted. "Like I don't know about that chunk of
metal on his chest, but I appreciate the discretion, Mulligan."

Roger stopped at the library door and gave him a nod. "Thank
you for your understanding, sir." He tapped the door and opened
it, ushering him in. "Mr. Featherstone, sir."

"Amos, good to see you." Shackleford rose and crossed to meet
Amos, grasping his hand in a firm shake. "Come in. Would you
like a coffee? Tea?"

Featherstone nodded. "Coffee would be appreciated. Thank you."

Shackleford raised an eyebrow at Roger.

"Of course, sir," Roger said.

He missed the opening statements but returned shortly with coffee and a collection of finger pastries, placing the tray on the low table between the two men. Featherstone leaned forward, elbows on his knees, while Shackleford sat back, hands on the arms of the chair. Both men wore frowns and neither of them spoke as Roger entered.

"Will there be anything else, sir?"

Shackleford raised a hand. "Stay for a moment, if you would, Mulligan. I'd like your opinion."

"Of course, sir."

"Tell him, Amos."

"It's this Griffin woman," Featherstone said. "I know he's got his heart set on finding a relative to leave this place to." He nodded at Shackleford. "But this woman has a reputation of being something of a charlatan."

Roger nodded. "I'm not surprised, given that website, sir. Is there a problem?"

Both men blinked up at him. "Care to explain that, Mulligan?" Shackleford asked.

"Well, sir, there are two ways to hide. One is to stay out of sight. Keep a low profile and lock the secret away behind doors. That's been your approach, I believe, sir."

Shackleford nodded and glanced at Featherstone, who shrugged in return.

"The other way is to hide in plain sight. Make the secret unbelievable and put it on display. If she has some mechanism for generating revenue through her less mundane skills, she'd need a way to account for that money without attracting the attention of the authorities, wouldn't she?"

Shackleford frowned but Featherstone's face went blank.

"What's her financial status, Amos?"

Featherstone bit his lip. "Comfortable. I couldn't get into her tax records but she doesn't appear to be hurting or living above her means. Has a leased walk-up in the trendier part of town. Pays her bills on time. Clean credit record with a score above 800."

"Marital status?" Shackleford asked.

"Divorced. Was married for a couple of years in her early twenties. No kids. Parents both alive, but her grandparents are all gone. Only sibling—a brother—died in a car accident when she was in her late teens. Drunk driver crossed the median."

Shackleford winced and looked at Roger. "So you're saying she's using this spiritualist thing as a front?"

"That would be my guess, sir. If she's getting cash somehow, having a business where the clientele pays in cash makes it easy for her to claim a few extra clients each day to account for the income."

"You're talking about money laundering," Featherstone said.

"Yes, sir."

"Is she dealing drugs, Amos?" Shackleford asked.

Featherstone frowned. "I didn't see any indication of it, but then, if she's any good, I probably wouldn't see it, would I? What makes you ask?"

"I'm trying to think of ways she might use her skills to generate revenues."

"What? Alchemy? Turning grass into grass?" Featherstone asked, a grin playing on his lips.

"Aspirin into acid?" Shackleford tossed back.

Featherstone frowned. "You think this is possible."

"I do," Shackleford said. "Having a business where people walk in and out all day?" He looked at Roger. "Mulligan?"

Roger nodded. "Yes, sir. It would make a good cover."

"You know a lot about money laundering?" Featherstone asked.

"Afghanistan, sir. Millions of dollars floating through an underworld that lived on black market drugs and weapons."

Featherstone nodded and sighed before looking at Shackleford. "How do you want to proceed, Joe?"

"I think it's time for me to visit Ms. Griffin."

"And do what?" Featherstone asked.

"I'm thinking I make an appointment for a reading and see if I can get one of my own."

Featherstone grimaced. "Is that wise?"

Shackleford shook his head. "Probably not. If she's got any amount of talent, she'll see through me immediately."

"Then what?" Featherstone asked.

"Well, at least we'll know."

"So will she," Featherstone said.

"Yes," Shackleford said and smiled. "And that might be a good thing."

Featherstone took a hefty belt of coffee and grimaced. "What are you thinking?"

"What is it? About three hours to get down there by car?" the old man asked.

"About that. Depends on rush hour."

Shackleford nodded. "Mulligan, book us a room for a couple of days. Something nice but not ostentatious." He looked at Featherstone. "We'll drive down, spend the night, get an appointment to see her, and take it from there. Any objections?"

"You're laying your cards on the table," Featherstone said. "Are you being a bit premature?"

Shackleford shrugged. "I'm too old, Amos. I'm right on the edge of 'too late' and don't want to take that chance."

"You're the boss. Anything you want me to do in the meantime?"

"Look up the ex," Shackleford said. "See if he has any leverage on her."

Featherstone nodded. "You're thinking you need to protect her from him if she comes into any amount of—say—inheritance?"

"Precisely."

Featherstone nodded. "I'll look into the parents, too. Never know."

"Probably wise," Shackleford said.

"When would you like to go, sir?" Roger asked.

"No time like the present." Shackleford looked at Featherstone. "How much time do you need?"

"I'll head back down today. A couple of days should do it." He took a sip of coffee and frowned. "Might want to book an appointment and then arrange the hotel around it."

Shackleford's eyebrows rose. "Is she that popular? I thought you said she was a charlatan."

"I said she had the reputation. For all I know, that's her talent and all the bad-mouthing is sour grapes."

Shackleford snorted. "Fair enough."

"You should still get an appointment. Sometime midweek next week, maybe," Featherstone said. "That'll give me time to sniff out the ex and take a look at the parents. Neither of them set off any alarm bells at first blush, but I wasn't focused on either of them."

"I'll take care of that, sir," Roger said.

"Thank you, Mulligan."

"Will there be anything else, sir?"

Shackleford shook his head. "Can you stay and visit, Amos?"

Featherstone leaned back in his chair, cradling his cup in his hands. "I've got some time."

"Carry on, Mulligan. I'll ring you if we need something."

Roger nodded and left them starting what sounded like a long-standing discussion about geopolitics.

Roger used his laptop and a throwaway spam address to book an appointment with Madam Dionysia for the following week. The number of booked time-slots surprised him a little, but midday, midweek offered the widest choices. He scrolled through the schedule, noting that the weekends were booked out for a couple of weeks. He wondered if that was because she didn't work weekends or if the most people had time off then. The form only accepted times from 10 a.m. to 7 p.m., in any case. It only asked for a name, phone number, and a question for Madam Dionysia. He pressed the submit button and was mildly surprised that she didn't ask for a credit card number.

A few minutes later his cell phone buzzed to let him know he had an incoming text. He opened it to read "Your appointment has been confirmed."

She seemed to know her business in the networked age.

He switched over to a hotel booking site and arranged for a two-night stay in one of their midrange suites. The price made him second guess Shackleford's instructions, but discovered that the cost of two separate rooms, even allowing for one economy and one high-end, wasn't that much different from the suite. His middle-class roots died hard, apparently. Shackleford called the price of the Mercedes "petty cash." Given the location of the house and the taxes he paid on it, Roger could accept that stance intellectually, but the numbers still made him swallow hard every time he thought about them. Saving money by scrimping on two nights in a hotel, even a hotel that charged four hundred a night, wouldn't make that much difference in the rarefied economic atmosphere that Shackleford House enjoyed.

He shook his head, used the house credit card, and booked the suite for the dates around the appointment.

He sat back and considered what Barbara Griffin—Madam Dionysia—might do when Shackleford walked into the room.

Featherstone met them at the hotel for dinner before the big day. Shackleford weathered the trip without difficulty. The Mercedes practically drove itself down the long, boring stretch of interstate. Once they'd been seated and the server took their orders, Featherstone leaned over the table. "The ex might be a problem."

"How so?" Shackleford said, settling his napkin on his lap after a quick shake.

"A bit of a boozer and a regular at the local marijuana dispensary. Employed as an account rep for a local boiler room. They're not high-paying positions, usually. They get a minimum plus bonuses for closing sales."

"Robo-calls?" Roger asked.

"Probably robo-dialed but yeah. Spam callers."

"They still use people for those?"

"Some do."

Shackleford looked back and forth between them. "Robo-calls?"

"Automated sales calls, generally sketchy," Featherstone said. "Fund raisers, credit card scams. During the political season, they're heavily used as supposed surveys but they're really usually hit pieces against the campaign's opponents, intended to put out un-flattering messaging with a veneer of 'does that change your mind?' questions layered on top."

Shackleford pursed his lips. "So, he's a problem?"

"Potentially. The decree doesn't list any support payments in either direction. When they broke up, neither of them had a pot to piss in so there wasn't much to fight over. Even so, it wasn't exactly amicable."

"How not amicable was it?" Shackleford asked.

"He cheated. She found out and kicked him to the curb. He wasn't happy with it. She was his meal ticket in a dead-end job in retail at the time."

Shackleford nodded and they paused the conversation while the server brought salads and drinks. When he'd moved on, Shackleford asked, "Parents?"

"Downsized nest in the burbs. She's a paralegal, twenty-plus years in the same small partnership. He's a couple years from re-tirement. High-school administrator."

"Anything to be concerned about?" Shackleford asked. "Does the mother have any talents?"

Featherstone shrugged. "Nothing that stands out to me. You might have a different perspective." He raised his eyebrows in a silent question.

"I'd have to see her," Shackleford said. "Where is this small partnership?"

"Strip-mall office halfway between here and there. Two old gals who'll probably retire when the mother's ready to hang it up. Wills, some small contract work, a minor amount of ambulance chasing. They handled Barbara's divorce for her. Basic retail lawyering, from what I've been able to put together."

"They close as a family? The Griffins?" Shackleford asked.

"Not sure," Featherstone said. "I don't have phone records on any of them and didn't have eyes on them during Thanksgiving." He shrugged. "I have no idea if they know she's a spiritualist."

Shackleford nodded. "Well, let's take it one step at a time. We'll go visit Barbara tomorrow morning. See where that gets us."

"You want me along?" Featherstone asked.

"If you don't mind waiting in the car, it might be useful to have you handy," Shackleford said. "Maybe we could swing by that law office and take a look at her mother."

Featherstone nodded. "We could do that."

The server returned with their meals, so they put business aside to enjoy the food.

Roger found a place to park the Mercedes a couple of doors down from Madam Dionysia's place, on a side street just off the main retail district. He went around to let Shackleford out of the vehicle; Featherstone stayed in the car.

"We'll be back shortly," Shackleford said.

"Take your time, Joe. You're paying me by the hour." He grinned and toasted them with his cup of carry-out coffee.

"Don't spill that on the upholstery." Shackleford grinned back.

They walked the short distance to her door, the aroma of bread and pastry wafting on the breeze from the bakery on the first floor. Roger pressed the button and waited. The lock clicked and buzzed, so he pulled it open and held it for Shackleford. "Do you want me to come up, sir?"

Shackleford shook his head, but stopped. "Actually, yes, please, Mulligan. It might be best."

"Very good, sir." He followed Shackleford's slow progress up the narrow stairs, at the ready in case the old man stumbled. It wasn't that Shackleford was frail so much as that Roger didn't want to take a chance with an eighty-something-year-old man on narrow steps.

At the top of the stairs on a simple landing was a plain wooden door. It clicked and swung open before Roger could knock. "Come in, gentlemen." A woman's alto voice came from the room beyond. Roger held the door open for his employer.

The morning sunlight through lacy sheers illuminated the room with a warm yellow glow. Barbara Griffin—or rather, Madam Dionysia—sat on a peacock chair of rattan, the flowing skirt of her sand-colored caftan draped around her legs. Her black hair crowned her in an artful coif corralled by a tiara of green stones that set off her eyes. She wore dangling earrings and a necklace of the same green stones. "This is unexpected," she said, tilting her head to look at Shackleford.

Shackleford gave her a small nod. "Good morning, Barbara."

She waved a hand at a pair of comfy looking chairs. "Have a seat, gentlemen. I'll forego the incense and theatrics." She looked at Roger. "You must be Roger Mulligan."

Roger left the nearer chair for Shackleford and sat beside him. "Yes, ma'am."

She nodded and turned her gaze to Shackleford. "And you must be the Joseph Shackleford he made the reservation for."

"I am," Shackleford said.

She pursed her lips and nodded, sitting back against the rattan— one elbow on the armrest, her hand raised in a languid pose, fingers flexing in an almost hypnotic rhythm. "What is it you want, Mr. Shackleford?"

"I want to know more about you," he said. "And your talent."

"I bet you do." Her gaze flicked to Roger and back to Shackleford.

Shackleford said, "You can speak freely." He settled himself in his chair and laced his fingers together on his chest.

"You already know more about me than I'm comfortable with, Mr. Shackleford. Who are you and why do you want to know?"

"Aren't you supposed to be the psychic?" Shackleford asked, his amusement evident on his lips and raised eyebrows.

"I am, yes," she said. "I can't read you. At all." Her forehead wrinkled in a frown. She looked at Roger and gave a short nod. "Mr. Mulligan, I can read." She gave him a tiny shrug, almost an apology along with a small smile, a quick flicker at the corners of her lips. "Thank you for your service."

Roger hated that phrase but smiled and nodded.

She looked back at Shackleford. "He thinks you're here to make me rich, Mr. Shackleford."

"I'm here because of your family tree." He glanced at Roger. "Check with him."

She looked at Roger again. "May I?"

"Yes, ma'am."

She stared at him a moment before the languid finger motions froze. "We're related?"

"We are," Shackleford said.

She frowned and shook her head. "I knew I shouldn't have turned in that swab."

"Why did you?" Shackleford asked.

"Gift from my mother. She's into the whole genealogy thing. Gave me a kit for my birthday and made me swipe it right there at the table." She shook her head and flicked her fingers as if waving at a pesky fly. "So? What do you want?"

"I want you to save my house," Shackleford said, his smile adding depths to the wrinkles on his face.

"From what?" she asked.

"A money-grubbing niece who wants to get me declared incompetent, challenge my will, and take control of Shackleford House so she can raze it and fill the lot with condos."

Her eyes widened, lifting her perfectly arched eyebrows halfway to her hairline. She glanced at Roger. "Again?" she asked.

"Of course," he said, only slightly nervous about what she might find while rummaging around in his head.

She gave him a nod and a smile. "I'll be gentle." She stared through him, her gaze in his direction but focused somewhere else, as her hand resumed its languid flexing. Eventually she looked away, but Roger wasn't sure how long that time had been. A second? A minute? Half an hour? He blinked several times, feeling as if he'd just woken up. Barbara blew out a deep breath. "Holy shit," she said. "Thank you, Mr. Mulligan."

Roger shrugged, not exactly sure what the correct protocol was for volunteering to have his brain rifled.

She looked at Shackleford. "Okay, I know what he thinks. You don't need me to save the house. You've got your foundation lined up to take over the place. What's your pitch?"

"First, while the foundation would take over the estate on my passing, I'm concerned that my niece would successfully challenge the will in probate and have it overturned in her favor as my only living relative."

"So, now you're looking to this cadet branch of the Shackleford clan to fill out your own family tree? You had to go back to the old country to find relatives?"

"Living ones, yes," Shackleford said. "More specifically, living ones with talent. How long have you known?"

Griffin shrugged. "Since I was eighteen. It made for an interesting college experience."

"Your parents?"

She shook her head. "Mother has some hint, just judging from the look of her. I don't think she knows. I can't read her, but my father's an open book." She grimaced. "Some things a daughter just shouldn't know."

"Do you know anybody else with talent?" Shackleford asked.

She shook her head again. "Every once in a while I'll see a face in a crowd that I think might have talent, but no. Nobody I know."

"I've never met anybody with your skill," Shackleford said. "Mine tends more toward physical manifestation."

"I have some of that, too," she said. "That trick with the door. Very useful for locking my dorm room when I didn't want to be disturbed."

Shackleford lifted a hand. "Can you do fire?" He snapped his fingers and a candle's worth of flame appeared over his thumb.

Roger swallowed, discovering the difference between believing Shackleford was a mage and seeing his magic on display.

Griffin glanced at him and winked, before snapping her own fingers to show a green-tinged flame over her own thumb. "Handy for lighting joints," she said.

They both folded their thumbs down, extinguishing their fires.

"But you can't read other talents," Shackleford said.

"Well, my pool is pretty limited. The only other one I know is my mother." She shrugged. "Now you."

"So how invested are you in this?" Shackleford asked, waving a hand at the room. "I suspect you do a good business."

"It's seasonal," she said. "I have a few regulars who cover my bills, but the tail end of winter is my best season."

"Really?" Shackleford said, tilting his head as if trying to roll an idea into place. "Any idea why?"

"I think it's a seasonal effect, to be honest," she said. "Most of them are looking for something to alleviate their inner darkness, although that's not how they see themselves. Some variation on cabin fever."

"Fascinating. So you probably haven't come across many instructional works."

"Instructional works?" she asked. "What? For talent? Is that what you're calling it?"

"Talent. Magic. Affinity." Shackleford shrugged. "Talent seems to be a common term."

Her eyes widened just a fraction. "You know others?"

"Oh, yes. Several dozen. There's an annual gala around the spring equinox."

She blinked, her eyes closing and staying closed for a moment before opening again. "A gala?"

"Well, it's low key. Not something one can advertise."

She laughed. "I suspect not."

"So, you didn't answer my question," Shackleford said. "How invested are you here?"

"Why?" she asked.

"I would like to have you come stay with us at Shackleford House."

Her eyes hardened around the corners. "And do what? Exactly."

"Well, you might help with my research, but mostly I'd like to have you in situ, as it were, so that you're not a lost relation coming out of the woodwork when I die."

She frowned. "Your research?"

He nodded. "I'm trying to find a way to get rid of a cursed object. So far no luck."

"Cursed object?" she asked, her face taking on an 'are you kidding me?' frown.

"For lack of a better term. Yes."

She stared at him hard for a few moments. "You're serious."

"Oh, yes. Very." Shackleford shrugged. "Youthful exuberance and false sense of immortality. It's been useful but now the bill has come due."

"And you want to try to beat it?"

"That's my thinking, yes. I don't know if it's possible," he said. "And honestly, if you're not interested, that's fine. I'm mostly interested in finding somebody who can care for Shackleford House and carry on the tradition."

"Tradition?"

"Pixies," Roger said.

They both looked at him.

He shrugged and looked back at Shackleford. "Somebody with talent needs to take over the house to look out for the pixies and fairies, don't they? Otherwise it's just going to be the foundation and they're not going to know what to do."

"Wait," Griffin said. "Honest-to-God pixies?"

Roger shrugged. "That's what he calls them. They deal with the house and the fairies do the yard work."

She stared at Shackleford. "Pixies?"

Shackleford shrugged. "Sprites. There are two tribes. I call them pixies and fairies. They don't object."

"How do you know this?" she asked, looking at Roger. "You don't appear to have any talent." She closed her eyes and put a hand up. "That didn't come out right."

"I understand," he said, a chuckle bubbling up from his chest. "I'm as mundane as they come. I have no idea. Mr. Shackleford suggested that the pixies didn't like my cleaning and how to get them back on my side. I did it. I may not be able to see them, but I know when there's dust. As long as they're happy, there's no dust, the floors stay polished, and the windows clean." He shrugged. "I still have to polish the silver and do the laundry. Seems a fair trade to me."

She lowered her hands and folded them together in her lap. She pulled a deep breath in through her nose, letting it out the same way. She frowned at Roger for a moment and then looked at Shackleford.

"So? What are you proposing? You going to adopt me?"

Shackleford laughed. "You're a little old for that and I suspect your parents might have something to say about it."

"Then what?" she asked.

"It's just what I said. I'd like you to come to Shackleford House and live. I want you to be a known presence when my niece visits. I'd like to recognize you as a relative and offer you the house and a position in the Shackleford Historical Preservation Foundation."

"You're going to just keep me in the manner to which I'd like to become accustomed?" she asked, with a wry smile. "Simply out of the goodness of your heart?"

He smiled. "Oh, I have very selfish motivations. First, it's not going to be easy for you to stand up to Naomi Patching. Once she learns of your presence in the house as the heir apparent, she'll do everything she can to dislodge you. We should probably have a conversation with your parents about your genealogy."

"No worries on that score. Mum has already tracked us back to the 1300s in Europe. No mean feat given the state of record-keeping. I'm sure she'd know who you are just by the name."

"Do they know about your talent?" Shackleford asked.

"I never really hide it, but I don't wear it on my sleeve. Seemed too risky."

He nodded. "It is. These days you probably don't have to worry about being a witch as much but being crazy? Yes. People will think you're crazy. Dementia, in my case."

"Are you?"

He shrugged. "I have good days and bad days. This is a good day. So far."

"It's the cursed artifact, isn't it," she said. It wasn't a question.

"At least in part. My doctor says I'm not suffering from any of the normal dementia symptoms. Apparently mine are unique ."

She nodded.

"You don't have to make a decision right now," Shackleford said. "Think about it. If you'd like to come to visit, we can put you up in a hotel so you can check out the place on your own terms."

"You realize this is nightmare territory, right?" she asked. "Single woman moving into a house with two strange men?"

Shackleford's eyes widened but Roger spoke. "I understand it," he said. "Read me."

She looked back and forth between the two and lifted her hand again, staring into Roger's eyes.

He swallowed hard and brought back the scenes he tried most to forget, letting them play for her, showing her his disgust.

After a moment she closed her eyes and clenched her raised hand
into a fist. After a moment she lowered her hand to her lap again
and opened her eyes. "It's a lot to think about."

Shackleford nodded. "I understand."

"You hardly know me. What makes you think I'll keep the place
after I get it?"

"Well, technically, the Foundation will own the building, unless
my niece manages to break the will. You may decide to bag it
all, take whatever money you can, and go off on a round-the-world
tour." Shackleford shrugged. "To be fair, you could do that any
time you wanted without sacking the treasury to do it."

She frowned and stared at Shackleford. "You're basically wanting me to be a pixie-sitter?"

He shook his head. "No, Ms. Griffin. I'm hoping that you'll see
the potential in being the Shackleford-in-residence. The house is
special. Its roots run deep into the land. You'll find resources there
you won't find anywhere else. You have talent. I can introduce you
to a cadre of people who can help you do more than you imagine."

"I can imagine a lot," she said. "You're sounding like this is
going to be the studio production of My Fair Wizard."

He laughed and nodded. "I'm sorry. That's true. I suppose I
am." He shook his head. "Just come up to visit. You have Mulligan's number. Arrange at least a few days. Perhaps a week. You
don't have to stay in the house. I would prefer you not do anything
you feel would be dangerous."

"If I might suggest, sir?" Roger said.

Shackleford looked at him and nodded.

"Perhaps a guide who's not us?"

The old man frowned. "Who are you thinking? Pettigrew?"

"No. Ms. Necket."

"Fidelia?" Shackleford's eyebrows shot up as his eyes opened
wide. "Of course."

Griffin snapped her fingers. "Gentlemen?"

Shackleford nodded. "Pardon us, Ms. Griffin. One of my oldest
and dearest friends is Fidelia Necket. She's talented. Very connected in the community. Even if you decide to pass on Shackleford
House, knowing her means you'll be tapped into the wider network
of talented people."

"Worldwide wizards," Roger said. "Ms. Necket is an amazing
woman. I've only met her once but I think you'd like her."

"What's it to you?" Griffin asked, looking at Roger. "Job security?"

Roger sighed and looked down at his hands. "My contract ends
soon. I don't know what I'll do after that."

She blinked. "You're not part of the deal?"

"I'm employed by Ms. Patching at the moment."

"He's being defeatist," Shackleford said. "I've offered to buy out his contract, but his deal is good and I have no qualms about letting my niece spend her treasure on a war I intend to win. I'll offer him a job as soon as his current contract pays off." He glanced at Roger. "I don't know if he'll take it, but I'll offer."

Griffin kept her hands folded in her lap and tilted her head to one side. "What would you do instead?"

He shrugged. "I'm looking into butler school."

She blinked. "Butler school?"

"Yes," he said. "Finishing schools for butlers. I think I'd need to get an undergrad in hospitality management first, but after ..." He paused. "After everything else I've done, I'm finding the job at Shackleford House to be rather satisfying."

Shackleford looked at him. "You might find it to be quite different with a larger household. You only have to look after me now."

Roger shrugged. "A larger household means a larger staff. A cook. At least one footman. Possibly doubling as chauffeur or valet."

Shackleford turned in his chair and stared at Roger. "You've given this a lot of thought."

Roger shrugged again. "I like having options and I'd just as soon avoid the adrenaline-driven ones."

"How do I contact this Ms. Necket?" Griffin asked.

"Let me touch base with her and see if she's willing to do it first," Shackleford said. "She's probably hip deep in the Fête d'Étoile right now."

"What's that?" she asked.

"Annual ball for the rich and talented," Shackleford said. "She's the chairman of the organizing committee this year." He glanced at Roger. "She hasn't contacted you yet, has she?"

"Me, sir? No. Why would she?"

"She's notorious for borrowing staff," Shackleford said.

"Would that be a problem, sir?"

"Just let me know if it happens."

"Of course, sir."

"This is sounding more and more like My Fair Wizard," Griffin said, her lips pursed. "It's not helping your case."

Shackleford nodded. "I understand. Tell you what. Can I hire you?"

"Hire me?" she asked. "You're already hiring me and your time is almost up." She glanced at an ornate clock on the wall above the door.

"Fair enough. How much would it take for me to hire your services for a week?"

"A week?"

He nodded.

"You know my rate," she said. "Or he does." She nodded at Roger.

"A hundred dollars an hour," Roger said.

She nodded.

"So, twenty-four hours a day, seven days. What's that?"

Roger did the math in his head. "A hundred and sixty-eight, sir."

Shackleford nodded. "So, at a hundred an hour that's seventeen thousand in round numbers?"

"Yes, sir."

He nodded again. "Very well. Ms. Griffin, I'd like to hire you for a one-week exclusive engagement in the city. I'll double your rate and pay you thirty-five thousand for the week plus expenses."

"How much?" she asked. Her eyebrows nearly reached her hairline.

"Thirty-five thousand. I'll even give you half up front, if you like. Half at the end of the week."

She sat back in her chair and laughed. "This just gets weirder and weirder. What do I need to do for this money?"

"Come to visit Shackleford House for at least an hour each of the seven days. Meet Fidelia Necket."

"Just meet her? I don't have to do anything with her?"

"Or with us, if you don't want to. I just want you to come see what it might be like if you owned Shackleford House. As a bonus, meeting Fidelia would widen your contacts in the talented world."

"She sounds too rich for my blood."

"If she is, you never have to see her again," Shackleford said.

Griffin frowned, looking first at Shackleford and then at Roger. "In writing."

"In writing," Shackleford repeated.

"Do you have a wingman?" Roger asked.

She blinked at him. "A wingman?"

He nodded. "Somebody you trust? A friend you hang out with? Somebody to watch your back?"

"Nobody who knows my talent," she said.

"Anybody you'd trust to tell?"

"Your mother?" Shackleford asked.

Her eyes widened at that suggestion. "What? No way." She shook her head.

"Anybody?" Roger asked.

"You're thinking I should bring my own witness?" she asked.

Roger lifted one shoulder in a shrug. "Somebody who knows you and knows what you're doing enough to help you escape if you feel like you need to." He paused. "You don't have many friends, I take it?"

She glared at him. "That's a little personal, isn't it?"

He shrugged. "I'm not judging. I'm with you. It's hard for me to make new ones after—you know."

She frowned, the glare not relaxing one iota. "You thinking you'll be my friend?"

"No, ma'am. I might be your butler, depending on circumstances, but that's as far as I go."

The frown relaxed a bit and the glare receded. "I don't have a wingman, no."

"What can we do to make you feel safer in this?" Shackleford asked.

"Contract, in writing. Half up front. Half at the end of the week. No shenanigans. You pay my expenses—food, hotel, clothing, everything I buy while I'm there." She settled back in her chair, a half smile on her lips.

"No," Shackleford said.

"No?" Her eyebrows went up again.

"That's a blank check I'm not writing," Shackleford said. "You could buy a house. You could buy a hotel." He shook his head.

"You can't afford it?" Her voice held a hint of challenge.

He shrugged. "Depends on the hotel, but they're a bad investment."

She blinked.

"Food, lodging—up to a thousand dollars a night—and a clothing budget," Shackleford said.

She blinked again. "Wait. Would I need a clothing budget?"

Shackleford shrugged. "Possibly. Knowing Fidelia, she's going to want to introduce you around." He shrugged. "Seven, five, add food. Round it up to fifteen thousand in expenses plus the thirty-eight thousand for your services? I'll need receipts for the expenses."

She stared at him for a long moment. "Make it seven thousand a day for seven days. No receipts. Same amount but I get to keep it all without screwing around with paperwork."

"Five thousand a day," Shackleford said.

"Six," she said.

He grinned. "Seven it is."

Her face blanked for a moment. "What?"

He shrugged. "I just wanted to see what you'd say. Forty-nine thousand for seven days of your time, Ms. Griffin. Half up front, half on completion. You'll make your own travel arrangements and pay your own expenses."

"In writing," she said.

"Do you have some paper?" the old man asked.

"You're serious," she said.

He nodded, a happy smile on his lips and a light dancing in his eyes. "Very much so."

She stared at him, her eyes narrowing, for several long moments before standing up and going through a door into the next room. She returned with a half dozen sheets of plain white paper and handed them to Shackleford. "Will this do?"

He nodded and stared at the top page for a moment before swiping his hand down its length. An elegant embossed, colored Shackleford House letterhead, complete with address and phone number, appeared at the top followed by a simple three-paragraph contract. At the bottom, signature lines with room for a notary block. He handed it to her.

She took the document in a hand that trembled just a bit. She read it and nodded. "I'll want this checked by a lawyer."

"I would expect nothing less," he said. "Would you like to do that now?"

"What? Today?" she asked.

He shrugged. "Do you have another appointment?"

She glanced at the clock. "Yes, actually, but my afternoon is clear."

"We can wait. I suspect you'll want your mother's attorneys to vet it? Or do you have your own?"

"You know where she works?" Her frown came back hard and fast, almost a scowl.

Shackleford shrugged. "Yes. And your father. I found you through your genealogy, remember? I wanted to find out more about you before I came down here." He shrugged again.

"And you're happy having this contract go through that firm?"

"Lawyer-client privilege," he said. "They're bound by it. I'm a wizard but that doesn't mean I don't have to follow the same legal rules as everybody else."

She glanced at the page. "I suppose," she said. "It does make disposing of the bodies a bit easier, though."

Shackleford looked up, his eyes wide in shock.

She grinned at him and he laughed.

"Lemme make a call," she said, taking the pages into the next room.

Shackleford smiled and hummed a little tune, looking around the room as if seeing it for the first time. "This is brilliant," he said as an aside.

"What is, sir? Having her come visit?"

"Oh, yes. That, too, but I was referring to this setup." He waved a hand around. "A thoroughly modern wizard."

"You're not playing Pygmalion with her, are you sir?"

He shook his head. "Not intentionally, Mulligan. I can see the potential, but she's a relative. The granddaughter I never had." He glanced at Roger. "Why? Thinking of setting your cap for her?"

Roger shook his head. "No, sir. She's out of my league."

"Why? Just because she's a wizard?"

"Well, that's part of it, sir, but if she's your heir apparent, I'll be her butler. That just wouldn't be right, sir."

Shackleford shrugged and gave him a small smile. "If you say so."

Griffin returned with the pages still in her hand. "Two o'clock. I assume you know where?"

Shackleford nodded and stood. "We do. Thank you, Ms. Griffin. Or would you prefer Madam Dionysia?"

She offered her hand and a smile. "Barbara is fine."

Shackleford shook her hand and headed for the door. "Two o'clock," he said.

Roger stood and gave her a small Jeeves bow. "Good morning, Ms. Griffin. A pleasure to meet you."

She nodded back. "Mr. Mulligan."

A wave of her hand clicked the door open. Roger held it for the old man before following him out and pulling the door closed behind.

When they stepped out into the bright morning sun, Shackleford glanced at Roger with a grin. "That was well done, Mulligan. I wouldn't have asked you to do that. Couldn't have."

Roger shook his head. "It was nothing, sir."

"It might have made the difference between success and failure, Mulligan."

"Then I'm happy to be of service, sir." He glanced up at the window. "She'll bring a breath of fresh air to Shackleford House."

Shackleford looked up, too. "That she will, Mulligan. That she will."

CHAPTER 15

The Wyverstone and Wrayvern offices occupied a spot in a rehabbed strip mall halfway between town and burb. A black logo of linked Ws covered the upper pane of the glass door. Vertical blinds filled the main window, blocking the view into the building. Roger looked down the line of storefronts which all seemed to hold some kind of office with the exception of a coffee shop/bakery on one end and a Korean take-out restaurant on the other. He parked the Mercedes one row out from the front of the building and checked the time. "It's 1:50, sir."

Shackleford glanced at Featherstone. "This the place?"

Featherstone nodded. "Esther should be coming back from lunch any minute. She takes a late lunch to cover the phones while the two lawyers are gone."

Shackleford nodded. "I thought this strip-mall idea had died out."

"Some have," Featherstone said. "Indoor malls and the big boxes cut into their business, but that coffee shop cleans up with all these offices. And Kim Bap there on the end keeps a fleet of drivers busy running Korean food into offices in town during the day and to the burbs at night. Whoever set this up was on the ball." He nodded at the Korean place. "There she is."

Roger watched an older woman in a gray pantsuit over a jewel-toned blue blouse stride along the sidewalk. She wore her hair pulled back and carried a black bag that matched her low-heeled shoes.

"She have talent?" Featherstone asked.

"A thread," Shackleton said. "Barely there. I doubt she's aware of it."

An older Ford compact, its navy paint faded and sporting a dent in the back bumper, pulled into one of the slots right in front of

229

the office. Barbara Griffin unfolded herself from the car, reached back and pulled out a large bag before slamming the door. The car chirped as she locked it. She smiled at her mother and met her halfway with a hug.

"So, they get along at least," Shackleford said. "Let's do this."

"You want me to wait in the car?" Featherstone asked.

"Anything you need in there?" Shackleford asked.

"Not that I can think of."

"Then yes, I think we can handle this. Relax."

As Roger got out of the car, he took note of the spicy aromas of Korean food mingling with the scent of exhaust in the chilly afternoon air. He walked around to the passenger side to hold the door for Shackleford. The two women turned to look at them, Esther Griffin with eyes wide and Barbara seeming to pay more attention to the car than the men.

"Would you like me to wait, sir?"

"Come with me, Mulligan. I'm a frail old man and you make a nice bodyguard." He shot Roger a crooked grin.

"Very good, sir."

Shackleford struck off toward the two women, Roger a half step back and to the side.

"Good afternoon, ladies," Shackleford said, nodding at Esther. "You must be Barbara's mother." He held out a hand. "Joseph Shackleford."

Esther shook Shackleford's hand after a quick glance at Barbara. "Good afternoon, Mr. Shackleford."

"Mum, this is the man who wants to hire me for a week."

"I gathered," she said looking Shackleford up and down before giving Roger the same treatment. "And you are?"

Roger gave her a short bow. "Roger Mulligan, ma'am. I'm Mr. Shackleford's butler."

The woman's eyebrows rose. "And chauffeur, apparently?"

"Yes, ma'am. Also cook and doorman." Roger smiled. "Shackleford House keeps a very small staff."

"You," she said.

"Yes, ma'am."

She nodded. "Well, let's go take care of business, shall we?"

Roger stepped to the door and held it open for them, following behind Shackleford as the group stepped into the carpeted foyer. A potted ficus stood guard just inside the blinds, surrounded by a phalanx of easy chairs. A solid metal desk held a computer, a potted African violet, and a handful of framed photos.

"Let me tell Patty you're here," Esther said. She glanced at Barbara. "You've never met her, have you?"

"No. Olivia did the paperwork for Dionysia."

Esther stashed her purse in the bottom drawer of her desk and disappeared toward the back of the office down a short corridor. Roger heard voices but couldn't make out any of the words. She reappeared with a smile and a smartly dressed woman in tow. "Patience Wrayvern, this is Mr. Joseph Shackleford and my daughter, Barbara."

Wrayvern extended her hand to Shackleford. "Call me Patty, please."

"I'm Joe," Shackleford said, accepting the handshake. "Thank you for making the time today."

"Glad to help." She turned to Barbara. "We finally meet. I feel like I know you already." She extended a hand.

Barbara stepped up and shook it. "Nice to meet you at last."

"I understand you have a contract you want vetted?" Wrayvern asked.

"Yes," Barbara said. "Services contract with Mr. Shackleford." She pulled a manila envelope from her bag, holding it out to Wrayvern.

The woman took the envelope and glanced at Shackleford before looking at Barbara again. "Which of you is the client here?"

Barbara raised her hand. "That would be me. I want to make sure this deal is covered properly."

Wrayvern nodded. "Okay. Good. Come on back with me." She looked at Shackleford. "If you'd have a seat while I consult my client?" She nodded at the collection of easy chairs by the ficus.

"Of course," Shackleford said, taking a seat.

Roger followed suit as the two women went down the corridor, Wrayvern already pulling the pages out of the envelope as she walked.

"Can I get you anything?" Esther asked. "Coffee? Tea? Water?"

Shackleford shook his head. "I'm fine, thank you."

"Mr. Mulligan?"

"No, ma'am. Thank you."

She smiled and took her seat behind the desk, tapping a few keys on her keyboard and consulting the screen. She picked up an earbud and hooked it over her right ear before focusing on the monitor again. Her tapping provided a quiet counterpoint to the low sound of voices coming from the back. After a few minutes, she stopped typing and touched her earbud. "Of course," she said and stood. She looked at Shackleford. "She'd like to see you now, sir."

Shackleford stood and Esther escorted him down the hall, returning after only a few moments.

"You sure I can't get you something, Mr. Mulligan?"

"I'm fine, ma'am. Thank you."

"You're really his butler?" she asked, taking her seat again.

"Yes, ma'am."

"Do you like it?"

"Ma'am?"

"Being his butler," she said, narrowing her eyes a little. "You don't seem like the butler type."

Roger shrugged. "It's been a learning experience. I find it quite satisfying, ma'am."

She smiled. "Pardon my curiosity," she said. "I've never met a butler before."

"I hadn't either before I became one, ma'am."

"What did you do before? If you don't mind my asking."

"I was an EMT for a couple of years. Army before that."

She nodded, doing that eye-narrowing again. "I can see that." She gave him a small—almost sad—smile. "Looks like you've taken the right path now."

"Ma'am?"

She shook her head and waved a hand in the air. "Nothing. An old lady's meandering. I was just thinking that being in the army and taking care of people when they're hurt—it must have been hard. I can't imagine what it was like. You seem quite content, even happy."

Roger smiled and nodded. "Thank you, ma'am. It was and I am."

Wrayvern came out of her office followed by Barbara and Shackleford. She breezed down the hall and into the foyer. Roger stood as she handed a document to Esther. "Make a copy of this for our files if you would, Esther?"

Esther took the pages and disappeared down the hallway.

Wrayvern looked at Roger. "You're Mr. Mulligan, right?"

"Yes, ma'am."

She nodded, giving him a solid up-and-down look before nodding again. She turned to Barbara. "You have my number. Anything goes west, call. Day or night."

"I will, Patty. Thank you."

Wrayvern smiled at Shackleford. "I'd be lying if I said I trusted you, Mr. Shackleford, but she does for reasons she can't explain."

Shackleford nodded. "I completely understand. I'm not sure I'd trust me either under the circumstances." He shrugged. "All I can do is be as transparent as possible about my motives and intentions."

Esther came back and handed the original to Wrayvern. "I'll start a new file for this," she said, waving the copy.

Wrayvern took the page. "Thank you, Esther. What do you think?" She glanced at Shackleford.

Esther looked at him as well, her eyes narrowing a little and a smile growing on her lips. "You look quite satisfied, Mr. Shackleford."

Shackleford beamed back at her. "I am, dear lady. Thank you."

"You take care of my girl, you hear?" Her warm smile made it clear that she believed he would do just that.

"I'll do my very best," Shackleford said. "She's family, after all. As are you."

Wrayvern's eyes widened and Esther nodded to Wrayvern. "We're related. Didn't you know?"

"Are you?" Wrayvern asked.

"We share a great-great-grandfather back in the old country," Esther said. "His sons came to America."

"Really," Wrayvern said. "How did you find this out?"

"DNA," Barbara said. "I took one of those swab things and so did he." She nodded at Shackleford.

Wrayvern blinked. "So now you're going to go work for him?"

"Just for a week."

She looked back and forth between the two of them. "You're paying an awful lot of money for services that aren't spelled out in that contract very well."

"You know the nature of her business?" Shackleford asked, nodding at Barbara.

Wrayvern's lips twitched, almost like she was holding back a smile. "I do."

"I need her to come do a spiritual assay of Shackleford House. It's imperative that I find out if the old pile is haunted before turning it over to the Shackleford Foundation."

Wrayvern pursed her lips and glanced at Barbara who nodded back. Wrayvern rolled her lips in, biting down on them and shrugging. "Consenting adults," she said after a moment.

Esther patted Wrayvern's arm. "It'll be fine."

"She's your daughter," Wrayvern said with a shrug. "I'm just her lawyer." She held out a hand to Barbara. "Good luck. Call if you need me."

Barbara shook the hand and nodded. "I will."

Wrayvern offered her hand to Shackleford. "Mr. Shackleford."

"Ms. Wrayvern," he said, shaking her hand with a small bow over it.

Wrayvern looked at the three of them—Barbara, Roger, and then a longer look at Shackleford—before turning on her heel and striding down the corridor.

"Don't mind her," Esther said. "Being distrustful comes with the job." She smiled and hugged Barbara. "You'll have to let me know how it goes. This must be very exciting for you."

"Thanks, Mum. I'll call you when I get settled. Hug Dad for me."

"I will." She offered her hand to Shackleford. "Very nice to meet you, Mr. Shackleford. Joe."

Shackleford smiled back at her and shook her hand. "Nice to meet you, too. I don't have that many relatives left. It's gratifying to have found you across the generations."

Esther beamed at him, perhaps blushing slightly, before turning to Roger. "Mr. Mulligan," she said, as he took her hand. "Take care of them."

"I will, ma'am. It's my job after all." Roger gave her the Jeeves bow over their clasped hands.

She shook her head, a knowing smile growing on her lips. "I think it's more than a job, Mr. Mulligan," she said. "I think it's your calling."

Roger smiled at her as she turned back to her desk with a grin. "Well, family time is over. I have work to do."

Roger held the door for Barbara and Shackleford to exit and followed them out.

Shackleford folded his copy of the contract once lengthwise and handed it to Roger before offering his hand to Barbara. "She's delightful."

"Ms. Wrayvern?" Barbara asked, taking his hand.

"Your mother. You know her talent?"

Barbara shook her head. "Does she have one?"

"Oh, yes," Shackleford said, the wrinkles at the corners of his eyes deepening as he grinned. "It's just a whisper. Just enough. If I hadn't known to look, I might have missed it."

"What is it?" she asked.

"She can read people. Even me." He looked at Roger. "She read you, too, didn't she?"

Roger nodded. "Yes, sir."

"But how?" Barbara asked. "I can't read people with talent."

"I suspect you can," Shackleford said. "I just think your strength masks it because you're used to going deeper."

She blinked at him. "What are you saying?"

He took a half step back and opened his arms as if to offer a hug. "Look at me. Do you trust me?"

Barbara blinked a couple of times but nodded. "Yes."

"Why?" Shackleford asked. "You can't get into my head."

She seemed to pull back onto her heels and her gaze focused somewhere in space. After a few moments, she said, "You've not given me any reason to doubt you."

"That's the thing," Shackleford said. "I haven't given you any reason to trust me, either. You didn't know me when you woke up this morning." He cocked his head to one side. "Now you trust me?"

Griffin turned her head to look at the office door. "She knew."

"Yes, my dear. I believe she did. Whether she understands the mechanic or not, your Ms. Wrayvern depends on your mother's talent and uses it. Probably has for as long as they've worked together."

They stood there for a few moments before Griffin shook herself and held out a hand. "I'll be in touch. Next week is light. I'll shift a couple of regulars around to free up seven days."

Shackleford beamed and shook her hand in both of his. "I'm looking forward to it."

"About the payment?" she asked.

"Oh, half in advance. Yes," he said and pulled an envelope out of the inside pocket of his jacket and handed it to her. "Here you are."

She took it and her eyes widened a bit. "Just like that?"

He shrugged. "You've signed the contract. I've done what I could to offer you my assurances that you'll be safe. You are—after all is said and done—family. Why not just like that?"

"You had that in your pocket the whole time?"

He laughed. "No, but we did have a few hours to kill. Banks can be slow but they're seldom that slow."

She stared at the envelope and laughed. "Of course." She shook her head. "I didn't think it through."

He laughed again. "Understandable. You've had an interesting day."

She nodded and slipped the envelope into her bag. "I have. Thank you again, Mr. Shackleford. I'm looking forward to visiting Shackleford House."

"No more than we are to having you visit, I assure you," he said. "Just let Mulligan know the particulars and we'll see you sometime next week, eh?"

She nodded and made her way to her car, glancing at the black Mercedes as she went.

Shackleford struck off across the parking lot, Roger a half step behind until they reached the vehicle when he stepped up to get the door. The old man looked at him, a half smile on his lips. "Something on your mind, Mulligan?"

Roger glanced at the Ford backing out of its slot. "You think she'll go through with it, sir?"

"I do, Mulligan." He watched the Ford pulling out into traffic. "That's a lot of money but it carries the promise of more." He grinned. "I don't think she realizes just how much more, but she'll want to get the second payment at a minimum."

Roger opened the door and Shackleford slid in beside Featherstone.

"Mission accomplished?" Featherstone asked.

"She'll be in town next week."

Roger closed the door and walked around to get into the driver's seat. The next couple of weeks would be interesting. He just hoped it wouldn't be the cursed level of interesting.

The front doorbell rang at precisely 10 a.m. Fidelia Necket waited on the stoop, smartly dressed in an elegant navy pantsuit over a cream silk blouse. Her gray hair hugged her head like a helmet of feathers. Roger smiled. "Ms. Necket. Thank you for coming." He held the door wide for her.

She smiled and entered. "How could I stay away, Mulligan? Joseph's letter said he's found a relative?"

"So it would seem, ma'am. He's expecting you."

She followed him up the stairs and into the library where Roger found Shackleford in his wheelchair, reading the green book. He froze in the doorway.

"What is it, Perkins?" Shackleford asked, a scowl on his face and the impatient snap in his voice boding ill for the interruption.

"Ms. Necket, sir," Roger said, stepping out of the doorway.

"Fidelia?"

She stepped into the room and frowned. "Joseph? How are you today?"

"What a pleasant surprise," Shackleford said, his pique evaporating. "I wasn't expecting you today, was I?"

"Yes, Joseph. You invited me." She glanced at Roger. "I would love a nice cup of tea, Mulligan."

"Of course, ma'am. It will only take a moment."

"We have another guest arriving?" she asked.

"Yes, ma'am. That's my expectation," Roger said.

"Well, bring an extra cup," she said and turned to Shackleford. "What are you reading, Joseph?"

Roger backed out of the room and closed the library door. "Why today?" he asked and headed for the kitchen, a knot of fear growing in his gut.

He brewed a pot of tea and loaded a tray with cups and saucers, milk and sugar. A small plate of shortbread cookies and another of the biscotti that Shackleford favored rounded out the presentation. He took the tray up to the library and deposited it on the low table in front of Fidelia. "Tea, ma'am."

Shackleford still sat in his wheelchair, but he'd set aside the book.

"Thank you, Perkins," Shackleford said.

Fidelia nodded to Roger. "Thank you, Mulligan. I can pour."

Roger gave a small nod and left them. He only got halfway down the stairs before the doorbell rang again. He sighed and tried to think of what he'd say to Barbara Griffin. He had no good answers when he swung the door open to find Naomi Patching on the stoop. "Good morning, Ms. Patching."

"Mulligan," she said, pushing him aside and heading for the stairs. "I trust he's awake?"

"Ma'am, I must insist," Roger stepped quickly to try to get in front of her, to block her path.

"No, Mulligan. I must insist," she said stepping around him and continuing her charge up the stairs. "If you touch me, that's assault, Mulligan."

"Mr. Shackleford has a guest, ma'am."

"A guest?" she stopped at the landing. "Who?"

Before Roger could parse an answer, she charged down the short hall and burst into the library, taking two strides into the room before stopping.

"I'm sorry, sir. I tried to stop her."

"It's all right, Perkins," Shackleford said, tea cup halfway to his lips. "Naomi, my dear. Cup of tea?"

Fidelia seemed completely at ease in her chair. "Ms. Patching. How unexpected. Yes, would you care for a cup of tea?"

Naomi stared at Fidelia for a long moment before looking at her uncle. "How are you today, Uncle?"

He toasted her with his teacup. "Quite well, thank you. Seems to be my day for visitors. Please, have a seat. To what do we owe the honor of your company?"

Naomi lowered herself into a chair beside Shackleford, casting short glances at Fidelia. "I came to ask about a family matter, Uncle."

He smiled. "Fidelia is like family," he said.

"No, Uncle. This is family business." She looked to Fidelia. "I'm sure you understand."

Fidelia finished pouring tea into the spare cup. "One lump? Two? Splash of milk perhaps?"

Naomi practically snatched the saucer from under the cup and had to steady it with her other hand. "I'd like to have a word with my uncle. Alone."

Fidelia placed her china on the tray and stood. "Of course. I'll just wait next door until you're through." She smiled at Mulligan as she passed, stopping at the door to glance at Shackleford. "We'll continue when you're ready, Joseph."

"Of course, Fidelia. I still want to hear about the planning session." He looked at Roger. "Perkins, see to Ms. Necket's comfort if you would."

"Yes, sir," he said and closed the door behind himself with a click.

Fidelia, already halfway to the upstairs parlor, glanced back at Roger. "Is she always like that?"

"More or less, ma'am."

She shook her head and beckoned him to follow. "You have any idea what's on her mind, Mulligan?"

"No, ma'am."

"Would you tell me if you did?" She grinned at him.

"No, ma'am, but I'd tell you I wasn't free to comment."

She nodded. "I suspect she found out about Ms. Griffin."

"The possibilities are endless, ma'am."

She snickered and rounded the corner into the upstairs parlor. "How long has he been like that?" she asked, lowering her voice and turning to face him.

"He was fine at breakfast, ma'am."

"Do these periods last long? When he's lost somewhere like that?"

"I've never seen one last more than a few hours, ma'am."

She nodded and pursed her lips, staring at the rug. "Aren't you concerned about breaking confidence?"

"You're an ally and a friend, ma'am. He needs as many of those as he can get."

She looked up at him. "And Ms. Griffin?"

"She's due any minute, ma'am."

"What did you think of her?"

"Formidable, ma'am."

Her eyebrows rose at that. "An interesting choice of words."

The front doorbell rang.

"I'll bring her up, ma'am. You can see for yourself."

She smiled and took a seat near the windows. "I'm looking forward to it."

Roger went to the door and opened it to find Barbara and her mother on the step. "Good morning, ladies. Won't you come in?"

They stepped into the hall, taking in the foyer with wide eyes. Roger pictured his own first look and smiled.

"Welcome to Shackleford House," he said.

"I hope it's all right," Barbara said. "I brought my mother after all."

"Perfectly fine," he said. "Lovely to see you again, Mrs. Griffin."

"Thank you, Mr. Mulligan, isn't it?"

"Just Mulligan is fine, ma'am. Tradition."

She narrowed her eyes at him for a moment and touched Barbara's arm. "Oh, dear."

"What is it, Mother?"

"I—I don't know," she said. "Is there a problem, Mr. Mulligan?"

"Mr. Shackleford has a guest at the moment. His niece called unexpectedly, but if you'd come with me, I have someone else who would like to meet you."

The older woman's face relaxed and she nodded.

Roger led them to the upstairs parlor where Fidelia Necket rose to greet them.

"Ms. Fidelia Necket, may I present Esther and Barbara Griffin." He turned to the Griffins. "Mrs. Griffin, Ms. Griffin, it's my pleasure to introduce you to Ms. Fidelia Necket, an old friend of Mr. Shackleford and your guide for your stay, Ms. Griffin."

Ester's eyes widened. "Guide?"

"Mr. Shackleford asked me to serve as a kind of chaperone," Fidelia said. "I'm familiar with the workings of Shackleford House and he thought that having another woman involved would help everyone feel more at ease."

Esther stepped forward to shake Fidelia's hand. "Very pleased to meet you, Ms. Necket."

"Delia, please. No need for formality here."

Esther nodded. "I'm Esther when I'm at home."

"You can consider this your home while under the Shackleford roof, ma'am," Roger said. "Is there anything I can get you? Tea? Coffee?"

"I'd love a cup of coffee," Barbara said.

"I wouldn't refuse a cup of coffee," Esther said. "If it's no trouble."

Roger looked at Fidelia. "Ma'am?"

"Coffee's fine, Mulligan. Thank you." She waved a hand at the chairs arrayed in front of the windows. "Shall we?"

They took their seats while Roger returned to the kitchen for the second tray of the morning. He chuckled to himself wishing he could be a fly on that wall upstairs. He hadn't expected Barbara's wingman to be her mother, especially on a work day, but he didn't feel terribly surprised. The Shackleford family seemed to have solid roots, even if some of the sprouts seemed a bit off.

It took him a few minutes to brew a fresh pot and load the tray with cups, sugar, milk, and cream. He arranged the items on the tray to his liking before the coffee finished brewing. He added a plate of finger pastries and some dishes and napkins before taking it back up to the parlor.

Fidelia smiled at his return. The Griffins seemed completely at ease—relaxing in their chairs.

"Ah, Mulligan. Just in time," Fidelia said. "Thank you so much."

Roger placed the tray on the table between them and gave a small bow. "My pleasure. Sorry for the delay. I needed to brew a fresh pot and some things can't be rushed. Shall I pour?"

Fidelia shook her head. "Thank you, Mulligan. I think we can manage."

"Is there anything else you need, ladies?"

"At some point we'll need a tour of the house," Fidelia said. "That can wait until Joseph is free."

"Of course, ma'am." Roger left them to the clinking of glassware and the low murmurs of conversation. He smiled to himself stood just outside the library door, trying to judge how matters progressed inside by the tone of the voices coming through the heavy wood. It didn't sound like they were fighting, but his distrust for Naomi Patching made him nervous. He waited as long as he could stand it and then tapped twice before entering.

Shackleford looked up, a scowl on his face, his lips pressed into a line. "What is it, Perkins?"

"Is everything satisfactory, sir?"

"Of course it is, Perkins. I would have rung for you had it not been."

"Sorry for the interruption, sir." Roger bowed and started to back out of the room.

"Just as well," Naomi said, placing her cup and saucer on the tray with a rattle of china. "I think we're done here. You can show me out, Perkins." She stood and gave Roger a smirk. She crossed to Shackleford, kneeling beside his wheelchair to pat his hand and forearm. "You rest, Uncle. You seem very tired today. I'll stop by again later in the week to make sure you're all right. How does that sound?"

Shackleford shook his head. "Dreadful, but I don't suppose I can stop you."

Naomi smiled. "Oh, Uncle. You know I just want what's best for you."

Shackleford snorted and turned his face away from her.

She patted his arm again and stood.

Roger stepped out of the doorway to let her precede him from the room and closed the door gently after himself.

"He's completely lost it, Mulligan," she said. "How long has he been like that this time?"

"He was fine at breakfast, ma'am."

She gave him a sour look and sniffed. She started down the stairs but stopped at the sounds coming from the parlor. "Is somebody else here, Mulligan?"

"Yes, ma'am."

Naomi glared at him and reversed direction, bolting down the short hall before he could get in front of her. She stopped just inside the door.

"Good morning, again, Ms. Patching. Care to join us?" Fidelia said, looking up from her coffee with a smile on her lips but steel in her eyes.

"What are you doing here?" Naomi asked, biting the words out.

"Well, I was having tea with Mr. Shackleford before you needed the room."

"Not you. Them." She pointed at the Griffins.

Roger saw Esther's eyes narrow for a moment before she put her coffee down on the tray and positioned her body in the chair as if to protect Barbara.

Fidelia tsked. "Manners, Ms. Patching. Manners. This is Mrs. Esther Griffin and her daughter, Barbara. We've just been discussing the history of Shackleford House over the centuries."

Color flushed up the back of Naomi's neck and ears, a visible warning of her anger. "Griffin," she said, spitting the word onto the rug. "Already?" She stalked a couple of steps closer.

Roger moved to get himself in front of Naomi, using his bulk to intercede. "Ms. Patching, this is inappropriate."

"It's fine, Mulligan," Fidelia said. "Ms. Patching is no threat."

"I see you, Fidelia Necket. You've been angling to get your hands on my uncle—and this house—for decades. It's not going to happen." She waved a dismissive hand at the Griffins. "I should have known you were behind this latest stunt."

"I believe that's quite enough, Ms. Patching. It's time for you to leave, ma'am," Roger said.

Naomi turned her fulminating gaze on him. "Or what? You'll throw me out? I have more right to be here than you do. I hired you, for God's sake."

"Yes, ma'am, you did, but you gave me the job of protecting Mr. Shackleford and this house. That extends to his guests." He paused. "I must ask you to leave now, Ms. Patching." He really didn't want to lay hands on the woman, but he was prepared for it. He'd certainly done worse in his life.

"You've already got one assault and battery on your record, Mulligan. Do you really want another?" Patching asked.

Roger gave her a small nod. "I take my duties seriously, ma'am."

"Technically, it's self-defense," Esther said.

Naomi turned her glare on the woman. "Who asked you?"

"Nobody," Esther said. "I just thought I should point out that Mr. Mulligan—in his capacity as butler—constitutes the de facto head of security for the building and it falls within his purview to protect the house and the people in it. As such, it's perfectly within the scope of his duties to grab you by the scruff of your neck and frog march you out of the building, if he determines you to be a credible threat to my daughter or me." She reached for the coffee again, not looking away from Naomi.

Barbara gaped at her mother. Even Fidelia gave the woman an admiring glance before turning her gaze back to Naomi.

"What are you, a lawyer?" Naomi asked.

"No. Paralegal. I work for lawyers. Domestic assaults are all too common, so I see a lot of case law." She sipped her coffee and stared back at Naomi.

Roger stepped between them, blocking Naomi's view. "Ma'am. Please." He gestured to the door with an open palm.

Naomi glared at him but turned on her heel and strode out of the parlor, Roger right behind her. She stopped at the door. "You listen to me, Roger Mulligan. That little bitch is not going to get this house. Am I clear on that?"

Roger opened the door and held it. "Good day, Ms. Patching."

She took a half step closer to him, getting right up into his face. "You cross me, Mulligan, and you'll regret it. Do you understand that?"

Roger schooled his features into as perfect a butler mask as he could manage. "Good day, Ms. Patching."

She ground her teeth together hard enough that Roger saw her jaw muscles bulge and heard the tiny scraping of her molars. "This. Is. Not. Over."

"Good day, Ms. Patching."

With one final glare, she spun and stomped out the door.

Roger closed it behind her with a firm thump, throwing the deadbolt for good measure. He turned to find all three women standing at the top of the stairs, looking down. "Is there something you need, ladies?"

Fidelia saluted him with her coffee cup. "Thank you, Mulligan. We thought you might need a witness." She glanced at the Griffins. "Or three."

"She's trouble, that one," Esther said.

Fidelia nodded. "We know, Esther." She turned and led the way back into the parlor. "Interesting story about the foyer, though. During the War of 1812, the British tried a blockade ..." Her voice faded out as they rounded the corner into the upstairs parlor.

Roger shook his head. The three of them together promised to make the next few days particularly interesting. He made his way to the library and knocked before entering. Shackleford sat, staring off into space. "Ms. Patching has left, sir."

Shackleford didn't move, just sat there—still in his wheelchair—gazing off, his eyeballs occasionally moving as if he might be reading something in his head.

"Sir?" Roger took another step into the room.

Shackleford's head nodded a couple of times, that small nod you make to yourself when you make up your own mind about something. He blinked rapidly and sat back. "Ah, Mulligan. Has that wasp left, finally?"

"Ms. Patching has left, sir."

"Excellent." He looked down at his chair and at the tea service in front of him. "Oh, dear." He looked up at Roger. "What happened, Mulligan?"

"You had a spell, sir."

Shackleford snorted and waved a hand at the chair, which changed back to a straight wooden chair while Roger watched. "I know that, Mulligan. What happened? I didn't need three cups for tea with Naomi."

"I discovered you when Ms. Necket arrived, sir. We expected Ms. Griffin shortly so I brought three cups. Ms. Patching arrived first."

"Delia? Is she still here?"

"Yes, sir. Next door in the upstairs parlor with the Griffins."

Shackleford's eyes shot open. "Plural?"

"Miss Griffin brought her mother, sir."

Shackleford grinned. "Did she? Have they been waiting long?"

"Almost half an hour, sir. Ms. Patching met with you alone."

"Did she?" He shook his head. "Can't do anything about it now." He stood and headed for the door. "Let's not keep them waiting any longer than necessary, shall we?"

Roger followed Shackleford into the parlor where he held out his hands to Esther. "My dear Mrs. Griffin. Please forgive me for keeping you waiting. Family business."

She stood and shook his hand. "Think nothing of it. Delia kept us quite entertained. I had no idea the house has such a rich history."

He turned to Barbara. "I'm so pleased you've come."

She stepped forward to shake his hand. "You're paying for it." She grinned at him. "I hope you don't mind I brought my mother as chaperone?"

"Nonsense. Of course not. That's why I asked Delia here to join us." He turned to her. "Thank you, by the way, in case I didn't mention that earlier?" He raised his eyebrows.

Fidelia waved him off with a smile. "We've had a lovely time getting to know each other, Joseph. Won't you join us?"

Roger picked up the cue and moved one of the lighter chairs over to their grouping.

Shackleford smiled. "Thank you, Mulligan."

"You're welcome, sir. Shall I fetch you a cup for coffee?"

Shackleford looked at the tray and nodded. "If there's any left?"

Fidelia lifted the carafe and gave it a testing shake before handing it to Roger. "You may need to fill this again, Mulligan."

He took it with a bow. "It will be just a few minutes to brew a fresh pot."

Shackleford settled back into his chair and crossed his legs at the knee. "We're not going anywhere, Mulligan. Thank you."

Roger took the carafe back to the kitchen and checked the time as he started the third pot of the day. He'd need to arrange luncheon for four soon. He ran some menu ideas through his mind. Soup and salad, perhaps some sandwiches? He made a mental note to ask if there were any preferences when he returned. While the mood upstairs seemed good, he couldn't quite shake the sense that Naomi Patching would make more trouble. He snorted. Of course, she'd make more trouble. What bothered him was wondering where that trouble might show up.

CHAPTER 16

They spent the remainder of afternoon touring the house, Roger leading the parade with the keys while Shackleford and Fidelia filled in the missing context for them. Both of the Griffins seemed slightly glazed by the time the tour ended in the atrium.

Esther, who had been flagging as the tour wore on, seemed to perk up in delight at the garden. She clasped her hands behind her back and wandered through the narrow paths, marveling at the plantings tucked into corners. "It's unbelievable," she said. She looked up at the trees. "These feel like full-sized trees and ancient."

"Some are more than a century old," Shackleford said. "The last time the house burned down was in the 1800s. This wing was built around them during that reconstruction period."

Esther shook her head and continued her stroll. Fidelia fell into step with her; the two of them meandered off into the garden, chatting.

Barbara, on the other hand, seemed almost shell-shocked, her eyes glazed as she stared at the plants, the trees, turning finally to Roger, then Shackleford. She blew out a deep breath. "You weren't kidding."

Shackleford shook his head, a smile reaching all the way to his eyes. "I wasn't kidding."

She drew in a deep breath and blew it out noisily. "And you want to leave this to me?"

"Yes," Shackleford said. "I think so."

"You don't even know me."

"That's one reason I wanted you to come visit. Ideally, to live here, but that's up to you."

"I wouldn't know what to do with it."

Shackleford shrugged. "There's really nothing for you to do with it. Just make it your home. I think I said before, I was going to leave it to the Shackleford Foundation so they could put it in the National Register to keep it from being demolished."

"Do you need me for that?"

"Not strictly speaking, no, but I looked for a relative with talent for decades," he said. "When I found you, it seemed like the answer to a prayer." He looked at Roger. "I have you to thank for that, Mulligan. If you hadn't installed the internet, I'd have never known of DNA testing."

"My pleasure, sir."

Barbara ran a finger down the trunk of the nearest tree and glanced over to where her mother and Fidelia bent over a planting of flowers deeper in the garden. "I don't know how to talk to pixies or fairies," she said, her voice low. "I assume they manage this garden?"

Shackleford nodded. "The fairies hold the garden as their home. Older than the house by centuries. Building the house around it protected it from being lost to development." He looked up at the spreading branches above. "I'd forgotten how relaxing the grove is."

"How does that work?" she asked.

"No idea," the old man said. "They sometimes tell me if there's a problem they can't handle. That doesn't happen often. Last time was ten years ago, before the condos came up to the property line. The pixies in the house? As long as they're given the respect they deserve, they serve the house. I know when they're upset." He glanced at Roger with a grin. "They like a little whiskey now and again."

"Will they talk to me?" she asked.

"I assume so," Shackleford said. "You've got the talent."

"I've got a talent," she said, looking around. "Is it the right talent?"

"Honestly, I don't think it matters," Shackleford said.

She blinked at him, her mouth half open. "What?"

"It's simple," Shackleford said. "You have talent that's been handed down for generations. You use it regularly. Consciously." He glanced over to Esther. "So does she, even though I don't think she's aware of it."

"So, what does that have to do with all this?" She waved a hand around in the air.

"You know that it's real. That there are people like me and Fidelia, and even if they never speak to you, you at least have some foundation for believing me when I tell you that the house and grounds are cared for by pixies and fairies."

Barbara stared at Roger for a moment. "You believe they're here, too," she said.

Roger nodded. "Yes, ma'am."

"And yet you don't have any talent that I can see."

"No, ma'am. I'll confess to a touch of envy, but lots of people have skills and talents that I don't have."

"What makes you believe they're here?"

The question startled a short laugh out of him. He looked up at the canopy above. "This room was locked away for the first few months I was here. I first visited it a few days ago. Look at it. Does it appear to be in a state of advanced neglect?"

She looked around. "No, but would it?"

Roger shrugged. "The trees? Maybe not, but the flowering plants? The grasses? They're not overgrown. I'll grant that the mosses and stones keep the plantings in check, but this place is natural without being wild." He shrugged again. "I have no trouble thinking that some kind of magic must be responsible—or at least a team of skilled gardeners. They're not coming through any of the doors in the house or I'd have seen them."

She nodded and looked around. "It is amazing."

Esther and Fidelia completed their circuit around the garden and rejoined them.

"Mr. Shackleford, this is amazing. Simply amazing," Esther said. "Do the trees stay green through the winter?"

"No, they're already changing color. They'll drop eventually," he said. "The temperature in here gets rather frosty and the days are pretty short because the garden has the house all around it. A botanist could probably tell you the reasons, but I just enjoy it."

"I'd forgotten just how lovely the garden is, Joseph," Fidelia said.

"I had, too," he said. "One of the downsides of living here, I suppose."

"What's that?" Fidelia asked.

"Well, I could come here any time. So I tend to think 'I could do that later' but then never do." He took a deep breath and blew it out in a satisfied sigh. "Perhaps I need to rethink that, eh?"

"You've enough space in this house for a few dozen people," Esther said. "Don't you find it lonely rattling around all alone?"

"I haven't, no." He shrugged. "I'm not alone, and I have my business to attend to." He smiled at Fidelia. "And friends who call when they're in town."

"What of you?" Esther asked, looking at Barbara. "You want to live here?"

As Barbara looked around, Roger saw some spark in her eyes as her gaze seemed to caress the graceful branches overhead. "That's what we're here to determine, isn't it?"

Esther nodded. "Yes, I suppose it is."

"It's just the first day," Shackleford said. "Why don't we just take it as it comes?"

"What were you planning for me to do this week, Mr. Shackleford?" Barbara asked.

"I'd like you to work with Mulligan here to come up with a plan for the future of Shackleford House."

Roger felt his eyes practically bulge in his head. Judging from Barbara's open-mouthed stare, she was as surprised as he.

Shackleford glanced at Fidelia. "Perhaps Fidelia would be willing to assist?"

Fidelia grinned. "You know I've wanted you to do something with this place for years, Joseph."

"It's settled then?" Shackleford asked.

Barbara held up her hands, palm out. "Oh, no. No, no. Not settled. What do you mean by come up with a plan? I thought you had a foundation all set up and ready."

He grinned. "I do. I've filed the paperwork. The foundation has been legally established as a not-for-profit public charity with the mission of preserving the history of the oldest continuously occupied location in the state."

"Then what are you expecting me to do?" she asked.

"I've hired you for a week," Shackleford said. "Yes?"

"Yes," Barbara said. "You hired me to evaluate the property, if I remember correctly."

"I believe the wording is more along the lines of 'what it might be like if you owned Shackleford House,' which is what I've just asked you to do, isn't it? Come up with a plan for what to do when you own it?"

Barbara looked at her mother.

Esther shrugged. "It seems reasonable to me, dear. If I were going to leave a mansion like this to somebody, I'd like to know what they planned on doing with it after I was gone."

"In a week?" Barbara asked.

"Only six days left," Shackleford said. "I don't expect miracles, but show me something." He grinned at her. "What do you say?"

Barbara looked at Roger. "You'll help?"

Roger nodded. "Of course, ma'am."

She looked at Fidelia. "Ms. Necket?"

"It's Delia, my dear, and I'd be honored."

She looked at her mother. "What do you think?"

"I think you've got your work cut out for you, dear." She smiled. "And I think I need to go back home to your father and my job. You don't need me here getting underfoot."

"You're not underfoot, dear lady," Shackleford said.

She shook her head. "This isn't my fight, Joseph. She asked me to come be a chaperone and I couldn't say no." She looked from Delia to Roger then back to Shackleford. "You people are possibly crazy, but you're not dangerous. She doesn't need a chaperone here any more than she needs a bodyguard at her business with all those strange clients." She paused. "Actually, she probably needs one there, more."

Barbara snorted. "Probably right."

"The other thing you should do is check out of that hotel and come live here," Esther said. She looked at Shackleford. "That's what you wanted wasn't it?"

"Yes, but I'm not blind to the appearances and the risks."

"I'll stay, too," Fidelia said. "Not like you don't have the room for it, and I foresee some late nights." She looked at Mulligan. "You'll have a few extra people roaming the premises. Can you manage with us?"

Roger felt himself grinning. "I'd love it, ma'am." he said. "Guest rooms or one of the suites?"

"One thing at a time," Barbara said. "Let me get checked out and move my stuff over. I don't have a lot with me. Mom can take my car back, and we can figure out how I get home at the end of the week."

Fidelia grinned. "A take-charge woman. This is going to be fun."

"When I get back, we can sit down and do a little brainstorming about how to handle the task. There's that parlor upstairs here, the one we were in this afternoon back at the main house. One of the classrooms would probably be the right place to set up planning since it's big enough for all three of us to work without disturbing Mr. Shackleford." She blinked and took a breath, looking around at all of them. "Sorry. Did I say something wrong?"

Shackleford frowned. "One thing."

Her face drooped. "I'm sorry—"

"It's Joe or Joseph. Not Mr. Shackleford." He grinned. "Uncle Joe if you like. We can sort the actual relationship if you like. It's probably fifth cousin Joe or something, but I'd be delighted if you just called me Joe."

She smiled at him and Fidelia covered her mouth with a hand, winking at Roger.

"I think it's a splendid plan," Shackleford said. "You're more than welcome anytime you want to stay here, Delia. You know that."

Fidelia nodded. "I do, and this seems like a good reason." She looked at Barbara. "You sure you'll feel safe here?"

Barbara looked at each of them in turn, then looked up at the trees. "Yes." She grinned. "My mother knows where I am and who I'm with so I'm pretty sure you won't try anything funny."

Esther laughed and headed for the doors. "Let's get a move on, then. If we hustle, I can be home in time for dinner."

Mulligan got in front and held the doors for the women.

Shackleford waved them on. "I'm going to just sit here for a bit, Mulligan," he said. Taking a deep breath, he settled on one of the benches that dotted the space.

Roger saw the Griffins off and turned to Fidelia. "Do you need to get an overnight bag or something, ma'am?"

"I have one in the car," she said. "Can I take it around back and park it in the garage?"

"Of course, ma'am. If there's anything you need, just ask."

"I won't be a moment." She followed the Griffins down the path and out onto the sidewalk.

Roger swung by his quarters and fetched the keys for both the back door and the garage before walking through to let her in. He only had to wait for a couple of minutes before an older model Taurus pulled into the yard, Fidelia Necket behind the wheel. He opened the door to the last bay and she backed into it smartly. She killed the engine and popped the trunk.

Roger closed the garage door and went to the back of the car. Two well-worn suitcases lay in the padded compartment along with a canvas duffel bag that looked a lot like the one he'd had in the army.

"Grab the small bag, if you would, Mulligan?"

He pulled the carry-on from the trunk. "Anything else you need in here, ma'am?"

She came back and looked in, shaking her head. "No, that will do. For now, anyway." She slammed the trunk and led the way back to the house. "You're looking forward to this, Mulligan?"

"I am, yes, ma'am."

"What would you suggest in terms of working space?"

"We have several choices, ma'am. The upstairs parlor is large enough, as is the commons area in the west wing. There are four classrooms. One has tables for working space in addition to the chalkboards and desks."

"What about the ballroom?" she asked. "We could set up a table in there to work on."

"Definitely a possibility, ma'am. It's a bit loud. Sound echoes in that empty room."

She nodded. "Good point. Do we have something like flip charts?"

"Not that I've seen, ma'am."

She hmm'ed and led the way back through the kitchen to the foyer. "Let's wait for Barbara to return before deciding on space."

Roger nodded and put the bag in the hall closet under the stairs. "We could order some flip charts, ma'am."

She shrugged. "I could take Barbara out to the supply store this evening if we need to. With just the three of us, it might be overkill."

"No such thing, ma'am." Roger spoke before thinking and flushed. "Sorry, ma'am. Old habits."

Fidelia frowned and cocked her head to the side.

"Ma'am?" he asked.

She raised a hand, index finger extended, and turned her head. "What's that sound?"

Roger stood still, letting the stillness of the house settle around him. He shook his head.

Fidelia continued seeking the source, sweeping back and forth until she turned to face the west wing doors. "In there."

Although Roger heard nothing he all but ran to the doors, threw one open and dashed into the garden.

Shackleford sat on the bench where Roger had left him, his faced turned to the light shining in from above. Tears leaked from his closed eyes, the wetness shimmering on his face.

Fidelia came up behind Roger and took one look before crossing to Shackleford's side. "Joseph?" Her voice came out as a whisper that seemed to echo through the little forest.

Shackleford shook his head, just the slightest tremor—back and forth once.

She started to reach for his shoulder but pulled her hand back. She looked over her shoulder at Roger, her raised eyebrows the only question she needed to ask.

Roger shook his head.

She sat beside him and put a hand over his where it rested on the bench. "I'm here, Joseph."

"I've missed you so," he said. "Why did you leave?"

"I'm sorry, Joseph," she said.

He lowered his head and brushed at his face with his free hand. "I loved you, Miriam. And you left me."

Fidelia's eyes widened. She released his hand and put an arm around his shoulders. "I didn't want to, Joseph."

"You didn't want to," he said, still not looking up. "We would have had a life together. Children. But you left me."

She pulled his shoulder closer and he sagged into her. She glanced at Roger, her own eyes looking suspiciously shiny. "Help me get him to his room."

Roger crossed the five steps to the old man's side and took his arm, pulling him up to his feet and looping it over his shoulders. He had to stoop a little to keep from putting too much pressure on the shoulder joint, but the old man came to his feet and allowed Roger to half carry him out of the garden and up the stairs toward the master suite.

The old man balked outside the library, straightening up and locking his knees. "No," he said. He pushed Roger away and waved the library door open with a gesture, bolted into the room, and picked up the green book from the end table as he took his customary seat beside the window. The book fell open in his lap and he stared at the page.

Fidelia stopped beside Roger at the library door, agape.

"Wrong book," Roger said, keeping his voice low.

"Wrong book?"

"Yes, ma'am. He reads that one when he's having one of his spells. He reads the brown one when he's himself."

She nodded.

Shackleford looked up as if seeing them for the first time. "Ah, Delia. What a surprise. Come in, come in. Perkins, some tea, please."

Roger gave his butler bow. "Of course, sir."

Fidelia nodded to Roger and entered the library, taking a seat across from him. "How have you been, Joseph?"

"It's been so long," Shackleford said. "How was K2?"

Roger closed the door and went to the kitchen to make the tea.

The library door clicked open by itself on his return, and he entered to find Shackleford standing at the window looking out. "Thank you, Mulligan."

"You're welcome, sir."

Fidelia looked up from her chair and nodded at the low table in front of her. "Thank you, Mulligan."

He smiled. "Of course, ma'am." He started to leave but Shackleford stopped him.

"A moment, if you please, Mulligan," he said without turning from the window.

"Yes, sir?"

"Miriam died. Sixty-odd years ago. I was devastated."

"You don't need to explain, sir."

He turned then and offered Fidelia a tentative smile. "I do, Mulligan. It's getting worse. I'm not sure how much longer I can maintain."

"Joseph," Fidelia said. "Come sit. Have some tea."

He looked down, thrusting his hands in his trouser pockets. "I don't know if I'll be able to come back again the next time."

Fidelia took cup and saucer, filling it with grace granted by years of practice. She held it out to Shackleford. "Your tea, Joseph."

He crossed to take the china from her, lowering himself into his chair. He sighed and took a sip, and a second, before putting the cup down again.

"There," she said. "What's this nonsense about not coming back?"

"Every time I go back, it's harder to come forward again."

"And every time it takes you back a little further?" she asked.

He nodded. "I used to think it was stealing my memories but it appears to be just pulling them out of me a little at a time." He looked up at her. "And the only way to stop is to die."

She sipped her own tea and glanced at Roger over the rim of her cup. "What's the deal with the different books?" she asked. "Mulligan says you read a different book. That green one."

He mirrored her action with his own cup. "Yes. I don't know why that happens. That one has nothing to do with cursed objects or demonic actions. I gave up on it a decade ago after years of study."

She nodded. "That's the answer."

He looked up, his gaze snapping to her face. "The answer?"

"Of course," she said. "It's the past. When the amulet takes you back, you forget that you gave up on it and pick it up again. I take it you put a lot of stock in it?"

He nodded, looking down at his cup and taking another sip. "I did. I was quite disappointed when it turned out to be a dud."

"Where's the new one?" she asked, looking around the room.

Shackleford nodded at the cushion on a nearby chair. "Under that pillow, I suspect."

Roger crossed to the chair and pulled the book from beneath the throw pillow, handing it to Fidelia. "It seems to end up there quite often, ma'am."

She frowned. "Curious." Placing her cup and saucer back on the tray, she took the book from Roger. She opened to the table of contents and scanned down the substantial list. "This seems to be a bit more on point, Joseph. Have you found anything?"

He shrugged. "There's a chapter on an artifact that might be this one. A black iron necklace that grants the wearer extra powers at the expense of their mental capacity."

She peered at him over the top of the book. "Might be?"

He shrugged again. "It's a sketchy report. The most salient fact being that whoever picked it up put it on and died when they took it off."

"And you think there might be some other black iron necklace?" she asked, lowering the book to her lap.

He glanced at Roger as if looking for support before shaking his head. "No, actually, I think that's it. There doesn't seem to be a way to lift the curse."

Fidelia frowned. "There's always a loophole. Always."

"That's what I thought, too," Shackleford said. "But this is old. Older than history. I'd think older than mankind, but that makes no sense at all."

"Really?" Fidelia asked.

"Who'd be around to put it on in the first place if not some person?" He smiled into his cup as he took another sip. "Some ape? An uplifted chimp? And where would it have come from? Iron working is relatively new in a cosmological sense."

"Do you mind if I borrow this?" she asked. "The green one, too?"

Shackleford shrugged. "Neither one has done me any good. You may as well give them a look." He pulled the green-covered work from the side table and handed it across. He smiled at Roger. "You'll have to guess if I'm not holding a book," he said.

"I'll cope, sir." Roger considered the issue for a few moments. He could usually tell if the old man wasn't there as soon as he opened his mouth. "Did you have a butler before Perkins, sir?"

"No, Mulligan. Parsons was my father's valet, but I hired Perkins when I first set up house."

"Was it that God-awful pile you had in Arizona?" Fidelia asked.

Shackleford nodded. "One of the first purchases I made after ..." He patted his chest. "After finding this."

"I remember it," Fidelia said. "I had no idea what possessed you—" She cut herself off and swallowed.

Shackleford snorted. "Precisely," he said. "It turned out to be a good decision, that house."

"Why?" she asked. "Wasn't it demolished or something?"

"It was. A land developer bought the property for a new shopping mall. I made a killing on it."

She blinked. "Really?"

"You saw the shape it was in," Shackleford said.

"Yes, that's why I couldn't understand why you bought it and why you actually lived there. You could have lived anywhere."

He shook his head. "Only if my father had coughed up the money. That was my first big deal. By the time I closed on it, I'd sunk nearly every penny I had to my own name into it."

"But you hired Perkins?"

He nodded. "Appearances. We lived frugally on my allowance. We were both much younger men."

"Why did you sell the seaside place on the Cape?" she asked. "Was that one of your investments?"

"You know that place is gone now, right?"

Her eyes widened. "No, really?"

"One of the Atlantic storms. Took out the whole bluff it was on." He shrugged. "I had the opportunity to buy a property in Connecticut and took it. Sold that place and rolled the money over. Two years later it sank into the sea." He sipped, smiling at her over the rim of his cup. "I still have the Connecticut house, if you're looking for a place to live."

She laughed and shook her head. "I'm happy in my condo. No staff to worry about. No grounds to keep. Frees me up to travel." She paused. "Is it empty?"

He shook his head. "Rented. I gave it to a management company to handle. Amazing how much people are willing to pay for a lease on a mansion." He shook his head. "It turns over about every three years as they come to understand that the reason they couldn't afford to buy one is the same reason they can't really afford the lease."

"Oh?" she asked. "What's that?"

"Not enough income," he said. "Lease siphons it off too fast so what looked like a good deal soon becomes an unrelenting burden." He sighed. "Money makes people stupid. They think that if they get a pile scraped together it'll grow on its own—and it can—but then they start to spend it."

"Ah, cash flow," she said.

Shackleford nodded and looked at Roger. "So, Perkins was the only other butler. If I call you Perkins, it's as likely habit as dementia."

"I understand, sir."

"We're going to have to clue Ms. Griffin in," Fidelia said.

Shackleford sighed but nodded. "At least she's talented. It won't seem like insane ranting."

The front doorbell rang.

"Speaking of whom," Roger said. "Excuse me, sir." He went down to open the door and help Barbara with her bags.

She stood on the stoop with a single large suitcase and a broad grin. She turned and waved to her mother in the car at the curb. When the car drove off, she turned back to him. "Well, Mulligan. Ready to get to work?"

"I am, Miss. Mr. Shackleford and Ms. Necket are in the library." He reached down and plucked the suitcase off the landing. "This way, Miss."

She stepped into the house and he closed and bolted the door.

"We've delayed deciding anything until you returned," Roger said.

"Appreciated, Mulligan. Thank you." She glanced at him. "It feels odd calling you by your last name. Does it bother you?"

He grinned. "That's all I've been called for much of my adult life, Miss. First the army and then as an EMT. It's not that much different." He looked down at his suit. "The uniform fits better."

"It feels so stuffy," she said.

He put her bag beside Fidelia's in the closet and nodded. "I'll confess I was a bit put off by it at first." He shrugged and opened his palm toward the stairs. "This way, miss."

"At least call me Barbara," she said. "You don't work for me."

"You're a guest of the house, miss." He started up the stairs and she fell into step.

"Barbara," she said.

"Very well, Miss Barbara."

She laughed, the sound echoing around the foyer.

He showed her into the library. "Ms. Griffin, sir. Should I begin dinner?"

Shackleford nodded. "Set it up in the small dining room, if you would, Mulligan?"

"Of course, sir." He looked at the two women. "Any dietary preferences I should take into account?"

"None for me," Barbara said. "I'm not a fan of boiled beets, but almost anything else."

Fidelia smiled. "Whatever you prepare will be fine, Mulligan."

"Very well. Thank you, all." He started back out and Fidelia patted the chair beside her.

"Come. Sit, Barbara. We have to talk."

Shackleford took a chair across from them.

Roger had time to see Barbara frown, glancing between them as she lowered herself into the chair.

Using some of his new skills, Roger prepared chicken marsala with rice and steamed green beans. The cellar contained a nice selection of wines and his reference materials suggested a red. He shook his head at the suggestion but as the chicken developed, he realized that a white wouldn't do. He opened a bottle of Collioure to let it breathe. Being a beer guy, he'd never heard of it before but he trusted the references.

While dinner cooked, he set the table, leaning heavily on the diagrams in his butler handbook to make sure he had the right number of forks and spoons in the right places. Given the length of time he'd been at Shackleford House, it felt good to try out some of the skills he had only read about.

The buildings on either side of the mansion blocked the late afternoon sun, so he adjusted the drapes and checked the lighting in the room.

As dinner hour grew nearer, he surveyed his handiwork and smiled to himself. "If they could see me now ..."

He returned to the kitchen to put the finishing touches on a green salad and push a frozen apple pie into the oven. It seemed a little like cheating, but he hadn't had a chance to try his pastry skills. Besides, the old man had them on standing order so he must at least expect to get one now and again.

A few minutes before the hour, he started a fresh pot of coffee and put on water for tea. He wasn't sure who'd drink which but felt compelled to offer both. He ached to know how it was going in the library but managed to stay busy with his duties. It wasn't unlike waiting for the brass to finish planning a patrol. At least people wouldn't be shooting at him in Shackleford House.

He hoped.

At the hour, he went up the stairs, knocked on the library door, and entered. "Dinner is served, sir."

The three of them sat with their heads together over the low table among the chairs. They all looked up. Roger felt a wash of relief run through him when Barbara smiled over her shoulder. He'd been concerned that she'd abandon them once she learned of Shackleford's problem.

"Thank you, Mulligan. It smells delicious," Shackleford said. "We'll be right down."

"Very good, sir." Roger went down and settled the salads around the table, placing a serving boat of fresh balsamic vinaigrette near the head.

Shackleford led the way into the dining room with Fidelia and Barbara walking behind, arm in arm. The image of some period piece movie flashed in Roger's mind, although Shackleford wasn't "dressed for dinner" and both women wore pants instead of gowns. The picture made him smile as he held the chair for Fidelia. Shackleford seated Barbara before taking his own chair at the head of the table.

Roger poured water for them. "Would anyone care for coffee? Tea? Wine?"

Shackleford looked at the table and then at his two dining companions. "I'm fine. Ladies?"

"Water's good for me," Fidelia said.

Barbara nodded. "Thank you, Mulligan. This is fine."

Roger stepped back, replacing the pitcher on a tray on the sideboard.

Fidelia asked, "So, where do you think we should work? How do you want to handle this project?" She helped herself to vinaigrette and handed the dressing boat across the table to Barbara.

"We need to break it down," she said. "Plan for a plan." She drizzled some dressing on her salad and passed the boat to Shackleford.

"I like the sound of that," he said. "I think I said it before. Use whatever you need from the house. If there's something we don't have, we'll get it."

"That's a pretty large blank check, Joseph." Fidelia speared a forkful of greens.

He grinned at her. "I'm not worried."

"I think the first step is to brainstorm what kinds of things we might do," Barbara said.

"Like what?" Fidelia asked.

Barbara paused, a cherry tomato halfway to her mouth. "Well, we have a lot of bedrooms. A bed and breakfast? A foster home, going back to the house's original purpose? It was a boarding school for a time, wasn't it?"

Shackleford nodded. "Long time ago."

"Replace the chalkboards with white boards and those classrooms would look—well, not like new with those antique wooden desks—but still modern enough."

"What would we teach? And to whom?" Fidelia asked.

"Just brainstorm now. We can refine later," Barbara said. "What do you think, Delia?"

"The ballroom is set up as a conference center. We could rent that out for business meetings. Small conferences," she said.

"I think they had that in mind when they set it up back in the 60s," Shackleford said.

"Do we know how many bedrooms there are?" Barbara asked.

"At least a dozen plus the servants' quarters upstairs and the butler's and cook's quarters," Shackleford said.

While they worked through their salads, Roger went to the kitchen and plated the main course, returning to the dining room with it on a lovely tray, each plate covered with a gleaming silver dome. He replaced the used salad plates with chicken and rice, getting appreciative smiles from Shackleford and Fidelia. After he served up water and wine, he took the dirty dishes back to the kitchen.

The meal progressed smoothly, Roger only half following the conversation as he made sure everyone had food and beverage. The brainstorming continued through dessert. Nobody complained about the store-bought pie; they seemed too engrossed in the planning.

As he poured the coffee, Shackleford looked up at him. "What do you think, Mulligan?"

"I think part of the plan might be to see what kind of need the city has," he said. "That would help focus the conversation."

"What kind of need?" Shackleford asked.

"Yes, sir. Are there hundreds of small conference centers going begging? Or are there professional organizations that don't have regular meeting spaces?"

"Oh, we didn't have that one on the list, did we?" Fidelia asked.

Barbara shook her head.

"We'd need to look into any licensing that might be required if we bring in guests," he said. "A bed and breakfast would need staff."

Barbara nodded. 'Yes. It would take some research into each of these ideas, but knowing what the city needs?" She nodded again. "Makes sense."

"Also scale," Fidelia said. "It's a lot of bedrooms for a residence. If we pick boarding school, how do we select students?"

"Can we even do that? What's this zoned for?"

"Residential, at the moment," Shackleford said.

"That's probably grandfathered in, though, isn't it?" Fidelia asked. "You're surrounded by multifamily buildings."

"Condominiums, to be precise," Shackleford said. "That's what Naomi wants this place to be."

"That can't happen," Barbara said.

Both Shackleford and Fidelia turned wide eyes on her. She sat back in her chair and swallowed. "Can it?"

Shackleford smiled. "I sincerely hope not. That's why you're here."

"Can we stop her?" Fidelia asked. "You know she's going to fight any will in probate."

"If I didn't think we could, I wouldn't be taking the steps I'm taking." He shrugged. "Anything is possible. Depends on whose palms get greased and how solidly we plan our defenses." He looked at Barbara. "You'd be the one in the hot seat."

Barbara shook her head. "I am far from an expert on rich people's problems."

Shackleford laughed and Fidelia hid a smile behind her coffee cup.

"Sorry, that might not have sounded right," Barbara said.

"No, no. Well and succinctly put," Shackleford said. "Here's what you have. Very deep pockets, which buy you the best expertise in the country. Need advice on bed and breakfast? Easy. Conference planning? Hire an expert for it."

"That's not going to work," Barbara said.

Shackleford raised his eyebrows. "Why not?"

"Parking," she said. "Unless you rent a parking garage somewhere and bus them in. The condo associations will complain."

"I thought you didn't know rich people's problems," he said.

She shrugged. "We're still brainstorming but it's pretty clear that a lot of this ignores the current regulatory environment."

"What kind of red tape did you have to deal with?" Shackleford asked.

"Not much at my place. Smaller town. Multi-use zoning including residential, retail, and even light industrial." She shrugged. "I needed to register with the state but it wasn't particularly onerous. Here? Who runs the city? Mayor and a city council? Zoning board. Building inspectors." She shook her head. "I'm guessing your niece will send all of them after us."

Shackleford grimaced and spun his coffee cup in its saucer. "True."

"So what do we do?" Fidelia asked.

Barbara's shoulders slumped a little and she leaned back in her chair. "Sleep on it?"

"It's a little early for bed, but we should probably figure out where we'll be sleeping," Fidelia said, grinning at Roger. "Suggestions, Mulligan?"

"The guest rooms in the west wing, ma'am. It would take only a few minutes to set them up for you, make the beds. Stock the bathrooms," he said.

Barbara looked back over her shoulder at him. "We've added to your workload."

"Nothing to concern yourself over, Miss Barbara."

Shackleford's eyebrows twitched at the use of her name and Fidelia smiled. "Do you have a preference, my dear?" she asked, looking at Barbara.

"Long as there's a bed and a bathroom nearby." She shrugged. "I'm not that fussy."

Shackleford caught Roger's eye. "If you'd make up the rooms on either side of the bath, Mulligan? It's not that far down the hall."

Roger nodded. "Of course, sir."

CHAPTER 17

Morning brought unexpected visitors to the front door—a bulky guy in an off-the-rack suit, backed up by a woman in a gray uniform with a "County Sheriff" patch on the shoulder.

"May I help you?" Roger asked.

"Are you Roger Mulligan, butler to Mr. Joseph Perry Shackleford of this address?" He paused to look up at the bronze numbers above the door.

"I am."

"I have a letter for Mr. Shackleford. Will you accept it?" He held up a business-sized white envelope.

"You have a summons for Mr. Shackleford?" He glanced at the sheriff's deputy.

"Yes," the man said.

"Mr. Shackleford is up. If you'd care to serve him directly, I can take you to him."

The man nodded. "The deputy is my witness."

Roger nodded. "I understand." He stood back from the doorway and held the door for them to enter, closing it behind them. "This way. Mr. Shackleford is at breakfast." Roger led them back through to the small dining room. "May I say who's calling, sir?"

The man glanced at him. "Who? Me?"

"Yes, sir."

He sniffed and shrugged. "William Quimby."

"Thank you, sir." Roger entered the dining room, interrupting the conversation. "I'm sorry to interrupt, sir. Mr. William Quimby and a deputy county sheriff to see you, sir." He stepped out of the way and Quimby entered, followed by the officer.

Shackleford rose and came around the table holding out his hand. "I'm Shackleford. Hand it over. Do you need me to sign for it?"

263

Quimby slapped the envelope into the old man's hand and nodded at the deputy. "She's my witness. Have a good day."

"Show them out, Mulligan."

"Yes, sir."

Roger ushered them out and made sure to lock the door behind them before returning to the dining room.

Shackleford looked up at him. "Some more coffee, please, Mulligan."

"Of course, sir."

He looked down at the document in his hand. "Next time, just accept the summons in my name, Mulligan. As butler you're an authorized agent for normal business." He waved the summons. "This is going to be normal business from now on, I expect."

"I will, sir."

"What's it for? Is she suing you?" Fidelia asked.

"Competency hearing." He shrugged and folded the document up, slipping it into the inside pocket of his jacket. "I expected it. Just not this soon."

Fidelia smirked. "We rattled her cage yesterday."

Roger took the coffee carafe around, filling cups as he went.

Shackleford shook his head, frowning. "Maybe, but I doubt that even my redoubtable niece can wrangle a motion in probate court in less than a week. This was foolish on her part."

"How so?" Fidelia asked.

"She needs to have a doctor's statement signed within thirty days of filing. I've only seen two doctors recently and neither of them found anything wrong with me."

"You expected this?" Barbara asked.

"Oh, yes." He nodded at Roger. "She hired Mulligan to be my caretaker." He looked up at Roger. "You'll probably be called as a witness."

"Of course, sir."

"I'll call Rexwood and have her look into it. I suspect we can get it quashed," Shackleford said. "In the meantime, what have you two cooked up?"

Roger worked around the table, clearing away the detritus of breakfast as they talked.

"Nothing new. The major assets are the classrooms, the dorm rooms, and the teachers' suites," Fidelia said. "That says 'school' to me, but I'm not sure how we manage that. The state's pretty rigid when it comes to who they let practice education."

"Something to look into," Shackleford said. "I have no idea what the regulations or liabilities are."

Barbara nodded. "Bed and breakfast is probably the next choice. We'd need to renovate, I think."

Shackleford took a sip of coffee and nodded. "Talk to me about this."

"We went back through the upstairs wings after dinner last night. They're clearly set up as some kind of boarding school. The classrooms, the dorm. Do you have any documentation on that?" she asked.

Shackleford pursed his lips. "It was before my time."

"Somebody must have kept records," Fidelia said.

"Like old ledgers, ma'am?" Roger asked.

All eyes turned to Roger. "Yes, Mulligan."

"I have some in my desk, ma'am. I never looked to see how far back they go."

"It's a start," she said, looking at Shackleford. "Can we look at them?"

"Of course," the old man said. "There might be some records in one of the warehouses, but finding them would take a miracle."

"Or allies," Fidelia said.

Shackleford raised an eyebrow. "Who'd you have in mind?"

"First things first," she said. "Let's see what we have in terms of ledgers. With any luck, that will give us a clue about what time frame."

Barbara shook her head, frowning into her cup.

"Something?" Fidelia asked.

"We're getting ahead of ourselves. Assume we're right. It was a boarding school. They had to be rich kids who weren't so rich that they got shipped off to some hoity-toity finishing school in Europe or one of the elite schools here."

"Or so rich they wouldn't hobnob with the merely wealthy," Fidelia said. "Also, remember—European travel was by steamship until recently."

Barbara nodded. "Yeah, even with that. Does it matter? Could we even consider it as worth doing?"

Fidelia's eyes widened and she put her cup into the saucer with an audible click.

Shackleford glanced at Fidelia before settling back in his chair, a bemused smile on his face and his fingers steepled over his chest. "Worth doing? Say more about that."

"Well, look," she said, looking up. "I'm pretty sure with enough money and the right people, we could probably figure out a way to teach a dozen kids. Teach them what?"

Shackleford shrugged. "Reading, writing, arithmetic?"

"Why?" Barbara asked.

"Why what?" Fidelia asked.

"Why reading, writing, and arithmetic?" she asked. "It's twelve people. Assume kids. Or maybe move them up to at-risk teens. What will we accomplish?"

Shackleford narrowed his eyes and tilted his head to one side. "Keep going. What do you want to accomplish?"

"I want to help people," she said, looking back into her cup.

A smile blossomed on Fidelia's face. "What do you want to help them with?"

Barbara shook her head. "I don't know. That's the problem. Maybe help kids with talent? I grew up completely lost. My teens were hell. I kept reading people and finding out how much they hated me or thought I was stupid or liked somebody else." She shook her head. "Flashes. I still have only the slightest idea of what I might be able to do." She glanced up at them. "You two do things that I'm in awe of. Pixies? Fairies?" She gazed around the room. "This house. It's like the damn thing is alive."

Shackleford blinked. "Alive?" He looked up at the ceiling, narrowing his eyes. "Can you read the house?"

Barbara shrugged and shook her head. "Not read. It's just kind of a background noise, like a refrigerator in the next room. You don't really hear it unless the house is quiet and it clicks on." She looked at Shackleford, then Fidelia. "You don't sense it?"

Fidelia shook her head. "I heard something yesterday." She glanced at Shackleford. "I don't know what it was, but I don't sense either the fairies or the pixies." She glanced up at the ceiling. "Nothing from the house, either."

"I hear the pixies," Shackleford said. "When they want me to. I can sense the fairies in the yard and atrium, but mostly I just let them be." He shrugged. "In my experience, we all have different talents and different levels of skill at those talents. I knew another mind reader once, but she was an old woman who lived in a cabin in the woods. She passed away a long time ago."

"How many wizards are there?" Barbara asked.

Shackleford shrugged and looked at Fidelia.

"I don't know, either," Fidelia said. "I have a list of a few hundred who attend the annual gala, but neither you nor your mother are on the list. Obviously."

"A few hundred?" Barbara asked, eyes wide.

Fidelia nodded. "Oh, yes. And more that I've heard of but aren't on the list."

"You know them when you see them, right? People with talent?" Barbara asked.

"Generally," Fidelia said. "A few have latent talent that's not visible. Every once in a while I've shaken hands with somebody and found a spark."

"So where are you going with this?" Shackleford asked. "Some kind of school for wizards?"

Barbara frowned and shook her head. "No. At least not here and I'm not sure it would help. If there are so many variations on talent, then trying to put together a curriculum to address them en masse would be doomed to fail before it even started."

Shackleford nodded. "So what then?"

"You're rich," she said, looking at Shackleford.

"I think we've established that," the old man said with a grin. "You're suggesting a charity?"

"No," Barbara said. "Well, maybe no. Maybe yes. I don't know." She scowled into her cup as if the answer might be floating in the coffee.

"Spit it out, girl," Fidelia said, a warm smile on her face. "I like the way you're thinking."

"With the house, we can help a dozen kids. How can we help a million?"

Shackleford's eyebrows shot up. "A big number, but only a fraction of the kids who need help on the planet."

"Help them with what?" Fidelia asked. "Wizards riding to the rescue to give them what we think is best for them?"

Barbara snorted. "That's worked out so well." She shook her head. "No. I don't know, but I'd rather give money to a school that can use that money to help a hundred kids than use the same amount to help a dozen who probably can already afford to get the help they need."

Shackleford pursed his lips for a moment before speaking. "Go back to growing up with talent. How did you navigate that by yourself?"

"I always had a high level of empathy, even as a kid. It just sort of went from that to getting deeper into their heads. Luckily, I have to actively look. It's not like some party in my head all the time."

"How many talented people have you seen?" Shackleford asked.

"Just a few. Less than a dozen before I met you. Nobody I knew to talk to. In the beginning, I'd see people walking by the house. They had a kind of glow." She smiled. "I asked my mother why some people glowed and others didn't. She didn't know what I was talking about. I remember being about ten or eleven and pointing to a lady walking by with a dog. She had this really cool aura thing around her. White and yellow and blue and red. It was pretty. When I pointed her out to my mother, she didn't see it. She just said, 'She's very pretty and quite talented, isn't she?' She said that. Talented. I asked what her talent was. Mom shrugged. 'Dressing well,' she said, as if that explained the glow."

"What if we asked the wizards?" Fidelia asked.

Barbara looked up at her. "Asked them what?"

"What they need. There'll be maybe a couple of hundred at the Fête. Most of them well off." She shrugged. "Most of us are."

"Really?" Barbara asked. "I wasn't until you found me. I'm still not. I'm comfortable. Run my little psychic business and it keeps me in incense and food."

Fidelia's shoulders dropped a fraction and she tilted her head a few degrees to the left.

"What if you're assuming that, because the ones you know are rich, most of them are?" Barbara asked. "How could we check that?"

"Go to a ball game," Roger said.

All eyes turned to him and he shrugged. "Sorry to interject, but if you can see it just by looking, go where there are a lot of people. Any large sporting event."

"How does that help us, Mulligan?" Shackleford asked.

"It answers the question of whether or not most wizards are rich. It'll give you an idea of how many there are. If the only ones at the event have expensive seats? I still don't know if that helps."

"What would you do with the place, Mulligan?" Shackleford asked. "You've been silent on the subject until now."

"Bed and breakfast," he said. "Exclusive. Expensive. Remodel the upstairs wings to make them luxury suites. We can extend the Wi-Fi network to cover the house with a few plug-ins. Put a real kitchen off the ballroom. Hire a chef to cook. Dress it up like an English manor house. Get some housekeepers and maids. A real butler. Some footmen." He shrugged. "Rich people will rent expensive suites in hotels with hot and cold running everything, but I suspect there might be people who'd get a kick out of being out of the limelight and having the chance to spend a few days with a butler and cook."

Shackleford and Fidelia both grinned, but Barbara frowned. "How does that help people?" she asked.

"It doesn't, miss. It answers the question of what to do with the house. With that out of the way, there's nothing preventing you from doing something else—something more altruistic, more philanthropic."

"You could even make that part of the sales pitch," Fidelia said. "Part of the proceeds go to help ... whomever."

Barbara fell back into her chair, gazing into the middle distance. "Could that work?"

Shackleford shrugged. "Do a preliminary plan on it. Bed and breakfasts were all the rage but now it's apparently whatever that silly Airbnb is."

Fidelia looked at him. "Where'd you hear that? I didn't think you ventured out of your library."

The old man sniffed. "I've seen the internet. That's how I found her." He nodded at Barbara.

Fidelia toasted him with her coffee cup. "Well done, sir."

He grinned. "Thank you, my dear."

"How would you even figure out the market for that?" Barbara asked.

"Hire a marketing research firm," Shackleford said. "You're working with deep pockets. I've always found that I can hire the expertise in areas in which I lack the background for much less than it would cost me to do it wrong."

"You've also had an advantage," Fidelia said, glancing at his chest.

He nodded. "True."

Barbara looked back and forth between Fidelia and Shackleford a couple of times. "Are you two hiding something from me?"

"We're not a couple, if that's where you're going," Fidelia said.

"It isn't." Barbara sat forward. "What's this about a competency hearing?"

"We've talked about this, haven't we?" Shackleford asked. "My niece wants me declared incompetent so she can become my guardian, tuck me into a home somewhere out of the way, and take over the estate and my finances. Her end goal is to get my money and assets and turn this place into the newest condos on the block."

"You seem a long way from incompetent, sir. How does she think this is going to play out in the court?"

Shackleford grimaced. "It will depend on the day, I suspect."

"The day?" Barbara looked around. "Why? Are you bad on Thursdays or something?"

Shackleford looked at Fidelia who shrugged and retreated behind her coffee. The look she gave him was clearly "you're on your own here, pal."

"First, I do not have dementia. Second, what I do have is a cursed artifact. I'm sure we talked about this before."

"Please keep going," Barbara said. "I'm not seeing where this dementia thing is coming from with your niece. Surely she's not seen you acting oddly."

Shackleford grimaced. "Actually, she has. When she's here, I'm in a wheelchair. I pretend."

Fidelia cleared her throat. Loudly.

"Sometimes I pretend," Shackleford said, glancing at Fidelia.

"And she's seen the real episodes enough to think that you're like that all the time?" Barbara asked.

"Basically," Shackleford said. "I haven't gone out of my way to disabuse her of the idea."

"So, if you go to court with a doctor's certificate that says you're not suffering dementia, and you can show the judge that you're lucid, what's the problem?"

"The episodes have become more frequent over the last few months. They're lasting longer. They're harder to bear." He looked down at his hands. "It's getting harder to come back from them."

"Recover afterwards, you mean?" Barbara asked.

Shackleford shook his head. "No, I mean get my mind back to the present."

"So you're afraid you'll have one of these episodes and think you're twenty years old again?"

He shrugged. "Basically."

"What's the day have to do with it?"

"They're worse and more common during the full moon." He shrugged. "Cliché, I know."

"Let me guess, the moon is full now?" Barbara asked.

Shackleford shook his head. "Nearly new. In spite of that, I had a serious episode yesterday while you were out."

"And if you take the artifact off, you die," Barbara said.

Shackleford nodded.

"If the judge finds in your niece's favor, even the fact that you've found me is likely to be discounted, isn't it?"

Shackleford nodded again.

"I'll be sure to cash the check quickly," she said.

Shackleford laughed. "Good idea."

"So we have two weeks to get the thing off you, right?" Barbara asked.

"That would be the idea, yes," Shackleford said. "I've been trying to figure out how to do that for the last twenty years."

"Or we try to delay the hearing," Fidelia said. "If we can get it delayed to the next new moon, we'd have a better chance."

Barbara shook her head. "I don't know. If you had a really bad episode just yesterday, what're the odds you won't have one today? Can you stack the deck so you don't have one in court?"

Shackleford sighed. "Not entirely. No."

"How do you reverse a curse?" Barbara asked. "You two are wizards, right?"

Fidelia shrugged. "They're not common. This one is ancient, from what I understand."

Shackleford nodded. "Old as humans on this continent, I think. I don't know what the power is behind it. I think of it as evil, but it might just be a function of the balance being maintained."

"Balance?" Barbara asked.

"Yes," the old man said. "I got a lot of good out of this curse. I'm paying the price now."

"What's the benefit if you die?" she asked.

"Somebody else will pick up the necklace," Shackleford said. "Like I did. They'll put it on and then they'll have the advantage and the cost."

"So it's a 'pay it forward' deal when you die?"

"In a manner of speaking, I suppose so," Shackleford said.

Barbara sat back in her chair, tilting her head to one side, some kind of processing going on behind her eyes.

"What are you thinking?" Fidelia asked.

"How dead is dead? And how do we pick it up without touching it?"

"Death is usually final," Fidelia said.

"Keyword. Usually." She looked at Roger. "You've brought people back from the dead."

Roger felt the blood drain from his face. "No."

"Yes," Barbara said. "You have. Flatlined, adrenaline push, zap 'em."

Roger swallowed hard. "Not. Happening."

"What are you thinking, my dear?" Fidelia asked, placing her cup in its saucer with a clink.

"He's an EMT. Emergency Medical Technician. He's trained in restarting hearts. He's done it at least twice here in the States."

Fidelia frowned. "Where else would he have done it?"

"Afghanistan," Roger said and blew out a deep breath.

"You're talking about killing me?" Shackleford asked in the same tone he might have asked "What's for dinner?"

"You don't sound surprised," Fidelia said.

He shook his head. "It's not the first thing that crossed my mind this morning, no, but I'd be lying if I hadn't thought about it."

She gasped. "You can't be serious."

"As a heart attack," he said, grinning at her. "You're not that much younger than I am. You know what I'm talking about."

She shrugged. "I'm planning for the end, yes, but I'm not seeking it."

"You don't have a chain around your neck that will kill you the next time you take it off."

"Granted," she said. "But still."

He waved her off. "Nothing like that."

"Sir, there is no way I am on board with anything involving you taking that thing off," Roger said.

"You did get that device the doctor recommended, didn't you?"

"Yes, sir. It's in the pantry, but that's a 'Hail Mary' tool when nothing else will work."

He nodded. "I understand. At my age, you like to have as many 'Hail Marys' in your pocket as you can."

Barbara frowned and reached across the table to touch his hand. "I didn't mean anything ..."

He chuckled. "I know." He patted her hand, his gnarled, liver-spotted hands looking odd against her smoother, lighter skin. "If, by some twist of fate, you find me dead on the floor, do not pick up the necklace with your hand."

"Could she help herself?" Fidelia asked. "Could you resist when you first saw it?"

The amusement drained out of Shackleford's face. "I had it around my neck before I even realized I'd picked it up."

Fidelia shrugged. "So, it's basically a time bomb for the rest of us as well."

Shackleford looked down and ran his fingers over his mouth. "I hadn't thought of that."

"Enough of this," Fidelia said, slapping the tablecloth with her palm. "You're not going to die between now and next week. We need to get one of your legal beagles on this trail and find out what she's planning. Do we have anything like discovery in this, or do we have to wait until the trial?"

"I don't know," the old man said. "You're right. Mulligan, would you book me an hour with Julia Rexwood. She should be in your book under legal advisors."

"Julia Rexwood, sir," Roger repeated, pulling out his notebook and writing the name. "As soon as I've cleared, sir."

Shackleford looked at the ormolu clock on the sideboard. "Her office should be open now. We can take care of ourselves while you make the call."

"Of course, sir." Roger went to his quarters to look up Rexwood's number and copy it into his notebook before going to the new phone in the cubby off the kitchen. Part of him missed the old black rotary with its weapons-grade handset, but punching in the numbers and hitting Dial made for a less error-prone method, since it allowed him to check the number on the screen against the one in his notebook.

The phone rang once before the call connected. "Julia Rexwood. What can I do for Shackleford House today?"

"Good morning, Ms. Rexwood. My name is Roger Mulligan. I'm the Shackleford butler. Mr. Shackleford asked me to book an hour of your time to look into a summons he's just received."

The line went silent for a moment, long enough that Roger looked to see if the call had disconnected. "Yes," she said. "Do you have the docket number and court?"

"Mr. Shackleford has it. I can get it for you."

"Please do."

"One moment." Roger pushed the hold button on the handset and went back to the small dining room. "She would like the information from the summons, sir."

Shackleford nodded and pulled the document from his pocket, holding out a hand for the phone. "Let me talk to her."

Roger released the hold and said, "Mr. Shackleford, ma'am," into the handset before handing the phone to the old man.

"Julia?" He listened for a moment and then read off the docket number and court information. "Yes, competency. Preliminary hearing." He nodded several more times without speaking. "If you need more than an hour, take what you need." He listened for a few more moments. "Let me know. Mulligan can drive me down to your office if you need me." He nodded a few more times. "Thank you, Julia. Good-bye." He handed the phone back to Roger. "She'll track it down and get back to us, probably later this morning." He folded the summons back up and slipped it into his pocket. "So where were we?"

"You're not going to die," Fidelia said. "At least not around us."

Shackleford nodded. "Fair enough. And bed and breakfast?"

"We need to hire a marketing team," Barbara said. "Do you have one of those in your book, Mulligan?"

"I can check, Miss Barbara. Would anyone like more coffee?" Roger made a fast pass around the table picking up dirty dishes and the now-empty carafe. "I'll make another pot."

Shackleford nodded. "I'd have another cup."

Roger nodded and headed for his quarters again, stopping at the kitchen to drop off the dishes and telephone handset. He had a suspicion he'd need it again soon. He picked up his Bible and checked the table of contents for consultants, finding "Consultants, Marketing" as a category with half a dozen entries under it. He shrugged and took the book back to the dining room. "It seems we have our choice, sir."

"How many?" Shackleford asked.

"Six, sir."

Shackleford held out his hand. "Show me, please, Mulligan."

Roger took the book to him and opened to the pages.

Shackleford took the book and tilted his head slightly upwards to read it. "All right," he said. "Most of these are sales agencies. They specialize in targeting advertising."

"Don't you need to know markets to do that?" Barbara asked.

"Yes, but they specialize in creating the ad campaigns once the markets are established. They'd be useful once we determine if there's enough interest in the bed and breakfast idea, but my concern is that they'd take the idea and try convince us to give them a million dollars to sell it before answering the question 'Should we?' I can't blame them. From their viewpoint, the answer is always 'Why not?' They're good. I recognize the names." The old man shook his head. "This one. Badger Ltd. Horace and Hecuba Badger. Brother and sister team, if you can believe it."

"Oh, I know them," Fidelia said. "Horace is a lovely man, and Hecuba's razor-focused and sharp as a new blade."

Shackleford handed the book back to Mulligan. "Call them. See what kind of availability they have, would you, Mulligan? You can drive Barbara and Delia over to see what they have to say."

"Of course, sir."

"You're not coming?" Barbara asked.

"No. This is your plan. I'll bankroll it, but it's up to you three to hash it out." He eyed Barbara over his spectacles. "Assuming you're interested in this to begin with."

Barbara opened her mouth as if to speak but closed it again without saying a word. She looked at Fidelia. "What do you think I should do?"

"I think you should follow your heart, my dear. Anything else is simply wasting your time."

Barbara looked at Roger. "Mulligan? Any opinion?"

Roger shrugged. "You've been paid for a week's worth of work, or will be. Spending it planning the house's future doesn't mean you need to be here for it." He paused for a moment. "It will just make it more difficult to walk away from a project you'll have invested yourself in."

Barbara blinked and stared at him for several moments. "Just like you can't walk away from being the butler," she said.

"Precisely, Miss Barbara."

Barbara nodded. "All right then. Let's build the plan. What do we do if we find the idea of a B and B is untenable?"

"Ask the Badgers what they'd recommend," Fidelia said. "They're bound to have ideas on how to leverage the estate."

"One step at a time," Shackleford said. "Go meet with them." He nodded at Roger. "Give them a call, Mulligan. Get it arranged for this afternoon if possible, but as soon as they can fit you in."

"At once, sir." Roger left them sitting at the table while he went to the kitchen and called the number listed.

The phone rang three times before being picked up. "Badger Limited. How can we help you?" a young-sounding man's voice asked.

"Good morning, My name is Mulligan and I work for Shackleford House. We have a marketing research problem that we would like you to address."

"Shackleford House? Mr. Shackleford needs us?"

"Technically, a working group he has designated to lay out a future for the residence, but yes, Mr. Shackleford will fund the project."

"One moment, please, Mr. Mulligan."

The line went silent with a click.

After maybe thirty seconds, a new man's voice came on the line. "This is Hector Badger. To whom am I speaking?"

"I'm Roger Mulligan, Mr. Badger. Butler at Shackleford House."

"Mulligan. I see. Is Mr. Shackleford available?"

"Yes, sir. One moment." Roger took the handset to the dining room, offering it to Shackleford. "Mr. Badger would like to speak with you, sir."

Shackleford took the phone and said, "Hector. How's the family?" After a short conversation he handed it back to Roger. "There you go."

He took the handset and said, "Mr. Badger. Mulligan here."

"Thank you, Mulligan. I needed to make sure you were who you said you were."

"I understand, sir."

"We have an hour open this afternoon at 2:30. Can you make that?"

"Of course, sir. 2:30 it is."

"Excellent. I'm looking forward to hearing what this project is about."

"We'll be there. Good-bye, sir." Roger hung up and nodded to Barbara. "We have an hour at Badger, Limited, at 2:30 this afternoon, Miss Barbara."

"You'll want to organize your thinking, perhaps lay out a series of questions you'd like to submit to them," Shackleford said.

"Do we have something like a notepad in the house?" Fidelia asked, looking at Mulligan. "Some loose sheets of paper?"

"Reams of printer paper, ma'am."

"Printer?" She looked at Shackleford, her eyes wide. "I'm impressed. I don't suppose we could use your computer?"

"Mine might be easier, ma'am. It's a laptop. I believe you could set up wherever you like in the main house."

Shackleford took the last swig of coffee from his cup and placed it back on the table, laying his napkin beside it. "That's my cue." He rose and smiled at Barbara. "I'll just get back to my research and leave you to it."

"You don't want to be involved?" Barbara asked.

"Oh, I will be, but I'm most interested in seeing how you tackle this problem." He smiled at Fidelia. "Don't corrupt her too much, Delia."

The old woman smiled back at him. "You know I don't go in for half measures, Joseph. Thank you for letting me be involved. I think this is the most fun I've had since planning my last safari."

"Kilimanjaro?" he asked.

She shook her head. "That was fun, too, but I went back a few years later and took a photographic safari into the high veldt. More of a trek, really, along the trail between Royal Natal and Cathedral Peak. Afterward I took a side trip into the Kalahari. Fascinating culturally, and the scenery?" She sighed. "Breathtaking. Not in the literal sense like above 14,000 feet, but amazing."

"Is there any place you haven't been?" Barbara asked, her eyes wide.

Fidelia shrugged. "Oh, lots. I haven't been to the Australian Outback yet. I may combine that with an Antarctic expedition. They're very hard to arrange unless you're willing to take the commercial tourist route."

Shackleford chuckled. "I'll be in the library if you need me." He looked at each of the two women with a broad grin. "Although I can't imagine what you two might need the likes of me for."

"Would you like anything, sir?" Roger asked. "I'll be up shortly for the morning chores."

"No, thank you, Mulligan. Just call me for lunch."

"Of course, sir."

Shackleford shared a smile all around and headed toward the library.

"You mentioned a laptop?" Fidelia said.

"Would you like it in the upstairs parlor?" Roger asked.

"If that's convenient."

"Of course, ma'am. I'll fetch it immediately." He took a stack of dirty dishes to the kitchen on his way through to his quarters. His morning routine would suffer for this diversion, but he couldn't help feeling excited by what it could mean for the house.

CHAPTER 18

The offices of Badger, Limited, occupied the fifth floor of a brick commercial building in the old part of town, not far from Shackleford's automobile warehouse. The receptionist—a twenty-something young man wearing a navy business suit, a crisp, pale blue button-down shirt, and a foulard tie—walked them to a freight elevator and took them up. "This used to be a factory," he said. "Aircraft engine assembly during the war, and then a food processing company took it over in the 50s. You can still smell the spices in the basement when the weather is damp."

The elevator let them out onto a vast open space with tall windows running from floor to ceiling. The polished concrete floors gleamed as if they were marble; sturdy concrete columns perhaps twenty feet high held up the roof.

A gray-haired couple met them as the doors opened. "Delia?" the woman said, a broad smile blooming on her face. "I didn't expect to see you here."

Delia led them off the elevator, offering a double-cheek kiss to the woman and to an equally pleased-looking man. "Hecuba. So lovely to see you. You, too, Horace." She turned to Roger and Barbara. "Let me introduce you to the rest of the project team." She grinned. "This young woman is Barbara Griffin, a long-lost Shackleford relative who's got some questions we'd like you to answer."

The Badgers each took a turn to offer a hand and greeting.

"The old man finally found an acceptable heir?" Horace said, his eyes dancing.

"Nice to meet you, Mr. Badger. Ms. Badger," Barbara said. Roger caught the slight squinting of Barbara's eyes and the way her shoulders lost some of their tension afterward.

Fidelia waved Roger forward. "This is Roger Mulligan. The new butler at Shackleford House."

Horace offered his hand. "We spoke on the phone, I believe. Nice to meet you, Mr. Mulligan."

Roger shook and gave a short nod. "And you, sir."

Hecuba followed her brother's lead and shook Roger's hand as well. "You're part of the project team?"

"I am, ma'am."

Hecuba looked to Fidelia with a question on her face that she didn't give voice to.

"After Perkins passed away, Mr. Mulligan took over looking after Joseph and the house. He's intimately familiar with the workings of the household and should prove invaluable for his insights," Fidelia said. "He's aware that we all share certain gifts and abilities."

Both Badgers' eyes widened in surprise and a small amount of alarm.

Roger gave them a small nod. "Discretion is key to my position. While I'm occasionally surprised, I'm equally delighted to find so many talents that I never knew existed."

"Well, let's go see what we can do to help Shackleford House today, hmm?" Hecuba said, recovering her equanimity. "If you'd come this way ...?" She led them across the open space, her footsteps echoing from the concrete surfaces all around.

She stopped at an oval conference table near the harbor-side corner of the building. A taller building a couple of blocks away obscured a bit of the view, but the afternoon sun shining on the working harbor made for a picturesque backdrop.

Hector took a seat on one long side and waved them into chairs. "So? What's the pitch?"

Barbara and Fidelia took turns laying out the situation. Roger watched as Fidelia managed to pull Barbara out of her shell and push her forward as the project lead, handing more and more of the explanation to her.

"So, that's it," Barbara concluded. "Mr. Shackleford would like to know what to do with the mansion. It's an amazing building, and keeping most of it unoccupied isn't really useful. Among the three of us, we believe an English estate theme with butlers and footmen, a cook and parlor maids, might be an appropriate use of the site, but we'd like to get a better idea of whether or not the project is viable from a marketing perspective."

"You've determined that the house can support it?" Horace asked. "The building is sound enough?"

"We believe so, yes," Barbara said. "We'll probably need a structural engineer to sign off on it."

Roger took out his notebook and made a note.

"Parking?" Hecuba asked. "How many guests are you thinking of?"

"There's a large loading dock at the end of the east wing," Roger said. "The drive and paved area together are big enough for at least ten cars, perhaps a dozen. We could park a few more behind the main house, and there's room for expansion in both areas if there's a need."

"So? Call it a dozen guest rooms with room for a single vehicle each. Six in each wing?"

"We'd need to see how the floor plans look," Barbara said. "The house isn't exactly symmetrical. I think we'd need to maintain at least a few of the family bedrooms, but yes, for planning purposes, call it twelve rooms."

"You'll have to check with the city codes office," Horace said. "I'm not sure what restrictions they've managed to saddle that neighborhood with as part of their gentrification."

Roger took out his notebook again and made another note.

"First things first," Barbara said. "If it's not a viable project from a marketing perspective, then we'd have to revisit."

"If you discover something that might be more useful or more interesting," Fidelia said, "we'd be interested in hearing about it. I suspect we've overlooked a great number of possibilities."

The Badgers looked at each other and nodded in unison. "Is there anything else?" Hecuba asked.

"Not that I can think of," Barbara said.

"Me, either," Fidelia said.

Hecuba looked at Roger. "Mr. Mulligan? You've been pretty quiet over there."

"We considered several options including boarding schools, but I really think a bed and breakfast is our best choice. Capitalization isn't an issue. We can charge what we need to in order to cover the expenses of the additional staff but we don't know if that high-end market of bed and breakfast is viable at ten to twelve rooms at something over a thousand a night."

"A lot would depend on the costs. How much remodeling would you have to eat?" Hecuba asked.

Roger ran the floor plan of the east wing through his mind. "It might be substantial," he said. "Depends on what we do with the rooms that are already there. The east wing may need to be gutted and redone from the walls in." That thought made him pause and look at Barbara.

She returned the concerned gaze.

"That's got you thinking, at least," Hecuba said with a smile. "That's good."

Fidelia looked back and forth between Roger and Barbara but didn't offer any additional comments.

Barbara took the meeting back to focus. "All of it depends on what the likely market is. That's what we need next."

Horace nodded. "I agree. Can any of you sign a contract for Shackleford?"

"I can take it to him for signature and return it today, sir," Roger said.

"I can," Fidelia said. She shrugged. "Durable power of attorney. He's got one for me as well. Long-standing, actually."

Horace nodded. "Let me get a contract and we can start today." He went over to a desk on the far side of the building.

"This is a big space for what you use," Fidelia said.

Hecuba smiled. "I love it. It echoes a lot, but when it's just us up here, we play music and it's like a concert hall. Sometimes we dance." She looked down with a shy smile before looking out the window. "View's not bad either."

"You own the whole building?" Barbara asked.

"We do. The basement is filled with our computers. First floor is rented office space. I've got one open if you're looking?" Hecuba raised an eyebrow.

Barbara grinned. "Not just yet, but I'll keep it in mind."

"Second and third are offices for our research teams. Fourth floor is our apartment."

"You live here?" Fidelia said.

"Really short commute time," Horace said, coming back with a single-page contract. "We got a zoning variance from the city to include our residence. It was cheaper than having to support another building." He slid the contract over to Fidelia. "Standard terms. We've done a lot of work for Shackleford over the years."

Fidelia scanned the contract and pulled a pen out of thin air to sign it. She turned the page around to the Badgers' side of the table.

Horace stared at her for a long moment.

"I told you. He knows," Fidelia said.

Horace looked at Roger who shrugged. "I work for Mr. Shackleford, sir. It's been an interesting few months."

Horace snorted a short laugh and took Fidelia's offered pen to scrawl his signature on the line. He handed her back the pen and picked up the paper, sliding it between thumb and forefinger. He pulled a second copy off the back of the first and handed the top copy to her. "We'll have a preliminary report in a couple of days."

"Can you email it to us?" Barbara asked, giving her address.

"Copy to me, too?" Roger asked, giving his.

"You have email now?" Hecuba asked.

Roger smiled. "We have internet at the house now, yes."

She smiled. "That will make things easier."

"What's your timeline on this project?" Horace asked.

"I've got five more days to come up with a plan for what to do with Shackleford House," Barbara said. "I could run a little long; but my goal is to have something within a week."

"Thought about tours?" Hecuba asked.

"Parking is an issue," Barbara said. "As Roger noted before, ten or twelve cars is our limit."

"Artist's residence?" Horace asked. "Long-term retreats. Writers, artists?"

"Could we generate enough revenue to cover the real-estate taxes?" Barbara asked. "They're called 'starving artists' for a reason."

"Not all who wander are lost and not all artists starve," Horace said. "But I take your point."

"Wizard school?" Hecuba asked.

"Thought of that, too," Barbara said. "I have no idea how to make that work. I'm self-taught—how would we identify students and how would they pay for it?"

Hecuba looked at Fidelia. "You know a lot of rich wizards with kids."

"Not that many. It comes back to how do you teach talent? Talented parents handle it for their kids. Sport talents have no parents to guide them."

"My mother has a thread of talent. I can see it in her now, but she can't see it in me," Barbara said.

"Now?" Hecuba asked.

"Growing up, I couldn't. I started developing in my teens, but I was probably twenty-five before I saw it in her."

"Something to think about," Horace said. "Is there anything else?"

"I'm good," Barbara said.

Fidelia stood. "We've taken enough of your time. We should let you get on with the project. Thank you, both."

"Our pleasure," Hecuba said, heading toward the elevator.

"How did you get involved with Shackleford House, Barbara?" Horace asked.

"I'm related to Mr. Shackleford. He tracked me down and hired me to come work with him for a week."

"Hired you?" Hecuba said.

"Yes. Consultant on the future of Shackleford House."

"She's the only talented Shackleford he's been able to find," Fidelia said, reaching out to give Barbara a sideways hug. "With any luck, he'll be able to keep the place out of his niece's property-grubbing paws."

"Naomi?" Hecuba asked.

"That's the one."

The two Badgers shared a look.

"She's bad news, that one," Horace said.

"How well we know," Fidelia said.

They arrived at the elevator as the doors opened, the young man from the entry smiling at them. "Going down?"

After another round of handshakes and a ride in the elevator, they emerged into the parking lot in the shaded canyon between buildings.

"Two days?" Barbara asked.

"They're good at what they do. I suspect they'll do a quick documentation search and see if there's any foundation to build on. With their talents and connections that won't take long," Fidelia said. "If they have to go out and sample, that'll take longer and be more expensive."

Roger held the car door for them. "What if they say it's not viable, ma'am?"

Barbara slid in first and Fidelia followed. "Then we reassess our goals," she said. "One thing we haven't considered is why we're doing it."

Roger closed the door and walked around to the driver's side. "Besides Mr. Shackleford's wish?" he asked, starting the car and getting them moving toward the street.

"Yes. Does he have a goal? Is it busy work to give Barbara something to do?" She reached over and patted Barbara's hand where it lay on the seat. "You're delightful, my dear, but would you have come to stay for a week if he hadn't hired you?"

"To be fair, he hired me to come stay at the house for a week and see if I liked it," she said. "It sounded skeevy to me but I'm making as much this week as I would in a year as a psychic."

Fidelia pulled back a little and turned sideways in her seat. "A psychic?"

"That's my talent," Barbara said. "I can read minds. At least in people without talent. I have a few other minor talents, but I figured out that I could make money as Madame Dionysia, Spiritualist. It was better than working retail."

"What's your background?"

"Grew up in a small town in Rhode Island. That's where Mr. Shackleford found me. Got good grades, studied business management at URI. With what I'm earning this week, I'll be able to sink my student loans, finally."

"Did you have your talent while you were in school?" Fidelia asked, a wry smile on her lips.

"Did I cheat on exams?" Barbara asked with a small chuckle. "Unfortunately, it never worked that way." She shook her head. "I did my own work."

"Meet any other talented people?" Fidelia asked. "I'd have thought a population of that size might have at least a few."

"I suspect they do. It's a big school. I kept my head down and my mouth shut for the most part. If they weren't in my classes or living in my dorm, I wouldn't have even seen them." Barbara sighed. "Being a psychic isn't the best talent to have in a hormone- and alcohol-laced soup. At the time, I didn't have nearly the level of control that I've developed since I graduated."

"Are all talented people single?" Roger asked, looking at them in the rearview mirror.

Fidelia snorted. "No. I was married for a time. Joseph was, too."

"I've had some relationships," Barbara said. "It was easy to tell when they soured."

Roger pulled the car into the drive behind the house and parked near the back door. He opened the doors for Barbara and Fidelia but when he unlocked the back door, both women paled.

"Oh, dear," Fidelia said.

"What's that sound? Sounds like a smoke alarm?" Barbara asked.

Roger shook his head. "I don't hear anything."

"Pixies," Fidelia said, bolting into the house. "With me, Mulligan."

The three of them raced into the foyer and stopped. Both Barbara and Fidelia kept turning their heads this way and that.

"I can't tell where it's coming from," Barbara said.

"I can't either." Fidelia's eyes narrowed until they nearly closed.

"Mr. Shackleford?" Mulligan shouted. He shook his head and mounted the stairs two at a time, making a bee-line for the library. He made a quick circuit around the room, checking behind the furniture and under the tables, before bolting to the master suite. He found the old man propped against the wall and sitting on the bathroom floor, naked except for the chain and pendant around his neck. He stared into space, eyes open, his hands palm up on his skinny thighs. "Sir?" He heard the footsteps behind him and stepped into the door frame to block them. "He's in here. Give me a moment."

Fidelia stopped, sliding a little bit on the polished floor. "Is he okay?"

Roger looked over his shoulder. "No blood. No broken bones. Let me get a robe on him." He stepped back into the bath and closed the door behind him. "Sir?" He pulled the old man's robe from its hook behind the door and held it open. "Mr. Shackleford?"

The old man didn't move.

Roger draped the warm robe over him backward, like a blanket. He pressed his fingertips against Shackleford's throat, finding the pulse to be strong and regular. He flashed a hand in front of the old man's face and his eyes blinked. He crouched down in front of him. "Mr. Shackleford? Can you hear me?"

Shackleford's brow furrowed and his eyes started blinking—regular pulses that were too long to be autonomous. Blink. Blink. Blink. After a half dozen or more blinks, his eyes closed, the wrinkles around them deepening. After a few moments, the old man drew in a long, shuddering breath and his eyes popped open. "Perkins. No. Mulligan. You're back."

"Are you, sir? Back I mean?"

His head wobbled on his neck, something between a tiny nod and a tiny shake. "I'm about halfway in each. It's ... odd. Like a dream." He looked around, just his eyes at first and then his head started turning. "I'm on the floor?"

"Yes, sir. Naked under the robe."

Shackleford glanced down and to the side. "That explains why my butt's complaining." He looked up. "Is it safe for me to get up?"

"I don't know, sir. Do you feel dizzy? Light-headed? Weak?"

Shackleford shook his head. "Not that I can tell."

"Let's see if we can get you off the floor and put that robe on properly."

Roger got under Shackleford's arm and pulled him to his feet, catching the robe as it fell off to wrap it around him correctly and cinch the tie around his waist. Shackleford seemed steady enough on his own to take the step to the john and sit on the closed lid.

"How are you doing, sir?"

Shackleford shrugged. "Whatever it was, it's receding quickly. Where are Barbara and Delia?"

"I suspect they're panicking on the other side of that door, sir."

He swallowed. "I'm fine," he said, raising his voice to a near shout.

"Okay," Fidelia's voice sounded strained, and right against the wood. "We'll wait in the library."

Roger heard their footsteps recede as he watched Shackleford regain his normal composure. As normal as it could be sitting on the can in the bathroom, anyway. "How can I help you, sir?"

"Where are my clothes?" he asked looking around the bathroom.

"Where do you usually get undressed, sir? I assume you were either in or about to get into the shower."

"Not getting out?" Shackleford asked, still scanning the room.

"No water on the floor. Your hair and beard aren't wet, sir."

Shackleford reached up to touch his beard then nodded. "Good thinking."

"Doesn't take Sherlock Holmes to see the obvious, sir."

Shackleford offered one of his small chuckles. "You'd be surprised, Mulligan."

"Was it the amulet, sir?"

Shackleford nodded. "Yes, I'm relatively certain. I'm also relatively certain that it's a problem." He looked up into Roger's face. "It's getting worse. I've never had an episode like this before."

"That you know of, sir," Roger said.

"Eh? What?" Shackleford asked.

"Well, I only knew you were in trouble because both Barbara and Fidelia heard something. Something loud. I couldn't hear it."

Shackleford frowned, his tongue flickering over his bottom lip. "Pixies?"

"Or the fairies. Or both," Roger said with a shrug. "Fidelia heard something the other day when we found you in the atrium, sir."

"So, your hypothesis is that I may have had other episodes like this—even when you were here—but you didn't hear the alarm?"

"Yes, sir. You could have come out of this on your own and I'd have never known. We have no way of knowing how many times or how often it's happened over the last five months."

Shackleford nodded, his brow furrowing. "Distressing thought, Mulligan. Quite distressing."

"It's happened twice in two days, sir. It could be a fluke."

Shackleford shook his head. "I don't think so, Mulligan. I'm afraid it's not. We go hours between speaking."

"I'm hesitant to impose on your time, sir. I have my duties to keep me busy."

"Yes, Mulligan, but it may be time to make those duties include a periodic check-in to make sure I'm still—well—me."

"As long as the two ladies are in the house, I should have plenty of warning." Roger smiled at him. "Now, do you need help dressing?"

Shackleford shook his head, seeming quite himself again. "I think I can manage, Mulligan. If you'd see to our guests, I'll be along shortly."

"Yes, sir." Roger left him sitting on the john and went through to the library.

Barbara and Fidelia looked up as he entered.

"How is he?" Barbara asked.

"Mr. Shackleford seems to have recovered. He's dressing and will be along shortly."

"You didn't hear the noise?" Fidelia asked.

"No, ma'am. I assume you heard some magically generated sound that I'm deaf to. The same as the other day in the atrium."

She frowned and worried her lower lip with her teeth. "That's a problem."

"Yes, ma'am. I just discussed that with Mr. Shackleford."

"What's a problem?" Barbara asked.

"Actually, it's twofold," Fidelia said. "One, we don't know how many of these episodes he's had. Mulligan has been here for months but can't hear either the pixies or the fairies. We don't know how many times he's had an episode like this."

"Are they dangerous?" Barbara asked.

Fidelia shook her head. "Not as such, no."

"The difficulty is that I don't know how long they last or how frequently they may be happening. Mulligan and I cross paths rarely over the course of the day," Shackleford said from the door. He nodded to Mulligan on his way to his normal chair, lowering himself and relaxing into it with a quiet sigh.

"What's the other problem?" Barbara asked.

"If they're more frequent than we know, it raises the possibility that it might happen while he's in court," Fidelia said.

Shackleford frowned. "That reminds me. We haven't heard from Julia Rexwood, have we?"

"Not to my knowledge, sir," Roger said. "Let me check the messages." He went to the upstairs parlor to check but found none recorded. When he got back to the library, Shackleford had the Badger contract in his hand and was scanning down through it.

"This was well done," he said. "Your work, Delia?"

"Hers," Fidelia said, nodding at Barbara.

Shackleford beamed at the younger woman. "Well done, indeed."

"Might I get refreshment, sir?" Roger asked.

Shackleford looked over at Fidelia and Barbara. "Tea? Coffee?"

"I wouldn't say no to either," Fidelia said.

"Coffee?" Barbara asked. "If it's not too much trouble."

"No trouble, Miss Barbara," Roger said.

Shackleford nodded and handed the contract to Roger. "Coffee it is, then, and would you file this, please, Mulligan."

Roger took the document and bowed. "Of course, sir. It'll be a few minutes."

He dropped the contract off on his desk on the way to the kitchen and set about putting the coffee tray together. The routine effort gave him something to do to assimilate the adrenaline spike he'd received by finding Shackleford sitting naked on the cold tiles of his bathroom. He took a few cleansing breaths while the coffeepot surged and hissed on the counter. How many episodes had he missed? There was the time he found the old man shirtless, and this one, but how many more? As the coffee huffed to the end of its cycle he took some solace in the idea that nothing serious had befallen the old guy yet.

He'd still make it a point to check on him at least once an hour when the women left.

Julia Rexwood called as Roger finished setting the table for dinner. He took the handset to Shackleford in the library and waited.

"Can they compel that?" he asked once the pleasantries had finished. He frowned and shook his head. "I see. It would have been nice to have some kind of notification." He glanced to Roger, and then arched a brow.

"They can't have gotten access to my records," Shackleford said into the phone. "How did they convince a judge to accept the petition? Don't they need some kind of justification?" He frowned and nodded for a few moments. "I see. So this is a preliminary hearing? Should I get a copy of my own doctor's report?" He nodded. "Of course. I'll have them send it to you." He nodded a few more times. "Anything else?" He nodded again. "Very well. Thank you, Julia." He handed the phone back to Roger. "Thank you, Mulligan."

"Well?" Fidelia asked.

"Preliminary hearing to see if there's cause to hold a full guardianship hearing," Shackleford said. "We're allowed to bring witnesses and submit documentation from our own physicians." He looked at Roger. "I'd like you to be there to speak on my behalf, if you would, Mulligan."

"I'd be happy to, sir." He paused. "I won't be able to lie, sir."

Shackleford grinned. "I wouldn't expect you to. Just tell them the precise answer to the questions they ask and you should be fine."

Fidelia raised her eyebrows. "Is that wise, Joseph?"

"I know my niece. Once they get Mulligan sworn in they'll ask him about my wheelchair and the episodes she's supposedly observed herself." He looked at Roger and lowered his voice. "Tell the court, Mr. Mulligan. Have you observed the interactions between Mr. Shackleford and Mrs. Patching?"

"Yes, sir," Roger said.

"How would you characterize those interactions, Mr. Mulligan?" Shackleford asked, keeping the lower voice going.

Roger smiled. "It was a rather convincing act, sir."

"You mean to say he was pretending, Mr. Mulligan?"

"Yes, sir. Right down to the wheelchair, which he only used when Mrs. Patching was in the house."

Shackleford smiled and nodded. "Easy. If they ask you anything beyond that, just answer with the truth, Mulligan."

Barbara pursed her lips and frowned. "They're not going to let off that easily."

"They have the burden of proof, my dear," Fidelia said. "But I agree. I'd expect some questions that will require a little more tap-dancing."

"No tap-dancing," Shackleford said. "Simple answers. Yes or no as much as possible. Julia will go over it with us before the hearing."

The front doorbell rang, interrupting the conversation.

"Speak of the devil," Shackleford said. "That's Naomi now. Probably coming to make sure I'm properly flustered." He nodded at Roger. "Show her in, Mulligan."

"Yes, sir."

Roger went to the door and opened it to find Naomi and Ted waiting on the stoop. "Mr. and Mrs. Patching," he said. "Mr. Shackleford is expecting you. Come in."

Ted blinked and his face blanked for a moment but Naomi smiled and led the way in.

"I just bet he was," she said.

Roger ushered them up the stairs to the library. "Mr. and Mrs. Patching, sir." He stepped out of the door frame to allow them to enter.

Naomi stopped short just inside the room and Ted nearly bumped into her. "You're still here?" she said, glaring at Barbara.

"Where else would I be?" Barbara asked.

"Your home?" Naomi asked, taking two steps into the room.

Fidelia stood and offered a hand to Naomi. "We haven't been formally introduced, have we? I'm Fidelia Necket. You must be the niece who's dragging him into court in a couple of weeks. Naomi, is it?" She smiled.

Naomi scowled and walked past Fidelia to crouch beside Shackleford's wheelchair. "How are you feeling, Uncle?"

He smiled in her general direction. "Naomi, what a surprise. And you brought Michael for a visit." He leaned over toward her. "Getting serious are you?"

Naomi smiled and patted the old man's forearm. "This is Ted, Uncle. My husband now."

Shackleford looked up, frowning at Ted and then back at Naomi. "Ted? What happened to Michael? He was such a nice boy."

Naomi sighed, a deep from-the-chest dramatic performance of a sigh. "We just didn't work out, Uncle."

"I'm sorry to hear that," Shackleford said. "What brings you to visit an old man this morning?"

"We were in the neighborhood and just wanted to stop by to see if there was anything you needed."

Shackleford shook his head. "How considerate, but I'm fine. Perkins here takes good care of me, and my niece has come to stay for a few months."

"Uncle, I'm your niece."

He blinked. "Really?" He peered into her face and then looked at Barbara. "She's also my niece, isn't she? Barbara?"

"No, Joseph, I'm just your cousin, several times removed," Barbara said, settling back on her easy chair with the tiniest of smiles on her lips and ice in her eyes.

Naomi shot a couple of daggers from her eyes at her before turning back to Shackleford. "Well, I'll leave you to your guests, Uncle. We just wanted to make sure you were all right."

"Very considerate," he said, smiling into space somewhere over her left shoulder.

Naomi stood, smoothing down her skirt before turning to Barbara. "You're not fooling anyone," she said, the final word grinding out between her molars.

Barbara smiled. "Don't bet on that, Mrs. Patching."

Naomi sniffed and turned to Fidelia. "Another gold-digger?"

Fidelia snickered and shot a glance at Ted before looking back at her. "Are you the pot or the kettle?"

Naomi blinked a couple of times before looking at Ted. "Come on, Ted. I think it's time we left."

"I couldn't agree more," Fidelia said.

"Won't you stay for dinner?" Shackleford asked. "Perkins can set the table for two more. Mrs. Morrisey always cooks enough for an army."

Naomi glanced back at him. "Mrs. Morrisey would never forgive us for barging in at the dinner hour, Uncle. Another time." She gathered Ted with a look and swept from the room.

"I'll be right back, sir," Roger said, following them out.

"Is he always like that?" Ted asked as Roger caught up with them halfway down the stairs.

"Only when Mrs. Patching is here, sir."

"Really?" Naomi asked, stopping at the foot of the stairs. "You expect me to believe that?"

"No, ma'am. I don't."

"Come, Ted," she said. "We got what we came for."

Roger beat her to the door only because she stopped halfway to let him catch up, a smirk dimpling her cheeks. "A few more months, Mulligan. Make it that long and you'll be a very wealthy man."

"Thank you, ma'am. I'm looking forward to collecting my bonus."

The self-satisfied smirk broadened on her face. "I just bet you are." She strode out of the house without a backward glance, Ted in attendance two steps behind.

Roger closed and bolted the door before returning to the library.

Shackleford sat in his straight chair with a grin plastered on his face. Fidelia smiled, but Barbara looked slightly dazed.

"Would somebody tell me what just happened?" Barbara asked.

"Unless I miss my guess, that was Naomi setting Ted up as a corroborating witness," Fidelia said.

"It wouldn't surprise me to learn she had a recorder in her bag," Shackleford said.

"She did," Barbara said.

Fidelia's eyes widened and she looked at Barbara. "Really?"

Barbara nodded. "Top of mind. The gloating was like treacle."

"All right then. She just violated state law by recording without consent. Anything she tries to introduce as evidence will be disallowed and opens her to a state felony."

"You sound like a lawyer," Barbara said.

"I have a juris doctor from Brown. Never practiced, but it's been useful."

Barbara blinked. "You have a law degree but you're not a lawyer? Why?"

Fidelia gave a little laugh and patted Barbara's hand. "Bless you, child. Even if I had been a lawyer I'd have retired a decade ago." She shrugged. "I had other interests and the money to pursue them. I really only went to law school to satisfy my parents.

Fascinating field, jurisprudence. Too many people confuse justice with fairness—or with right and wrong."

"Isn't it?" Barbara asked.

Fidelia grimaced and shook her head. "Not exactly. Finding justice is establishing equitability under the law. The finding might not be actually fair to one or more parties, but it's declared so by the law."

"How is that fair?" Barbara asked.

"Sometimes it's not, but fairness is weighed on the scales of justice and the laws are heavily weighted by men." She shrugged. "That's why so many women have trouble with the law."

Shackleford laughed. "Sorry. It's too true to be funny but the phrasing caught me."

"Dinner will be ready shortly, sir."

"Thank you, Mulligan. I'm looking forward to whatever you've cooked up tonight. I've been smelling something delicious all afternoon."

"Roasted chicken, sir. I hope you like it."

CHAPTER 19

Fidelia, Barbara, and Roger made the trip to Badgers, Limited, on Wednesday. The receptionist took them up to the fifth floor, where the Badgers greeted them. "Sorry to drag you down here again, but we thought you might like the full report," Horace said. "In short, it's good news." He waved them into their seats and turned on a monitor on the table.

"We started with some basic assumptions about travel and income. It's not too surprising that the richer you are, the more you travel, but only up to a point," Hecuba said.

"After a certain income level, people come to you," Horace said. "Which isn't to say the highest income people don't travel. As nearly as we can tell, anyway. There are so few really rich that it's almost impossible to get a good sample." The screen showed the number of people at a particular income level. "The good news is that with over a million people earning half a million or more, we believe there might be a reasonable market for your themed bed and breakfast idea. The royal treatment, as it were."

"There's bad news in here somewhere," Barbara said.

Hecuba grimaced, but nodded. "Yes. The price point per night. There are suites around the world that top out above twenty thousand a night, but they're in prestige locations. Generally in landmark buildings or in special locations like the Hotel Wilson in Geneva or the Burj Al Arab in Dubai. At two thousand a night, you're asking as much as the royal class suites in the luxury hotels. There aren't that many in town, which might be a good thing under normal circumstances," she said. "In this case, those rooms are going empty at least half the time."

"Business people who come to the city regularly often have condos or town houses as tax deductions. They'll have places where they're known, or they take rooms on the upscale, more secure

295

floors with concierge service. If you're earning half a mil a year, the chances are good that you know how to control expenses, especially business expenses." Horace advanced the slide. "Richer people travel more than people who don't make as much, but where a household earning under a hundred thousand might travel once a year on vacation and three times a year on business that's paid by their employer, the upper tier—we cut off at half a million a year—travel only slightly more and mostly on business. When they take vacations they travel farther and stay longer, but the majority of those people aren't traveling more than ten times a year and their stays are three to five days."

"So, there might be a market," Fidelia said. "But we have a problem in that we need to reach out to the people who aren't traveling strictly for business. We probably can't attract the vacation traveler. It's not like this is a destination city."

"There's about a twenty percent chance that you could fill ten rooms at two thousand a night at least half the time," Hecuba said. The screen flipped to the new graphic. "That's the same as if you charged a thousand a night, but the actual projected income takes it down to two hundred."

"Which is about half the going rate for some of the best hotel rooms in town," Horace said.

Roger felt his brain glazing over with the numbers and probabilities.

The slide changed again. "At a thousand a night, you get thirty percent," Hecuba said. "Again, that's only filling the rooms half the time."

"I think we have your point," Fidelia said. "Few hotels book more than seventy per cent of their rooms and those are predominantly the cheap seats."

The Badgers exchanged a glance then both nodded. "About right, yes."

"What's the price point for us to fill seventy percent of the rooms at least eighty percent of the time?" she asked.

"Probably around five hundred a night," Horace said. "We didn't run a lot of numbers, but the best case we found was in that range between four and five hundred."

"So if we went to five hundred and ran at sixty percent occupancy, that's only three thousand a day," Barbara said.

"Yes," Hecuba said. "Break even estimates say you'll need to keep average daily expenses—fixed and variable—under that."

Barbara and Fidelia shared a look. Fidelia shrugged. Barbara looked at Roger. "Thoughts?" she asked. "I'm apparently as boggled as you are."

"We'd need more than just the décor and ambiance," he said. "We'd need a draw beyond the Downton Abbey crowd."

Hecuba smiled. "If you can find that, you'll be well on the road."

Fidelia nodded and stood. "Thanks. You've given us the shape of the problem. We'll have to think about what you've found out."

"We'll email the full report to Shackleford House," Horace said.

They shook hands all around and left the building. Once ensconced in the car, Barbara sighed.

"What are you thinking?" Fidelia asked her.

"I'm thinking this may not be the right path and I don't have any idea what a better one might be."

"You don't need to turn a profit," Fidelia said. "Just breaking even would reduce the costs of the house considerably."

Barbara frowned. "What do you mean?"

"You have any idea what the property taxes are on that place?"

"A thousand a day, in round numbers." Roger said, glancing back in the rearview mirror. "I pay the bills."

Barbara gave a little cough.

"We don't use much electricity or water. They're more variable. Just the main house is about what you'd expect, but if we open up the wings and have more people turning on lights and flushing toilets, that's going to add up, but I'd be surprised if it went up to a grand a day."

Fidelia sat back in her seat and gazed out the window. "So, in theory, that might work."

"What about the cost of staff?" Barbara asked. "I don't want to be running a sweatshop."

"Figure two hundred a day per head, so five people is a thousand a day," Fidelia said. "You'd have to pay the butler and cook more, but the footmen and maids could still earn a decent wage. They're basically your bellhops and housekeeping."

"Would the pixies approve?" Roger asked, making the turn into the alley behind the house.

Fidelia pursed her lips and shrugged. "I don't know. We'll need to check with Joseph."

"What's the issue with the pixies?" Barbara asked.

"They live in the house," Roger said, easing the car up to the back door. "They handle most of the routine maintenance like dusting and polishing the floors. According to Mr. Shackleford, they also apparently play pranks on people they don't like."

"This is all new to me," Barbara said. "Delia?"

Fidelia shook her head. "They're basic sprites. We've given them the name 'pixie,' but they're helpful entities who live with talented people. The bigger the place, the more room there is for them. Shackleford House probably has a lot of them just because it's huge by modern standards and it's been around a very long time."

"I never noticed any in my place," Barbara said.

"You might not have had enough of them to be noticeable. I suspect you have at least a few, but until you get enough of them, their efforts are lost in the noise of day-to-day activity." She looked out at the house as Roger pulled to a stop. "This place probably has thousands of them. I suspect it's attracted every pixie in a hundred-mile radius."

Roger got out and held the doors for Barbara and Fidelia. "I'll just put the car away and join you in the library. Mr. Shackleford will be interested in what we've learned. I'll bring up a pot of tea."

By the time Roger got the tea brewed and into the library, the two women had filled Shackleford in on the findings.

"So what's your take on this, Mulligan?" he asked.

"I think that this is a huge asset to be left unused. I think we're on the right track with a bed and breakfast, but I'm not sure that the right answer is being open to the public, sir."

Shackleford's eyes widened and he grinned. "Say more."

"Well, sir, the Badgers indicated that all the highest end rooms have a draw. We can refit the house as an English manor, assuming the pixies won't mind—or can be bribed to accept the remodeling."

"Leave the remodeling to me, Mulligan," Shackleford said.

"Yes, sir. We have the furnishings already," Roger said. "Am I right that there's a warehouse full of antiques that came from various periods in the house's history, sir?"

"You're correct, Mulligan."

"So that's enough for the décor and accent pieces, in terms of furnishing. We may need to invest in new mattresses and linens, but we have more than enough bed frames in the house already." He paused. "We need a draw. Depending on what that is, we may have to adjust our plans in terms of what we remodel the house to."

Fidelia took her tea and settled back into her chair, crossing her legs at the knee. "What kind of draw?"

"I don't know but the atrium is one of a kind, ma'am. I'm not talented but even I can feel it when I go in there. I'd spend all day there if I could." He shrugged. "It just seems to me we should be looking at that as our centerpiece, not the house."

Barbara frowned at him. "Can I see what you're thinking?"

Roger nodded. "It's all jumbled, but sure."

She nodded and raised her hand, letting it flutter in the air for a moment before her eyes widened. "I think I see."

"Can you tell me, Miss Barbara? Because I'm not getting anything to stick."

"You're thinking something along the lines of a spiritual retreat? Something like that?"

"Yes," he said. "Something like that. A place where people could come and meditate or do yoga or whatever."

"Centered on the atrium," Fidelia said.

"Yes, ma'am. We're looking for a draw. A draw is something not available elsewhere." He shrugged. "You'd know better than I would, ma'am, but I'm guessing there's not another honest-to-God fairy forest inside any other building in the city."

She snorted a short laugh. "Probably not in North America."

"So? Can we make that the draw? How do we package it? Who do we package it for?" he asked. "Who do we try to sell it to?"

"What's your goal?" Shackleford asked over the top of his tea cup. His eyes twinkled.

"The best use of the building," Barbara said. She glanced at Roger before looking back at the old man. "I had no idea this place was so expensive to live in."

Shackleford shrugged. "I have simple needs. I make do."

Barbara almost did a spit take with her tea, managing to contain the damage at the last second. "Simple needs? You live in a mansion. You have a butler and ride in a Mercedes limo?"

"To be fair," Fidelia said. "He lives in two rooms and barely left the second floor for months until this week. The car is a bit expensive, but he has a reputation, an image to uphold. Roger's only here because of Naomi."

"Thank you, Delia," Shackleford said. "The only real extravagance is this library." He looked around at the shelves. "Might be one of the largest collections of magic-related works in the Western Hemisphere. I know of one in the Czech Republic that could rival it, but I haven't kept in touch with him."

"Ianos Kovalik?" Fidelia asked.

Shackleford nodded.

"He's coming to the Fête this year, assuming he can get a visa through the State Department in time." She smiled. "You should attend, Joseph. When was the last time you came?"

"I don't dare," he said, looking into his teacup. "I don't know if I'd be myself."

Fidelia sighed and her shoulders slumped. "Are you going to hide here in this library until you die?"

He looked at her, a sad smile in his eyes. "Quite likely."

"You've got a court date you'll need to keep," she said.

He nodded. "That could be my undoing." He looked around at each of them. "This could all be for naught."

"So, what's our plan, Barbara?" Shackleford asked after Roger finished clearing the dinner dishes. "Tomorrow's your last day."

Fidelia leaned forward, elbows on the table, her coffee cup cradled under her nose. She smiled at Barbara with light dancing in her eyes.

Barbara, for her part, looked less than excited. "We've hammered and tonged this all week," she said. "Without some kind of goal, it's got all the structure of mashed potatoes."

Shackleford nodded. "I understand that. So, what's the goal?"

Barbara frowned at him. "You won't tell me."

"I asked you for a plan for Shackleford House, didn't I?" He shrugged, a self-satisfied smile on his face.

She growled at him—only half in jest. "A plan to do what? The possibilities are endless."

"If this was your house, what would you want to do with it?" Shackleford asked.

"Reduce the overhead," she said, almost immediately.

"Why?" He came back at her just as fast.

"You're paying a thousand a day, just in taxes. I have no idea what the utility bills must be. Are the fairies making the water to keep the atrium going? Because that's a lot of water."

"You're not suggesting we do away with it, are you?" Shackleford asked.

"No. Of course not. It's ..." Words apparently failed her at that point because she just shook her head.

"Look through the lens the other way, my dear," Fidelia said.

"The other way?" Barbara asked.

"Yes. You're looking at how much it costs to keep the house running. What are the benefits?"

Barbara blinked several times. "I thought that was what we were trying to plan for. Some benefit for the place."

Fidelia's shoulders flexed in an expressively exaggerated shrug. "You've already mentioned the atrium. It's home to a tribe of fairies. The house is home to nations' worth of pixies. The atmosphere in this place is—quite literally—magical. Surely, you've felt it."

Barbara looked at her coffee cup and nodded. "Yes." She cast an apologetic glance at Roger. "I can't explain it, but yes, I've felt it."

Nathan Lowell

"Then what's the real issue?" Fidelia asked. "Roger and I have gone where you've led us all week. I thought we had a half-decent plan with the bed and breakfast."

"It's the expense," Barbara said. "You heard the contractor. Just putting in the kitchen would be over a hundred thousand. The upstairs remodeling, at least that much again."

"Amortized over ten years, that's less than you might think," Shackleford said.

"Then there's staff and insurance." Her eyes went wide. "My God, how much is the homeowner's insurance on this place?"

"Stop," Shackleford said. His voice was low but the command snapped through the room.

"Sorry," Barbara said, folding her hands on the table in front of her.

Shackleford's lips tightened and Roger watched the old man's jaw muscles clenching. He closed his eyes. The sound of his breathing all but echoed in the silence. His left hand clenched into a fist where it rested on the table.

"Joseph? Are you all right?" Fidelia asked.

The old man's head made a tight twitch to the side and back.

"Can we help?" Fidelia asked.

He made the head shake again.

The feeling of helplessness left Roger with the sour taste of bile in his throat. He wanted to check the old man's vitals but as long as he was still breathing, Roger didn't dare touch him.

After what seemed like hours, the tension drained from Shackleford's body. First the tight frown smoothed to normal, his jaw relaxed and his shoulders sagged. Then his fist opened and his hand pressed palm-down on the tablecloth. The steam engine hissing of his breath through his nose lost some of the pressure and slowed. Last, his eyes opened and a tiny smile tugged his lips. "Well," he said. He looked around the table and up at Roger. "Delightful meal, Perkins. My compliments to Mrs. Riggs."

"I'll tell her, sir."

Shackleford looked at Fidelia. "Is there something wrong, Delia? You look pale."

Fidelia sighed and reached across to pat Shackleford's forearm. "You're having one of your episodes, Joseph."

He nodded. "Yes. It will pass."

"Wait, you know?" Barbara asked.

Shackleford looked at Barbara, a heavy frown working his forehead into a veritable storm of furrows, his gaze raking her face. "Who are you?"

"I'm your cousin Barbara," she said.

The frown lessened just a bit but his head moved in a slow shake—back and forth, back and forth. "I don't know you." He looked to Fidelia. "Should I?"

"Yes, Joseph. She's your cousin."

"Fascinating," he said, looking back at Barbara. "Time travel isn't all it's cracked up to be. Will I meet you in the future?"

Barbara lifted her hand and the rolling movement in her wrist flexed all the fingers in turn as she stared at him. Her eyes narrowed. "Yes," she said, her voice faint and whispery. "We'll meet in the future."

A beatific smile lit up the old man's face. "I feel you trying to rummage," he said. "I'm looking forward to your memories."

Barbara's hand clenched into a fist and her eyes shot open wide. "No." She threw herself back in her chair. "No," she said again.

"You can take it, you know. He's old and weak. He won't stop you." The words rolled from Shackleford's lips, like oil filming across a pool of water. The old man's smile reached all the way to his eyes. "He'd welcome the release and think of the power you'd have."

Barbara looked around at Fidelia and Roger. "Help."

Fidelia launched herself from her chair and knocked Shackleford sideways to the floor, chair and all toppling to the parquet in a clatter.

Shackleford oofed as he hit the floor and lay there long enough for Mulligan to reach his side, crouching beside him as Fidelia pulled the chair upright again.

The old man looked up, blinking and shaking his head. "Perkins? What happened?"

"You fell, sir. Are you hurt?"

"Only my pride, Perkins. Help me up, would you?" He rolled onto his back and held an arm up for Roger to pull him upright enough to get his feet under him. Roger helped lift him to his feet and into the chair. Shackleford looked around the table. "Clumsy of me. Did I have too much wine with dinner?"

"No, Joseph," Fidelia said. "You just turned too quickly and the chair got away from you."

Roger looked to where Barbara sat stone-still in her seat, eyes clamped shut as tightly as the white-knuckled fist she still held in the air. "Miss Barbara?"

She nodded. "Need a moment."

"Is she all right, Mulligan?" Shackleford asked.

"Just needs a moment, sir," Roger said.

Fidelia reached over and took Shackleford's hand. "Are you all right, Joseph? Nothing banged or bruised?"

"I'm fine, Delia." He looked at his right shoulder, brushing at it as if to clear away any floor dirt. "Embarrassed more than anything."

"You didn't bump your head?" she asked.

He rubbed his hands along the sides of his head and over the top. "Nothing is sore. It would be if I banged it, wouldn't it?"

Fidelia relaxed, her shoulders falling back and a smile replacing the frown. "Yes. Most likely." She glanced at Roger, the relief plain in her face.

"You would, sir. I saw you hit the floor, you mostly caught yourself. Please tell me if anything starts hurting?"

"I shall, Perkins. I shall." He squared himself to the table and watched Barbara for several moments.

As if feeling their collective gaze on her, she said, "I'm all right." As she sucked a deep breath in through her nose, her eyes popped open. She blew the breath out her mouth in a whoosh. "There. Sorry. Had a cramp in my brain."

"Are you all right?" Fidelia asked.

Barbara nodded. "Yes, I think so. It was just ... unexpected." She looked at Shackleford. "You took a nasty tumble."

The old man nodded. "I may retire early this evening. Leave you young people to entertain yourselves."

Fidelia snorted. "I'm not that much younger than you."

He smiled at her and reached over to pat her hand. "Keep reminding me, Delia. Keep reminding me. With luck, one day you'll catch up with me."

"But you wouldn't be here to see it," she said.

He chuckled. "Be careful what you wish for." He looked at Roger. "I'm going to bed, I think. Today took a lot out of me."

"Let me walk you up the stairs, sir."

"I'm not an invalid," Shackleford said, standing up from his chair. "I'm sure I can climb a set of stairs."

"I'm sure, too, sir, but just as a safety precaution? For the ladies' sakes? It would make them feel better."

"It would, Joseph," Fidelia said. "You just had one tumble. I'd hate to think of you having another."

Shackleford sighed and motioned to Roger. "Come on, then. Sooner started, sooner done, eh?"

Roger walked a half step behind the old man all the way up to his room. "Can I help you with your jacket, sir?" he asked.

"Thank you, Perkins. Yes. Just hang it up there." He waved in the general direction of his wardrobe and held the bedpost while he toed off his shoes. "My pajamas? Where are they, Perkins?"

Roger went to the dresser and pulled a set of pajamas from the third drawer. "Sorry, I didn't get a chance to lay them out for you yet, sir."

Shackleford shook his head. "My fault for disrupting the schedule." He stripped off his tie and took off his shirt and undershirt.

Roger handed him the pajama top, picking up the tie to smooth and hang in the rack for pressing while dropping the clothing in the hamper for the next laundry.

Shackleford navigated the change from trousers to pajama bottoms by himself while Roger turned down the bed and placed the old man's robe and slippers in their customary positions. Shackleford slipped into the bed, pulling the covers up to his chin and faded off to sleep before Roger could say anything else.

Roger stood there for a few moments, wondering if there was something else he should be doing for the old man. Unable to think of what it might be, he left the room, flipping off the light and closing the door behind him.

He found Fidelia and Barbara in the library, both with wide, concerned eyes.

"How is he?" Fidelia asked.

"He seems fine, physically," Roger said. "He's still calling me Perkins, but he's sleeping."

"Should he sleep?" Barbara asked. "If he has a concussion ..."

Roger shrugged. "If he had bumped his head, even a little, I might be worried about it. I didn't see anything that looked like a bump on his head and I was looking right at him when he fell. He hit the floor on his shoulder and arm."

"I feel terrible," Fidelia said. "It was the only thing I could think of to do."

"You did good," Barbara said. "I shouldn't have tried to read him. I knew better, but I thought maybe I could get through. Maybe find something to help him." She closed her mouth and swallowed hard. "Yeah. Not a good move on my part."

"We discovered something," Fidelia said. "At least sometimes he has a warning that it's coming."

Roger nodded. "It's probably too soon to say he always has a warning."

"Agreed," Fidelia said. "It's still more than we knew this morning and gives us a chance in court."

"How so?" Roger said, envisioning Shackleford being overtaken in front of the judge.

"Well, we can interrupt the proceedings if it seems as if he's in physical distress." Fidelia shrugged. "He looked like he was having a heart attack or something there for a few moments."

"Or something," Roger said, nodding. "We'd know what was coming, even if the court didn't."

"Would it be enough?" Barbara asked.

Fidelia shook her head. "I don't know, my dear. We'll have to play it by ear."

"Will you be glad to get home?" Fidelia asked.

Barbara looked around the foyer, up at the ceiling far above and down at the parquet floor. "I don't know."

Fidelia's eyebrows rose. "Really?"

Barbara shrugged. "It seems odd, but this already feels more like home than my apartment ever did. That was always just a place to be on my way somewhere else."

"How long have you lived there?"

Barbara's gaze focused in the middle distance. "Can it be ten years already?"

"And it's not home?" Fidelia asked.

"It's funny. I used to think so, but I guess I'm a bit spoiled by this place." She smiled at Roger. "Thank you, Mr. Mulligan. It's nice to feel a little spoiled."

"Just Mulligan is fine, Miss Barbara, and you're very welcome."

Shackleford stepped forward and held out an envelope. "Here's the final payment," he said. "You've more than met my expectations for your stay." His lips held a smile but his eyes held a sadness. "You're welcome here any time. Having you here has been an absolute delight."

"We didn't come up with a plan," she said, holding her hands behind her back. "I didn't earn that."

Shackleford shook his head. "The plan wasn't in the contract now, was it? That was just something I tacked on once you were here."

"But the contract only said I should come and stay a week and get to know the house."

The old man's smile widened and he pushed the envelope closer to her.

"He's got you, my dear," Fidelia said. "Take it or he'll just deposit it directly to your bank."

Barbara reached out and took the envelope, holding it in both hands and staring down at it for a long moment. "Thank you." She swallowed and nodded. "Thank you. I've certainly had an education over the last few days."

"The Fête d'Étoile is in a few weeks," Fidelia said. "If you'd like an invitation, I can send you one."

"You could come up and stay with us," Shackleford said. "You always have a place here."

Barbara took a quick breath and slipped the envelope into her purse. "I should get going. The car is waiting and it's a long drive."

Fidelia offered her hand, shaking Barbara's in both of hers while giving her a cheek kiss. "It's been lovely to meet you. You know how to reach me if you need to, right?"

Barbara nodded. "I do. And do send an invite to the Fête. Thanks to this week, I can probably afford to attend without embarrassing myself." She gave Fidelia a little grin that carried as much excitement as self-deprecation.

Shackleford's smile tilted a little more toward sadness as he stepped up beside Fidelia. "I'm just a foolish old man, but I'm sorry to see you go. Anytime you want to come visit ..." He shrugged and held out a hand.

Barbara took his hand and pulled him in for a hug, planting a solid kiss on his cheek. "A handshake isn't enough, old man," she said, drawing back to look into his eyes. "Neither is 'thank you.' You've opened my eyes to a world I never knew existed."

Shackleford patted her back and nodded. "Please come back to see us when you can."

She pulled back from him, almost reluctantly, before turning to Roger. She straightened and tilted her head back a little, a pretend princess at court. "Thank you for everything, Mr. Mulligan." She held out her hand.

Roger stepped up to shake her hand with a small bow over it. "A pleasure working with you this week, Miss Barbara. I look forward to your return." He had a little lump in his throat that just wouldn't swallow away. "Let me get your bags." He stepped to where the luggage waited and took it in hand.

Shackleford himself stepped up to hold the door. Barbara led the way down the path to the waiting limo at the curb.

"He really didn't have to do this," she said over her shoulder. "I could have rented a car and driven myself."

Roger shook his head. "You know better, Ms. Barbara. He's a bit odd, but his sense of duty runs deep."

The trunk popped open as they reached the gate and a liveried driver came around to hold the passenger door. "Good afternoon, miss. I'm Yvonne. Please let me know if there's anything I can do to make your ride more enjoyable."

"Thank you, Yvonne." Barbara slid into the car and gave a little final wave to Shackleford and Fidelia standing on the stoop before Yvonne closed the door with a solid chunk.

Roger slid the bags into the trunk, nodding to Yvonne who came back to settle them where she wanted them. With a final nod, he went back to the sidewalk, watching as the limo pulled out onto the street and disappeared in the distance. With a sigh he returned to the house, the lavender between the stones reminding him of the first time he'd walked the front path. Shackleford and Fidelia waited for him on the stoop. Together, they re-entered the house.

"It's going to seem quiet without her here," Fidelia said.

Shackleford nodded. "I hadn't expected to become quite so fond of her so quickly." He sighed. "Suppose she'll come visit?"

Fidelia shrugged. "Fate is funny, even when we're the butt of her jokes." She paused. "You know, I should head home, too."

The old man sighed. "I know. I've imposed on your better nature for a week. Thank you for this, Fidelia."

"I want you to attend the Fête this year," she said.

Shackleford sighed and opened his mouth to speak but she shut him down.

"No excuses, Joseph. You'll be among friends. You'll know most of them."

He pursed his lips and shook his head. "Not many of them know of my little problem." He patted his chest. "I'd just as soon keep it that way."

"It's still a few weeks away. Perhaps between the two of us we can find a solution that doesn't kill you in the process."

Shackleford snickered and offered his arm to her. "Well, back to the library then. We should figure out where to look."

She took his arm and they strolled across the foyer to the stairs. "I think there's something in those two books that we haven't figured out yet," she said.

"I'll bring a tray up momentarily, sir. Coffee or tea or both?"

Shackleford looked to Fidelia with a raised eyebrow.

"Coffee would be fine, Mulligan. Thank you," she said.

Roger made his way to the kitchen, already missing Barbara Griffin's presence in the house. He couldn't put his finger on it but the house just felt emptier, maybe a little sadder, without her there. "Madam Dionysia, indeed," he said to the empty kitchen. He pulled an empty saucer down from the cupboard and put it on the counter as a reminder to give the pixies a treat later.

Julia Rexwood—an imposing woman in late middle age, wearing a dark business suit, her brunette coif shot with gray—met them at the courthouse and took them through the metal detectors. "Just try to relax," she said, taking Shackleford's arm. "They'll pass you."

Roger and Fidelia followed behind as witnesses. Roger couldn't help feeling a bit sorry for Barbara, waiting by the phone back at her home. Rexwood explained for everyone's benefit. "This is actually a preliminary hearing to determine if your niece has cause to become your guardian and whether or not there is sufficient evidence for a full hearing."

"I appreciate this, Julia," Shackleford said.

"You'll appreciate my bill, too, Joseph, but that's for later." She grinned at him. "We're up in about half an hour, but I have a conference room where we can wait." She looked at him. "Are you feeling well?"

Shackleford shrugged. "Nervous. Silly, I suppose, but there it is."

She patted his arm where hers linked with his. "We've got this part nailed. Just consider that the judge has the authority to pull the plug on the whole thing, but not the authority to find against you. Your worst-case scenario after the hearing is that you have to undergo some court supervised testing and come back for the official hearing. Best case is that it ends today."

Shackleford nodded, but Roger didn't like the way the old man was breathing.

Rexwood led them down long corridors dotted with groups of people in suits interspersed with uniformed officers keeping an eye on everybody. A middle-aged woman and surly young man sat on a bench along one wall. A group of people stopped talking as Rexwood approached. One of them nodded to her. She nodded back, but didn't speak. Eventually they came to a door which she opened and held for them. "Here we are."

The room held a table with a half dozen chairs around it. Rexwood parked Shackleford in the closest one, and crouched by his side. "Nobody should come through that door but me or a uniformed officer of the court," she said. "Anybody else comes in, you don't speak to them, understood?"

"Understood," Shackleford said, swallowing hard.

She frowned at him. "Are you sure you're all right?"

"Just a little light-headed," he said. "All the excitement, I guess."

Rexwood glanced at Fidelia and stood. "Keep an eye on him?"

Fidelia and Roger both nodded. "He's safe with us," Fidelia said.

Rexwood took another frowning look at Shackleford who waved her off. "I'm fine," he said, frowning back. "Take care of the legal pieces. That's enough for you to worry about."

Fidelia crossed to take the chair next to Shackleford. "We'll just amuse ourselves for a while, Julia. Thank you."

The attorney still frowned as she left the room, taking one last look at Shackleford before closing the door behind her with a click of the latch.

"Don't fuss, Delia," the old man said. "I'm fine."

He didn't look fine. Roger counted the old man's breaths while watching the second hand tick on the big clock on the wall. The old man looked pale and kept swallowing hard.

"What should we do about Ms. Griffin, sir?" Roger asked, trying to get Shackleford's attention.

The old man looked up at him. "Do about her, Mulligan? What do you mean?"

"Are you considering changing your will, sir?"

Shackleford nodded and his frown relaxed a bit. "I am. I need to do that this week. The house seems to like her, don't you think, Delia?"

"I'm not as tuned to the house as you are, Joseph. She is a lovely young woman. She'll grow into Shackleford House given time."

"Grow into?" Shackleford asked.

"Having a house like that is rather a large responsibility, don't you think? Especially for somebody who never had to manage a household beyond her apartment before."

Shackleford nodded and looked at his feet. "I hadn't thought of that. You're right." He glanced at her with a grin. "As always." He patted her hand and then reached up to massage his left shoulder, rolling it around a little.

"Trouble, sir?" Roger asked, not liking what he saw.

"Musta laid on it wrong last night," Shackleford said, sitting upright and rolling both shoulders. "Just a little sore."

Fidelia raised an eyebrow at Roger who gave her small shake of his head. A bubble of worry edged up inside him, but simple stress on the old guy could account for all of it.

"Do you think her plan for a bed and breakfast has merit, sir?" Roger asked, trying to steer the conversation back to Barbara.

"I do," he said. "I'm not sure it's on the mark just yet." He patted his chest. "I usually know when the answer is right. It's close, but not quite."

They looked up at a tap at the door and Rexwood came back in. "We've got about ten minutes before they'll call us. How are you doing?"

"I'm doing just fine, Julia," Shackleford said, an edge to his voice. "Stop worrying about me. I'm old but I'm not going to keel over on you." The outburst seemed to leave him panting for breath.

Roger took half a step forward. "Sir? Are you all right?"

Shackleford looked up at Roger, a scowl on his face. "Didn't I just say I was fine, Mulligan?"

"Yes, sir, but you don't look fine."

The old man's eyes suddenly squeezed closed and he curled in on himself. He would have fallen to the floor if Roger hadn't been close enough to catch him and put him on his back. He pressed a finger to Shackleford's neck before putting his ear to the man's chest. "Cardiac arrest. Call 911," Roger said, his training kicking in as he tilted the old man's head back, checking his airway. No breaths. He placed his palms together on Shackleford's chest but felt the amulet under the shirt and realized he needed to get that out of the way before compressing. He glanced up at Rexwood. "Go! 911. Now."

The woman broke for the door and pulled out a cell phone.

"Door," Roger said, stripping the old man's shirt off his chest, exposing the necklace.

Fidelia jumped over Shackleford's legs and pulled the door closed.

"Stay there. Hold it shut," Roger said. He lifted the amulet up and pushed it over Shackleford's shoulder.

"What are you doing?" she asked.

"I need room to work."

"Take it off him," she said.

"What? No. He'll die."

"He's already dead, Mulligan. Take it off him or I will. We can bring him back."

"You're mad," he said. "How did he get it through the metal detector?"

"They'll take it off him at the hospital and God knows what will happen then," Fidelia said. "It's not metal, Mulligan. It's magic. Take it off him now."

The ticking clock reminded Roger that time never worked in the patient's favor. She had a point. They'd never leave the metal necklace on him once they got him into the ER. It wouldn't be the first thing they did, but they'd pull that metal off before they did very much. He took a deep breath and pulled the necklace up over Shackleford's head. The chain seemed to slither out from under the old man on its own.

"Yes," Fidelia said, lunging for the necklace. "Give it to me."

Roger looked up just in time to avoid Fidelia's grasping hand. He pushed her away with his free hand and held the necklace away from her. "No." He only got the one syllable out before she came for his face with her nails. He batted her away and she fell, tripping on her heels and sliding a bit on the polished linoleum. Without thinking, Roger took the chain and looped it over his head, tucking the amulet into his shirt pocket to keep it from swinging.

"What did you do?" Fidelia asked, pushing herself up from the floor.

Roger started compression, counting in little grunts. He ignored her question, but kept an eye on her as he pressed and counted. He paused and gave two rescue breaths. "You could help here," he said, getting back to compressions. He counted aloud, focused on his hands, the movements. The old man's bones felt brittle under his skin, but Roger kept going.

Fidelia moved to Shackleford's head, holding his head at the right angle. "Sorry. I got it."

Roger nodded and hit his count, pulling his hands back.

Fidelia blocked Shackleford's nose and gave him two breaths while Roger caught his.

It seemed like hours, but within five minutes the building EMTs showed up and took over from Roger and Fidelia. Uniformed officers moved them out of the small room and into the corridor.

Rexwood stood at the front of the small crowd, eyes wide as she tried to look into the room. "How is he?" she asked, pulling Roger and Fidelia aside. "What happened in there?" She lowered her voice and looked around to see who was near. Looking back to Roger, her gaze focused on the black chain running around his neck and traced it down to his pocket. "What have you done?"

Roger looked at Fidelia. "Is she okay?"

Fidelia nodded.

"If he comes back, they'll take him to the nearest ER where they'd have taken it from him without knowing," Roger said.

"What do you mean 'okay'?" Rexwood asked.

"He wanted to know if you were talented," Fidelia said.

Rexwood seemed to see Roger for the first time. "My God. You're not."

Roger shook his head. "Definitely not. I doubt I could even do a decent card trick and don't ask me to sing."

"But you're his butler."

"Yes, and trust me when I say it's been a learning experience, but that's not really important right now." He turned to see that the EMTs still bent over the old man, but he heard the charging whine of a defibrillator just as one of the officers closed the door.

"Is he going to recover?" Rexwood asked, glancing at the door.

"He may not. Cardiac arrest isn't something you get over, as a rule. We don't know the rules of engagement for this." He patted his pocket. "Was he dead enough already that removing it wouldn't matter?"

"Spill," Rexwood said. "What happened in there? I was coming back with the EMTs when something nearly knocked me down."

"It was that," Fidelia said, nodding at the necklace. "As soon as it came off him, I felt it, too, and tried to grab it." She colored. "I—I don't know what came over me."

"You didn't feel it?" Rexwood asked, looking at Roger.

"Nope. Cold metal. I took a chance and put it on."

"How's it feel?" Fidelia asked.

"Heavy, but I don't feel any different, other than I'm burning through an adrenaline spike and my hands are going to start shaking soon."

"You know you can't take it off," Rexwood said.

Roger looked down at it and shrugged. "I wore dog tags for years. It's only a little bulkier."

Fidelia looked at him hard but before she could speak, Rexwood's phone rang.

"All right, then, this is going to throw a wrench into the docket, but I suppose unconsciousness and cardiac arrest count as a valid excuse."

The EMTs opened the door and rolled the gurney into the room to take Shackleford, still apparently unconscious, out to the waiting ambulance. One of them came over to the little group. "You were with him when he collapsed?"

"Yes, sir," Roger said. "I'm his butler, Roger Mulligan. This is Fidelia Necket, close family friend."

"Either of you have power of attorney?"

"I do," Fidelia said.

"Can I get a consent to treat?" he asked, thrusting a clipboard into her hands.

She took it and signed in a flowing script. "Where are you taking him?"

"Mercy Medical," he said. "It's closest."

"Will he make it?" she asked.

The EMT shrugged. "He's breathing on his own, but his ticker is complaining. We'll do what we can but we have to roll."

"Of course," Fidelia said.

The EMT hurried down the corridor, speaking into his shoulder mic as he wove between the puddles of onlookers still clogging the passage.

"Come on," Rexwood said. "They just called our number."

"We still have a hearing?" Fidelia asked, eyes wide.

"We'll have to appear. Fastest way to get the delay while he's recovering. The hearing will go on, so we'd better get there before Naomi has the judge convinced we're a no-show."

CHAPTER 20

The hearing room wasn't exactly what Roger expected. The judge wore her robes like she'd been born to them, but she waited in a high-backed office chair at the head of a long table. The room smelled of floor wax and despair. Naomi sat beside a lawyer-looking guy at the judge's left hand. She had a stack of documents in front of her.

Rexwood led them to the other side and took a seat beside the judge. "Sorry we're late, Your Honor."

The judge nodded. "I understand there are extenuating circumstances."

"Your honor, under the circumstances, we'd like to request a delay until Mr. Shackleford is well enough to attend."

Naomi narrowed her eyes at Roger and scowled at Fidelia, but she didn't speak.

The judge looked at Julia with a raised eyebrow and turned to Naomi's side. "Under the circumstances, Mr. Lassiter, I'm inclined to grant the delay."

"No," Naomi said. "Your honor. This is just a delaying tactic."

Roger felt his jaw drop and Julia started to respond but the judge held up a hand. "That's an astonishing remark, Ms. Patching, given that your uncle was just taken out by ambulance by EMTs."

Naomi nudged her lawyer.

"We believe we have sufficient evidence to justify a full hearing, Your Honor," he said. "Even if Mr. Shackleford were here. If it please the court, we'd like to proceed."

The judge made a sour face but looked at Julia. "Ms. Rexwood?"

Rexwood leaned over to Roger and Fidelia. "Well?"

Roger pulled his notebook out and held it below the level of the table and wrote a question. "Can we get it dismissed without him here?"

Rexwood shrugged.

Fidelia took the pen to scrawl "We can win if it goes to the full hearing." She nodded at Roger. "Let's see if we can quash it now and save the trouble."

"You sure?" Rexwood asked.

Roger shared a glance with Fidelia. They both nodded.

"Very well, Your Honor," Rexwood said.

The judge picked up a small gavel, tapped the table, and read the docket number and officialese from the paper in front of her. Duty exhausted, she turned to Naomi's side of the table. "Mr. Lassiter, your case?"

"Your honor, we believe Mr. Joseph Perry Shackleford is both physically and mentally unable to care for himself. We ask that his niece and only living relative, Ms. Naomi Patching, be appointed as his guardian."

"Evidence, Mr. Lassiter?"

"He is wheelchair-bound, unable to dress himself, and suffering from dementia, Your Honor."

"Evidence is more than words, Mr. Lassiter." She looked at Naomi. "You're Ms. Patching?"

"Yes, Your Honor."

"You're his niece?"

"Yes, Your Honor."

"You claim to be his only living relative?"

"Direct relative, yes, Your Honor."

"I thought you were his niece, Ms. Patching."

"I am, Your Honor."

"Then you're not a direct relative. You're the child of one of his siblings, aren't you?"

"Sorry, Your Honor, I misspoke."

The judge nodded but shut Naomi down by turning to Rexwood. "I understand Mr. Shackleford met with a misadventure, but would you care to offer your case, Ms. Rexwood?"

"He's hardly wheelchair-bound. He walked into court under his own power today."

"Impossible," Naomi said, slapping the table.

The judge cast a sour glance at Lassiter, who passed it on to Naomi.

"Continue, Ms. Rexwood, if you would." Her gaze never left Naomi.

"Mr. Shackleford dresses himself every morning. He is sometimes a bit confused as to the day of the week, but I confess to the same weakness, Your Honor. It hardly counts as dementia. Further, I have a report from a geriatrics specialist who confirms that Mr. Shackleford has none of the clinical characteristics of any of the conditions often attributed to dementia."

Lassiter frowned at Naomi, who shrugged in return.

"May I see that report, Ms. Rexwood?"

"Of course, Your Honor." She slid a sheet of letterhead from her folder and presented it to the judge.

The judge read down through it before passing it to Lassiter. "Your comments, Mr. Lassiter?"

Lassiter looked down through the document but kept a poker face. "This would have come out in discovery, Your Honor."

"I would have expected you to have your own, Mr. Lassiter."

"I'm sorry, Your Honor. We were unable to compel Mr. Shackleford to attend our physician without a court order."

"Tell me, did you ask him, Ms. Patching?"

"Yes, Your Honor. More than once."

"What was his reply, Ms. Patching?"

"He declined, Your Honor."

The judge gave her a wry smile. "Thank you, Ms. Patching." She looked at Rexwood. "Anything further from you, Ms. Rexwood?"

"We see no legitimate grounds for granting guardianship to a man who may be old but still manages a multinational portfolio of businesses."

"Thank you, Ms. Rexwood." She looked at Naomi. "Do you have anything to add? Something that might give the court some leverage in this matter?"

"He's been wheelchair-bound for months. Every time I visit him, he's in a wheelchair with his blanket and book. He never knows who I am, calls me by other relatives' names, and can't even keep his butler's name straight." She took a breath. "Your Honor."

"Thank you, Ms. Patching," she said, glance at her sheet before looking up at Roger. "You're the butler in question, I take it, Mr. Mulligan."

"Yes, Your Honor."

"What are your qualifications as butler, Mr. Mulligan?"

"None to speak of, Your Honor. I was hired because I am an ex-Army medic and have EMT training."

Her eyebrows rose slightly at that. "A bit of a change, isn't it, Mr. Mulligan. High octane adventure to greeting visitors?"

"Yes, Your Honor."

"Tell me what you do, Mr. Mulligan."

"My duties involve caring for the house, its occupants, and guests, Your Honor. I have a regular round of duties depending on the time of day and the day of the week."

"I see, and have you observed this behavior between Mr. Shackleford and his niece?"

"I have, Your Honor."

The judge blinked. "You have?"

"Yes, Your Honor."

She worked her tongue around in her mouth a little, a smile not quite suppressed. She took a breath and asked, "Can you tell me the first time you observed this behavior, Mr. Mulligan?"

"Yes, Your Honor. I can."

"Please do, Mr. Mulligan."

"The first time I met Mr. Shackleford in person, Your Honor. Ms. Patching took me to the library. Mr. Shackleford was in a wheelchair. He called Ms. Patching by some other name that I don't remember and sent her away for something from the kitchen."

The judge blinked. "How long ago was that, Mr. Mulligan?"

"About five months ago, Your Honor. I have the dates in my phone, if you'd like to know them."

"At the moment I'm more interested in what Mr. Shackleford had to say after Ms. Patching left the room."

"He asked me why I wanted the job, Your Honor. I told him I needed the money. He asked me a few other questions before Ms. Patching returned."

"And on her return?" the judge asked.

"He cussed her out for bringing the wrong thing from the pantry and sent her back with a stern message to the cook, I think."

"You're not sure about what part?" the judge asked.

"The stern message to the cook, Your Honor. It was one of his favorite pranks."

"Pranks, Mr. Mulligan?"

"Shackleford House has no cook, Your Honor."

"But he sent Ms. Patching to deliver a message, at least on one occasion?"

"Yes, Your Honor."

"Doesn't that seem a little off to you, Mr. Mulligan?"

"It did at first, Your Honor."

"What changed your mind?"

"As soon as she was out of the room, we resumed a normal conversation. He gave me an opportunity to ask him questions about the job. Anything, actually."

"Did he seem rational to you, Mr. Mulligan."

Lassiter leaned forward, "Your honor?"

She waved him down. "Leading the witness, not qualified to answer. Noted. Overruled. Mr. Mulligan? How did he seem to you?"

"Like the kind of man I wanted to work for, Your Honor."

She narrowed her eyes at him and gave him the stare for a good minute without speaking. "That must have been a pretty big hurdle for a combat vet, Mr. Mulligan."

"It was, Your Honor."

"So your contention is that Mr. Shackleford deliberately misled Ms. Patching?"

"Yes, Your Honor. That was only the first time."

"You seem pretty sure of the happenings for having it be five months ago, Mr. Mulligan."

"Yes, Your Honor. It was an important day for me."

"Why is that, Mr. Mulligan?"

"I don't sign million-dollar contracts every day, Your Honor."

Naomi slid back in her seat while the judge and the two lawyers all turned round eyes on Mulligan.

"You make a million dollars as a butler?" the judge asked.

"My monthly stipend is five thousand, but if I keep the job for a year, I receive a million-dollar bonus."

The judge looked at Rexwood. "Did you know this?"

Rexwood shook her head. "No your, honor. First I've heard of it."

The judge looked at Roger, her head tilted to the side. "Do you realize that this information is potentially prejudicial to your case, Mr. Mulligan?"

Roger looked at Rexwood who stared back at him, her lips pressed together like she was trying to hold in a scream. "No, Your Honor. It never occurred to me."

The judge sighed, blowing it out slowly between pursed lips. "You didn't think that a million dollars might color your opinion of the man paying for it?"

Roger frowned. "Mr. Shackleford didn't hire me, Your Honor."

Naomi pushed back a little farther from the table while the judge picked her jaw up.

"Who hired you, Mr. Mulligan?"

"Ms. Patching, Your Honor. She and her husband. Five thousand a month and a million-dollar bonus if I kept him alive for a year until they could get him into a home in Colorado."

The judge looked at Rexwood. "Did you know any of this?"

"No, Your Honor. I've been working on the basis that the request is baseless on its face."

"You can't prove that," Naomi said.

Lassiter turned to her but the judge beat him to it.

"He doesn't have to prove anything, Ms. Patching. This is only the preliminary meeting to determine if there is sufficient reason to convene a formal hearing." She looked down at her notes. "You claim he is wheelchair-bound, Ms. Patching."

"He's always met me in the library in a wheelchair, Your Honor. What was I supposed to think?"

"Ms. Rexwood claims he walked in under his own power, Ms. Patching. Are you suggesting that she might be mistaken?"

Naomi looked at Rexwood and then Roger and finally Fidelia. She swallowed hard but stiffened her spine. "It should be easy enough to prove, Your Honor."

"I agree, Ms. Patching." She looked to the uniformed officer at the door. "Officer Quinlan, would you check the security footage for the time that Ms. Rexwood's party checked in. I want to know if Mr. Shackleford walked through the metal detector."

"Yes, Your Honor." He stepped out, and another officer took his place.

Naomi looked more than a little pale.

"Ms. Patching, you further claim that Mr. Shackleford cannot dress himself." The judge looked over the top of her glasses. "Do you have any corroborating testimony? Evidence?"

Naomi shook her head. "No, Your Honor."

"Mr. Mulligan, what other staff does Shackleford House have?"

"None, Your Honor. I'm the only one."

"No valet for Mr. Shackleford?"

"No, Your Honor. I tend to his clothing but I've only helped him out of his clothing once. I helped him get a robe on once when he'd fallen in the bath and needed assistance getting up."

"In five months?" the judge asked.

"Yes, Your Honor. He's eighty-something but a rather independent individual."

"He thinks he's a wizard," Naomi said, leaning forward. "Ask him," She pointed at Roger. "Ask him."

The judge's expression flickered between a frowning annoyance and a bemused smile. "Mr. Mulligan?"

"Yes, Your Honor. He thinks he's a wizard."

Rexwood looked at him, her eyes round as silver dollars.

"You don't think that's strange, Mr. Mulligan?"

Roger shrugged. "Not particularly, Your Honor. People think all kinds of things. I knew a soldier in Afghanistan who thought he was immortal. Wounded a dozen times. Never bothered him a bit."

"What happened to him?"

"Improvised Explosive Device, Your Honor. Took him, his vehicle, and four of his men."

"Do you think Mr. Shackleford is a wizard?" the judge asked.

"Your Honor," Rexwood said, holding up a hand.

"You're going to prevail, counselor. I want to hear what he has to say."

"I believe Mr. Shackleford believes he's a wizard, yes, Your Honor."

"That wasn't what I asked, Mr. Mulligan."

"My mental state isn't a question today, Your Honor."

She leaned over the table and raised her eyebrows. "Do you really want to go there, Mr. Mulligan?"

"Yes, Your Honor. I believe he's a wizard."

"Do you have any evidence to that effect?"

"No, Your Honor."

"Then why do you believe it?"

"As Ms. Rexwood says. He's old but he's brilliant. He manages a portfolio that generates so much revenue that he can afford to live alone in a mansion with a real-estate tax bill that's more than most people's mortgages. He replaced his fleet of antique autos with a quarter-million-dollar limo and called it petty change. He's living in the oldest continuously occupied property in North America and has done so for at least two decades with little more help than his butler. That's pretty wizardly to me, Your Honor."

"Being rich doesn't make him a wizard, Mr. Mulligan."

"No, it doesn't, Your Honor. But you asked what I believe. I can't speak to what he is, other than a decent man who always treated me well and seems to have more on the ball than half the people I know."

The judge leaned back in her chair and nodded. "Well parsed, Mr. Mulligan."

"He's a good man. He's old. He may not survive into this evening. He's not senile. He's not helpless. He's done a good job making Ms. Patching think so, but it's not true."

The judge nodded and looked at Fidelia. "You are?"

"Fidelia Necket, Your Honor."

"Your relationship to Mr. Shackleford?"

"Longtime family friend, Your Honor. We share durable powers of attorney."

"Why is that, Ms. Necket?"

"We're both old, Your Honor. Neither of us has a spouse or significant other who can make the decisions that people sometimes can't make for themselves. I trust him with mine. He trusts his with me."

"How long have you known him?"

Fidelia shrugged. "I don't know. Half a century, give or take a decade. He was the older brother I never had growing up. I must have been in my twenties. I'll be eighty-two this summer."

"What do you bring to this meeting?" the judge asked.

"I thought I was coming to offer moral support," she said. "And to see Ms. Patching's face when he walked in on his own."

As if on cue, the officer came back into the room and nodded to the judge.

"Officer Quinlan?" the judge asked.

"He walked in, Your Honor. By himself."

The judge nodded. "With that, my work here is done," she said. "Request denied. I find there is insufficient evidence to proceed to a formal hearing in the matter of the guardianship of Mr. Joseph Perry Shackleford. Unless one of you has anything further to add?" She stared hard at Lassiter.

"No, Your Honor," he said.

She looked at Rexwood.

"No, Your Honor."

"Good," she said, gathering her paperwork and thrusting it into a folder. She stood and left out a door in the back before Roger even got halfway to his feet.

"You're not getting another penny," Naomi said, leaning over the table on both hands.

"So, you're going to breach your own contract?" Roger asked. "And you're announcing it in front of—" he looked around. "Four officers of the court?"

She opened her mouth but Lassiter cut her off. "Before you say another word, leave the room."

She glared at him and opened it again, but his lips pressed together and he returned her glare, his eyes wide and threatening mayhem.

With a hmph she turned on her heel, striding out the door that the handy officer held for her.

Lassiter sighed and offered a hand to Rexwood. "That went well, Julia. Congratulations."

"She's a live one, Phil."

"She's paid off my house. I can't complain too much." He shook his head, gathered his papers and followed her out.

Rexwood put her folder back in the brief case and ushered them out. "We need to find out how he's doing and let him know he's in the clear."

The three of them rode over in Shackleford's Mercedes. Roger dropped them at the hospital entrance and found a place to park. He got back in time to catch Fidelia holding up a sheet of paper and her driver's license. "I'm the one who signed the consent to treat. I have the paper. This is Mr. Shackleford's lawyer. What else do you want?"

Roger stood back because it looked like Fidelia might be about to completely lose her head.

The receptionist looked around and pointed down the hall. "ER check-in is that way, ma'am."

"Thank you," Fidelia said. She turned to Rexwood. "I thought this was supposed to solve these problems." She shook the page in her hand.

"She's just doing her job, Delia. It's not an everyday occurrence." She linked arms. "Come on. Let's see if we can find him." She gathered Roger with a glance and he followed them down wide hallways, the faint smell of disinfectant fighting with the air freshener.

When Fidelia presented herself to the ER desk, the attendant took one look at her, the documentation, then nodded. "Is one of you Mulligan?"

Roger raised a hand. "That's me."

"He's been asking for you," she said. "Waiting room right around the corner. I'll let them know you're here." She waved a hand and smiled.

"Wanna bet the front desk called ahead?" Rexwood asked, leading the way around to a large waiting room with comfortable chairs filled with anxious-looking people staring at the newcomers.

Fidelia shook her head. "No bet." She sighed. "Now I feel bad."

Rexwood patted her arm. "If he's asking for Mr. Mulligan, that's a lot better than the last time we saw him."

They found two seats together and Roger stood nearby. Rexwood tried to get him to take her seat but he shook his head. "In theory, they'll be coming for me shortly, ma'am."

Roger's suit attracted a lot of attention and he felt a bit self-conscious in it for the first time. It had become second nature to him to wear it much as his fatigues had been. He let the day's events replay in his mind while he waited, feeling the weight of the necklace around his neck and resting on his chest under his shirt. It didn't feel as bulky as he first thought it was. He pulled out his notebook and made a reminder to call Barbara Griffin to let her know the latest news as soon as he returned from seeing Shackleford, but then had a better idea and leaned forward to speak to Fidelia.

"Ma'am? Might I suggest that you call Barbara and let her know the outcome of the legal case?"

Fidelia glanced up at him. "Good idea, Mulligan. She's probably pulling her hair out. Thank you." She rummaged in her bag for her phone.

Rexwood leaned in. "Who's Barbara?"

"Long story," Fidelia said. "She's one of Joseph's lost relatives. He found her recently on the internet, if you can believe it."

"Lost relatives?" Rexwood asked, brow furrowed for a moment before her eyes widened. "A talented relative?"

Fidelia smiled at Rexwood as she pulled the phone out of her bag. "Yes. Rather talented at that."

Rexwood settled back in her chair, an oddly contemplative look on her face. "Did Patching know?"

Fidelia nodded. "Found out the first day she was at the house. The summons came very shortly after." She scrolled through the screens until she found the contact and pressed the button, holding the phone to her ear. After a moment, she said, "Barbara? Delia Necket." She paused listening. "It's over. Case dismissed or refused or whatever."

Roger heard the happy sounds coming from the phone, even over the low-level angst in the room.

"That's a little more complicated, my dear." Fidelia said, after another pause. "I'll call you back as soon as we know more." Fidelia nodded a couple of times. "Yes, cryptic. I'm sorry. I'll explain more when I can. Give me an hour and if I haven't called you back, call me." She smiled into the phone. "I'm sure Joseph would be delighted." She listened and nodded. "I'll ring off now, my dear. Talk soon." She pressed the disconnect button and looked at Roger. "She asked if it would be all right if she came back to Shackleford House."

Roger smiled. "I'm sure Mr. Shackleford would be pleased, indeed, ma'am."

A little boy playing with a plastic truck on the carpet by Roger's feet tugged on the leg of his trousers. "Hey, mister? Are you a butler? You sound like a butler."

Roger grinned down at him. "Thank you, young man. I am a butler."

The boy's eyes widened. "Really? They're not just in movies and stuff?"

Roger nodded. "Really."

A pale woman in capri pants and a mis-buttoned blouse hustled over to the boy. "Ethan! What are you doing?" She looked at Roger. "I'm really sorry he bothered you."

"He was no bother, ma'am."

She gave him an uncertain nod and glanced at Fidelia and Rexwood. "I hope it's not too serious," she said.

"Thank you. Best wishes to you, ma'am."

She nodded again and took the boy by the upper arm, scooching down to pick up his truck. "Stay by Aunt Rosa, all right?"

"But we've been here forever," the boy said, drawing out the "ver" as only a child could. "When can we go home?"

The woman hugged him to her side. "I know, mijo. I know. Soon as we hear about your mama, okay?"

"That man's a butler," he said, glancing back at Roger.

"You shouldn't bother people, strangers, mijo. It's not polite. Come, sit over here with us and play with your truck."

Fidelia looked up at Roger. "You made rather a big impression, Mulligan."

"So it would seem, ma'am."

A young-looking doctor with old eyes stepped around the corner and every face turned in his direction. "Mr. Mulligan?"

Roger lifted a hand. "That would be me."

"If you'd come with me, Mr. Mulligan?"

Fidelia and Rexwood rose and followed them.

The doctor paused and glanced at Mulligan with a raised eyebrow.

"Ms. Necket holds Mr. Shackleford's power of attorney and Ms. Rexwood is his attorney, Doctor."

The doctor nodded and changed course. "In here," he said, holding a door open to a small consultation room just off the hall.

They trooped in and the doctor closed the door behind them. "I'm Doctor Oswald. Joe's been asking for Mulligan ever since he woke up." He kept looking at the three of them like he wasn't quite sure what to make of the three well-dressed people in his ER. "The EMTs said somebody was giving CPR when they arrived. Was that you?"

"Yes, Doctor," Roger said. "Ms. Necket handled the breathing and I did the compressions. Ms. Rexwood went for help."

"You probably saved his life, although his ribs aren't going to be much fun to live with for a few days."

"Will he be all right?" Fidelia asked.

"He's stable," Oswald said. "It probably comes as no surprise to you that he's rather old ..." He paused to grin at them. "For a man his age, he's in remarkably good health."

"Heart disease?" Fidelia asked.

"We'll need to do some more tests." The doctor thrust his hands into his pockets. "We're going to put him in ICU overnight, but if he's still stable by morning, we'll move him up to a room in the cardiac care unit."

"How long will he be here?" she asked.

"Depends on what we find in the next few hours. Typically it's three or four days. We'll do round-the-clock monitoring on him." He paused. "We have financial counseling available, if that's a concern?"

Fidelia shook her head. "Planning purposes only, Doctor."

"I have to ask you ladies to wait in the waiting room for a little longer?" He sounded apologetic. "Mr. Mulligan won't be long." He opened the door and ushered them out.

"Give him our best, Mulligan," Fidelia said and followed Rexwood out, leaving Mulligan and the doctor.

Oswald smiled. "Follow me." He led the way in the opposite direction through a maze of curtained alcoves, all apparently occupied, until they got to the end of the row. The doctor slipped behind the curtain, holding it open a bit for Roger to follow.

"Mulligan. Thank God. What happened?" Shackleford lay on one of the hospital beds, the head of it raised slightly, an IV line in one arm and a wiring harness line running out from the neck of his gown.

Out of habit, Roger scanned the readouts and nodded to himself. "You had cardiac arrest, sir."

The doctor eyed Roger. "You can read that?" he asked, nodding at the monitor on the wall.

"I'm a licensed EMT, doctor." He shrugged. "Long story."

The doctor snorted a laugh. "I bet. I'll leave you to him. Five minutes. You know the drill already, don't you?"

"Yes, Doctor."

The doctor nodded. "Call button if you need it." He pointed to the remote hanging on the headboard before he disappeared between the curtains.

"Mulligan. Where is it?" Shackleford's voice sounded like little more than a croak.

Roger patted his chest. "Here, sir. It's safe."

The old man's eyes widened and the monitor in the corner showed an extra couple of points on his heart rate.

"Easy, sir. It's all right." He reached down and gently pressed Shackleford's forearm. "You keeled over. Ms. Necket and I started CPR while Ms. Rexwood called for help. Ms. Necket convinced me to remove it from you but I had to put it somewhere." He shrugged. "Next thing I knew, it was on me."

Shackleford sighed and his eyes blinked. He looked old and frail against the white pillow and sheets but his green eyes shone clear and bright against his pale, wrinkled skin. "Court?"

"The judge threw Naomi's case out, sir."

Shackleford smiled. "Really?"

"Yes, sir. We came right from the courthouse to here. The ladies are in the waiting room. You asked for me, so they let me come in."

"I'm going to be here a few days, Mulligan."

"Yes, sir. The doctor told me. They want to know what caused the heart failure."

"They won't find anything," Shackleford said.

The note of certainty surprised Roger. "Why do you say that?"

Shackleford glanced at Roger's chest. "It's not there anymore."

"What are you saying, sir?"

Shackleford lowered his voice to a whisper. Roger had to lean down to hear him over the monitors and other equipment. "It spoke to me. It told me ... well ... it told me lots of things over the years, but it told me good-bye. Next thing I know I'm here." He gazed into Roger's eyes and nodded a couple of times as if to emphasize his words. "It tried to kill me."

Roger pressed on Shackleford's forearm. "It didn't succeed."

"I have you to thank for that, Mulligan." He glanced at Roger's chest again. "But now you've got it."

"Yes, sir, but it has a problem."

"What's that?" Shackleford asked, his brow furrowing.

"I'm not talented. It has no link to me."

Shackleford's eyes flashed open and his mouth opened. "It can't reach you."

"I had to wrestle Ms. Necket for it when it came off your neck, sir, but as soon as I got it on, she was able to fight it. I haven't heard anything from it myself. Haven't felt anything rummaging around in my mind. Nothing, sir."

Shackleford's eyes narrowed and his tongue ran along his lower lip as it always did while his brain was working. "I'll want to hear about that wrestling match. Later. You've had nothing from it? At all?"

"Nothing, sir." Roger touched the disk where it lay under his shirt. "It feels a little smaller than I thought it would, but that's it."

"Show me," he said, glancing at the curtain. "Quickly. They'll be back in a minute to kick you out."

Roger unbuttoned one button and reached in to pull out the amulet, making sure to keep it far enough away that Shackleford couldn't touch it.

The old man's eyes widened and then narrowed. "It is smaller."

Roger looked down to see for himself. He wasn't sure whether it really was smaller or if he had just become used to it. "Perhaps it'll fade away to nothing, sir." He tucked it back into his shirt as the doctor came through the curtain.

"Time," the doctor said. "Your lady friends are going to be frantic. You better go let them know."

Shackleford held out his hand to Roger. "Thank you, Mulligan."

Roger shook the old man's hand. "My pleasure, sir. Can I bring you anything from the house?"

"He can have his own pajamas, small electronics with earbuds, books," the doctor said. "I've just cleared it with the floor nurse. You can visit him tomorrow in the Cardiac Care Unit."

Roger nodded. "Thank you, Doctor. We'll see you tomorrow, sir."

Shackleford raised a hand in farewell as Roger slipped through the curtain.

Roger collected Fidelia and Rexwood with a nod and a smile. "He's doing well. I expect him to remain himself for the foreseeable future. If you're ready, we should probably make room here and I can tell you about it on the way back to the courthouse so you can retrieve your vehicles."

Roger returned to an empty mansion for the first time since he'd stepped into Shackleford House nearly six months before. He pulled a saucer from the cupboard and lifted the stopper from the decanter of whiskey he kept in the pantry for just this purpose. He poured a little into the dish and, after a pause, poured one finger in a glass for himself. He stoppered the decanter and put it back on its shelf. He picked up the glass, angling it so the heavy liquor flowed along the side of the crystal, the late afternoon light shining through the amber. Lifting the glass, he offered a toast. "Thank you," he said. "To better times." He took a sip and savored the rich burn as it slid down.

He spent a few quiet moments communing with his drink, leaning back against the sink and surveying his domain. Who would have thought he could have found peace after ... everything. His mind balked at rehashing all the things that had come before. He took the last drops from the glass and rinsed it in the sink before turning to his duties. He'd need to pack a bag for Mr. Shackleford's hospital stay and he still had his normal routine to complete for the day. He probably wouldn't get it all done but with Shackleford out, it gave him an opportunity to give the library a good going over.

He smiled to himself and got back to work.

Chapter 21

After almost a week, Roger went to the hospital to retrieve Shackleford. The doctors had apologized for keeping him, but as Shackleford had predicted, they couldn't find anything. They kept him a couple of extra days "just to make sure," but when they started talking about an extended stay, the old man put his foot down. Roger found him in his room—the normal hospital room instead of the cardiac unit where he'd been for the previous couple of days.

Shackleford sat in the straight chair, dressed and combed, tie tight. "Ah, Mulligan. The doctor hasn't been around yet, but I suspect he'll be here shortly. How are things at the house?"

"Very good, sir. At least I haven't heard any complaints." Roger smiled.

Shackleford chuckled. "How did it feel to have the place to yourself?"

"We got along famously, sir. I took the liberty of giving the library and your suite a good airing out while you were gone. I haven't had any pranks pulled on me yet, so I trust I haven't stepped on any spiritual toes."

Shackleford's eyes danced with his smile. "Libations?"

"Even a drop for the outside help, sir. I'm relatively sure they're happy."

The doctor came in, an older man in a white coat with the obligatory stethoscope in the pocket, a tablet in his hand, and a red folder under his arm. He nodded to Roger, extending a hand. "You're Mulligan, I take it?"

"Yes, Doctor."

"John Delacroix," he said. "Nice to finally cross paths with you. You administered the CPR?"

"With some help, Doctor."

"Good man," he said. "Well, Joseph? You ready to get back to your own bed?"

"I am, sir. Looking forward to it."

The doctor grinned and made a notation on his tablet computer. "If you'd just sign here, we'll get an orderly up here to roll you out."

Shackleford scrawled his name in the appointed box and handed tablet and stylus back to the doctor. "I have a packet of care instructions," he said, holding up the folder. "Who wants it?"

Roger held out his hand. "I'll take it, Doctor. Anything I should be aware of?"

"There's a note here that you're an EMT. Is that right?"

"Yes, Doctor. I'm certified, but I work for Mr. Shackleford now."

"You have an AED at the house?"

"I do. I know how to use it. Should I expect to?"

The doctor looked at Shackleford, his lips pursed. "Beats the hell out of me," he said. "I'm seeing none of the typical pathology that would indicate cardiac arrest. He clearly had one, but from all appearances, his heart just stopped on its own for reasons I can't begin to guess." He shrugged. "Kills me to say that, but honesty compels me to admit I have no idea why and I can't say it won't happen again." The doctor sighed. "There's a schedule of exercises for him in there. Take it slow at first, no heavy lifting. Diet and exercise cures a multitude of ills," he said.

Roger nodded. "His primary care gave me a list as well. Working on his balance and core."

"Are you doing them?" the doctor asked, looking at Shackleford.

The old man gave a sheepish shrug before shaking his head. "We've been rather busy of late."

The doctor nodded and gave him a wry "Uh huh." He looked to Roger. "The more he moves, the longer he lives."

Roger nodded. "I'll remind him of that, Doctor."

The doctor grinned and offered his hand to Shackleford. "Good luck, sir, and I hope I never see you again."

Shackleford shook the doctor's hand and smiled back. "Nothing personal, Doctor."

Delacroix chuckled and headed for the door, holding it open for the orderly entering with a wheelchair.

"Your chariot awaits, Mr. Shackleford," he said, rolling the chair up to him. He looked at Roger. "You the driver?"

"Yes, sir."

"Patient pickup right at the end of this wing. If you're in the main lot, there are signs. Follow the one for Cardiac and we'll meet you down there in a couple of minutes."

Shackleford didn't have much to say on the ride home. Roger kept
an eye on him in the rearview mirror but the old man seemed happy
just riding along, watching the world scroll by his window.

As they made the turn into the alley, Shackleford said, "It's
been half a century since I put that damned thing on. It feels odd
not to have it. I still feel like it's there."

"I felt the same way when I got rid of my dog tags, sir." Roger
made the turn into the tarmac behind the house. "Although they
were lighter than this."

"Is it still shrinking?"

"I don't know, sir. I can't tell if it's shrinking or if I'm just
getting used to it." He pulled up to the back door and parked. By
the time he got around the car, Fidelia and Barbara stood in the
doorway so when Shackleford stepped out he got the full blast of
happy smiling women.

"What's all this?" Shackleford said, a smile breaking out on his
craggy face like dawn on a rock-bound coast. "Delia? Barbara?
What are you doing here?"

"Where else would I be, Joseph?" Delia asked.

"Don't you have a safari or something to do?"

Delia shook her head. "Wrong season. I've got a trek planned for
the Gobi Desert in a month, but I don't have to be in Ulaanbaatar
for a few weeks yet."

Barbara looked at her, jaw dropping a little. "Really? Outer
Mongolia?"

"Why not? I've some friends who trek the Dzungarian Basin
every year. I'll be joining them for their annual pilgrimage."

Shackleford still stood, one hand on the car door, staring at
Barbara. "I didn't expect to see you either. What are you doing
here?"

Barbara shrugged. "I talked with Delia and she said it would
be all right for me to come back for a while. I don't have to stay—"

"No," Shackleford said. "No, it's not just all right. It's wonder-
ful. I had no idea you'd even consider it. Let's get inside where I
can sit."

Fidelia took him by the arm and walked him into the house,
leaving Roger to get the bag from the trunk.

"Is he really all right?" Barbara asked as Roger placed the bag
inside the back door.

"The doctors don't know what caused it. He's had the normal
reactions to cardiac arrest, but they can't see anything beyond an
old, relatively healthy heart."

"No," she said, glancing at his chest. "Delia said you took the amulet." She looked up at him.

"I did."

She stared at him for several long moments. "Are you all right?"

"As far as I can tell, I'm suffering no ill effects from it, Miss Barbara."

She gave a small nod. "What will you do now?"

"Put the car away and begin preparing luncheon," Roger said.

She laughed. "No, I mean, now. He's not in danger anymore. Will you stay on as butler?"

The question caught Roger flat-footed. "Why wouldn't I?"

"From what Delia said, his niece isn't going to pay you anymore."

Roger shrugged. "We have an enforceable contract. If she reneges, she'll be paying me double."

"Wait. What?"

"When she hired me, I had a friend help me rewrite the contract. It was a dumb contract and I think she knew it. We made some changes to list specific duties and responsibilities. We also added a default clause so that each party paid a penalty if they breached the contract. If I failed to hold the position for the year, I owed them all the money I'd earned on the job."

"Ouch," she said.

Roger nodded. "But if they breach, they owe me double."

"So they'd owe you two years of salary?"

"And two million dollars," Roger said.

Her jaw dropped. "You're getting a million dollars?"

"My completion bonus. If I serve as butler for a year, they owe me a million. Why on earth would I quit now?" He smiled. "If you'll excuse me, Miss Barbara? I need to put the car away and begin luncheon."

She picked her jaw up with a snap and a nod. "Of course, Mulligan. Carry on."

Roger gave her his best Jeeves bow and set about carrying on.

CHAPTER 22

Roger pulled the car up to the front of the hotel's convention center doors, taking his place in a line of limousines picking up the well-dressed and bejeweled crowd. Whatever magic they used to line up the guests and cars seemed to be working. He spotted Shackleford with Fidelia on his arm and Barbara at his side waiting in the portico for their turn at the curb.

He pulled up and a hotel doorman opened the passenger door.

"Shotgun," Barbara said, standing back a bit while Shackleford handed Fidelia into the back and slid in alongside her.

The doorman closed their door and then opened the front for Barbara. "Have a good evening, Miss. Thank you for coming," he said.

She gathered the skirts of her gown and slid in beside Roger, tucking her feet in to clear the door before it closed.

Roger rolled the car out of the way while giving everybody a chance to buckle up, then pulled out of the entry, joining the line at the parking lot exit.

Fidelia leaned a little forward to speak to Barbara. "Did you have a good time, my dear?"

Barbara's laugh filled the car. "Oh, my. You have no idea."

"Young Carton seemed quite taken with you," Shackleton said.

Barbara shrugged. "He seemed more taken with himself, I thought."

Fidelia snorted. "And here I thought you couldn't read talented people."

"Did I miss something, Delia?" Shackleford asked.

"No, Joseph. Let's just say, Sheldon Carton may be nearly forty but he needs to outgrow being a frat boy."

Shackleford chuckled. "Fair. I think I was probably closer to sixty myself."

In the rearview mirror, Roger saw Fidelia kiss Shackleford's cheek. "You were never a frat boy, Joseph."

"Thank you," Shackleford said. "I think."

"Who did you find most interesting tonight, my dear?" Fidelia asked. "Your first time in the big pool as it were."

Barbara sat back in her seat, looking out the passenger window for a moment before turning back to look at her. "They all seemed so earnest."

"Earnest?" Fidelia asked.

"Yes, as if they had something to prove to the new kid. The men in particular but even the women. I had the distinct impression that the claws were sheathed but that I needed to watch my step."

Shackleford laughed. "Perspicacious of you. There's always a bit of jockeying for position when you get more than three talented people in a room."

"You know who seemed most interesting?" Barbara asked, after a moment.

"Do tell, my dear."

"The Staggs. Jonas and Cecelia?"

Fidelia grinned. "Cecily. Why them? I'd have thought you'd have found more in common with some of the younger talents."

"I don't know," Barbara said, gazing out the side window again. "Chemistry, perhaps. That and they weren't trying to be interesting."

Fidelia gave a short chuckle. "Well, you were the belle of the ball this year, my dear. The woman of mystery who appeared beside the most reclusive talent in a decade."

"Oh, don't tease the girl, Delia," Shackleford said. "Your sponsorship to the club, as it were, was at least as intriguing as showing up with me."

"Hm. Perhaps," Delia said. "Perhaps."

"Now that the Fête is behind us," Shackleford said. "What are your plans?" He nudged the back of Barbara's seat.

"Who, me?" she asked, turning to look back between the seats.

"Yes, you. Delia's off to Ulaanbaatar in a couple of days. What about you?"

Barbara sighed and looked around the car at each of them in turn. "Would you think it terribly ungrateful of me if I went back to being Madame Dionysia for a time?"

"Not at all," Shackleford said. "Not at all. As long as you know you have a home with us at Shackleford House whenever you want it."

"Thank you, Joseph," she said, blinking and looking out at the cityscape as they wound their way back into town.

"What about the bed and breakfast?" Fidelia asked.

Barbara looked at Roger and smiled. "That was Mulligan's idea. I think it's a good one, but none of you need me underfoot for that."

Roger glanced at her. "You are always welcome, Miss Barbara."

"Thank you, Mulligan," she said, settling back into her seat.

The remainder of the drive passed in quiet contemplation until Roger pulled up to the back door of the house and shut off the car.

He walked around to open the door for Shackleford and Fidelia before opening the door for Barbara. "Here we are, Miss."

"Age before beauty," Shackleford said, smiling at her.

They stood there in the chill of the early spring night, looking up at the house.

"This will be yours one day, you know," Fidelia said.

Barbara looked up at it and nodded, before casting a smile at Shackleford. "Not for a long while yet, I hope."

Shackleford smiled back, a bit sadly. "Sooner rather than later, I fear."

Fidelia took his arm and nodded at the door. "Don't get maudlin on us, you old fool. Open the door before we catch our deaths out here."

Shackleford cleared his throat and nodded. The door popped off its latch as Roger went back to the car to settle it in the garage.

He came out to find Shackleford waiting for him at the back door. "What about you, Mulligan?" the old man asked.

"Sir?"

"What are your plans?"

"I need to make sure you're all settled for the night, sir. I think the pixies need a bit of libation given the last few days of excitement."

"That's not what I'm talking about, my boy. Don't play the fool."

Roger nodded. "I have a few more months of my contract with your niece. If she pays off as she should, I'll need an investment advisor to shelter some of that windfall from the government. If she doesn't, I'll need a lawyer."

"Fair enough. Then what?" The old man tilted his head to one side, his eyes shining behind his spectacles from the light above the back door.

"Then I'll have to see if Shackleford House still needs me, sir."

Shackleford smiled at that and nodded a couple of times. He patted Roger on the arm and turned to the house. "Good man, Mulligan. Good man."

He disappeared into the house, leaving Roger to stand on the back stoop looking up at the city-washed sky above for a moment.

A feeling of contentment settled on him as he listened to the night traffic on the streets around him and the occasional rustle of the still-bare limbs of the two oaks in the back. He nodded to himself and entered the door, closing and locking it securely. He followed the sound of voices up the stairs and into the library. "Might I offer a nightcap, anyone?" he asked.

"Nothing for me, Mulligan," Shackleford said. "I'm for bed. I don't remember the last time I stayed out so late. My old bones need to stretch out. Ladies?"

"Nothing for me," Barbara said. "I need to get out of these shoes and put on some real clothes. Storybook princess is fun but I'm about to turn into a pumpkin, I think." She stopped to kiss Shackleford on the cheek and give Fidelia a hug. "Thank you both for this evening. It was magical." She grinned. "Not that way."

"Good night, my dears," Fidelia said, as Shackleford followed Barbara out of the library.

"May I get you something, ma'am?" Roger asked.

Fidelia shook her head and blessed him with her smile. "I just wanted to say thank you, Mulligan. Not just for—" She nodded at his chest and the amulet hidden under his shirt. "That was above and beyond," she said. "But for being here for Joseph when he needed it. For staying when others might have run."

Roger gave her a small bow. "It has been my pleasure, ma'am." He paused for a moment. "To be honest, I think I needed him as much as he needed me."

Her smile warmed and she crossed to give him a peck on the cheek. "It's not proper, I know," she said. "But thank you, Mulligan."

"You're quite welcome, ma'am."

She sailed from the library and headed down the hallway toward her room, leaving the door open.

Roger made a quick pass, collecting the glasses and straightening the pillows before taking the tray of dishes down to the kitchen and placing them in the dishwasher. He still needed to make a turn around the house to shut off the lights and make sure the house was secure, but he took down a saucer and placed it on the counter. The pixies had earned their whiskey.

He might even join them.

The Golden Age of the Solar Clipper

Quarter Share
Half Share
Full Share
Double Share
Captains Share
Owners Share

In Ashes Born
To Fire Called
By Darkness Forged

Milk Run
Suicide Run
Home Run

South Coast
Cape Grace
Finwell Bay

Tanyth Fairport Adventures

Ravenwood
Zypherias Call
The Hermit Of Lammas Wood

Awards

2011 Parsec Award Winner for Best Speculative Fiction
(Long Form) for *Owners Share*

2010 Parsec Award Winner for Best Speculative Fiction
(Long Form) for *Captains Share*

2009 Podiobooks Founders Choice Award for Captains Share

2009 Parsec Award Finalist for Best Speculative Fiction
(Long Form) for *Double Share*

2008 Podiobooks Founders Choice Award for *Double Share*

2008 Parsec Award Finalist for Best Speculative Fiction
(Long Form) for *Full Share*

2008 Parsec Award Finalist for Best Speculative Fiction
(Long Form) for *South Coast*

Contact

Website: nathanlowell.com
Twitter: twitter.com/nlowell
Email: nathan.lowell@gmail.com

About The Author

Nathan Lowell first entered the literary world by podcasting his novels. The Golden Age of the Solar Clipper grew from his life-long fascination with space opera and his own experiences shipboard in the United States Coast Guard. Unlike most works which focus on a larger-than-life hero, Nathan centers on the people behind the scenes—ordinary men and women trying to make a living in the depths of interstellar space. In his novels, there are no bug-eyed monsters, or galactic space battles, instead he paints a richly vivid and realistic world where the hero uses hard work and his own innate talents to improve his station and the lives of those of his community.

Dr. Nathan Lowell holds a Ph.D. in Educational Technology with specializations in Distance Education and Instructional Design. He also holds an M.A. in Educational Technology and a BS in Business Administration. He grew up on the south coast of Maine and is strongly rooted in the maritime heritage of the sea-farer. He served in the USCG from 1970 to 1975, seeing duty aboard a cutter on hurricane patrol in the North Atlantic and at a communications station in Kodiak, Alaska. He currently lives on the plains east of the Rocky Mountains with his wife and two daughters.

Made in the USA
Middletown, DE
30 October 2024